A yellow arc cut thr
They all bailed out of
the deck as the snapp
in the air above. The c
itself. Sparks hissed in
ting hard orange light. The discharge arched and
twisted and abruptly split, shaped into . . .

"Human shape!" Viktor said.

The shape was like a bad cartoon, never holding
true for long. Elongated legs, wobbly head, arms
that flailed in crimson disorder . . .

Julia felt her heart thump. "They can see us!"

PRAISE FOR RECENT NOVELS
BY ONE OF SCIENCE FICTION'S
MOST ACCLAIMED AUTHORS
GREGORY BENFORD

THE MARTIAN RACE

"Compelling . . . convincing . . . ranks among [Benford's] best."
—*Locus*

"Taut, plausible, and full of ideas."
—*Kirkus Reviews*

"[Benford] writes plausible, hard SF as well as anyone on the planet."
—*Publishers Weekly*

more . . .

BEYOND INFINITY

"Impeccable . . . a wonder-filled adventure."
—*Denver Post*

"Dense, lively . . . With its thoughtful extrapolation and mind-bending physics, this book reinforces Benford's position as one of today's foremost writers of hard SF."
—*Publishers Weekly*

"A hard SF author without equal."
—*Starlog*

THE
SUNBORN

Also by Gregory Benford

Fiction:

Beyond Infinity
The Martian Race
Eater
The Stars in Shroud
Jupiter Project
Shiva Descending (with William Rostler)
Heart of the Comet (with David Brin)
A Darker Geometry (with Mark O. Martin)
Beyond the Fall of Night (with Arthur C. Clarke)
If the Stars Are Gods (with Gordon Eklund)
Against Infinity
Cosm
Foundation's Fear
Artifact
Timescape

The Galactic Center Series

In the Ocean of Night
Across the Seas of Suns
Great Sky River
Tides of Light
Furious Gulf
Sailing Bright Eternity

Nonfiction:

Deep Time: How Humanity Communicates
Across Millennia

GREGORY
BENFORD

———•———

THE
SUNBORN

WARNER BOOKS

NEW YORK   BOSTON

Copyright © 2005 by Abbenford Associates
All rights reserved. No part of this book may be reproduced in any form or by any electronic or mechanical means, including information storage and retrieval systems, without permission in writing from the publisher, except by a reviewer who may quote brief passages in a review.

Warner Books

Time Warner Book Group
1271 Avenue of the Americas, New York, NY 10020
Visit our Web site at www.twbookmark.com

Printed in the United States of America

Originally published in hardcover by Warner Books

First Paperback Printing: February 2006

10 9 8 7 6 5 4 3 2 1

To Robert Forward, Charles Sheffield, and Hal Clement

They showed a scrupulous respect for the culture, methods, and findings of science, no matter where these led.

PART I

RAW MARS

The world will never starve for wonders; but only for want of wonder.
—Gilbert Keith Chesterton

The sun's seethe broke upward, flaring into a fountain of fire. A colossal magnetic arch trembled, rubbery and snaking with scorching energies. At its very top the lacy magnetic fibers ruptured. Virulent plasma poured forth, fleeing the star in furious jets. The angry spout curled and spat, thundering into the vacuum, spreading, whipping into fresh filaments. White-hot, it splashed and spun. Yet from this violence came structure. Crackling traceries writhed and coiled together. Bright strands peeled from the outrushing flow. Howling ferocity fought, expanded, and then cooled as the billowing plume rose. Lacy arrays came and went as magnetic forces struggled against the blaring heat of plasma now unleashed. Here and there, fields weaved and knotted. Order arose in the sprawling, swelling teardrop. Internal wrath dimmed. The plasma gout sped outward from the parent star, rushing into the realm of planets, bringing stormy funnels, wriggling and fighting. A red world lay in its path, unshielded, its ancient rock cloaked only by a thin film of gas. Yet life clung there. Frothing with great, seething energies, the tempest roared toward it.

1.

FIRM, FRIENDLY, POSITIVE

JULIA TURNED HER BEST SIDE toward the camera, a three-quarters shot, and spread her arms. Okay, maybe a bit theatrical, but she had the backdrop for it.

"Welcome to Earth on Mars!" She always opened firm, friendly, positive. She swept an arm around, taking in the stubby trees with their odd purple-green leaves, the raked mounds barely sprouting brownish green patches, and above it all, the shiny curve of the dome, a hundred meters high. Beyond the dome's ultraviolet screening hung the dark bowl of space. The somber cap was always there, reminding them of how little atmosphere shielded them.

"We showed you the inflation of the big dome a month ago, the planting of trees right after—now we have grass."

Not any breed of grass you've ever seen before, though; it's a genetically modified plant more like a dwarf bamboo, and technically bamboo is a grass, just a really stiff one, so . . .

"It'll be a while before we can play football on it, true. We're pretty sure nothing like grass ever grew on the surface of ancient Mars, even back in the warm and wet period. So this prickly little fuzz"—she stooped to stroke it—"is a first. It'll help along the big job that the microbes are doing down in the ground already—breaking up the regolith, making it into real soil."

Was she sounding strained already? It was getting harder to strike the right level of enthusiasm in her weekly broadcast to Earthside. She could barely remember the days, decades before, when she had broadcast several times a day, sometimes from this same spot. But then, they had been breaking new ground nearly every day. And betting pools on Earth gave new odds every time they went out in the rover, for whether they'd come back alive. Usually about fifty-fifty. The good ol' days.

She smiled, strolling to her right as Viktor panned the camera. She had to remember her marks and turns, and to keep out of camera view the crowd of camp staff watching nearby.

Viktor called, "Cut, got sun reflecting in the lens."

"Whew! Good. Let me memorize a few lines . . ."

She was glad for the break. It was getting harder to sound perky. The Consortium people had been grousing about that lately. But then, they had done so periodically, over the two decades she and Viktor had been doing their little shows. Media mavens had some respect for The Mars Couple (the title of the Broadway musical about them), but the long shadow of the Consortium, which had backed the 2018 First Landing (the movie title), wanted to keep them on the air for the worldwide subscriber base— and always pumping the numbers higher, of course. Axelrod, still the head of the Consortium, The Man Who Sold Mars (the miniseries title), and now probably the wealthiest man in the solar system, played diplomat between them and the execs Earthside. Exploration? Discovery? Yes, they still got to do some. But a safari that turned up nothing new—like the Olympus Mons fiasco (*Climb the Solar System's Highest Mountain!*)—could drive down Consortium shares, send heads rolling at high corporate levels, and make headlines. So she and Viktor tried not to think too much about the eternal media issues. It never really helped.

Viktor was fiddling, changing camera angle, and here came Andy Lang, trotting over with his studied grin. "Julia, got an idea for a last shot."

"What is it?" She looked beyond him and saw the two arm wings Andy had brought from Earth the year before, bright blue monolayer on a carbon strut. "Oh—well, look, we've done your flying stunt three times already."

"I'm thinking just a closing shot." He gestured up to the top of the dome, over a hundred meters above. "I come off the top platform, swing around the eucalyptus clump, into Viktor's field of view—after you do your last line."

"Ummm." She had to admit they had no good finishing image, and Earthside was always carping about that. "You can do it?"

"Been practicing. I've got the timing down." He was a big, muscular guy, an engineering wizard who had improved their geothermal system enormously. And a looker. Axelrod made sure to send them lookers. After all, thousands volunteered to work here every year. Why take the ugly ones when the worldwide audience liked eye candy?

Julia looked up at the ledge platform near the dome peak. Andy's earlier flights had gone around the dome's outer curve, pleasantly graceful. The eucalyptus stand at the dome's center was her pet project. She insisted on some blue gum trees from her Australian home, the forests

north of Adelaide. Earthside dutifully responded with a
funded contest among plant biologists to find a eucalyptus
that could withstand the sleeting ultraviolet here. Of
course, the dome helped a lot; chemists had developed a
miracle polymer that could billow into a broad dome,
holding in nearly a full Earth atmosphere, and yet also
subtract a lot of the UV from sunlight—all without editing away the middle spectrum needed for plant growth.

The blue gums were a darker hue, but they grew rap-
idly in the Martian regolith. Of course she had to prepare
the soil, in joyful days spent spading in the humus they
had processed from their own wastes. The French called it
eau de fumier, spirit of manure, and chronicled every centimeter of blue gum growth. She'd sprouted the seeds and
nurtured the tiny seedlings fiercely. Once planted, their
white flanks had grown astonishingly fast. Their leaves
hung down, minimizing their exposure to the residual
hard ultraviolet that got through the dome's filtering skin.
But their trunks were spindly, with odd limbs sticking out
like awkward elbows—yet more evidence that bringing
life to Mars was not going to be easy.

She considered. Andy was a media hit with the ladies
Earthside, if perhaps a bit of a camera hog. She had been
giving him all the airtime he wanted lately, glad to off-
load the work. "Okay, get on up there."

She checked the timing with Viktor while Andy shim-
mied up the climbing rope to the peak of the dome and its
platform, the big arm wings strapped to his back making
him look like a gigantic moth. They moved location so
that Andy would be shielded from Viktor's view until he
came around the clump of whitebark eucalyptus trunks as
Viktor panned upward from her concluding shot.

In a few minutes more they were ready to go. Julia wondered if she could ease out of this job altogether, letting Andy the Hunk take most of it. She made a mental note to tactfully broach the subject with Axelrod.

"Positions!" Viktor called. Andy nodded from the platform, wings in place. "On," Viktor said.

Without thinking about it Julia hit the same marker where she had left off. "You can't imagine how thrilling it is to walk on Martian grass, without a space suit, breathing air that smells . . . well, I won't lie, still pretty dusty. But better, yes. To think that we used to test the rocks here for signs of water deposition! Once the raw frontier, now a park. Progress."

Of course, the hard part was turning regolith rocks and sand into topsoil, but that's booooring, yes. Earthside had developed some fierce strains of bacteria that could break down all comers—old running shoes, hardbound books, insulation, packing buffers—into rich black loam almost as you watched.

She ducked as a white shape hurtled by, narrowly missing her head. "Chicken alert!" she said lightly, gesturing toward it with her head. It squawked and flapped, turning like a feathered blimp with wings. "Who would have thought chickens could have so much fun up here, in the low gravity? They find it far easier to fly here than on Earth. Of course, we brought them here so we could have fresh eggs, and they do lay, so we predicted that part correctly. But we don't always know everything that's going to happen in a biological experiment. This is the Mars version of the chicken and egg problem."

Viktor smiled dutifully; they'd shared this little joke

before. The Earthside producer would more probably wince. *Okay, back to the script.*

She waved a hand to her right, and Viktor followed the gesture with the camera, bringing in the view of the slopes and hills in the distance, beyond the green lances of the eucalyptus limbs. The slopes were still rusty red in the afternoon light, far beyond the dome that sloped down to its curved tie-down wall eighty meters away. They stood out nicely with the green eucalyptus foreground. The other trees—ranging from drought- and cold-resistant shrubs from Tasmania to hardy high-altitude species—almost made a convincing forest. The "grass" was really a mixture of mosses, lichens, and small tundra species, too. A big favorite of the staff was "vegetable sheep," soft, pale clumps from New Zealand's high country. Convincing to the visual audience—*a golf course on Mars!*—but also able to survive a cold Martian night and even a sudden pressure drop. The toughest stuff from Earth, made still more rugged with bioengineering.

Axelrod had insisted on the visuals. *Make it look Earthy, yes.* She had worked for years to make the inflated domes support life, and there was still plenty to do. Making the raw regolith swarm with microbes to build soil, coaxing lichens onto the boulders used to help anchor the dome floors in place, being sure the roots of the first shrubs could survive the cold and prickly alkaline dirt . . . Years, yes, grubbing and figuring and trying everything she could muster. For a beginning.

Pay attention! You're on-camera, and Viktor hates to reshoot.

"Ah, one of my faves . . ." She altered course to pass by a baobab—a tall, fat, tubular tree from Western Australia, with only a few thin, spidery limbs sprouting from its top, like a nearly bald man. Early settlers had used them for food storage, take shelter, even jail cells. On Mars they grew spectacularly fast, like eucalyptus, and nobody knew why. Aussie plants generally did better here, from the early greenhouse days of the first landing onward. Maybe, the biologist in her said, this came from the low-energy biology of Australia. The continent had skated across the Pacific, its mountains getting worn down, minerals depleted, rainfall lessening, and life had been forced to adapt. A hundred million years of life getting by with less and less . . . much like Mars.

"For those of you who've loyally stuck with us through these—wow!—twenty-two years, I say thanks. Sometimes I think that this is all a dream, and days like this prove it. Grass on Mars! Or—" She grinned, tilting her head up a bit to let the filtered sunlight play on her still-dark hair, using the only line she had prepared for this 'cast. "Another way to say it, I started out with nothing and still have most of it left. Out there—in wild Mars."

Not that this little patch is so domesticated. It's how we find out if raw regolith can become true soil, and what will grow well here.

"Already, there are environmental groups trying to preserve original, ancient Mars from us invaders." She chuckled. "If Mars were just bare stone and dust, I'd laugh—I never did believe that rocks have rights. But since there's life here, they have a point."

This was just editorial patter, of course, while Viktor followed her on the walk toward the fountain. It tinkled and splashed in the foreground while she approached, Viktor shooting from behind her, so the camera looked through the trees, on through the clear dome walls to the dusty red landscape beyond. "I like to gaze out, so that I can imagine what Mars was like in its early days, a hospitable planet." She turned, spread her hands in self-mockery. "Okay, we now know from fossils that there were no really big trees—nothing larger than a bush, in fact. But I can dream . . ."

She smiled and tried not to make it look calculated. After a quarter century of peering into camera snouts she had some media savvy. Still, she and Viktor thought in terms of, *If we do this, people will like it.* That had been a steadier guide through the decades than taking the advice about exploring Mars from the Earthside media execs of the Consortium, whose sole idea was, *If we do this, we'll maximize our global audience share, get ideas for new product lines, and/or optimize near-term profitability.*

She paused beside the splashing fountain. She plucked up a cup they had planted there, and drank from it. "On Earth you can drink all the water you want and leave the tap on between cupfuls. Here, nobody does." She smiled and walked on. "You've seen this before, but imagine if it were the only fountain you'd seen in a quarter century. That's why I come here to read, meditate, think. That—and our newest wonder . . ."

Let them wait. She had learned that trick early on. Mars couldn't be chopped up into five-second "image bites" and leave any lasting impression. She circled around the constant-cam that fed a view to Earthside for the market that wanted to have the Martian day as a wall or window in their homes. She knew this view sold especially well in the cramped rooms of China and India. It was a solid but subtle advertisement.

Crowded? Here's a whole world, only a few dozen peo-
ple on it—well, actually, about ten dozen—and it has the
same land area as Earth. A different world entirely.

Things were different, all right. The dome was great,
the biggest of several, a full 150 meters tall. It would have
been far more useful in the first years, when they still
lived in apartment-sized habs. Now her pressure suit was
supple, moving fluidly over her body as she walked and
stooped. The first expedition suits were the best of their
era, but they still made you as flexible as a barely oiled
Tin Man, as dextrous as a bear in mittens. The old helmets
misted over unless you remembered to swab the inside
with ordinary dish soap. And the catheters had always
been irksome, especially for women; now they fit
beautifully.

Outside, the wind whistled softly around the dome
walls. Another reason she enjoyed the big dome—the
sighing winds. Sounds didn't carry well in Mars' thin atmosphere, and the habs were so insulated they were cut
off from any outdoor noise.

The grass ended, and she crunched over slightly
processed regolith. Lichens could break the rock down,
but they took time—lots of it. So they'd taken shortcuts
to make an ersatz soil. They mixed Martian dust and small
gravel-sized rock bits with a lot of their organic waste,
spaded in over decades—everything from kitchen leftovers to slightly cleaned excrement. Add compost-starter
bacteria, keep moist, and wait. And hope. Microbes liked
free carbon, using it with water to frame elaborate molecules. She and Viktor had doled it out for years under the
first, small dome before even trying to grow anything. The

Book of Genesis got it all done in six days, but mere humans took longer.

She hit the marker they had laid out—a rock—and turned, pointing off-camera. "And now—*ta-daah!*—we have a surprise. The first Martian swimming pool."

Okay, no swimming pools in Genesis—but it's a step.

"I'm going for my first swim—now." She shucked off her blue jumpsuit to reveal a red bikini. Her arms and legs were muscular, breasts midsize, skin pale, not too many wrinkles. Not really a babe, no, but she still got mash notes from middle-aged guys, somehow leaking through the e-mail filters.

Hey, we're looking for market share here! She grinned, turned, and dove into the lapping clear water. Surfaced, gasped—she wasn't faking, this really was her first swim in a quarter century—and laughed with sheer pleasure (not in the script). Went into a breaststroke, feeling the tug and flex of muscle, and something inexpressible and simple burst in her. *Fun, yes—not nearly enough fun on Mars.*

Or water. They had moved from the original base camp about eighteen years before. Once Earthside had shipped enough gear to build a real water-retrieval system, and a big nuke generator to run it, there seemed no point in not moving the hab and other structures—mostly light and portable—to the ice hills.

Mars was in some ways an upside-down world. On Earth one would look for water in the low spots, stream channels. Here in Gusev water lay waiting in the hilly hummocks, termed by geologists "pingos." When water froze beneath blown dust, it thrust up as it expanded, making low hills of a few hundred meters. She recalled how

Marc and Raoul had found the first ice, their drill bit steaming as ice sublimed into fog. Now Marc was a big vid star and Raoul ran Axelrod's solar energy grid on the moon. Time . . .

She stopped at the pool edge, flipped out, and sprang to her feet—*thanks, 0.38 g!* "The first swim on Mars, and you saw it." *Planned this shot a year ago, when I ordered the bikini.* She donned a blue terry-cloth bathrobe; the dryness made the air feel decidedly chilly. "In case you're wondering, swimming doesn't feel any different here. That's because the water you displace makes you float— we're mostly made of water, so the effect compensates. It doesn't matter much what the local gravity is."

Okay, slipped in some science while their guard was down.

"Behind all this is our improved water-harvesting system." She pointed out the dome walls, where pipes stretched away toward a squat inflated building. "Robotic, nuclear-powered. It warms up the giant ice sheets below us, pumps water to the surface. Took nine years to build— whoosh! Thank you, engineers."

What did the water mean? She envisioned life on a tiny fraction of Mars with plentiful water—no longer a cold, dusty desert. Under a pressurized dome the greenhouse effect raised the temperature to something livable. Link domes, blow up bigger ones, and you have a colony. They could grow crops big-time. Red Kansas . . .

A gout of steam hissed from a release value, wreathing her in a moist, rotten-egg smell. Andy had put the finishing touches on the deep thermal system, spreading the upwelling steam and hot water into a pipe system two meters below the dome floor. Their nuke generators ran the system, but most of the energy came for free from the magma lode kilometers below. Once the geologists—"areolo-gists" when on Mars, the purists said—had drilled clean through the pingos and reached the magma, the upwelling heat melted the ice layers. Ducted upward, it made possi-ble the eight domes they now ran, rich in moist air. Soon they would start linking them all. She smiled as she thought about strolling along treelined walkways from dome to dome, across windblown ripe wheat fields, no helmet or suit. Birds warbling, rabbits scurrying in the bushes.

In the first years their diet had been vegetarian. It made sense to eat plant protein directly, rather than lose 90 per-cent of the energy by passing it through an animal first. But from the first four rabbits shipped out they now had hundreds, and relished dinner on "meat nights." They'd have one tonight, after this media show.

"So that's it—life on Mars gets a bit better. We're still spending most of our research effort on the Marsmat—the biggest conceptual problem in biology, we think. We just got a new crew to help. And pretty soon, on the big nuke rocket due in a week, we'll get a lot more gear and supplies. Onward!"

She grinned, waved—and Viktor called, "Is done."

She had waited long enough. She shucked off the bathrobe and tossed the wireless mike on top of the heap.

"Am still running."

"Check it for editing," she said quickly. "I'm going to splash." She dove into the pool again. Grinning, Viktor caught it in slow-mo.

Julia rolled over onto her back and took a few luxuri-ous strokes. She caught Andy's kick off the platform and watched him swoop gracefully around the dome. It was still a bit of a thrill to see. They kept the dome at high pressure to support it, which added more lift for Andy. He kept his wings canted against the thermals that rose from the warm floor, camera-savvy, grinning relentlessly.

Even with the lower gravity and higher air density, Viktor and Julia had been skeptical that it could work. But Axelrod and the Consortium Board had loved the idea, seeing tourism as a long-term potential market.

And Andy did look great, obviously having a lot of fun, his handsome legs forming a neat line as he arced above. He rotated his arms, mimicking the motion birds make in flight, pumping thrust into his orbit. His turn sharpened into a smaller circle, coming swiftly around the steepled bulk of the big eucalyptus. His wings pitched to drive him inward, and wind rippled his hair. Julia watched Viktor follow the accelerating curve with the camera, bright wings sharp against the dark sky. Good stuff.

But he was cutting it close to the tree, still far up its slope. The Consortium Board had chosen Andy both for his engineering skills and for this grinning, show-off personality, just the thing to perk up their audience numbers.

His T-shirt flapped, and he turned in closer still. She lost sight of him behind the eucalyptus, and when he came within view again, there seemed to be no separation at all between his body and the tree. Ahead of him a limb stuck out a bit farther than the rest. He saw it and turned his right wing to push out, away, and the wing hit the limb. For an instant it looked as though he would bank down and away from the glancing brush. But the wing caught on the branch.

It ripped, showing light where the monolayer split

away from the brace. Impact united with the change in flow patterns around his body. The thin line of light grew and seemed to turn Andy's body on a pivot, spinning him.

The eucalyptus wrenched sideways. It was thin, and the collision jerked.

He fought to bring the wing into a plane with his left arm, but the pitch was too much. Julia gasped as his right arm frantically pumped for leverage it did not have. The moment froze, slowed—and then he was tumbling in air, away from the tree, falling, gathering speed.

The tree toppled, too.

In the low gravity the plunge seemed to take long moments. All the way down he fought to get air under his remaining wing. The right wing flapped and rattled and kept him off-kilter. His efforts brought his head down, and when he hit in the rocks near the pool, the skull struck first.

The smack was horrible. She cried out in the silence.

Andy had not uttered a sound on the way down.

2.

BOOT HILL

THE TRADITIONAL DUNE BUGGY with the shrouded body crawled slowly up the small hill. Footprints had made the entire area smooth, and the cortege followed a well-worn path. The stone cairn, which they'd erected twenty years ago when the first mission landed, had had many visitors. Also by tradition, the burial would be late in the day. Boot Hill looked out over the red and pink and brown wilderness of Mars. With the domes of the colony in the distance the mourners were reminded of the strangeness of their new world and surrounded with the beauty of a Mars sunset. It was a fitting send-off to a fellow explorer and served somehow to lessen their grief.

Julia well remembered that small party of five who'd established the graveyard with the mounds for Lee Chen and Gerda Braun. Today there were twelve mounds and ten times as many mourners. Every time they did this the line was longer.

We lost Alexev in a fall, Sheila Cabbot in an electrical failure. And, of course, two aerobraking tragedies. Andy is the thirteenth.

Over the years they'd added far more graves than Julia had ever wanted to see, and had to expand the original boundary circle of rocks several times. *None lost to disease yet. All accidents.* She reached the top of the hill and scanned back along the line of suited figures trudging up the rise. The newcomers were easy to pick out, stumbling slightly in an uncertain rhythm. The efficient "Mars gait" took a bit of time to master. Also, the harsh reality of Mars was likely hitting them full force for the first time. The younger ones tended to babble in times of stress. The chatter in the suit mikes was unsettling; she switched hers off.

Someone Julia didn't immediately recognize was scanning a small vid around the scene. Most everything they did was recorded; she should have been used to it by now. But she still chafed under the watchful lens eyes. It seemed like an intrusion here, just to make a fleeting news item Earthside. But then, Andy had loved the spotlight. He wouldn't mind.

She looked carefully at the figure holding the vid. Still no recognition.

We've really grown; I used to know everyone instantly, just by gait and size. Usually without looking at their suit markings. Hope this guy is new, and not someone I've forgotten.

Viktor jogged her arm, and she turned back to the ceremony.

She leaned over and touched her helmet to his. "Who's the guy with the vid? Is he new?"

"Didier Rabette. From machine shop. Here two years already."

One of the geologists was a lay preacher, and she'd volunteered to officiate. That, too, was new; they were really beginning to specialize. *Progress.*

The ceremony was brief but effective. Julia thought suddenly about navy sea burials. Regrets, but the mission must continue.

She let the bulk of the crowd leave, stung anew by the suddenness of death. She never got used to it: how someone you'd just talked to, or someone who had always been there, was now gone. She still held internal conversations with her parents, although both were gone. Her father had slowly declined from one of the newly emerging killer viral diseases, the zoonosis class that migrated from animals to humans, fresh out of the African cauldron. It was really no surprise when he died. But her mother's death had been sudden: a brief respiratory illness, one of the "new" flus that roamed the crowded Earth, and she was gone in less than a week. From "doing fine" to "done for" in just over twenty-four hours, actually.

Julia realized that even if she'd not been 50 million miles away, she likely would not have rushed to her mother's bedside, because the course of the disease had been so ambiguous, the decline so sudden. At least, she thought ruefully, it helped assuage her guilt a little. But now Andy—plucked from them in a heartbeat. As a biologist she understood intellectually that evolution requires death; if all the original forms were still around, there would be no room for the new ones. But emotionally it was very hard to understand.

Afterward, on the way down, she was surprised by how large the colony looked. In the gathering dark, lights twinkled in the distance, stirred by the dusty breeze. "Mars City" was beginning to take shape.

3.

THE MARS EFFECT

"WE MUST MEET WITH the new ones," Viktor said crisply the next morning over breakfast in the compact cafeteria. "First thing today."

They were sitting at their usual table, and nobody in the crew sat with them, by tradition. They were the founders, after all. Julia sometimes waved some of them over, but usually she and Viktor wanted privacy. It reminded them of the early years, when the two of them had had Mars to themselves. No one within 50 million miles. They'd staved off the lurking fears of abandonment and ever-present danger by creating their own private reality. By focusing closely they became the whole world to each other.

As they had come into the cafeteria, the audio switched to some gospel music, an unusual choice for her, but it fitted her current mood. "Trouble of This World" by Bill Landford rang gracefully amid the clatter of breakfast.

In the two days since Andy's death a numb, gray pall had descended. Julia and Viktor had taken full responsibility, and meant it. The Consortium Board, meeting in emergency session, had rejected that explanation. Andy had flown inside the dome over a hundred times. Hang-glider enthusiasts around the world had endlessly rerun the pictures of Andy's tight glide, and they emerged with a consensus: he had cut the margin too fine. Andy had never flown that tight a circle around the eucalyptus before. He had simply misjudged.

The vast Martian subscription audience felt the same. There had been the usual abrasive commentary, asking whether Julia and Viktor had simply lost their judgment from the long years of running the Gusev Mars Outpost, but that was so expected that nobody paid attention.

Not that any of it helped Julia and Viktor. They did feel responsible, and no media mavens could change that. "Trouble of This World" mournfully underlined their mood. Julia sipped coffee and let her doubts well up within. It was better to let the feelings wash over her and live in them fully, knowing they would pass.

They had found long before that music knitted together the small community here, made it seem less isolated from humanity. The occasional disputes over what to play—the opera buffs thought Wagner for breakfast was fine—were worth it. Today it certainly helped to hear a chorus singing quiet spirituals over the breakfast clatter.

She said nothing and gazed out the big window. Their table commanded its view, taking in the big new dome to the left, and beyond it the dozens of lesser domes, habs, Quonset huts and labs and depots. All with sandbags atop to shield against the solar wind and cosmic rays that sleeted down here eternally. Tracks crosshatched the whole area, and color-coded, suited figures moved everywhere in pressure suits.

Ugly, she had to admit. Immediately she looked beyond the bustling colony. There lay beauty. The roll of dark hills across the crater floor blended into the bright talus slopes that swept up into the craggy crater walls. A kilometer up, the rocky edges of the crater blended into a pink-brown sky that quickly faded into black. She never quite got used to that sky—blacker than ebony and holding a sun hard and bright against the dim backdrop of stars.

Raw Mars, still out there.

She got homesick, of course, often triggered by the similar desert landscapes here. On summers in her girlhood her family had returned to a small town of one thousand in The Mallee region of north Victoria. There were unending games with the kids of the town, flitting among the blue gum trees along the shaded billabongs. The dry heat had seemed to swarm up into her nostrils like a friend, welcoming her back into carefree summer.

There was cracker night, with fireworks shooting off in backyards and the town square. The dads drank XXXX beer and lit fuses with glee. Dogs hid whimpering under beds, and crowds *ooh*ed at bursting stars. The best part was the scary moments when something went wrong. Once her father somehow set fire to an old dunny in the yard, and the heavy stench of old dung came rising out of the pit when they hosed it down.

Her grandest adventure, carried out against the fearsome warnings of the boys, had been the Great Ascent of the grain silo. She'd waited until nobody was about in the late afternoon, and the door stood ajar at the base of the empty, echoing 120-foot concrete tower. There was only pale wheat dust inside, awaiting the harvest, but as she went up the narrow ladder with no rail, the dust made the rungs slippery.

When she reached the first landing, her right foot slipped on the slick dust and she fell to one knee, snatching at the step and barely holding on. That deserved a pause, but the light was fading inside, so she started up the next ladder, and without pause the next. The great cylinder above seemed infinite, and the six ladders took her at last to a narrow platform that capped the roof. She peered out across the chessboard fields and to the east sighted the next silo, gleaming crimson in the sunset. To the west was the next silo, and she imagined them marching all the way to the vast Nullarbor, the null-arbor land of no trees that stretched a full thousand miles.

Then she looked down. Her younger brother, Bill, waved up at her. He must have followed when she sneaked away. He was right below, staring up. He made his ghoul face, eyes wild. She spat a big gob—her mouth was dusty—and watched it dwindle away, skating on the breeze. He danced away, laughing. She was amazed, in her last long glance about, at how her feeling for the land changed just by getting above it. For the first time she sensed herself as a tiny creature on a great turning sphere beneath a forgiving star.

Back inside, on the way down, she slipped again and hung on with one hand. Somehow, though her heart thumped, she did not feel fear. When she got home, her brother told on her and they both got a spanking, her for the climbing and he for telling. But worth it, oh yes . . .

Back to business. "Sorry, you were saying . . ."

"We must meet with new people," Viktor said.

She sighed. "I suppose so."

He grasped her hand and squeezed. "Andy would not want the work to stop."

"Um. Earthside wanted—"

"Forget Earth."

"I've got a desk of work to do—"

"Will wait."

She recalled the schedule. Always the schedule. "Look, we've only got a day left before—"

"I know, excursion." His face split with the familiar warm grin. "We've got descent scheduled at that new vent, site C4."

"And it's taken us a month to arrange it."

"To overcome Consortium rules, you mean."

"It's like they don't want us—you and me—to ever go out again." She slurped up some coffee without taking her eyes from the view. His magic was working. She was getting back into life.

He shrugged, and his slight smile crinkled at the edges, joining the spidery lines that now laced down from his eyes. "We are too famous to lose."

"So we have to sit inside *forever*?"

Viktor's slightly lifted eyebrows reminded her that he knew well the edge in her voice. She could see him carefully look into her eyes and use the old tricks. "We not let them do this."

"They can't ship us back." After decades at 0.38 g, returning to Earth would be agony. Or maybe worse. Nobody knew the long-term effects of returning, whether the stress to the body could ever be compensated.

Viktor nodded. "Is advantage, in a way. We can't go home, so we sit here."

She snorted. "Museum exhibits."

"Axelrod sent message, said to talk to the new ones right away. Especially this"—he consulted a scribbled note—"Praknor person."

"Come on, he can't set schedules from the moon; we got away from that years ago."

"Said was important," Viktor went on stolidly, his hedgehog maneuver she knew so well.

"We had the usual welcoming ceremony, made them Martians, the water ritual, the reception—"

"I think is mostly political"—for Viktor this was the ultimate criticism—"and we must."

"Let them look around while we're gone. It'll save time if they have a feel for—"

"Must."

"Um."

"Must." Viktor was right, of course. She remembered the videographer she hadn't recognized at the funeral; was she out of touch?

So right after breakfast they met with one Sandra Praknor—efficient, neat, intent, with a hawklike look to her. She was a science manager, her dossier said, a field that had risen to prominence recently. Research had gotten so complex back Earthside that a whole layer had grown to mediate between the actual researchers and the resources they needed—computational, simulations, data analysis, and most of all the artificial design intelligences.

Science manager? She was already overseeing the colony's extensive research program. It made sense for that job to be on-site rather than at the Consortium. Paperwork was boring, even though it was all digital and Earthside-AI-assisted, but overall, the job was enjoyable; it let her vicariously experience all the studies going on, folded in with the huge Earthside effort. Even if they didn't get to go on all the expeditions themselves, she thought ruefully. Viktor was right: there was increasing resistance Earthside and on the moon to their engaging in "risky" behavior.

She had sardonically observed, reading the dossier, "Praknor has a 'cross-science degree'—what's that?"

In person it was even harder to tell what areas Praknor knew. The Consortium had hired her away from a major lab, and she had a crisp, executive style. She opened with remarks about Andy, condolences, and hopes that the death did not compromise the future of exploration.

Julia carefully put aside her emotions. She focused on Praknor's face, trying to read it but getting nowhere. Midlength dark hair, rather mannishly cut; the expression in the eyes too solid for a younger person; an open face that told nothing. As Julia opened her mouth to speak, Praknor threw her hair back. It flounced in the light gravity, reminding Julia of all the irritating blondes she had competed with in school. Julia's hair didn't work well that way, too fine, and the gesture alone still set her teeth on edge.

She made herself focus on Praknor's manner, trying to read it. In her previous job this woman must have been used to ordering the scientists around. She had a certain managerial blandness. No tics, no nervousness; just resolve. She wondered if Praknor could be caught off-guard. And where was her enthusiasm?

"We've had twelve deaths," Viktor said simply. "That did not slow us."

Praknor nodded and then went on and made the expected complimentary remarks. She mentioned how she had as a teenager set out to go into exobiology, a field that came of age with their discovery of the Marsmat. "I hope that will help me improve the program here," she concluded.

Viktor said warily, "Improve how?"

She gave them a thin smile. "Chairman Axelrod hired me personally. He wants me to impress upon you the necessity to find products for export. We of the Consortium cannot depend upon our product lines and the research investment of ISA to sustain us here indefinitely."

To Julia this was transparently a prepared speech, and Viktor's slow blink told her that he thought so, too. "Such as?"

Praknor smiled again, or rather the mouth did; the eyes stayed the same. "Your Marsmat foods idea—well, it hasn't panned out."

"Does not taste good," Viktor said. "And was Earthside idea, not ours."

"I sent those samples back for scientific purposes," Julia said evenly. "Not for Axelrod to start a product line."

"Well, I wasn't with the Consortium then," Praknor said, opening her laptop slate and consulting it.

She went into another carefully phrased opening statement about the need for all levels of the Consortium to co-operate in developing new "revenue avenues." At this point Julia tuned her out.

Mars had some resources, but few that were worth shipping to Earth. The first hit was some "Mars jewels" they found in the volcanic layers dotted around Gusev Crater. Pale, with mysterious violet motes embedded in milky teardrops, they commanded huge prices for a few seasons. Some flecked sulfur-laden stones later became fashionable. The perennial sellers were the "blueberries" the '04 rovers found, just hematite—but *Martian* hematite, so worth a thousand bucks a gram. Still, novelty only lasts so long.

Viktor had thought of another sideline, one that Axelrod liked especially. He had systematically rounded up all the parachutes that had slowed the dozens of landers, rovers, and provisions carriers that had landed in Gusev over several decades, ever since the first one at Christmas, 2003. The silky parachutes were seared by ultraviolet and solar wind particles, dirtied with red dust—and made grand T-shirts for the fashionistas on Earth.

Later, Axelrod cut a deal with several governments and made an even greater profit by returning to Earth the original rovers and landers still standing on the surface. These went to museums and private collectors. "Think of it as being able to buy the *Niña,* the *Pinta,* or the *Santa María,*" went one of the glossy upscale brochures.

Some lesser billionaires had bought heat shields and other pieces discarded in the era of automated exploration.

Apparently they made handsome "found techno-art" displays in the entrance foyers of big corporations. Then Axelrod sold off the Original Four's actual pressure suits, their houseware ("Dine as they did!"), even their worn-out flight jackets, T-shirts, and jeans. Raoul had reported in a letter that at a cocktail party reception a man had come up to him and proudly pointed out that he was wearing the very loafers that Raoul had used in the hab. They did not go well with the tux he was wearing, but the man didn't seem to care.

Julia kept her distance as much as possible. At first she had been cheerful about the whole commercialization thing, but Axelrod's relentless marketing wore her down. Even hundreds of millions of kilometers away, it got to her. She clearly recalled unwrapping supply drone packages and finding plastic supermuscled action figures that bore caricatures of her and Viktor's faces. Then there was the movie, miscast and scripted by writers who mostly knew four-letter words but no science. The animation series had been no better. Julia recalled all that in a flash, studying Praknor's assured manner, and wondered what would come next.

"The jewels are still a steady item, but my main effort will be to supervise more studies on the . . ." Here Praknor slowed, eyes flicking from Viktor to her slate, and Julia knew what she was going to say.

"Mars Effect," Julia finished for her.

"Uh, yes, I—"

"Does not exist," Viktor said.

"Our data—"

"Comes from good healthy lifestyle," Viktor said, following the line they had agreed on. "Plenty work, exercise, light diet, clean air. Also, we were picked because of good health and physical condition. Plus smarts."

Praknor said, "For years there was excess hydrogen sulfide in the agro domes where you two worked."

Viktor dismissed this with a wave of his hand. "All filtered out now."

"Before its effects were properly studied," Praknor said exactly, "in coordinated trials."

"Stunk, was its effect," Viktor said.

"You're not suggesting that *hydrogen sulfide* confers a health benefit, are you?" Julia asked. Her first experience of high school chemistry had been an experiment that made those rotten-egg fumes. She'd laundered her clothes every day, in the first dome years, to get the stink out.

"Something must explain your extraordinary longevity, as confirmed again in last year's Maxfield Index study."

"That index has a huge variance," Julia said to buy time.

"It is universally recognized as a reliable indicator of expected longevity," Praknor said primly. "You two have consistently scored very high in"—Praknor began ticking off items on her fingers—"reflexes, physiochem, metabolic rate, endurance, comprehension speed, precancer indicators—"

"All normalized to Earth," Viktor said. "And for large samples. Here is sample of two."

"Mr. Axelrod feels it is a powerful indicator. So do a lot of other specialists. Your bodies are not showing the sag and weakening of the general population—"

"Lower gravity," Julia said.

"—and I'm sure you aren't dyeing your hair." To their

puzzled looks she said, "No gray. *That* certainly isn't due to mechanical effects."

"Genetics," said Julia. "In my family we don't get gray until we're in our eighties." She turned to Viktor. "What about you?"

He shrugged, a carefully blank expression on his face.

Undaunted, Praknor showed them on her slate a complex, three-dimensional data contour map. It was a tall hill, color-coded so that at the crown a yellow-green spot marked out the *Mars sample* range. "You two, exposed to higher radiation doses and ultraviolet for over two decades, are doing better than 99 percent of the global population."

"Most of that population is starving in Asia," Viktor said conversationally.

"Comparison with the Euros shows the same," Praknor shot back.

"Too rich diet, too little exercise," Viktor countered mildly.

"Look," Julia said, equally mildly, "Axelrod has been pushing this idea hard for, what, six, eight years? So he can sell berths and luxury suites in his Mars-Orb."

"Sales prompted by your own results," Praknor said, visibly not letting herself get roused. "Starting with the tests *eleven* years ago."

They had been shrugging off this issue for years. It had seemed just another of the Earthside fads that ran for months and then faded. But now in Praknor's firmly set jaw Julia could see trouble.

The worst visitors to Mars by far had been the Med Study Team, which had arrived all enthused with testing and "optimizing" the physical conditioning effects on

Mars. This was in the days when Earthside still thought 0.38 g was bound to cause physiological damage—a holdover from the NASA programs that had endlessly obsessed over zero g, without ever doing centrifugal-gravity tests. The Med Study Team brought with them stationary bikes, with which they hosted "spinning" competitions, and talked up how much they were all going to learn about the Mars Effect. That awful two years climaxed in a group "spinning climb" called Mt. Everest Week. Everybody in base (a lucky few were out on an extended foray for samples, and spared) gathered in the dining area, which sported Tibetan prayer flags and burning candles. (The effrontery of burning anything on an oxygen-starved world hadn't occurred to the Med Study Team, of course.) The big screen showed the real Everest views, tracing their imaginary progress with little flags on an inset map. They all pedaled furiously, sweating, spinning, and the Med Study Team made measurements. They were supposed to be making an internal journey, while literally going nowhere. A team member dumped dry ice into buckets of water to simulate Himalayan mists as the team leader announced after four hours that they were "ascending" the peak.

Viktor got there first. Everyone in the team took this as clear proof of the Mars Effect. Julia took it as adaptation, no more. But with Viktor's victory she had enough clout to do something. The team wanted to stay, but she and Viktor used their immense leverage in Earthside media to leak their irritation. They said they could study any Mars Effect on their own, thank you. The Consortium stalled only a bit. The Med Study Team went back to Earth on the next boost, and she had never been so glad to see the back of anyone in her life.

The Mars Effect talk had surfaced repeatedly after that. True enough, the physical exams showed that she and Viktor were not losing their resilience. The aging Earth-side population in the advanced nations had driven a huge industry devoted to prolonging life spans, and their diagnostics now had great predictive value. The battery of tests could warn aging managers when to retire, how to optimize their remaining years, even what genetic markers foretold about their probable death modes.

So the "Mars Effect" had emerged as she and Viktor stood up well in the tests, capturing yet more media attention. Axelrod had seen a profit awaiting and began his orbital retirement resorts. After all, the man had built himself into a multi-billionaire from media empires and real estate. Without him the first Mars expedition would probably never have happened. After NASA's big blowup on the Canaveral pad Axelrod had seen opportunity where others saw only disaster. He had put together the bones of the Consortium, coaxed money from dozens of lesser billionaires, and used leverage in the U.S. Senate to make NASA sell off their useless surplus—since, as everyone knew, NASA wasn't going to Mars, anyway.

For such a man, setting the orbital health resorts' centrifugal gravity exactly at 0.38 g, plus advertising them with vids of Julia and Viktor bounding in joyous, long steps over the Martian plains—well, that was just marketing. It settled the Mars Effect into the collective mind. She almost regretted making those videos. Almost; it had been great fun, especially in their first mad romps without suits inside the first areodomes.

"The Mars Sat is the most profitable sector of all Mr. Axelrod's innovations," Praknor recited. "Further tests would strengthen our advertising campaign even more."

"So how many rich folks *bolshoi* retreats has he now in Earth orbit?" Viktor asked mildly. He tried to be blissfully uninformed of matters commercial.

"Seven. I am here to increase that number by nailing down the physiological studies, and . . ."

She had caught Viktor's wary look, eyelids lowering. "And to ask if you would be a . . . donor."

There was a long hush in the small conference room. "Of?" Julia asked into the silence.

"Mr. Axelrod ordered a market survey for new Mars products. The number one item, wildly popular in trials, was . . . sperm donation."

Julia and Viktor blinked together. At last Viktor said, "From? For?"

"We've had some offers from the, uh, Founder's Movement."

Julia could not suppress her laugh any longer. It came rolling out in her old brassy Aussie style, a roaring bark that rattled the room and only ebbed into a cackle as her air ran out. "That's the lot that want 'genes from the best and brightest,' right?"

"Yes." Praknor apparently did not think this was amusing, because, of course, it did involve money.

Julia said, "And Viktor's gotten some offers?"

Praknor said, "Indeed. Some as high as $50 million."

"Does that include cost of shipping?"

Praknor did not get it. "Yes. Frozen—"

Viktor joined Julia in gasping, thigh-slapping glee.

Praknor sat there staring at them until it wound down. "It is a serious offer."

Viktor made a solemn face and asked, "How is sample to be got?"

"I'm sure you know," Praknor said stiffly.

"And you are sent to gather it?" Viktor asked innocently.

Praknor's mouth took on a stern curl. "If you're not going to take this seriously . . ."

"Should we?" Julia shot back. "This man—to whom I happen to be married, I might note in passing—has spent over twenty years in a high-radiation environment, in stressful conditions, and is well past reproductive age—"

"And is desired by many women. He is intelligent, rugged, brave, famous—"

"Ah, is the famous does it." Viktor grinned.

Julia kept talking right over them. "—and should *not* be regarded as a profit margin item on *any*body's budget."

Silence. Looking into the other woman's face, she sensed how disconnected they were from Earthside's culture. To pay for famous sperm! The very idea curled her lip. Yet Praknor considered it a reasonable business proposition. Praknor finally filled the hush with, "I can see I am not going to get cooperation from you on improving the margin here—which, incidentally, is negative. Quite negative."

"We have lost money from beginning," Viktor said.

Julia, cooling down, added, "Since we decided to stay on here, and let the nuke take Raoul and Marc back. But Axelrod found a way to keep us resupplied through the lean years. Now he seems to think he has to make a buck."

"The stockholders want to see improved profitability," Praknor said evenly.

"Why do I sense another agenda here?" Julia spread her hands.

Praknor looked at them both without blinking. "Perhaps we need to meet again, tomorrow. Give you time to think these ideas through."

"We think fast here," Viktor said.

"Let's meet tomorrow, same time, okay?" Praknor said with utterly hollow brightness, tone rising on the last words.

"Uh, I suppose so," Julia said dubiously. Another meeting like this was going to be even worse. "I just don't think we agree on which way the outpost has to go."

"We are merely capitalizing on the two most famous people on Earth," Praknor said in a friendly tone.

"On Mars," Viktor corrected.

Julia and Viktor never regretted staying on Mars; the whole sweaty, frenetic hubbub on Earth repelled them even then; now it was unimaginable.

She recalled an e-letter from Marc shortly after he'd returned to Earth, sentiments echoed by every other returned Marsnaut.

"You rush into big halls," he had written, "and right away there are reporters and legions of devoted waiting, and they want you to talk. You're there to radiate certitude, and they want lots of that. Even though you've become a walking mouth that shakes hands and you don't really have conversations because everybody wants pronouncements. You are the center of attention of every room you enter and it gets old, old, old. 'What's it like out there?' gets asked a thousand different ways, and it doesn't help to answer, 'Read my book," because they already have, and yet want more. They want a meta-you, the complexity of your experiences shrunken down to recycled moments and phrases: explorer, adventurer, authority on everything above the atmosphere.

"You start to notice that as your image swells, the actual *you* gets smaller, lost. It's a queen bee life, with handlers and lawyers and worse. Compliments rain down on you and it's embarrassing. You do 'events' at which nothing happens except you talk. You enter to applause and make the same opening jokes and pretend it is all happening for the very first time, because it is for them. Even adulation stops thrilling you after a while. The threshold rises, and routine superlatives wing by you with no effect. You don't really know whether they're clapping for you or for the meta-you, enshrined in history yet still walking around, looking for the way offstage.

"After you run out of talk and the questions run down, too, out come the cameras. Everybody wants a picture taken with you, and your fixed grin doesn't matter. Celebs move with an aura around them, and to step inside that halo for a moment, get it frozen into digital, is a kind of immortality for them, you suppose, from their excited eyes. They come up to you and flatter you beyond all believability. So many want a precious moment with you, some with whispered theories about alien life and others about God, somehow. So your exit is measured out in ten-second bursts of sudden intimacy. Some might even be genuine if you had time to stop and let all the others fall away and just talk to this one real person.

"No moment goes unrecorded, even down to the farts getting up onstage and the nose-blowing when you have a cold. The camera lenses follow you into the men's room. You get advice shouted at you on the street, most of it hopelessly vague ('Get more funding for Mars!') or uselessly narrow ('Get behind mission profile redesign at Huntsville'). You're the boy in the bubble and the walls are always transparent."

She took the letter out and read it to Viktor every few months. It worked wonders when their morale was low.

4.

VENT R

JULIA TRIED TO FORGET the whole hour with Praknor, which had seemed like a day, by tending to the rabbits. She fed them, petted them, and tried not to think.

In the last two decades they had mined ice, inflated high-tech greenhouses, and grown crops, and were never in danger of lean diets. But sending meat 100 million kilometers was pricey, so early on they asked for rabbits. The vegetarian movement had continued to grow Earthside, so there were demonstrations, some violent, against shipping rabbits or any other living, high-protein source.

In reply Viktor made a video showing how much grunt work they did in a day, with his voice-over saying, "Hard labor needs solid food."

It worked. Omaha Steaks won the bidding to ship big canisters of beef and the fish Julia preferred to Mars, at their expense. Axelrod actually made a profit on the deal.

The rabbits mated avidly, leaping about, giving them both pets and a long-term meat source.

Julia saw no contradiction between caring for the animals and later slaughtering them, but then, she was a biologist. Which wasn't a lot different from being a farmer. And while she had longed for a cat as a pet, she knew the price in meat to feed it.

Viktor came in and sat beside her while she stroked a big white female named Roberta. "Forget her," he said, rubbing her neck.

"Hard to do."

"She got nowhere."

"Just like the other ideas, yeah," Julia said, grinning with false cheer.

This wasn't the first weird marketing attempt. Years back there was the idea the Consortium had flirted with for a while: send small interest groups to Mars. The "high concept" was that members of the newest Earthside social movement, polyamory—multiple loving partners, with few strings attached—were just the sort to colonize. They were "high-novelty-seeking individuals," so they needed alternative sexual hijinks over the long journeys, or so the argument went. And many of them were wealthy, some from Hollywood, and so could buy their own passage. Further evidence of a society with far too much time on its hands, Viktor had remarked. But there was some sanity left Earthside. The media got wind of the Consortium's marketing research and headlined this as the "sex, drugs, and rock 'n' roll in space agenda," and the marketing director got fired. Mercifully.

"I been thinking," Viktor said softly, his way of introducing a new idea. He stroked a big male rabbit thought-fully. Julia realized it was the one they had named Andy.

"You want to get away," she guessed.

He chuckled. "Wife always knows what husband is thinking, before he does."

She twisted her mouth. "Um. Tell Praknor?"

"She is busy talking to Earthside. We should not bother her."

"I heard there's a big solar storm on the way, too. It might cut off some of the low-frequency bands to Earth-side, the data streams." She grinned. "Praknor will be busy with that, too."

"So . . . let her show up for our meeting, find us gone."

Happily she said, "I *like* that."

The Vent R team of eight was ready, details delegated. Viktor quietly mustered them and got a liftoff time, 0600 the next day. Julia and Viktor were nominally in charge, but they had picked a young biologist, Daphne Newmar-ket, to call the stages of the descent. Daphne was a lab whiz and had done some limited descents in Vents A and C, nearby. She had a ready smile and ample muscles, in-fectious enthusiasm, blond hair tied back in a ponytail, and at times made Julia feel a thousand years old.

They all went about their tasks without a word to the newbies, particularly Praknor, who was busy setting up her own office and grousing about its size. The bigger habitats adjoined the first domes, affording views and much more space than the rambling, added-on hab Viktor and Julia shared. They used the minicams distributed through the outpost to be sure Praknor was preoccupied by staff and learning the endless details of life inside the linked cans and domes.

After the first expedition, the Consortium had reached an accord with their losing Chinese-Euro competitors, the Airbus Group. Once the race for prize money idea worked, big-time, it became the model for all further solar system exploration. In the Vent R descent team were a Brazilian, a Chinese, and an Indian veteran biologist and medical tech, Vaquabal. Those countries plus a dozen others had paid into the International Exploration Coalition, though the Consortium and Airbus still played major roles, grandfathered in—after all, they had put up the money and talent when no single nation would.

At 0530 they met in the assembly building, a half-cylinder of carbon composite laid flat side down at the edge of the landing field. The three other crew members were old hands, and they made quick work of the systems checks. Their biggest suborbital lifter was ready, maintenance crew certified, and they loaded swiftly. Gear slid into slot-carries, secured by bungee cords and clamps.

Julia got a good seat in the observing bubble. Viktor was copilot, running inboard systems monitors the whole flight. He would have liked to fly the bird, but the Consortium had its protocols . . . The liftoff was a steady rumble below them that pressed them at 3 g's, the rusty land falling away quickly. Mars had just enough atmosphere to allow some aerodynamic lift in the rocket plane, so they spent five minutes flying due west and then flipped and began the parachuted descent. A rumbling burst at an altitude of three kilometers settled them down without a jar in rumpled terrain.

First, suiting up. Unlike the old days, this was now almost a pleasure. Julia's skinsuit was a marvel of elastic threads that slipped on like velvet.

She and Viktor checked and rechecked their seals, oxy, temp. The newer staff rolled their eyeballs a bit, and Julia knew they were thinking, *Hey, the new systems self-monitor, y'know.* And she did know, but decades of triple-checking did not wear off. One of the job specs for astronauts was an obsessive-compulsive profile. No longer, it seemed. Someday, she was sure, one of the bright, techno-savvy types would end up gasping for air in a remote canyon. There would be a panel review and, *my, my,* a new malf route would be discovered.

Second, out into the big rover that rolled forth from their rear cargo bay. There was far more room inside, thick radiation shielding by water in the walls, and eight big tractor wheels. She could close her eyes and imagine she was in a limousine. Viktor insisted on driving, as usual.

Finally, out. Immediately Julia breathed easier. Here was raw Mars. Smooth basaltic flow below them, nonfriable, visible in the belly cam. They crossed low sandy basins ringed by ruddy hills, scribbling tracks across the belly of an ocean now 100 million years dry.

The vent mouth was a few klicks away. Viktor wanted to pick up the local geomonitors he had sent over by rocket months before. He yanked each of the silvery lances out of the ground, using the rover robo arm. The crew read them and downloaded their data into a diagnostic program.

After the fifth geomonitor, Viktor turned over driving the rover and studied the analysis screens. Frowning, he said, "These show same pattern we saw in Gusev."

Uchida, a sharp-eyed geologist, asked, "The magnetic field strength?"

Viktor pointed to colored lines that peaked several times over the last several months. "Local magnetic fields go up, so does vapor pressure in the upper Marsmat chamber—only hours later. Same delay when fields fall."

Uchida called up a figure on an inset window. "Here's the cause, I bet. We've got lotsa satellite data on this. Here's a figure from a paper on the anomalies in the south. In the north the solar wind flows smoothly around, as it does on Venus. But the incoming solar wind veers around these field peaks—"

"Look like magnetic mountains," Viktor said, running his eyes down the sheets of data, histograms, and plots beneath the cartoon figure, checking, checking. The usual scientific acronyms could not obscure the flow of incoming solar winds—like the big one currently blowing—around pronounced mountainlike peaks in magnetic field.

"Question is, what causes them? The geologists say it's magma sheets, cooled off into magnetized rock."

Viktor looked at Uchida skeptically. "You are geologist."

"Yeah, but the agreement between this data and what we know about the magma from seismology, well . . ." Uchida shrugged.

"Not good," Viktor said.

"The trouble is, it varies with time." Uchida produced curves showing the rise and fall of the "magnetic mountains"—not everywhere, but in certain spots around Mars. Long silence.

"And here's the local vapor pressure at those places."

"Um." Viktor studied the curves. More silence.

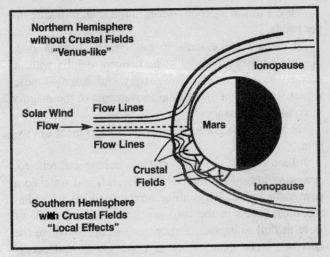

"Julia, what do you think?" Viktor said.

Distracted by the view, she studied the curves. Physics had never been her strong point, and she had no idea why the local magnetic fields should vary. But they did, the red line peaking every few weeks, the blue line of vapor pressure following. "Correlations don't have to mean cause," she said.

Uchida asked, "Which means . . . ?"

"Maybe there's magma underlying this whole area, moving now and then. When it flows in, the magnetic field rises. It melts deep layers of ice, which percolates up into the mat chambers."

Uchida pursed his lips. "But there are waves, too. Magnetic waves." He showed them different curves, these labeled with dates. Long sinusoids pulsed for hours, then faded. They combined at times, shaping into complex waveforms.

"Hey, I'm not a geophysicist," Julia said, throwing up her hands.

"It doesn't make sense to me, either," Uchida said. "Using the magma model"—he nodded to Julia with, it seemed to her, totally unnecessary diffidence—"these waves would come from fluid movements of the magma in constricted passages."

He and Viktor got into an extended technical discussion.

Julia turned to the big port view bubble and relaxed, preparing herself for the coming descent, and watched a new vista unfold. Crystalline strata sparkled with diamondlike facets in the hard sunlight. Sullen lava flows were as dull as asphalt in spots, and in others where the dust had worn them, shiny as black glass. And everywhere, reds and pinks in endless profusion, myriad shades depending on composition, time of day, and angle of sunlight. The crater cliffs began as brooding maroon ramparts at dawn, then lightened to crimson at noon and slid into blood red in the afternoon's slanting rays.

Ayers Rock on Mars. I went so far away and found myself still at home.

In the red twilights of the long years here she had recalled her girlhood in Australia. Not the rural summers with relatives north of Adelaide, with their droughts, brush fires, and smelly sheep, no. Nor the flies and hard work. Instead, the wide skies and wildlife returned to her in memory. The eucalyptus trees were beautiful and endlessly varied, with names like rose-of-the-West, yellow jacket, jarrah, Red River gum, half mahogany, grey ironbark, and especially the ghost gum, which she soon learned was *Eucalyptus papuana*, appearing in its silvery grace on postage stamps, calendars, and tea towels. They framed the human world of tea-colored, dammed-up ponds, of hot paddocks of milling sheep, of rusting, corrugated sheds tilted into trapezoids—trees standing as silent sentinels at sunset, glowing like aluminum in the settling quiet.

On impulse she had ordered a didgeridoo, the ancient echoing instrument of the Aborigines. It came at her personal expense in their fourth shipment—at nearly a million dollars, but they were rich in what Viktor called pseudomoney, from the book and interview rights; though Axelrod seemed to get most of it. The slender tube was labeled in the manifest a "wood trumpet," but it sounded nothing like that.

Some Aboriginals had complained that women were not allowed to play didgeridoos in their culture, that she was showing disrespect, but when worldwide sales of didgeridoos and concert tickets rocketed, they fell silent. She learned the trick of holding air in her bulging cheeks and breathing it out while her lungs drew air in, so that she could maintain a long, hollow tone. The skill was unique; normally people never needed to speak while they breathed. The long, low notes fit into her memory of the great Australian deserts, and when she played, the notes somehow sang also of red Mars.

Watching Gusev Crater through the wall screens—which improved in resolution and size with every upgrade, so that these days it was as though they had a bay window in each hab room—and playing the didgeridoo, called forth her sense of bleak oblivion. The spareness of deserts had always made her mind roam freely. She could find fresh perspectives on her field biology that way, and in those years had made her reputation as the central authority on the Marsmat. Labs Earthside worked at her behest, comparing Marsmat DNA to Earthly forms.

Somehow in her mind her girlhood and Mars blended. She had come to see biology as the frame of the world in those girlish years—the whole theater, in which vain humans were only actors. Mars confirmed this. On Earth, knowing biology quietly brought order to the ragtag rustling of people, ensured that their lives had continuity with the hushed natural world.

Just as it could to Mars. On that article of faith she had built their years here together.

Over a rise and there ahead the Vent R opening yawned, faint sulfur stains spreading from its mouth. The sharp ridges framing this canyon could not dispel the sensation of spacious wealth. Satellite observations had first detected vapor here, then found hints of vent chemicals. Sure enough, the lambent light glowed through an early morning fog before them. Iron-dark stains mingled near the vent splashes of yellow and orange. Red slopes nearby rose up and darkened to cobalt, then into indigo. Evidence of other ventings, long ago?

A dust devil in the distance wrote a filigree path across the rusty plains. She had always wanted to somehow sense their sandstorm sting and the moist kiss of the dawn fogs. All this time, and she had never felt Mars on her skin. *Not quite.* Then she recalled the hard days of the second year here, just before the first return launch—which she and Viktor declined. There had been one emergency, when she had been forced to run from their first, collapsing greenhouse—headed for the hab's lock in a stretching minute of panic that she would never forget. Raw Mars, sucking at her lungs, drying her skin—

"Looks like an easy one," Viktor called out as they ground to a stop beside the broad mouth of the thermal vent. Splashes of yellow and dingy brown marked the sand near the mouth. He pointed. "Vapor deposition from active periods, too."

Uchida was robo-master, and he put them to work unloading. Julia paced around Vent R, letting her senses take in details it was easy to miss. Inside a suit made it harder to get the feel of a new vent, the traceries of vapor deposition, stains, erosions. Nothing could live on the surface, of course, in the stinging oxidants and lethal ultraviolet. But the Marsmat could not contain its moist hoard perfectly.

Gusev Crater had thermal vents because the huge ancient impact had cracked the underlying layers, letting magma worm upward. The best place to go deeper into Mars seemed to be at the bottom of Valles Marineris. That great stretched scar cut deep and broad. The barometric pressure there could even allow a briny slush on a summer afternoon, melting long-frozen chemical reserves and maybe letting Marsmat get close to the surface.

She was curious about how the mat had used the deadly surface for an energy source without getting stung by the ultraviolet and alkaline dusts. There were whole conferences Earthside on just that basic physiological riddle. To get any work done here, she had to keep an open mind. Mars did not reward fixed preconceptions.

She looked up at the hard black sky. Faint filigrees fought up there. *Probably ionization curls,* she thought, *from the solar storm streaming past Mars right now and slamming into the thin atmosphere.*

Survey done, she went back to grunt labor. Compared with decades before, the rover's cable rig was first-class. It worked from a single heavy-duty winch, with a differential gear transferring power from one cable to the other depending on which sent a command. It was the same idea as the rear axle in a car and saved mass.

Four telepresence robots were standing beside the fissure. They had six spindly arms, four stubby legs, and a big central control box, all in sleek polycarbon, and she no longer found them odd. These had done the first study, lowering themselves on cables to check for life. Long experience had shown that letting 'bots do a lot of the roving saved time and accidents.

Sometimes Julia wondered if Mars could have been explored at all without plenty of 'bots. Sitting warm and snug in the habs, she and Viktor and rotations of crews from Earth had tried out dozens of candidate vents.

In two decades they had found that most fissures, especially toward the poles, were duds. No life within the top kilometers, though in some there were fossils testifying to ancient mats' attempted forays. Natural selection— a polite term for Mars drying out and turning cold—had pruned away these ventures. The planet's axial tilt had wandered, bringing warmer eras to the polar zones, then wandering away again. Life had adapted in some vents, but mostly it had died. Or withdrawn inward.

Not this vent, though.

Somebody back at Gusev made the 'bots all turn and awkwardly bow as the humans approached. Julia laughed with the others, and, as if right on cue, Praknor came on the comm. No preliminaries.

"You deliberately stood me up."

"Sorry, it was a scheduling mix-up," Julia said.

"I cannot believe—"

"Hey, got work to do here. Talk later." Julia cut off the long-range comm frequency and switched to local, 2.3 gigahertz. And felt an impish joy that turned up her lips. When she told Viktor, he smiled, too, with an expression she had come to cherish. Long relationships had their rewards.

First, as always, they set up the base camp. The team was quick and precise, hustling in the forward-leaning trot that was the most energy-efficient way to move on Mars. Every expedition now, there was new tech to make jobs easier, like the ball tents. She watched them deploy, nearly without human effort.

Under pressure any object wants to shape into a sphere. The ball tents took advantage of this. The ball was made of a flexible, thermally insulating material that could take wear and tear, especially the constant rub of dust. Light wires or ropes anchored the ball to the ground as an air tank inside inflated it, with the people already inside. A small chem cracking plant squatted beside each ball, running steadily to split the atmosphere's CO_2 for oxygen. Adding hydrogen from water let the cracker build up stocks of methane gas and oxygen, which could then burn to drive the rover. To get powerful methane fuel demanded only the CO2 plus water from buried ice, which was everywhere. With energy, all the chemistry became easy.

The robots had already arranged the electrical power

supply, comm and computation center, and other backups, all now standard for a descent. Telepresence had come a long way. Bossed from the Gusev tele-team, robots helped the humans put two tanks apiece on their lines, double-clamping them meters above the personal yokes. She did not like the idea of that much mass ready to fall on her and checked the clamps three times. Even robots make mistakes; maybe especially robots.

She got into the yoke, all sized and adjusted for her. Like putting on a jacket now, easy. Her shoulders ached a bit, maybe from her swimming. She had gone back to the pool a few times, whenever she started brooding about Andy Lang. Exercise erased cares.

"Is ready?" Viktor called. Everyone answered, "Aye!" and they began. The watch crew back at Gusev sent them a salute, a few bright bars of John Philip Sousa.

Backing down the slope, playing out their cables, Julia looked up into a bowl of sharp stars—always there, even at high noon. The 'bots got the oxy tanks past the Y-frame that routed the lines. There was a neat get-around, far easier than the awkward old days.

Rappelling, bouncing in the light grav, having fun. Down the first hundred meters in good time, just playing out the monofilament cables in a straight drop. She and Viktor were lowest and went down fast, clicking on their suit lamps as the light from above faded. After weeks of indoor work it actually felt good to be *doing* something— clean, direct, muscles and mind.

A large folded diaphragm lay at the bottom, where the fissure took an abrupt turn sideways. "Pressure seal," Julia said, and Viktor nodded.

"Four-leaf design," Viktor observed, playing a strong

beam of light over the interleaved folds. "Not see that one for a time."

Julia took several pictures. "Pretty thick. Got little grapplers at the edges, see? Sturdy."

In the girlhood Australian ecology, water was the rare resource. Underground Mars, its pressure was precious. Life evolved to seal off passages, allowing a buildup of local vapor density. Then it could hoard the water and gases it needed, building up reserves from the slow trickle from below.

The mat kept itself secured from the atmosphere with folded sticky layers, preventing moisture loss. The vaults below were thick with vapor, but by ordinary gas dynamics that could not be sustained for long. The valve *must* cut off the losses to the surface, to manage this eerie environment. A pressure lock.

But how did the valve know to close? How to respond to pressures and moisture densities? She was convinced that the glows and vapors somehow carried messages, organizing this whole shadowy realm. Biological organisms always had good sensors for toxics they made, their own wastes. The mat exhaled methane and probably had sensors that opened its valves at the right time—or so said a paper with her name on it, and she was halfway convinced. Still, progress in deciphering the mat's meanings had been painfully slow, these two decades.

This mat valve was classic, grown at a narrow turn in the vent. As nearly as Julia and other biologists had been able to determine, these were like Earthly stomates, the plant cells that guard openings in leaves. Plants open or close the holes by pumping fluid into or out of the stomate cells, changing their shape.

Still, analogies were tricky, because the mat was not a plant or an animal—both Earthly categories—but rather another form of evolved life entirely. Not just another phylum, but another kingdom altogether. Some thought it should be classed with the Earthly biofilms, but the mat was hugely more advanced.

Daphne knelt beside a pool covered with slime, next to the valve. The top was a crusty brown, and it dented when she poked it with a finger. Underneath it was most likely a pool of water.

"Standard defense against desiccation," Daphne said. Julia had written a paper on that, but she said nothing as Daphne teased apart the mat and scooped up some of the underlying liquid in a sample vial and tucked it into her pack. *Let them work,* she thought. *Anyway, independent confirmation is always good.* Julia's paper had concluded that the pools of liquid in mats supported mobile algal colonies, like *Volvox* and other pond life on Earth. But maybe this one would prove to be different, a local adaptation. Mars was a big place.

Julia swept her handbeam around. The mat hung here like drapes from the rough walls. Viktor was taking high-res pictures. "The upper lip of the mat flows down," Julia pointed out. "It covers this pool, keeps it from drying out. We've seen this at about every site."

Daphne scooped out some of the filmy water and put it under her hand microscope. "Wow, mobile algal colonies—like *Volvox*." She took samples.

Julia smiled and walked Daphne through the controls of the pulser. Viktor showed one of the crew how to rig the electrical leads to the dark tan wedges of the diaphragm.

The best place was along the thin fans, ribbed like the underside of a mushroom.

This was one of the big controversial issues, the subject of many Earthside review panels. Many biologists thought that any tampering with the mat was immoral. Certainly, they said, jolting it with currents could cause major damage.

But there was no other way to get into the inner chambers. From the start Viktor and Julia had used what worked. For two years they had held out at Gusev on their own, making several descents and setting the protocols followed in dozens of later descents. Julia had reasoned by analogy with some attractive little white sea urchins, *Lytechinus,* from which she had extracted eggs and sperm, back in grad school days. Back then she'd used a standard technique, running a small current through the water, stimulating the urchin's topmost pore—which duly released its eggs or sperm. The urchins hadn't seemed to mind, and neither did the mat, decades later.

Earthside howls of protest meant nothing to them. "Theory easy when your life not on the line," Viktor had said in a public message at the time. There were demonstrations, people wearing Viktor masks, carrying signs saying *Torturer* and *Martian Criminal, Mat Murderer.* When an interviewer asked about these, Viktor just laughed. They both published a *New York Times* opinion piece, reasoning that there were probably many chambers threading Mars, and the mat was large and robust—or else it could not have survived since the warm, wet era over 3 billion years ago.

Certainly current was better than squirting the valve with oxygen, as they had at first, in an emergency. That had caused visible damage, killing some of the mat, turning it dead gray. "Field trumps theory," Viktor had said.

Viktor triggered the voltage impulse. A hushed silence, just the wheeze of breathing coming over the comm. Then the leathery folds slowly withdrew, inching back, contracting like muscles.

The capacitor was a bulky wedge on Daphne's backpack; she was tall and muscular. She peered intently at her ammeter, careful not to overstress the thickly interwoven tissues. Viktor changed the pattern of the pulser, looking for the best sequence. The folds showed no particular response, but they did sluggishly open. The diaphragm took several minutes to spread, forced by the current flow. A two-meter passage yawned. Pale vapor poured from the opening.

"Nineteen milliamps at 0.35 volts," Daphne called crisply. Then in a different tone she whispered, looking at the slow withdrawal, "Wow . . ."

Julia remembered that this was Daphne's first fresh vent. She had trained on Vent A, the "classic" entry where they discovered the mat system. She was doing a thesis on the mat's reaction to repeated violations of its integrity by humans—oxygen exposure from leaks and exhalations from their early suits.

Though Daphne had been here a year, Julia did not know how the woman felt about the whole idea. After all, they were rupturing the mat's system. Some biologists argued for a go-slow strategy, checking to see when a vent opened of its own accord and venturing in only then. They had tried that for a year and got in a grand total of two descents. On the second one they'd had to electrically trigger the diaphragm to get back out. Julia and Viktor had argued the issue in endless interviews and position memos. In their view it basically came down to whether they did any research or not, whether humanity ever learned more about the mat.

The United Nations had even gotten into the matter, solemnly instructing the Consortium to stop all mat activities. That got them headlines, but they had no way to enforce their words. Axelrod retaliated by declaring that either the U.N. back off or he would lay claim to Mars. He left ambiguous whether he meant the whole planet or just part. This Mexican standoff never got resolved. After a while the Consortium gave the nod to resume descents. The incident stimulated the founding of the International Space Agency, though the contributing nations carefully kept control away from the U.N., of course.

Only years later did the world discover that Julia and Viktor had conducted a dozen descents without telling anybody. When they published their results, there was a predictable furor, but that died away, too. Most biologists had decided that staying in perpetual high dudgeon over matters several hundred million kilometers away was pointless.

"Honor of first entry goes to . . ." Viktor played out the suspense for a moment, before bowing. "To Daphne."

She was thrilled. The diaphragm was well clear of her body when she dropped down on her cable. She followed her endless drills and immediately mounted a belaying assembly on the wall below.

"It goes vertical again," she called. "Come on through. I'm on a bare ledge, easy standing, no mat underfoot."

The entire crew followed her and fitted their cables through the assembly so they would have a new, common descent point. All these procedures had been worked out by mountaineering experts Earthside and many trials Marside. They kept mechanical damage to the mat at a minimum. Already, overhead, the diaphragm started easing back together, trying to get a seal around their cables. It wouldn't work, because the cables still needed to have free play.

Still, it was reassuring to see the mat here trying the same solutions that Julia had seen elsewhere. It wasn't injured, or else it couldn't respond so quickly. Plus, it was further evidence that the mat system exchanged information globally, or else had evolved this defense mechanism so long ago—against what?—that it was instinctive. Despite decades of wondering which explanation was right, she did not know.

Julia paused for a moment. Mars was *tiring*. Whether this came from the unrelenting cold or the odd, pounding sunlight (even after the UV was screened out by faceplates), or the simple fact that human reflexes were not geared for 0.38 g, or some more subtle facet, nobody knew. But today she was feeling it. She and Viktor were nearly twenty years older than the rest of the team, and she wished for a moment that the Mars Effect would kick in right now.

Down into inky depths. They passed by lush mat. Gray sheets, angular spires, corkscrew formations of pale white. These stuck out into the upwelling gases and captured the richness. Some phosphoresced in pale blue and ivory. Other brown growths had earlike fans to catch moisture, a common feature. One spindly, fleshy growth looked like the fingers of a drowned corpse, drifting lazily in the currents . . . She got it all on vid.

The Mars-studies industry Earthside had classified all these types, coining terms like "extensors," "fungoidal extrusions," "asymmetriads," "symmetriads," and, inevitably, "mimoids" for the times when the mat copied something human. Usually the mat made a rough humanoid shape, as had happened in the second Vent A descent, in the first expedition. But now and then they were greeted with blocky copies of instruments, backpacks, tools. Somehow the mat could sense these, leading to a whole school of thought among biologists that the mat had optical sensors.

So far they hadn't found any. That might be because, despite Viktor's Mat Murderer image, he and Julia had not taken many samples. They respected the mat. Several scientists had died while studying it in the first expedition.

"Notice how large and complex the structures are," she called to the crew. "Daphne, that's a purple spore-thrower at your left."

"Check. Big, multiple pods. Wow."

This was half exploration, half a training exercise. Daphne was bright and quick, and Julia wanted to cultivate her as a long-term member of Gusev. She always needed more biologists than she had, especially for descents.

Giving a guided tour of a place she'd never been before felt a bit awkward, but she had been on dozens of descents, and training was essential. Most of the crew would return to Earth within a year or so, before the trial of returning to full g became too much. They had to learn and work before then. She could tell by their expressions that they were still in openmouthed awe, even though the others had several descents between them. Was she getting jaded? No, she reassured herself, just accomplished. An air of certainty calmed the others.

The harness and yoke under her arms was new and wonderfully flexible, giving her freedom. They worked their way around a protrusion. Daphne led the way— slow, steady, letting their eyes pick out telling details. The brown and gray mat was getting thicker on the slick, moist walls. The rest of the team followed, leading a new batch of climbing 'bots they'd use for recon later.

Julia was happy to leave that to others; her whole interest here was to sense a certain something she could never define. Call it *presence*—the looming feel of the mat, the sensation of being inside its workings. Julia supported her weight easily with one hand on the cable grabber, while she guided down the rock wall with the other. She concentrated. *Every moment here will get rehashed a millionfold by every biologist on Earth . . . and the ones on Mars, too.*

"Everybody ready for beams off?" Daphne called. She waited the full minute called for in the protocol. Then: "Switch off!"

All around them a pale ivory radiance seeped through the dark. Tapestries of dim gray luminosity. Julia knew the enzyme, something like Earth's luciferase, an energy-requiring reaction she had done in a test tube during molecular bio lab, a few thousand years ago. She recalled as a girl watching in awe "glowworms"—really fly larvae— hanging in long strands in New Zealand caves, luring insect prey.

The mat grew ever larger and thicker on the rock walls as they went lower. Mat species covered most of the tube walls now, gray and brown and black, with occasional bursts of orange and blue. They stacked thickly on every available out-jut, then worked up the verticals.

Just ahead, thin sheets of mat hung like drapes. Wisps of mist stirred when they passed by. Unlike scuba gear, their suits did not vent exhaled gases, so they could not poison this colony of oxygen-haters. In the first explorations she and the others had done just that.

They reached a branching point and elected to go horizontally into the widest opening. Their beams cast moving shadows, deepening the sense of mystery. Within minutes they found orange spires, moist and slick. Beyond that were corkscrew formations of pale white that stuck out into the upwelling gases and captured the richness. More pale, thin membranes, flapping like slow-motion flags. The bigger ones were hinged to spread before the billowing vapor gale. Traceries of vapor showed the flow, probably still driven by their opening the diaphragm.

A few steps more and they were in a murky vault that stretched beyond view. As Daphne's lamp swept around, vapors reflected back its glare. Perhaps fifty meters above, mat sheets hung from the ceiling of a vast cavern. Under their beams this grotto came alive with shimmering luminescence: burnt oranges, dapplings of vermilion, splashes of turquoise. A long silence.

"H-how big is this?" Daphne whispered.

Viktor said, "Can't see the walls."

Julia looked down, careful of her footing. "Or the floor, through this vapor."

"Beams off in one minute," Daphne called.

All around, a complex seethe of radiance. Julia knew that on Earth, mats of bacteria luminesced when they got thick enough. Quorum sensing, a technical term. A way for the bacteria to take roll. A lot of Earthside biologists thought that explained this phenomenon. But they had never stood in shadowy vaults like this—the thirteenth such large cavern found in over twenty years of exploration. To see the rich, textured ripples of luminosity that slowly worked across the ceiling and down the walls was to stand in the presence of mystery.

Another silence. Julia and Viktor knew this moment well, had experienced it in the company of many other crews who came and went through the decades.

Again Julia felt the churn of somber, slow luminosities stretching into the foggy darkness beyond their lamps' ability to penetrate. There was a sense of silent vitality in the ponderous ferment of vapor and light, a language beyond knowing. As a field biologist she had learned to trust her feel for a place, and this hollow of light far beneath a dry world had an essence she had for decades tried to grasp, not with human ideas, but by opening herself to the experience.

They snapped out of it. She let the others work, keeping to the side. Sample taking, vids to shoot, measurements of distance and density and pressure; the usual. There was an advantage to standing apart and watching the humans grub about at the bottom of the vast grotto, their lights spiking here and there like fingers probing. At least they didn't talk much.

A movement in the ceiling caught her eye. Pale tan strands came lacing through the mat, stretching like tendons. They made a mass that tilted and worked. Tubular stalks slid, fibers forked into layers, shaping, shaping. An outline seemed to bud up, shimmering and moist.

Julia's heart thumped. *Again.* A palpable sense of struggle, of concentration into this one focus . . .

The others saw it. They froze. "My . . . God," Daphne whispered. "I've read your accounts, seen the pictures, but . . ."

Julia had not seen the mat do this for several years. On the second descent of their first expedition the mat had made the same human outline, after two people had died of oxygen loss while exploring Vent A. She knew what to expect but found she was holding her breath. And here came that old prickly feeling again, washing over her skin.

Two rough protrusions sprouted at the top. At its base two more protrusions, slabs of dark mass extruding with aching effort into thicker tubes. At least three meters long, in all. And from the upper sides, above the two thickening tubes that now jutted from each side, a third blob, crusted as thick as tree bark, pulling itself out.

Viktor said it. "Human shape."

No mistake. The mat was responding, as it had before, to their entry. No one had died on a descent since that first strange incident, so the intent could not be malicious.

Daphne said softly, "It's so big . . . ?"

To Julia her voice sounded dry. "It's the mat's impression of us."

"How can it see us?" a crewman asked.

"It must sense enough to work out our outlines."

"Eyes?" he asked.

"The glowing is common," Julia said. "From surface webbed tissues, fed chemically by the substrate." She was sure they knew this from the scientific literature, but it was something else to actually see it, deep in a gloomy cavern. They could be asking questions for the same reasons people talk in haunted houses. "Apparently it communicates through its chambers with light. How far, we don't know."

There was more talk, but she just looked at the slow-moving mass. Parts of the mat looked somewhat like giant tube worms, such as those found deep in undersea vents on Earth. But there the analogy ended. The old questions rose in her, still unanswered. Sentience? Of some kind. Enough to control its environment.

But sentience implied some kind of selection pressure. She and Viktor had proposed that rationing the meager water resources could drive selection, and predictably, dozens of papers had criticized that. But did it have intelligence? Whole symposia had been devoted to just that issue. Julia had stopped accepting invitations to deliver interplanetary keynote addresses to those.

Viktor said, "We are thousand kilometers from other vents. Yet it knows to do this."

Daphne said, "And right away."

Julia aimed her own microcam at the shape and carefully swept the area to take it all in. Was the mat glow stronger around the form? "This looks about the same as the other manifestations. It'll probably stay here until we leave, as before."

"The entire planet is connected?" Daphne asked. "How?"

"With these glows?" Viktor answered, not moving, just watching the shape. "Or chemical signals? Or—notice those seams of iron in the walls? Conducts electricity pretty well."

One of the crewmen asked, "Was this what it was like when it . . . killed those two?"

Viktor said, "Was, yes. We never knew what happened, and has not happened again. Maybe was holding them, feeling all over them. Had covered some of their suits. Maybe to find out what they were. Anybody's guess."

Julia said, "Enough. Time to get back to sampling." Then she sent a private comm to Viktor. "What was that about the iron?"

He came closer, so she could see his grin. "You told me way back, in your minilectures, 'member? First sign of life in fossil record was iron oxides, locking up the oxy that the first life breathed out."

"So those layers—" She waved a gloved hand at the bloodred seams that ringed the cavern, and which the mat species conspicuously did not cover. "You think they're evidence of the early origin of life here?"

"A side issue. I think like engineer. Occurs to me, how to send information from Vent A to here? Chemicals, hard to send so far. Glow—like relay stations through thousand kilometers of caves? Hard. No. But wait—" Viktor's eyebrows lifted. "Layers of iron conduct electricity. Send signals through them, you have global network built into planet."

She blinked. "You never mentioned this before."

"Never thought of it before—until just now."

"Um. If the geologists work on it—"

"No need geologists. Already have the magnetic data, right? I showed you. Something funny about this vent, right in middle—yes, look."

She followed his pointing finger. The Marsmat definitely clumped close to the seams, without covering them. And the mat was thicker here than she had seen in any vent so far. "How's this explain your data? Big, long-pulse electromagnetic waves?"

Viktor shrugged—visibly, despite the suit. "Not sure. When don't know, do experiment."

"Huh? What?"

"We pulsed the pressure flaps, to open. Use same capacitor on those iron layers"—he gestured enthusiastically—"see what happens."

"Uh, now?" Descents were elaborately planned nowadays, and this had not been discussed.

"We have oxy. Others, crew, are doing routine work. Let's."

She eyed him skeptically. She loved this guy, but he was sometimes crazed. He gave her the big, broad grin, and she laughed. Maybe he was just being male; testosterone seemed to drive guys onward.

They got it rigged surprisingly quickly. Viktor was never happier than when he was tinkering, trying something new. Come to think of it, so was she. They attached long black shielded leads to two nearby strata, only a few meters away. Viktor drilled short holes into the stone and sank stub contacts into them. She suspected he had thought of this experiment before, else why bring just the right gear? But let it go. The red bands were of some basaltic iron-oxide-rich layers, probably over 3 billion years old—or so said one of the team, the geo guy.

Following protocol, Julia alerted Gusev about what they were trying. Gusev objected right away and pointed out that none of this had even been discussed in preplanning meetings. She told them they were going to do it, anyway. The Gusev operations officer—the OO, whose always-seeing-trouble motto was "oh-oh"—started sputtering.

Viktor called out on their comm line that ran up the monofilament to the winch. Reception was good, another vast improvement over the relay system in the first expedition. He went through Expedition Control and alerted the satellite superintendent to focus their orbiting arrays on the vent area. Those had originally picked up the odd low-frequency emissions during a routine orbital scan of the whole planet. Again objections. "Now Gusev acts like Earthside," Viktor said, grimacing.

Julia nodded, having fun. "Everything in triplicate." More like playing hooky from school than research, yes.

Viktor told them to just do it. Then he turned the capacitor system voltage to the max. Daphne asked why. "Big losses in strata, resistive load, have to overcome. Prob'ly won't work. Get nothing. Still—" and he closed the switch.

No drama. Some sparking for a second at the lower connection, then nothing but the hum of the electromotor discharge. Viktor kept it on for ten seconds, off for five, on for ten, then started a more complex pattern.

"What's the point of this pulse pattern?" Julia asked.

"Just trying things."

"You really hadn't thought of this before, had you?"

He grinned, lines crinkling deeply around his eyes. "You always say I'm tinkerer. So I do."

He kept this up for minutes, watching the pulser readouts intently, and they got a heads-up call from the OO. Julia was off checking on the team, and when she came back over to his "experiment," Viktor said, "Orbital low-frequency antenna is picking up emission. From here."

Julia felt a thrill, plus confusion. "Why? What's going on?"

"Stimulate a system maybe."

Julia frowned. "Some sort of—what?"

A team member said over comm, "How about some kind of induced resonance?"

Julia had no idea what that meant. Viktor said carefully, "More likely, somebody answering."

It took a moment for her to get her head around the idea. Viktor started switching the settings on the pulser. "I'll run a sequence, move around the parameter space," he muttered to her. She could not keep up with his moving hands, the readings for volts and amps. "System has high inductance."

"Which means?"

"Responds slowly. So I go to longer pulses, see what high voltage gets us."

He held the pulser to thirty-second sine waves. Minutes passed. The OO called through: higher emissions from the satellite antenna, also now in thirty-second waves. "Is echoing," Viktor said triumphantly.

"What's echoing?" Julia asked. "Do you think the mat has some capacity to—"

Crackling came from the stub contacts. Julia looked toward them and saw some vapor steaming out from the rock. "What?"

Viktor quickly turned down both volts and amps. "Funny. We are not putting much power through—"

The crackling got louder. Sparks at the contacts.

"Breakdown voltage?" Viktor asked, staring at the vapor now boiling from the contacts. "Our pulser, we're not near that level. Must be coming *in.*"

Julia heard a humming from the capacitor. Green sparks jumped out from the iron seam. "What's—" Then it exploded.

5.

THE STROMATOLITE EMPIRE

BRINGING VIKTOR UP had taken forever, like hours ticking in the back of her mind. Julia had lost it once, shouting at them, pulling at his harness to get it right, trying to be everywhere at once. Literally—she ran up beside him on the monofilament, holding on to the yoke and hanging beside him to see that the pressure seals on his wounds did not come off or start to leak.

Early on, she had popped one of her emergency pills, called blue devils by the crew. Hers were custom-designed and kicked in within a minute. She ordered the rest of the team to follow suit and was surprised to find that they already had. *Way ahead of me . . .*

It was hard treating injuries inside a suit. The only thing to do was to apply pressure wraps around it and seal off the fluid seepage through the woven skinsuit. Still, blood oozed through. Somehow. She spent the whole ascent tending to him, getting them around rocky obstructions, calling to Gusev for help when his shoulder wound opened and started spattering blood onto her visor.

It sprayed from the pressure differential, not because he was suddenly blowing an artery. She learned that only

minutes later, of course—no help when the blood spattered on her visor and helmet and she could not see much,
then smeared it trying to clear her field of view . . . and
she panicked. Flat out panicked, no apologies, just plain
losing it in the middle of a dark vertical cavern with only
her to look after him.

He was unconscious, thank God, and could not hear her
frantic panting, her spitting-mad swearing. She had
clicked off her comm, anyway, out of pure carelessness, a
clumsy amateur error.

Only her training saved her, and maybe him. She
moved quickly. Halfway up, leveraging him around a
tricky turn, she realized that she was calm again. And
though she was fretting below the surface, on top she was
alert, quick, crisp. The blue devil at work. But even it
couldn't stop her from worrying.

The trouble with doing in-suit medical was you
couldn't see more than the patient's face, or the wound,
couldn't do any diagnostics much beyond blood pressure
and pulse rate—which were visible on the suit backpack
readout. Plus you were fighting the damned vacuum all
the way. Slapping biomed patches on, and then self-
sealants, was just about all anyone could do.

As they came over the lip of the vent, residual moisture
on their suits froze to rime and fell as a dusting of snow.
The flakes fumed away within seconds, but Julia lost her
hold on Viktor and he spun out over the mouth and
groaned. She cursed herself and let the others secure him.
She felt exhausted, heart hammering. They got Viktor into
the rover at last.

They split up into the four who would remain to finish
the descent research and the four who would fly Viktor

back. Vaquabal knew plenty more medical than Julia, so he did most of the work on Viktor, right after liftoff.

Three wounds, all bloody, seeping. Blood pressure low, unconscious, heart rate rapid, and Viktor's eyes jerked alarmingly behind his eyelids. Vaquabal moved with assurance. Julia handed him things from medstores and did not have nearly enough to do, so she fidgeted and checked the med display screens, most of them unintelligible. Just before they landed, Vaquabal said, "He's stable. I will do the surgery."

"It's necessary?"

"We must dig out bits of shredded suit and capacitor."

"How far in?"

"Not far, I think." Suddenly he beamed. "He is in no real danger now, you know."

She made herself take a long breath. "No, I didn't."

Despite Vaquabal, the operation took a long time, and, worse, he would not allow her in the surgery. There were qualified nurses, after all, he argued. And she was tired and needed to lie down. All this was doubtless true, but none of such advice could she seem to make use of. Instead, she paced and her mind spun and she could not even make any conversation longer than a few sentences.

Earthside sent probing questions. Julia had gotten used to having minor incidents blown up into media fodder, but this was real and she wasn't having any, thank you. The time delay was tens of minutes in this part of the orbital cycle, a season when Julia and Viktor avoided talking with Earth at all. One never quite got over the need to get some response back. And the solar storm was blowing gouts of plasma, flooding some of their links with static. The sun was going through rough weather, spewing out big, noisy torrents.

Julia sent terse messages to Viktor's relatives, none of them close any longer, and hers as well. Then Axelrod got on the big screen.

"What was he doing?" Axelrod asked after the usual extending of concern.

"Sending pulsed electrical currents into an iron seam," she began, and tried to explain, but she was not in the mood.

So she signed off. As if waiting for a cue, Praknor appeared. The woman seemed to have a talent for showing up as something of far greater importance was about to happen—the expedition planning, the descent itself, and now this.

Julia kept her face frozen while Praknor voiced the same sentiments as Axelrod, and then said, "Assuming Viktor recovers—"

"Assuming?"

A two-second pause, then: "Of course, he's going to be fine, but I meant—"

"What?"

"—that it underscores the concerns we all have Earthside—"

"You're on Mars."

"—that you've been risking yourselves here for decades, for an entire generation, in fact—"

"We live here."

"—of course, and this just underlines the extent of the unknowns, so many unknowns, and—"

"Unknowns are why we're here."

"—that you both are *so* famous now, that any possible

injury to you gets big news coverage, doubts about the entire program, causes Consortium stock to plunge—"

Julia snorted sardonically.

"—and such oscillations in profitability are just not in tune with a structurally modern multiworld corporation—"

"The only one, actually."

"—that you both, when you've really had time to consider the issue in full, should consider giving up this risky life and—"

Julia gave her a long moment, but nothing more came out. "And?"

"Mr. Axelrod really needs you on the moon."

"Why?"

"Because it's a lot safer. And there are a lot of doubts about the whole Lunar Enterprises profile. Having big names in charge—"

"We're not CEOs. We're explorers."

"—will shore up public confidence in that entire arm of the business."

Julia let a few seconds trickle away. People respond differently under pressure, and—"You just gave away your whole agenda, right?"

Praknor looked suddenly stunned. "Yes. You needed to know. And in a high-stress time like this, you deserve to have all the cards on the table."

Julia let herself down easily into a chair. "This is some kind of new management technique, right?"

Praknor betrayed a morsel of uncertainty, her lips working. "There's a big nuke on its way. Axelrod wants you on it on the return trip."

"What?"

"You wanted to know. The spacecraft just barely made the orbital window to get here."

"And *we* don't know?"

"It's corporate confidential."

"But not an utter state secret, because you—"

"Mr. Axelrod instructed me to broach—"

"Julia?" Vaquabal was at her elbow.

Julia spun toward him, shoving Praknor away. "How—"

"He is fine. Awake now."

Julia turned back to Praknor, eyes flashing, breath fuming. "We're going to goddamn well live forever, y'know."

Viktor didn't want to dwell on the accident. "Just another data point," he said. "Goal is to look for pattern."

"Um," she said. He already had a laptop and was fooling around with the magnetic data. She said nothing about Praknor, just sat and let him play. He had lost a fair quantity of blood and taken penetrating wounds at hip, right shoulder, and left side. The suit had absorbed a lot of the blast, and its tight-woven threads stopped the wound from rupturing out into the low pressure. He sat up in the crisp white sheets and shrugged off questions about how he was feeling. The point, he gruffly let her know, was not to feel, but to think.

Julia knew this mood was the best signal he could give her about how he felt. She said softly, "I'll talk to the mission analysis people—"

"You, we, never believe them," he said. "They have data, but we were *there*. Big difference."

"Something went wrong with the capacitor, they're saying."

Viktor managed a dry chuckle, hands crinkling the sheets. "Voltage surge came from iron layer."

"Um. Why?"

"You notice how mat looked?"

She closed her eyes, her method of recalling a scene in the field, learned from long experience. "It . . . fluoresced."

"*Da.* What else?"

"Green sparks."

"*Da.* I check, use physics tables, is right color for simple voltage breakdown in water vapor and carbon dioxide, at low pressure."

She patted his hand. "You always do the numbers first."

"Keeps you honest. So, at the pressure we measure, what voltage breaks down that gas?"

"Um, lots."

"Quantitative, is 640 volts per meter."

"I'm supposed to be, what? Impressed?"

"I was sending couple volts into seam."

"No chance the capacitor just failed?"

He shook his head sadly at her ignorance. "Discharge came from seam, not capacitor."

"So what went wrong?"

"Nothing. Somebody got, maybe, enthusiastic. Somebody trying to get through."

"To . . ."

"To answer, *da.*"

The whole Praknor behavior pattern was another matter. Julia could see that the woman had already rubbed a lot of the outpost staff the wrong way. She had already spent a half year in narrow quarters on the way to Mars, and plainly the stresses—despite plenty of Earthside training—had compressed an already overcontrolled personality into strata of anxieties.

Confinement had a way of telescoping relationships and tensions. On Mars, if the staff had had to stay inside for most of the time, it would have become a barking asylum. That was why Earthside carefully studied possible crew members; but the stress of passage to Mars was even worse, and far less easy to project from Earthside simulations. The whirling stellar void visible on interior screens, the looming prospect of aerobraking—knowing that two had failed in the last twenty years, killing the crews—these unsettled the mind. So why had Earthside sent this new-style manager type, whose specialty seemed to be intimidation? Somebody didn't understand that explorers were not corporate types, so they had risked random personal chemistry—*nitro, meet glycerin, you're going to have a blast.*

She had a sudden hunch. Praknor had been sent as a special emissary. Axelrod had probably smoothed the way for her, and now Gusev Outpost was paying the price in crew friction.

Another piece of data: Julia checked with Outpost Control, and, indeed, they were pumping extra-big volumes of water up from the ice sheets below Gusev, filling the plastic-lined subsurface reservoirs they had labored for years to install. Mars ran on energy from nuclear thermal units and plenty of water. With those they could do all the chemistry they wanted. It also meant easy refueling for a fast-turnaround nuke.

The incoming nuke was "corporate confidential,"

which meant that Axelrod had yet another trick up his sleeve. There were a few more days before it landed, ten klicks away, at the pumping station. So Julia avoided Praknor and worked away in the lab. It could be her last chance to do biology that mattered.

The Stromatolite Empire.

Dreaming, she was standing on mud flats at low tide. Volcanic cones towered over a haze of gray ash, the landscape lit by spurts of hot lava. Streams of lava hissed into a shallow dark sea. Waves whipped by high winds pounded basalt cliffs. Hummocks of basalt stood on the shoreline, glistening when the fitful sun struck them with highlights of crystals. Gray-green life had begun on these mounds, clinging, fighting for nutrients in a violent land. Clouds parted for a moment, and she looked up, expecting to see the moon's pale face. Instead, a blue-green sparkle danced in the turbulent air. A swollen crescent moon leered at the yellow horizon. Earth.

And maybe Mars, even earlier.

The Stromatolite Empire.

She studied the research summary squirted up from Earth at her request. She had not thought of looking at the data on stromatolites in this way before, but as soon as she did, plenty of researchers were willing to help, so this arrived within hours.

Life on Earth had taken off after an excruciatingly slow start. Though simple cells began within about 400 million years after the planet had cooled off enough to allow it, they took 2.3 billion years to get around to making complex ones—eukaryotes—with machinery in a nucleus.

Another 400 million years plodded by before simple sea-weeds arrived. Stacking cells together to make more complicated plants was apparently a tough invention, taking 600 million years more. Only when all this was in place, barely 600 million years ago, did the Cambrian explosion of species occur, and complexity took off on its exponential rise.

But by the time all this runaway action started, the plants had flooded Earth's atmosphere with oxygen, making things tough on the anaerobes. So they had mostly retreated underground, where they still thrived down to depths of several kilometers. Having a blanket of poisonous oxygen over the surface had probably inhibited them. So she thought of looking back, at the microbial communities which had survived through almost all the Earth's history—stromatolites.

As an undergraduate in Adelaide she took a trip to see what they looked like and was astonished that they seemed to be just like rocks. Irregular, encrusted columns of rock.

For decades now she had seen just such bulging columns of microbial life, deep in the Martian caverns. Forms on both planets used DNA to pass on their genomes, but there were myriad differences. Earthside biologists were still fighting over the implications of this, most of the discussion going right by her at high velocity. She was an author on dozens of papers, arguing both sides of the issue, with titles like "Identity and Evolution of Martian Vent Endosymbiotic Methanogens." (After the first few, Viktor did not want his name on such tongue-twisting papers and did not even read them anymore.)

Either Mars had sent life's early kernels to Earth, in

shards blasted out by incoming meteorites, or the other way around.

She didn't care all that much which way the argument would turn out. It was *all* wonderful.

Geologists gauged the growth of modern Earth stromatolites by seeing how much they had covered over old soft drink bottles from the 1920s—about a millimeter a year. The microbial mats were slow, careful, with the gingerly care of the vastly elderly.

And when poisonous oxygen appeared, they had lapsed. Their species numbers fell, but unlike the vast run of all life, they did not die out. Along a few shores and lake beds, the mats still waited patiently, much reduced, in their warm salty ponds, waiting to again dominate the oceans . . .

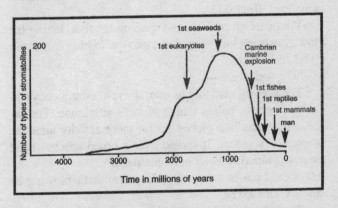

She remembered her dream. Stromatolites on Mars? As the thin atmosphere chilled and drained away to space, the microbial colonies had to retreat. Into the soil. But without the competition of the oxy invaders from above, they had not suffered the losses their Earthly brethren had to endure. They could spread in the larger caverns and rock pores the light gravity Mars allowed, find new ways to develop, make a network that now wrapped in labyrinthian caverns through the planet. Perhaps they were not now separate species, but something that Earth had never seen: an integrated organism, based on cooperation, the Martian Way.

Viktor hobbled into the conference room, leaning on Julia, scorning the crutch she offered. The physicist Brad McMullen was waiting for them, the display screens around the room alive with colors. Uchida was working at a keyboard.

"We're getting plenty of those signals from the Vent R area, sir," Brad said.

Viktor let go of Julia and spun on his foot, letting the low grav bring him around and into the waiting chair. "No 'sir.' Just 'Viktor.' "

"Uh, well, here—"

The activity map told its own story: low-frequency signals, magnetic pulses really, of large amplitude. The orbital antennas had picked up far more activity after the capacitor accident. It spread over a broad spectral band and was tapering away only gradually.

"Could not be from this solar storm that's blowing by us?" Viktor asked.

Brad shook his head. "We're getting surges from that, sure. The storm plasma emits higher harmonics, which can screw up our readings on the ground—but we can filter that out."

An orbiter had even caught a burst of light from the

original vent, Vent A, at the time of the electrical surge at Vent R.

Viktor beamed. "See?" he said to Julia. "The somebody who answered is trying to find us."

Julia eyed the display suspiciously. "What's the team at Vent R report?"

Brad said, "Plenty of light coming from the mat. They've wormed their way into some pretty big caverns—one bigger than a basketball stadium, Daphne said—and they can see all the way across the thing, just from the mat glow."

"Damn," Julia said. "I should *be* there."

"They send pictures?" Viktor asked, and she knew it was to distract her. Brad nodded and popped some up on the screens. Julia gasped at the brilliant ivory glow, the steepled vastness above, long streamers of mat growth hanging in billowing orange banners, hollows and shadows and flickering luminosities, like a thousand candles lighting a stony cathedral.

"Something wants to talk," Viktor said with a slow smile. "To do the talk magnetic."

Praknor skipped the introductory smile this time. "I've been instructed to curtail your exterior expeditions."

Julia had warned Viktor, but still his nostrils flared. "No descents? Preposterous."

"The corporate Accident Review Board has reviewed your conduct," Praknor said evenly, looking at Viktor with a remote, steady gaze. "You conducted an unapproved experiment involving high voltages—"

"Couple volts, milliamp currents," Viktor said.

"—endangering all personnel, and suffering potentially fatal wounds. All without review, or ever a suggestion of prior advisement."

"Was field experiment." Viktor leaned forward significantly, clasping his big hands in front of him, eyes narrowing across the table at her. "You have done such?"

"I am a cross-science specialist, and I know procedures must be followed in every hazardous environment. So does the Consortium."

"Um." Viktor raised his eyebrows. "Very impressive terms, but is not fieldwork."

Praknor gave each word weight. "Without. Proper. Procedures."

"That is nature of field. New things happen."

"I'm afraid the Consortium views this entire incident as a severe wake-up call. You two are our primary assets. The Consortium cannot allow you to risk yourselves."

Julia had been holding herself back, but now said as mildly as possible, "Don't you think that's up to us?"

Praknor said evenly, "We all have the highest respect for you. Your faces are known globally, your—"

"We are just people trying to do a job."

Praknor looked stymied, her lower lip turning in, teeth pressing the blood from the whitening red. She blinked, making a decision. "All right, then, here it is. Mr. Axelrod wants you back on the moon."

A moment's silence, then: "Why?" Viktor demanded. "Nothing we can do there."

"You'll be safe, secure, you can retire."

Viktor looked more puzzled than affronted. His brow wrinkled, looking like the grain in a weathered board left outside. "Too young to quit!"

Praknor's face softened just a bit, her eyebrows rising.

"Frankly this isn't a middle-aged game here. Never was. It's tough."

Julia stiffened. "We know that better than anyone."

"I'll skip over the early days, when, as I recall, Viktor got hurt in a vent. Julia, just last year you sprained an ankle. Three years ago Viktor broke an arm."

"Accidents, is all—"

"Happening more and more often to you two—"

"—and all better now," Viktor finished. "And what about Mars Effect, eh?"

Praknor took a breath, soldiered on. "Still—"

"Moon is boring!" Viktor slammed his hand on the table. "Is dead!"

Praknor said, "I didn't want to put it this way, but Axelrod said to use trumps, so—I'm just relaying word here. It's a Consortium decision, not revocable. You're going home."

"Moon is not home," Viktor said quietly.

"You can't go to Earth, the gravity would immobilize you."

"Moon is boring! Nothing to do."

Julia said mildly, "The big microwave antennas the Consortium's building, the solar cell farms—they're built mostly by robots, right?"

Praknor nodded quickly. "You could learn all those new technologies, supervise—"

"Plenty robots here already," Viktor said. "Not good at exploring. Maybe putting up Tinkertoy microwave antennas is okay for them. Not us."

Praknor tried a quick, unconvincing smile. "How about taking it easy for a while? You could fly in the new pressure dome they're putting up—"

"Like Andy?" Julia shot back.

Praknor stiffened. "I didn't think you would bring that up, since it was under your directive that he—"

"Hey, it was his idea, and he had plenty of experience." Julia was sorry she had said it the instant it was out. Even if it was indeed true.

Praknor said slowly, "That's not how the Consortium sees it."

When they were alone, Viktor was surprisingly calm. "We start publicity campaign, right now. Go to Earthside media."

"I agree," Julia said, though she had a sinking feeling. "Let's go through the Consortium publicity office. We know them."

"Even so, they'll block us. Maybe capture the broadcast."

"Not if it's an interview."

"Um. Maybe best, yes. I'll send inquiry to some friends, start them working on it."

"We need a big splash."

"I'll play up my injury, maybe say I can't travel." He grimaced. "Is lie."

"A media untruth." Julia patted his hand.

They tried to get back to work.

But Julia could not stop thinking about the fluorescent-lit, acronym-ridden, numbing culture she saw on the vid. Some would slop over onto the moon, certainly. Any civilian with the bucks could buy a week or two there in the "pleasure domes"—though the orbital Mars Sats were the big draw and cheaper. Even the thought of rubbing up against a steady stream of such people made her tired.

Mars never had. She wasn't young anymore, for sure, but there were moments when she still felt youthful jolts of inexplicable exhilaration, energy mixed with yearning, a certain simmering sense of invincibility. Maybe it was Mars. Here you needed rugged confidence, or else you'd cower in your hab, afraid of the whole wide world outside. So she and Viktor had developed their own aspirations, steady like a faith that did not need expression, a hope that could sting like chlorine.

Without Mars, she knew she would never feel that way again.

Daphne found Julia, intersecting her in one of the subsurface corridors. "Hey, got some results," Daphne said brightly.

Julia blinked at her. The Vent R descent seemed like an age ago, though it was only a week. "Uh, great."

Daphne's "office" was a tiny compartment. They wedged in as Julia reflected on the comparatively vast spaces she and Viktor occupied. "We got a good long way down, over a klick," Daphne said. "Into side channels, too."

On the wall a satellite photo appeared, overlaid with blue lines. "Here's the subsurface map. Got most of it with those climbing 'bots we took down." The lines followed a jagged but mostly radial pattern, fanning out from the Vent R mouth. "And now we add the magnetic field data, waves emitted from—"

Orange lines appeared. They were broader, mostly patterns of cross-hatching. "They follow the mat," Daphne concluded triumphantly. "Not perfectly, but close enough that it can't be an accident."

"Striking." Julia peered at the cross-hatching. "The magnetic waves, the low-frequency emissions Viktor has been working on—this is where they come from?"

Daphne was a biologist like Julia, but Mars staff had to be versatile. She said, "I know, I can't see any reason why they should overlap—but they do."

Julia smiled. Daphne was a lot like her younger self, plunging ahead. "So the mat uses electromagnetism, too?"

Daphne traced with her fingers some of the lines, thinking, not answering right away. "Seems unlikely, doesn't it?"

"Evolution is inventive."

"There are electric eels that use charge to find and shock prey. But waves . . ." Daphne shrugged. "What's that saying of yours?"

Julia wondered if the staff thought of her and Viktor as pontificator has-beens. Then she realized that, indeed, she did have stereotypical remarks. Like "Correlation may not mean causality?"

"Yeah, that. I remember hearing that the disease rate in Europe goes up with temperature. But it's the insects carrying the diseases that respond to temperature, get more active—not the weather making people sick."

"So the mat may not respond to magnetic fields directly?"

Daphne spread her hands. "Sure, I—"

"But then, what blew our capacitor?"

Viktor called her, and she found him collapsed on their bed. "You're overdoing it."

He ignored her. "Got a squirt from Earthside, mysterious."

"Axelrod." Not a question.

"Assistant to him. Said the moon antenna system launched a powered sail toward us."

Julia sat on the bed and felt his brow. Maybe a little warmer than usual. "This soon? I thought they weren't going to have the power transmission system up and running for years."

Viktor thumbed on their wall screen. A deep-space picture, magnified to the limits of resolution. A silvery disk hung in the black. Below it, hanging by struts like a spiderweb, was a small golden package. "To boost this lightweight package to high velocity takes only a few antennas. Axelrod said to send this as test package."

Julia had paid little attention to the grandiose Consortium plans. The collision between global climate change and rising energy demands was the biggest international issue Earthside. Storms were wrecking cities, the ocean was lapping at dikes, Kansas was a desert and India had floods. Yet the cheapest path to prosperity was to burn cheap coal and let somebody else worry about the accumulated carbon dioxide in the air. A classic tragedy of the commons—profit was private, waste was communal.

And here came the Consortium to the rescue. Viktor's next picture showed the beginnings of the microwave antenna network Axelrod's web of companies was building. Eventually it would trace around the moon's disk, as seen from Earth, because that gave the highest focusing of the incoming microwave beams. Those beams would strike football-field-sized receivers, just chicken wire really. The induced power in those wires would feed directly into Earth's power grid—cheap electricity.

The original power would come from the harsh sunlight hammering at the moon's surface. Captured in huge solar panels, fed to the microwave antennas, the energy source would be in its way an environmentalist's dream: the environment affected would be a quarter of a million miles away from Earth.

But that was a decade in the future, at least. Robots were making the solar panels on the moon, extracting iron from the lunar regolith with magnets, making wiring from it, building the antennas. Nearly all raw materials they got from the moon itself. Julia hadn't even realized that they had any of the big lunar antennas up and running, but there they were—big wire cups on slender stalks, light in the lunar gravity. They pointed skyward and radiated power to the silvery sail.

"Pushed it out of orbit around moon," Viktor said, thumbing through more images of the sail. "Gave it speed. Sent it into long orbit for Mars."

Julia arched eyebrows, impressed. "Nice toy demo, but—"

"Its job, they say, was to get here before that big nuke."

"Huh?"

"Nuke had already left when Axelrod decided to send this," Viktor said. "To beat its time in getting here."

"Why?"

"That is the mystery." Viktor grinned, though she could see he was bone-tired.

"Just showing off, I bet."

He waved this away. "Squirt from Earthside says not. Axelrod wants me to pick it up when it aerobrakes."

"What? Why—wait, you can't do it."

"Orders."

"You're in no shape—"

"They said we should both get it. For our eyes only."

He grinned, always happy when intrigues got more complicated.

"When's it get here?"

"Two days. Sail burns up on entry. Payload chutes down. Trying to set the package—that little golden-wrapped thing, you saw?—down in Gusev."

"Three days before the nuke." Julia frowned. "Damned funny."

"I like mysterious."

6.

LAST TRAIN OUT OF DODGE

TO KEEP HER MIND off their situation, she puzzled over the Vent R incident. Science beat politics every time.

Viktor had pointed out the biggest clue: the correlation between water vapor pressure near the site and the magnetic waves.

Except for birds who used the magnetic field to find their way on migrations, Earthly life mostly ignored magnetism. A few bacteria carried minute bits of iron and appeared to orient in a magnetic field, but how it helped them was unclear. She shook her head; would evolution have produced the same answer to the riddle of survival on Mars as on Earth?

She sat and thought and watched the Martian landscape as sharp shadows stretched across the afternoon. A thin filament of cloud towered in the distance. Sure enough, it was in the right direction for Vent A. The mat was opening its thick seals again, following a pattern no one had deciphered yet. She added one more data entry to her slate; this was the first venting in several months. And nobody knew why the mat did it, though there were plenty of theories. Vapor pressure . . .

The early discovery of methane in the Martian atmosphere, at ten parts per billion, had suggested that life might be the source—but it was not a clear proof. Scientists could always rummage around and find other interpretations, which in turn suggested further tests, and that was the dance of science itself.

Maybe a recent volcanic eruption had vented the methane from the warm interior; that happened often on Earth. Or perhaps, since comets were known to have methane ices, one had blundered into the atmosphere. And a calculation showed that the water vapor in the Martian atmosphere, kindled by ultraviolet, could react with the methane and erase it in a few centuries. So any volcanoes or comets had to be recent events. But in the hundreds of thousands of orbital photos there seemed no clear evidence for recent volcano ventings, or impact craters from comets. So the issue had drifted along without clear, sharp confirmation for any view. Until the Marsmat discoveries.

Now they knew that the Marsmat could send signals over great distances, hundreds of kilometers at least, far larger than any single mat. They had seen that in Vent R, when the humanlike image shaped up out of the mat on a first visit.

Why communicate over such scales? To sense a coming pulse of hydrogen sulfide vapor from deep below, tell the entire network, and make ready? A clear survival value in that, she supposed. Could organisms evolve such detailed response in this harsh place? Could an Earthly biofilm do it? Maybe biologists had never noticed. On Earth mats like the stromatolites were considered to be early, primitive forms with severe limitations and no future. The biofilms had just been outrun by other forms in the rich, warm, wet oceans.

Julia went out to the big greenhouse and gardened to clear her mind. They all went to the greenhouse when they were tired of the endless sunset hues of Mars. Or when they longed to see something alive that wouldn't talk. That first whiff of greenhouse air was a great morale boost. Greenhouses processed air better than any filter, carrying a particular fresh scent unlike Earth, undefinable, more raw. She would miss it.

She barely nodded to others working. Privacy was precious, and they'd adopted the Japanese habit of not intruding on one another's space unless by mutual agreement. She skipped the fields of wheat, rice, and potatoes, various beans, lines of broccoli and tomatoes. These looked ordinary, and then she walked under the canopy of carrot stalks so green they changed the Marslight.

No one could predict what the combination of low gravity and low sunlight would do; some crops died, others became green gushers. There was something very calming about being surrounded by green leaves and vines, all nodding gently in the endless updraft. To strengthen trees and stalks, they had to run breezes, fake winds. She recalled how, in the early years, she and Viktor had taken advantage of the absence of others, off on rover trips, to make love amid the churning plants—exciting, though chilly. It'd always been a big turn-on for her to look over the shoulder of a lover into the swaying foliage of a tree. Viktor said it showed she was a real primitive.

She worked with her hands to free her mind—pruning, harvesting, helping. Even a biologist had to keep reminding herself that life found ways nobody could foresee. Growing up in Australia, she had marveled at lizards in the deserts that absorbed water through channels in their feet, because they were most likely to come across moisture in shallow damp spots. On the other hand, nature made its creatures narrow of purpose.

Silently she joined a team that was harvesting corn. It was good, solid work, letting her hands go and have fun while her mind could idle, running on its own. Cut, sort, bag . . .

One winter she had gone out on a Girl Scout trip, and they had stayed overnight in a bush farmhouse with a tin roof. In the night birds thumped heavily onto the roof, because when they looked down from their migrating patterns, it reflected the moon and so looked like an inviting pond. She had rushed outside and found dazed ducks, given them water, and off they had gone—no doubt to make the same mistake again, because nature saw no point in giving them the processing power to learn from experience, much less to tell others of their kind. If there had been many tin roofs, they would never have made the migration, never made new ducks. Nature had not made them too narrow, not this time.

Too narrow . . . Could evolution have found a way to give the mat some use for the magnetic field waves? It sounded crazy.

Julia was thinking so hard about this that the burst of hand-clapping startled her. When she brought in a bushel of picked corn, her coworkers applauded. "Fastest picking I've ever seen," a man said. Julia was startled. She had not even noticed.

Sitting in the cafeteria, nursing a cup of coffee, a young woman from the bio section asked, "Mind if I sit down?" The room was crowded. Julia waved her into a chair. Stephanie, she recalled, a biochem type. They had even been on a dozen-author paper together, on how the Marsmat used sulfur for energy.

"Nothing much to do," the woman chatted on. "I'm a sexile for the next few hours."

"Uh, what?"

"Exiled for sex. My roomie has a guy in."

"Uh, oh." At first Julia blinked, affronted at this sudden bolt of intimate detail. Then she realized that this was another effect of living in a tight little base, however grand the views were outside. Unavoidably, formal hierarchy dissolved under the rub of informal daily life. See the commander daily slurping coffee and washing dishes, and pretty soon he doesn't look like the leader anymore. Even legends did scut work—or should.

The woman started happily chattering, and her talk went in Julia's ear and out the other. Only when the other woman started to notice did she make an attempt to respond. Julia was busy realizing how out of touch with the younger staff she was. *Could Praknor be right? Time to hang it up?*

*   *   *

Praknor tried to put her foot down over their excursion, eyes flashing. "No, it's ridiculous."

"Axelrod said we are to recover package," Viktor said.

"You can barely walk!"

"I'll do the walking," Julia said. "The route is along one of our standard drives, and I can do the driving, too."

"It's twenty-three kilometers—"

"We leave at dawn, back in plenty of time."

Praknor sat very still. "I believe we must define just who is now in charge here."

Julia said in a deliberately conversational tone, "Well, I hardly think it's a dichotomous choice. Still, no need getting our knickers in a twist when we can defer to Earthside on this one, eh?"

Earthside would be very surprised to be asked; tight control of excursions had faded away years ago. But she was counting on the fact that Praknor was so green she didn't know what the routine was.

Viktor picked this up. "And can talk to staff, too."

Praknor sputtered, but Viktor's intuition proved right. The staff would support the venerable Marsnauts, not a fresh manager who hardly had her Earthside smell worn off.

Julia sent a long message to the Consortium, and Praknor wrote one even longer. Off these went. Experience proved the rule: Earthside dithered for hours. Praknor got distracted with work. Nudge nudge, wink—

So they went. It helped that everybody was talking about the new results from the Pluto expedition, and a bit distracted. Nobody asked questions. The ISA discovery of a biosphere there had electrified them all. Julia had no idea what to think about the Pluto reports. The biology seemed impossible. But then, so had the news that the solar system's bow shock was moving inward. She had long before learned to let the outer world go on, without her attention. She put aside everything and focused on the task at hand—always, on risky Mars, a good idea.

Going out, Julia noticed how much of the landscape was now rutted and marked by the ever-busy humans. She could see the towers of their water-drilling fields in the distance. Some pingos nearby were thoroughly excavated, both for bio-signatures in the deep ice deposits and for geological data; then the ice was harvested, leaving holes yawning like mouths. Not far from them was the crumpled descent package.

This was yet another miracle of design. Hardly the size of a coffee table, the smart, carbon-fiber shell had survived the blistering plunge by flying itself. Stubby wings let it use the infalling energy to bank and lift, gaining the time to locate Gusev. Viktor insisted on parking only meters away, so she had a very short walk. The announced reason for this flight was some vital small parts for a malfed pressure control system, and they were indeed most of the payload mass. But when she lifted the parts out, there was a cylinder at the back. On it in big stenciled letters was FOR JULIA AND VIKTOR ONLY. In Axelrod's hand.

She got it back into the rover, and inside was a rolled-up letter. "It's so like Axelrod to send an old-fashioned letter rather than an electronic squirt," she said, opening it.

"Hang the expense," Viktor said. "Is also much more secure this way."

They read it together. "Now will be much fun to talk to Praknor," Viktor remarked.

*　　*　　*

"I can't believe it," Praknor said.

They showed her the letter. Axelrod had even written it by hand; he never trusted the security of digital media and more than once had been proved right. Praknor read it over twice.

"The big nuke is for heavy Mars hauling, yes." Viktor began, as usual, by illuminating the tech angle. "Will land with plenty supplies, rovers, support gear. But will take off with water in holds."

"This is insane," Praknor said quietly.

"Maybe, but is orders." Viktor even smiled.

"I thought, I was told, I was to prepare you for transfer to the moon. But, but—to send you to Pluto!"

"They need help," Julia said. "Nobody there has experience dealing with alien life, communication—"

"And *you* . . ."

Praknor didn't finish her sentence, but Julia knew how it went: *You over-the-hill types are going to ride out there in the biggest, best nuke yet built, to help? When young people like me are available?* Ah, the arrogance of youth!

"We are only part of it," Viktor said crisply. "This nuke has crew, supplies needed on Pluto, just needs us for maybe helping with the communication problem. And Axelrod, he has money in his mind, too."

Praknor shook her head. "There's no money to be made at Pluto. That's an ISA expedition."

Julia suppressed a smile. The whole nuclear rocket program had emerged from military, commercial, and exploratory arms. The Mars Prize itself had been the first step toward true international cooperation, and it had drawn two entries: Axelrod's Consortium from the USA, flying in big chemical boosters, and the Euro-Chinese end run, using a nuke.

After that, it seemed obvious that merging abilities and assets, with economies of scale, could make space a far easier enterprise. Ultimately that cooperation had formed the International Space Agency. Axelrod's can-do personality had driven much of it. Julia spoke with him nearly every week, still, but her memories of him were over two decades old now and fading. But she was sure that the man would never do anything that did not hold at least the promise of profit.

"You forget the ice asteroids," Viktor said.

Praknor just looked perplexed, so he went on. "Inner solar system was dried out by early, hot sun—the T Tauri stage, is called. Sun's light pressure blew lots of light elements out, so the gas giants are all beyond the asteroids— and even 'roids are dry. To develop inner solar system, need light elements—water, carbon dioxide, methane. There are whole chunks of that orbiting out beyond Neptune—the Pluto expedition found lots. Tested a few. Axelrod wants to move some in, far in—to here—so Consortium can use."

Praknor snorted with derision. "Move asteroids? Wouldn't it take huge energies?"

"No, little needed. 'Roids out there move with orbital velocities of maybe one, two kilometers per second. Slow. Take that away, they fall straight in toward sun."

"But even a small change, for such a huge mass—"

"Use nuke reactor. Melt some of ice, heat, blow it out back, makes rocket. Use the 'roid's own ice to move it. Cheap."

Praknor blinked, her mouth pursed, and then she stiff-ened. "That's what the board thinks?"

"Axelrod says so in his letter," Julia added. "Me, I think he wants to get all the help he can for the Pluto expedition. After all, it's getting plenty of media attention—distracting people from what we're doing here."

Praknor said slowly, "He wants to get back in the game."

Julia could tell by the subtle sag of Praknor's shoulders that she was accepting defeat. "If he can supply water to people in the asteroid belt between Mars and Jupiter, he can capture all the mining industry. There are more metals available in the belt than in the outer crust of the Earth."

"But is more," Viktor said, eyes crinkling.

"What?" Praknor was guarded, already hammered heavily by this torrent of news.

"On Pluto expedition is his daughter. And they are in deep trouble."

Before falling asleep, cuddling close, Julia said thought-fully, "Didn't these last few days seem, well, a bit odd?"

"How you mean?" Viktor was sleepy.

"First we get Praknor, who made a mess of dealing with us. Got our backs up."

"Axelrod is not diplomat."

"No, he's an order of magnitude better than mere diplo-mats. He's a conniver."

"How you mean?" Viktor turned off his light and got his skeptical look on his face. She knew that he would lis-ten for maybe a minute, then close his eyes and drift off to sleep. Very efficient.

"Praknor pushes us all out of shape by threatening to

ship us back to the moon. She believes it, too, and is the most abrasive person I've ever seen sent out here."

"Um." He did not open his eyes, but he said slowly, "So we think this is first of new breed."

"And she can point at the big nuke, due in soon."

"Last train out of Dodge."

"Huh?"

"I been watching movies. Westerns."

"Oh. Then Axelrod slips in this fast sail message, absolutely authentic, in his own hand."

"Personal touch."

"Good cop, bad cop."

Viktor chuckled. "Praknor, very bad cop. Good cop saves us from a routine life on moon. Holds out Pluto, where the action is right now. The nuke is already partway there, see? Energetically Mars is third of the way to Pluto."

She ran her hands over his back. "I love it when you talk technical."

"I know this."

She made a rude noise. "So we're to be part of a grand expedition, helping out his own daughter—and the Consortium can play it as a rescue plus science."

"Sells well."

"You got it. Great story, featuring our famous, fave heroes from the Mars Race."

"Is what Axelrod intended all along. Moon was phony choice."

She slapped his ass cheerfully. "And now we're glad to grab the chance! A month ago I'd have resisted leaving Mars at all."

"Now we are ready."

"Yes, we are."

"Axelrod smart guy."

Julia nudged him. "Plausible, right?"

"Does not matter."

"What? Why?"

"Because he could just order us to. But this way we're enthusiastic. Much better to have employees who want to do the work, *da*?"

She felt offended. "We're not employees!"

"To Consortium we are." He rolled over and put both arms around her. "Let them play their manager games. We have the fun. Is all that matters."

PART II

THE FAR DARK

Immensity is its own justification.
—William Rotsler

1.
THE ZAND

LIGHT—PALE, BLUE COLD, little more than star-shine—crept over the gray ice plains. Dancing blue and green auroral sheets shimmered in the deep blackness above. On the dayside skyline a turbid yellow stain swelled at the hard brim of the world. Then a sudden blinding-bright point threw stretched shadows across the hummocked land. The seventy-seven hours' night was over.

Sunlight, waxing yet still wan, laid siege to a rampart of spiky white needles. Temperatures edged up from the night's 96 degrees Absolute that made everything here rock-solid. Even the methane ice hills loomed like rumpled blue steel.

But the coming of the sun—now a pinpoint only as bright as a streetlight a block away—changed the landscape. Methane needles caught the sunglow, and their sharp crystalline spearpoints curled, sagged, slumped. Gray vapor rose to meet the tepid dawn. It met even colder, drier air from Darkside that came sliding in on a rushing wind.

Methane rain fell in wobbly dollops, spattering on black ice. The zand awoke.

It peered out at the slow awakening of a slumbering land. Its body stirred. These bleak days were not remotely like the warm breath of summer, now long lost. Centuries would elapse before Pluto again saw methane ice sublime into its pink haze. The grinning crescent of Charon above loomed large but was still too small to hold its gases. The eons had stripped Charon of its methane, leaving bare, rock-solid water ice. During the richly remembered summer Charon had grown a pearly vapor tail like a comet, while still stolidly performing its gravid waltz with Pluto. Now its vast, pocked plains yawned above as each world rotated with the other, face-to-face. Like dancers forever doomed to the same pace, the ice world's cycle repeated every 6.4 days.

Surface relays kindled by the sun sent crisp neural discharges coursing through the zand's body. The spherical shell that had sealed it from the long night split and retraced. Brittle rods clacked, withdrawing inside, finding fresh socketings in an internal skeleton. Pulpy organs sluggishly awoke. In such deep cold, only organic solvents could ooze to a slow, throbbing pulse.

The zand turned its ice-glazed lenses directly toward the hard point of radiance. This prickly stimulus was just barely enough. *Radiance.* Aided by energy hoarded through the bitter night, thick motor rings of muscle along the zand's daytime body began to pulse. The great beast moved. Sluggishly.

Just before easing into sleep the night before, the zand had marked an outcrop of foodrock and carefully covered it with snow. Now the ever-thickening rain beat upon the cache. The zand splashed through rivulets to the top of the knoll, fighting the humming wind that blew toward the dawn. As it struggled uphill, the chilly breeze seemed to be always against it.

Finally the top. Stiffly the zand extruded its blower and drove the rest of the damp, melting snow off the outcrop.

Nothing. Something had harvested this lode in the long night.

Darksiders. One had gotten by their fragile lines. Perhaps to do damage elsewhere?

Despair swept through it. Darksiders could slip through because the zand were all weak, terribly weak.

Then it put all thought aside and rested. Dizziness spun through the long body. Each move sapped its precious stores, and it knew now that it had used too much from its small stock of energy. This was going to be a very near thing.

It mustered more chemical energies within itself and went on. Its legs creaked and trembled.

Desperately it turned its head to scan the area for food. From this hummock it could see farther. The world's gentle curve was obvious from this height. If it found nothing, it would not live out another day.

There! On the horizon black spore cases popped open. Nitrogen, compressed and pent up all night, blew out the tiny cells locked inside. The plant's shell was as hard as the zand's own night armor, but it was designed to rupture at dawn.

Most of the hard seeds fell on barren ground and died. A few spun in long arcs toward the zand. This landed them at the base of the knoll. They instantly burrowed in. Ravenously, ecstatically, they ate. From their positive poles hissed the buoyant lifegas the zand so badly needed. Within their bodies the powerful solvent released by their banqueting reacted with their cell-stuff, yielding other, heavier gases. They split, dividing to multiply. Wriggling, they squirmed deep into the porous foodrock and spread across the rumpled face, their surging mass smothering it in a brown carpet.

The zand edged closer, waited for the right moment—and struck. Greedily it sucked in deep savory drafts of the zesty life-giving gases they gave forth. The brown mat curdled and died.

The zand's sick weakness vanished. The smoldering furnace of metabolism now ignited, and its fires sent waves of strength surging along its entire body.

For the first time since waking, the zand reared fully upright. Its spindly arms shook defiantly at the cold sky. Its chilled mind now fully unlocked. Loudly it trumpeted a hymn of praise to Lightgiver. That majestic Source of all life now floated entirely clear of the curved horizon, still shrouded in rising, swirling blue-white vapors and the driving, big-dropped rain.

Something fluttered out of the cloaking mists. A flapper, it must be, riding the turbulent mist currents toward the outcrop to steal from the dawn's wealth. The zand tensed to fight.

But it struck the ice, smacking and rolling. The big dark mass came thumping and tumbling to rest at the edge of the foodrock, sending cold steam purling up from where it lay.

Dead? More important—*new*. Strange. Round like Lightgiver, or like the zand itself at night, but smooth, shiny, hot. It even melted the rock-hard ice beneath it. In its polished surface the zand saw itself, grotesquely distorted.

Heat was wealth. The zand hungrily reversed its blower-organ and vacuumed the thing into its forward orifice.

Then came the first shock. This thing was heavy, throbbing, worse than a large flapper. Dull pain throbbed through the zand's alimentary tract. Its first impulse was to spew the offensive lump forth. But the zand had not survived countless nights to greet Lightgiver by merely obeying its impulses. It hunched closer to the outcrop and scooped up a generous helping of spicy mites. At once their furious body chemistry gave aid to its own. A fuming corrosive kindled in their first digestive stage. This syrup bit into the strange sphere. The shiny skin fumed and bubbled.

The zand's inward discomfort transmuted into a heady glow of well-being. Strange, vibrant tastes rippled through its body. Nothing except Self-merge had ever given it such joy.

It verged on delirium. Dimly, through a curtain of pleasure, it felt the rain of wobbly drops ease, mists lifting to unveil the hard, hot glory of Lightgiver's face. Ruby melt fluid trickled from warming rocks. Digestion simmering, the zand felt flooded as never before with power and hope. Turning its back to the wind, it sloshed away from the knoll where it had very nearly died.

Without a pause it dove into the dawn sea. Waves broke across it, bringing warmth. The sky brimmed with Lightgiver's promise. It was at peace.

It wondered where the shiny sphere had come from. Over the horizon, toward Lightgiver. An excellent puzzle to solve on such a fine day. It moved steadily, legs clacking, storing lifegas and burngas from the brimming fresh air. Radiance filled it.

Breathing in deeply, it broadcast a rejoicing morning song.

2.

CALLING HOME

SHANNA PUT ON the last movement of Beethoven's Fifth and turned up the gain.

Ludwig von Cornball, they had called him back at Moonbase One. Hipitude: post-postmodern irony. All because she played ol' Ludwig so much—but who was more appropriate? What spirit better expressed the grandeur of an expedition to the edge of the solar system?

She could well visualize Dr. Jensen tut-tutting at this latest display of childish dramatization. But Moonbase and Jensen—and more to the point, her father, the Great Axelrod—were electromagnetically five hours and twenty minutes away. Physically, even at high nuclear impulse, they were well more than a *year* away.

For now, within the survival limits set by her spacecraft—*Proserpina*, yes, *hers*, even if she did have to pretend to egalitarian methods with the crew, *her* crew—she could do what she damn well pleased. With a happy sigh she relaxed into her hammock and gave herself up to the symphony's triumphant chords.

Still, indeed, she *was* on watch.

With a foot she pushed off against a bulkhead and swung slowly in the ship's light centrifugal gravity, eyes on the wall screen. Ludwig had never imagined a place like this, yet the music fit.

Pluto was dim but grayly grand—lightly banded in pale pewter and salmon red, save where Charon cast its huge gloomy shadow. Massive ice sheets spread like pearly blankets from both poles. Ridges ribbed the frozen methane ranges. The equatorial land was a flinty, scarred ribbon, rock hemmed in by the oppressive ice. The planet turned almost imperceptibly, a major ridgeline just coming into view at the dawn line.

Observers on Earth had thought Pluto, Charon, and the sun could only line up for an eclipse every 124 years—but in 2029, to the utter surprise of Earthside astronomers, both the satellite's orbit and the planet's axis had begun to drift. By the time Shanna's mission launched in 2044, Charon was eclipsing the sun regularly each Plutonian day. Axes were tilting. Whole worlds were spinning up.

Strange, but just the beginning, thought Shanna. *The game's afoot, Watson.*

Even from Earthside satellite observatories—forty Astronomical Units away—it was obvious that Pluto was warming. The spectral bands of its nitrogen atmosphere showed steadily rising temperatures, working up toward the heady heights topping 100 degrees above Absolute Zero. (Or more than 300 degrees Fahrenheit below zero, for the American audience; when *would* they go metric?) All this, despite Pluto's steady retreat from the sun as it followed its 273-year, highly elliptical orbit. Into the far dark.

Nobody had expected the warmth. Or the steady intrusion of the interstellar gale, pushing in on the sun's own solar wind. That steady pressure was simply the plasma and gas that coasted between the suns, pressing against the prow of the sun's own wind, as the sun swept through the galaxy in its own orbit, about the galactic center. What the astrophysicists called the pause point——which meant where the solar wind met its equal and fought end-lessly—that point was edging in, steadily. Against an un-seen pressure from beyond the stars

Why was it coming in? How? Nobody knew.

And how typical of Pluto and its moon that they should thus confound Earth's experts—who had warned her that this remote, small, cold world would be dull, the myster-ies arcane. Yeah, yeah, yeah: gray, dim, frigid. (*Hadn't she had a boyfriend say that once? And he'd been so wrong . . .*)

They—all the astrobio experts, and the outright as-tronomers, too—hadn't seen any of the mystery here, the magic. *Fine, let 'em stay home.*

Shanna wondered about the glorious filmy auroras. They alone were worth the trip, even though a beetle-browed congressperson from one of the finance commit-tees would hardly have agreed.

Had the great, luminous auroras been here before . . . well, before what? Nobody had a clue what was driving the warming. Or the steadily incoming pressure.

Could the auroras be involved? They were much like Earth's—sheets of excited molecules radiating, stirred by the incoming sleet of solar wind particles. But these danced far faster, rippling with vibrant colors, like flap-ping flags.

She let the view absorb her for a last few moments. Each of her fellow crew—the two Kares, Chow-Lin, and Ukizi—had a specialist's fascination in the frigid vistas. But they were asleep, and she had a whole planet to her-self.

She was not the theoretician of the crew at all—rather, she was mission biologist/medical, a marginal pilot . . .

and now captain. The physicist who had been captain, Ferrari, died in a freak accident while working aft near the combustion zone, with the robots who tended the nuclear engines. They'd lost three 'bots, too, which were harder to get along without than Ferrari, in her opinion, though she kept quiet on that score.

A disaster, yes—but despite Earthside's hesitations, she had assumed command, leaving to Jordin Kare the primary piloting jobs. It had been touch and go there for a week, as they drove outward at a steady 0.3 g acceleration. (*Hey, maybe they'd pick up a little Mars Effect in the bargain.*) That was a huge rate; if they'd had the fuel to keep to it for the whole outbound trajectory, they'd have gotten here in three months. As it was, the mission had very nearly been called back when Ferrari died. It had taken all the sweet-talking she could muster to deal with both crew and Earthside, plus arm-twisting by good old Dad. *Never forget that,* she thought ruefully.

So now, though nobody liked it all that much, Shanna was in charge. Astronaut type, subspecialist in biology and medical, a practical bio degree, though not really primarily a scientist—but a general science fan, yes. Jordin and Mary Kay Kare, they were the real secret strength out here—the tech types who could repair anything but weren't narrow. The rest of the crew tended the big, roaring bulk of *Proserpina* and didn't take a lot of Shanna's time, luckily. She wasn't really a manager type.

The symphony ended with stirring punch. She could not resist the pleasure of slapping her hand down. A heartbeat later a musical chime—rigged by Shanna in protest against the usual peremptory beeping alarms—told her that the data gathered since *Proserpina*'s last radio contact had now been encoded and kicked back toward Moonbase One. She tapped a key, giving herself a voice channel, reciting her ID opening without thinking. "Okay, now the good stuff, gang. As we agreed, I am adding my own verbal comments to the data I just sent you."

They had not agreed, not at all. Many of the Pluto Mission Control engineers, wedded to their mathematical slang and NASA's jawbone acronyms, felt that real, live human commentary was subjective and useless. Ephemeral stuff. Let the expert teams back home interpret the data. But the public relations people loved anything that tickled the public's nose.

"Pluto is a much livelier place than we ever imagined." She took a breath; always good to have a clear opening statement. "There's weather, for one thing—a product of the planet's six-day rotation and the mysterious heating. Turns out the melting and freezing point of methane is crucial. With the heating-up the mean temperature is high enough that nitrogen and argon stay gaseous, giving Pluto its thin atmosphere. Of course, the ammonia and carbon dioxide are solid as rock—Pluto's warmer, these days, but still incredibly cold, by our comfortable standards."

There was the sound bite maybe. Now the technical.

"Methane, though, can go either way. It's a volatile gas. Earthside observers found methane frost on the surface as long ago as 1976—anybody remember?—and methane ice caps in 1987. They speculated even then that some of it might start to thaw as the planet made its closest approach to the sun. Well, it did, back in the late twencen— and still does, every Plutonian morning. Even better, the methane doesn't just sublime—as it was supposed to because of the low atmospheric pressure. Nope, it melts.

Then it freezes at night. That makes it a life-supporting fluid, in principle."

Now the dawn line was creeping at its achingly slow pace over a ridgeline, casting long shadows that pointed like arrows across a great rock plain. There was something there she could scarcely believe, hard to make out even from their thousand-kilometer-high orbit under the best magnification. Something they weren't going to believe back Earthside. So keep up the patter and lead them to it.

Their crew had debated how to announce this for days—with no result. So now that they were sleeping, she would. Earthside deserved to know, she reminded herself. It wasn't an ego thing at all. But still . . . she was the captain.

"Meanwhile, on the darkside there's a great 'heat sink,' like the one over Antarctica on Earth. It moves slowly across the landscape as the planet turns, radiating heat into space and pressing down a column of cold air—I mean, of even *colder* air. From its low, coldest point—the pressure point—winds flow out toward the dayside. At the sunset line they meet sun-warmed air—and it snows. Snow! Maybe I should take up skiing, huh?"

It was hard, talking to a mute audience. And she was getting jittery. She took a hit of the thick, jolting Colombian coffee in her mug. Onward—

"On the sunrise side those winds meet sunlight and melting methane ice, and so it rains. Hard. Gloomy dawn. Tough weather—and permanent, moving around the planet like a veil."

She close-upped the dawn line, and there it was—a great gray curtain descending, marching at about the speed of a fast car.

"So we've got a perpetual storm front moving at the edge of the nightside and another that travels with the sunrise."

As she warmed to her subject, all pretense at impersonal scientific discourse faded from Shanna's voice; she could not filter out her excitement that verged on a kind of love. She paused, watching the swirling alabaster blizzards at twilight's sharp edge and, on the dawn side, the great solemn racks of cloud. Although admittedly no Jupiter, this planet—her planet, for the moment—could put on quite a show.

"The result is a shallow sea of methane that moves slowly around the world, following the sun. Who'da thought, eh, you astro guys?" A slight slam at the astrophysicists, who had foreseen none of this. Who could have, though?

"Since methane doesn't expand as it freezes, the way water does, methane icebergs just sink." *Okay, the astro guys know that,* she thought, *but the public needs reminders, and this damn well was going out to the whole wide bloomin' world, right?* "Once it freezes, it sinks. So I'm sure it's all slush a short way below the surface, and solid ice from there down. But so what? The sea isn't stagnant, because of what that big ol' moon Charon is doing in its synchronous orbit. As big as Charon is—and as close to the planet as it's gotten since its orbit shifted, bigtime—Charon makes a permanent tidal bulge directly underneath it. Think of a big ridge of fat liquid, swarming over the whole planet."

Like the Earth ocean tides, she thought. *But much bigger, and somehow strange.* "And the two worlds are trapped, two dancers forever in each other's arms." *Like the Earth-moon system, only Charon's far bigger in relation to Pluto.* "So that bulge travels around from daylight to darkness, too. So sea currents form, and *flow*, and freeze. On the night side the tidal pull puts stress on the various ices, and they hump up and buckle into pressure ridges. Like the ones in Antarctica, but *much* bigger."

Miles high, in fact, in Pluto's weak gravity . . . A huge wedge soaring to the dark sky. Marching toward a dim horizon, grinding, grinding. *Strange* . . .

But her enthusiasm drained away, and she bit her lip. Now for the hard part.

She'd rehearsed this a dozen times, after all the arguments with the other crew—and still the words stuck in her throat. After all, she hadn't come here to do close-up planetology. An unmanned orbital mission could have done that nicely. Shanna had come in search of life.

Five decades before, in the twencen and its aftermath, the life-is-everywhere advocates had not had any real evidence. Until the Marsmat discovery in 2018. And the success of the SETI program, picking up a faint message. Then the skies opened.

Attention pored over those mysteries, and in turn back on the old problem of communicating with dolphins, whales, and the like. By then there was a whole academic discipline devoted to reading the well-nigh unreadable.

Well, maybe that would help the ship coming out now, on *Proserpina*'s tail, with a crew of has-been Marsmat folk. But for now she had different news.

The theory and code developed to wrestle with the SETI message's elegant mumbo jumbo was known somewhat condescendingly as Wiseguy. It had discovered that the SETI signal was a repeating "funeral pyre"—left behind to proclaim the wonders of an extinct civilization, thousands of light-years farther in toward the galactic center. Applied to the microwave emissions from Pluto, Wiseguy suggested an intelligent origin. Coherent, ordered emissions, it said—yet a code Wiseguy could not break. Nor could any human.

But those signals were refracted and damped by the plasma streams billowing forth from the sun, so the Space Array near Earth got only glimmerings of the Plutonian emission. This was enticing—even convincing—to the converted. The International Space Agency had decided to go full out and send a manned expedition, putting Wiseguy within range.

She paused, held her breath almost as if she expected a chorus of sighs, groans, shouts. But the community that had hoped she would find a striking refutation to the naysayers—that band was clustered around a view screen an unimaginable distance away.

"This isn't a chemical biosphere at all. That's why it can exist."

She coughed, excused herself self-consciously from people who would not hear the cough until five and a half hours hence. Then she made her voice more brisk, scientific.

"Mind you, the heating is the real point. There's some driver in the whole magnetosphere, and I think we've found it. A current is flowing in from farther out. I'm talkin' way, *way* beyond Pluto's orbit. Maybe from the Oort cloud—that's the junk left over from the formation of the solar system, out where the comets come from."

To her ears this chatty bravado rang false, but maybe it would play better back Earthside.

"We've detected some pretty huge currents in toward Pluto. And little old Pluto packs a wallop, too. It's got a strong magnetic field, nearly perpendicular to its spin axis—we sent you the data on this already. It's a generator, like Uranus. And out here in this neck of the woods, any energy source is big news."

She stopped, sensing the skepticism these last sentences would provoke six hours from now. She sighed. This was even harder than she'd feared. Her mind kept lurching off on tangents, spilling out scientific data and ideas. Behind the facade she was a fountain of emotion. Could they tell?

She took a deep breath and changed the subject. "And in the atmosphere there's a lot more free hydrogen than a planet this little ought to be able to hold. At some spots on the dayside we've measured gaseous carbon dioxide, although it all ought to be frozen. There are also some strange spectral lines—"

Shanna caught herself before saying what those lines seemed to show. She was not ready to make that leap of faith; not yet. "Anyhow, since my last report to you I have sent down one of the smaller probes. It landed on a little hill, one about to be submerged by the just-melting methane sea's froth. Smacked down next to an ice crag which I'm pretty sure is ammonia and carbon dioxide. Telemetry will tell all. The probe reported to me faithfully until an hour and a half ago, and then . . ." She paused to gather up her courage, imagining her father's famous Axelrod rumbling, avalanche-on-the-way belly laugh and Dr. Jensen's deep-grooved frown. Even though both her mentors were more than 6 billion kilometers away, they were with her as she framed her next sentence. Taking a deep breath—

"And then I—I believe something ate it."

3.

THE WAY OF THINGS

SLANTING LONG IN PALE shades of crimson and violet, Lightgiver's rays broke through thinning, rosy methane clouds as the rains of morning slackened. Still the zand swam tirelessly on toward Rendezvous with the others of its kind.

Joy! It had not felt this strong for many, many long days. Vigor and potency throbbed through it. When it found another of the zand and they Self-merged—as usually happened before day's end—there might even be a Birthing this time. How wonderful that would be!

Sudden, tearing pain lashed at the zand's belly. The hooked head of a borer twisted into the hole it had gouged. Agony lanced up from the wound. The borer's tail whipped the red sea into foam, powering the parasite's body around and around and *in, in,* deep and terrible.

The pain soared, and the slow, seeping faintness began. The zand's automatic neural defense system took over. Lifegas and burngas sighed from its side compression chambers into its central canal. A neural impulse connector parted, zapping a spark. Lifegas and burngas ignited in a jet of searing fire. The zand lifted up and away, out of the sea.

The borer clung on, its narrow winding body writhing and lashing against the much larger zand. The living rocket left a trail of ivory, a plume freezing into ice crystals. The zand rose. Air pressure dropped, sucking the borer from its hold. It fought and held and then tumbled away into the sea.

The zand struggled to breathe, to live. Air rushing past soothed the seeping wound. *Lightgiver be thanked for fast reactions,* the zand thought.

It trimmed its course to swing back down toward the sea, feeling strength return. It was still charged with the rejuvenating energies, sucked from the strange thing it had eaten earlier that morning. The land below lay rumpled and veiled by the dawn's mist.

The zand was tempted to remain airborne. *Fly! You live! Fly!*

But it would need its lifegas later on, should there be no food at Rendezvous. By now most of the rockfood on the dayside was submerged beneath the lapping sea of warm red methane. But later the sea would die, going sluggish and then rigid with cold—as it always did. The day would warp on and wrap up into night, leaving the methane to freeze again, promise denied. Only the surge of tides could stir it. And even that was pointless, without real warmth.

Such was the Way of Things. Peace lay in resignation to this truth.

Again it sang a canticle to Lightgiver, weaving strand-songs in with its general praise. To the almighty Nourisher of the World it gave its own specific thanks at having been spared for further life. The zand vowed to the sky that it would teach young zand to revere Lightgiver's holy name, should Lightgiver see fit to grant it a Birthing.

It banked on vagrant winds and sang. Ecstasy. Banked and sang.

A faint voice interrupted its meditations. The zand responded with its own distinctive pulses, *rip-rap-tink*, and received in return a conversational rush of joy from another zand. Old One had evidently survived the night again.

Old One—*there*, in the dark sky.

By mutual agreement both zand sealed themselves in firm raps of closing membranes. They expended enough of their precious lifegas to lift and float them just above the surface of the sea, resting.

"I am glad you have survived another day," the zand began, as was proper for a younger person to say.

"And I also, that we greet one another, You the Younger. We may not look forward to an indefinite number of such days," Old One replied.

"Am I always to be the Younger?" the zand asked.

"Relish it," the Old One said. "Such a name does not come again."

Life on their ever-changing world was precarious, but Old One's tone implied something far more comprehensive and profound. In the Younger, intellectual curiosity—with an undernote of fear—prevailed over the deference due to age. "Explain," Younger begged.

They hovered over the lapping sea. Winds snarled, buffeting them.

"Think back, youngling. Think back to your last Birthing. How did Lightgiver look in the sky?"

The young zand pondered. Self-merge and Birthing were such all-absorbing experiences that one did not, at the time, pay much attention to one's surroundings. Not even to Lightgiver?—the zand's conscience prodded, and a twinge of shame filled it for its evident lack of devotion. And then it remembered.

"Lightgiver was brighter—and warmer—and . . . and . . ."

"And *larger*?" Old One prompted.

"And larger, yes. A bit."

"Now let me share something with you before I die."

Old One brushed aside its companion's polite protests. "No, no—listen! I cannot go through many more days and nights of gorge and sleep, gorge and sleep. So attend me while you can, and tell this to the other zand. I *am* the Old One. Probably the oldest in the world. And I have watched the skies with care. Beyond the cycle of dark and light that we know is a far longer cycle. We have no proper way to measure it. But I have thought this out, and I can tell you that Lightgiver moves in and out, from Its greatest width to Its narrowest. All this great cycle occurs in more than fourteen thousand of our short cycles of light and day. I myself have seen two of these greater cycles."

"That much?" Younger was amazed. It almost lost its purchase upon the winds that lofted them above the dawn sea.

"Yes—a great long while."

"You must have learned—"

"I learned this—that while Lightgiver is at Its farthest and coldest, the ice does not melt, and there is no sea, and even in full day *all life sleeps*."

Younger again nearly lost itself upon the winds. This

was a dark idea, as black as the world's somber nightside itself.

Younger sensed a weariness in Old One's soul, a weight of pure remorseless time itself. So it tried to express cheer: "And then Lightgiver comes back? Yes? And is close and warm, and life wakes again?"

"Yes. But in the first of these long cycles—great ages, through which I have lived—we numbered eight thousand zand. We lost some to borers and flappers and starvation, and, of course, each night—then as now—some never made it through to the morning. Once in that cycle came a great raid from Darkside—"

"Then! It is—!"

"Yes, youngling, the story told in the epic chant is true. Intelligences exist back there, feeding on Lightgiver knows what—and we drove them off in the terrible battle of which legend tells, with much loss of life."

"But . . . the Birthings?"

"Almost enough to maintain our numbers. But not quite. And so there remained more than seven thousand of us, lean and hungry, when that long cycle reached the Great Night. When even at full daytime, all freezes."

Younger felt awed. "You all . . . slept?"

Looking toward the gathering day, Younger could see broad plains of warming rock, glimmering beyond the methane sea. And in the distance, strange high towers that it could not understand. Could they be a part of this grand narrative, the tale Younger was privileged to hear from the Old One itself? It hoped so. It hoped for some scrap of meaning in all things.

"Yes, and Lightgiver shrank to Its smallest size—I assume, for, of course, I could not watch during the frozen time. Then Lightgiver began to grow again, to the point at which It could again give us warmth and zest. But as the second cycle began, fewer of us awoke. *How many zand are there today?*"

The daily Rendezvous ensured that all of them knew. "Yesterday there were 3,441."

"*Half* what there were before the last long freeze. And Lightgiver bestows less warmth and light every day. Your personal experience is that of other zand: Self-merge leads to Birthing only when our world is most warm."

"So we do not grow in numbers sufficient to replace ourselves?"

"Yes, and then the long cold time takes a further toll. If three thousand of us live until the next great freeze begins, far fewer still will wake for the start of the next warming cycle. Fewer still will see its end. A dark day will come, therefore, when no zand at all will meet at Rendezvous, ever again."

Terror shook the younger zand. "And if *none* of us wake and feed, who will be here to sing Lightgiver's praises?"

"The flappers and the borers, perhaps," Old One savagely replied. Then, more gently: "Go, youngling; I have told you. Go to Rendezvous! Tell the others! May you have good Self-merge, with a Birthing and many young. Salute!"

With a hiss the young zand deflated, dropped into the sea, and began almost desperately to swim. In moments Younger was gone into the pink dawn mists.

Old One had felt the warming, kindling steady and true through the long turns of the world. The past was cold, the future warm. Why? What did those who ruled this world, the gods of darkness, mean by all this? Why the Darksiders, who came to kill so many?

Heat was good, bringing life to the world.

Warmth was the Good.

The Darksiders came always in from the night sky and, once here, killed without mercy. From the Dark came Evil. Why?

Buoyed by lifegas, the Old One floated and pondered the many seasons of joy and pain it had seen.

4.

DISBELIEF

A RED LIGHT WINKED ON: *she's here.*

John Axelrod crushed out his cigar stub, hurriedly shoved it and the ashtray into a bottom desk drawer, and turned up the air circulator. Position had its perks.

In a few moments Dr. Jensen would be walking in, and there was no point in adding to the psychiatrist's expectable irritation. To the traditional medical and moral arguments against smoking had lately been added a snob objection as well: tobacco use had come to be associated by Euro-Americans with the tropical world's urban hells, where people still smoked because it was the only pale pleasure they could afford.

The sealable double door swung open and Hilge Jensen stepped over the threshold. She was in her hospital whites, not her office wear. As usual, she started in as though they had been only momentarily interrupted, even though it was fifteen minutes since he told her to come talk this out in person.

"Look," Hilge said in her quick, flat tones, "consider her personality profile. Smart as a whip, and she paid for it in the usual coinage—isolated with the elite in school, socially a bit slow. Raised by a grandmother because neither of her own parents could be bothered—"

"Need I remind you that we are speaking of my own daughter here?" Axelrod kept his voice flat and objective, he hoped. "That's a very inexact description of my family situation to boot."

"Well, of course—" Hilge blinked, recalculated. "But I am trying to be analytical—"

"Proceed."

"Well, she has a problem with authority—"

"A mild way to put it." Axelrod kept his face calm, but he sure as hell didn't feel that way. Shanna was his daughter by his second wife—he'd had four wives before realizing that a workaholic life that involved commuting to the moon was incompatible with having a family. Wife number three was a gold digger without motherly instincts, and number four was a beautiful ice queen (what had he been thinking?) who couldn't deal with such a headstrong child. Shanna had ignored both of them, he knew, recognizing that they were likely to be temporary. His mother, the imperious Norma, was the most constant person in Shanna's early life, and eventually she'd gone to live permanently at his childhood home with her. And managed to grow up.

No, don't relive that again. Focus. "Very . . . mild."

She read his expression and hurried on. "So she learned

early to live alone, after her parents divorced, the usual problems—live with others and like it."

"I know this." Still objective. *Faster to let her run on than challenge everything she says.*

"Uh, yes. She takes on a late-teenage persona under pressure because that's the mode she used before she started astronaut training. Solitary tech interests, which she covers in social settings with a jaunty air, exuberance masking anxiety—again, fairly standard personality strategy—"

"I do remember your reports," he said dryly, still hoping to short-circuit the lecture.

Hilge's eyes jittered. "Uh, sure, but we knew she could fit well into that crew. Plenty of leadership skills, well demo'ed in earlier flights—"

"And now she's reverted to an old pattern, the bright-eyed-kid personality—I caught it, just listen to that broadcast. Loaded with false voice signatures!" He liked the quick blink Hilge always gave when he used her own jargon back on her. Did she think he'd made billions without having instinctive people-reading skills?

"Uh, yes—and along with it comes the early idealism. She *wants* to find life on Pluto. There aren't any green men or red princesses on Mars, just a mat. So she's bound there'll be something like them on *her* planet. And when people start acting out their fantasies—"

He flared. "You think she's hallucinating?"

"She's a long way from home, rest of crew asleep, talking away, tired—"

"She's a trained astronaut." He tried to keep his voice flat.

"But these descriptions—" Hilge spread her hands,

raised eyebrows. "The astronomers say nothing like this is—"

"Well, they haven't been there, have they?" He made himself be mild and steady again. "So what're we supposed to do? You can't give her word-association tests when it's five hours between the first word and her response, and another five hours before you can throw her the next word."

"Uh, her medication—"

"I know you snuck some of your pharm stuff into some of the mission foods."

"It was recommended—after long flights—"

"So we suggest some menu changes? She'll smell that right away." A pattern he had heard before, drugs as panacea, even the new smart drugs that everybody said were precision, zero side effects. Some damn doctor had even suggested some for himself. He'd stormed out of the office, of course. Alcohol, small doses at the end of the day—that was all the chemical help he needed, thank you.

"Mr. Axelrod . . ."

He held a hand up to give himself time to get back to equilibrium. In Hilge's blank look—yep, that's what she was going to suggest next—he saw he would get no help from her. Pluto, he mused, sighing. The name conjured up either horror—the stern, just, and unforgiving Roman god of Hell—or else low humor: Mickey Mouse's floppy-eared dog.

Yet Shanna had wanted to go there for so long. Other little girls' idols included holomovie hunks and vid-song stars. His daughter's started and ended with Clyde Tombaugh, the gangly farm kid from Kansas with his homemade telescope who had gone out to the Lowell Observatory early in the twencen and found Pluto within a few years . . . with a high school education.

Dr. Jensen was only the latest in a long line of psychosnoops who had pestered Shanna all her short life with their *why* questions. Who knew? Axelrod's decades as an executive had taught that there would never be any clear answers to the deepest motivations, including his own. Maybe *especially* his own. The rational carapace everybody wore was a shell, and should be left that way. Intact.

The problem for those skeptical therapists and soul-probers had been that Shanna was not, and never had been, unfriendly or antisocial. A quick, lithe athlete, she had played on school teams, easily made friends—but on her own terms and not because she couldn't bear to be alone. So the "psychodynamicists" skipped "Why Pluto?" and went directly to "Why do you want to be away for so long?"

"She is not following cooperative methods," Hilge said flatly. "She had the rest of the crew dancing to her tune at first. Now some barely tolerate her."

Axelrod grinned. People had been barely tolerating him for most of his career. "My daughter! Maybe she's dancing to the music of the spheres."

"We must do something."

"I repeat: Shanna may be right. Ever think—"

The red light came on again. "Hell. That damned new press secretary. He insisted on seeing me before we go on the air."

Hilge shifted gears; her voice became low, slow, and grim. "I know. *I* asked him to be here. Shanna's actions are also, unfortunately, part of a much larger problem. I'll let him fill you in."

Press Secretary Harvell Swain walked in with the air of one on a mission. Axelrod hid his grimace behind a palm, faking a small cough. NASA had forced Swain on him in return for clearing away bureaucratic logjams. Axelrod longed for the grand old days when Mars was there for the taking, when NASA was glad to be out of the spotlight because they had muffed their own programs so badly. Mere interplanetary exploration was easy compared with the nasty art of political infighting . . .

Tripping over the threshold on his way through—he was a recent Earthside import, not yet used to lunar doors or the lunar energy-saving walk—he stumbled up to the desk, nodding formally to both Hilge and Axelrod. "I have come here to tell you that the press conference this evening must be called off."

"Something the matter technically?" Axelrod countered.

"No. But we can't air that report from Astronaut Shanna."

"What do you mean, can't?"

"Listen—years we've been sweating out this mission. Some politicians are still calling the whole thing a boondoggle, that the Pluto mystery is just scientists playing games. So now the captain says they've found life. In a single-person broadcast!"

"Great find, I'd say."

"That's exactly the point!" Swain shot back. "So aliens turn up just now? Just when Congress is wondering if the whole issue is a hoax?"

Axelrod had seen the usual skeptics making a lot of

noise in the media, as excitement grew with *Proserpina*'s approach to Pluto. There had never been data that couldn't be read several ways. The welfare lobby eyed NASA's ballooning budget and made a few phone calls and *presto*, there were perfectly reputable scientists who didn't believe the solar pause point was moving inward. No threat there, they said. So why all these dollars "sent out beyond Saturn"—as though *Proserpina* carried tanks full of cash, not water?

"You don't really believe any of that hoax stuff, do you?" Axelrod asked with slow calm.

"It's too neat! They aren't going to believe her. And if you try to back her up, they won't believe you, either."

Axelrod knew the uses of being a hedgehog. He let the clock run.

The press secretary subsided, winded. Then he wound himself up for another try. "Look, Mr. Axelrod. I've given this thing all I've *got*. I laid a lot of groundwork on Earth before coming up here. Human-interest stories about the project, the works. 'Outer darkness defied for a dream by plucky girl and loyal crew'—the works."

"Young woman," Hilge automatically corrected.

"Sure, but she looks like a girl, face it. And we all know why she got on this mission at all."

An uncomfortable silence. Axelrod thought of saying, *Sure, the whole world does—because she's Axelrod's daughter.* "Saying it aloud here could still be dangerous, y'know." The new robotic microbugs could fly in through the ventilator ducts, crawl in along walls, stow away on an incoming briefcase or trouser cuff. So even in his own office he had to keep his mouth circumspect. Modern times!

Swain said nothing, just nodded. Copying the hedge-hog strategy?

"Okay," Axelrod allowed, "intrepid explorer of our last frontier, check. In the horse race for Truth, Science comes way behind Perceptions."

"Exactly. That's what you pay me for."

"The taxpayers pay you, not me."

"But you can fire me. They can't."

"Touché. But you realize, don't you, that we have here more than an oral report? Shanna sent us data, pictures. Plenty of which I have already begun sending down to the *New York Times* database. Also to the BBC."

To Axelrod's surprise the press secretary stood his ground. "And *you* realize, don't you, sir, that data nowadays can very effectively be faked? *That's* what they will think down there."

So much spunk all of a sudden? What, Axelrod wondered, *does he know politically from Earthside that I don't?*

Time to take the offensive. Axelrod stood up to his full height, which was considerable; a ploy he rarely had to use. "Look, there's this religion that broke away from my own a couple of thousand years ago. It and mine haven't always gotten along. But its founder once said, *Ye shall know the truth, and the truth shall make you free.* Free! Hell, if we can't stick with that, civilization—scientific civilization—might as well go out of business. We are going on this evening as scheduled, and take our chances with whatever Shanna says."

"But it's only, how can I—"

"Do it." He stood there and gave them the long, firm

look, knowing it would sink in. But he was thinking of years before, when all this had started.

Appropriately the desk announced, "Ten minutes."

"Dad, I need your help to get on the Pluto mission." Shanna looked at him with that direct way she had, mouth pursed.

Objections instantly crowded his mind. God, he was so glad to see her. How long had it been? How many months this time? And now she wanted to do . . . *what*?

To cover his confusion, he looked out of the window at the hot July afternoon. Huge shadowy thunderheads were crawling across the sky. All that thick, moist atmosphere out there . . . One g made him feel heavy and out of sorts—maybe he was spending too much time off-planet. Or maybe coming back was the problem.

She broke into his reverie. "It's everything to me. It's what I've always wanted to do. I've just *got* to go." He heard a familiar urgency in her voice. *Only child . . . never gave her enough time . . . maybe now I can make up for it.*

"Dad? It's not like I'm not qualified; you know I am."

His mind had drifted from the coming storm outside to the old one inside him. Still, he resisted the impulse to make up for past sins. "What makes you think I can pick the crew? It's an ISA mission, after all."

She laughed. "Yeah, and who bankrolls ISA? The Consortium."

"An oversimplification. The ISA money is from the big nations."

"Who come hat in hand—"

"We just got the jump on space technologies, that's all—so we license them to ISA."

"Look, Dad, everyone knows there would be no International Space Agency without you. You can't play coy with me." She flashed her engaging, wry smile. *The power children have over you . . .* "You're not testifying here, y'know."

"It's too dangerous. There are huge unknowns. Let someone else go."

"You sent people to Mars almost twenty years ago; it was even riskier then."

"They were all trained NASA astronauts—"

She jumped in. "And there was a $10 billion Mars Prize to win."

"Do you think I risked their lives for the money?"

"Do you think I'm not as qualified as a NASA astronaut?"

"You're not an astronaut until you've been through NASA training," he said quietly, "no matter how good a pilot you are."

It was an old argument between them. Axelrod had beaten NASA to Mars, but he'd always been careful to use their resources whenever possible. *Borrow from the best.*

Their astronaut training, for example. He hired only government-trained astronauts for Consortium missions. None of the orbital pilots from the little companies. Then the privatization of space that followed the initial Mars landing led to new ways of training pilots. NASA's way was to train people on the ground, then send them into space. As soon as there was ready private access to space, off-planet rocket jockeys could be trained in orbit directly. Better than ground training, yes. Shanna was one of these; a veteran of three years of orbital flights and moon trips. Under an assumed last name she'd worked her way through training and landed a job with Flights to the Stars, delivering tourists and cargo to orbital hotels and moon resorts. It was an old division—like the merchant marine and the navy.

She was visibly trying to keep calm. "The ISA has announced an open competition for the crew; it's not just for 'nauts."

"And you're going to enter," he said mildly to cover his inner confusions.

"Rumor is the Consortium gets to choose one of the crew."

"Rumor is rarely accurate. We've agreed to underwrite one."

She plunged forward, eyes big. "I want you to pick me."

"Do you think I'd risk my own flesh and blood—"

"Especially one you ignored for years—"

"I had a business to run, damn it." He slammed his fist on the desk. "You were well looked after. I made sure of that."

"Dad." There was a tremor in her voice he'd never heard before. Eyes watery. "I've never asked you for favors; never traded on your name. But this is so important I . . . I need to load the dice." She looked directly at him.

"Why do you want to do this? Seems to me you have an interesting life as it is."

"The Pluto mission is a great adventure! My job is just"—a shrug—"spacebus techy, medical."

"You've never even been to Mars. Go there for adventure! I'll be glad to make that happen for you."

"Other people are doing Mars. I want to go where no one has ever been."

Axelrod's mind was racing down nervous hallways. *If I don't help her, will she forgive me? What if I turn her down and she makes it on her own? Can I make sure she doesn't get chosen?* He shook his head. *She has such passion for this, how could I? Such idealism—wait a minute . . .*

"If you're the Consortium's representative, you'll have to act like it," he said slowly.

"Meaning?"

"Being a private enterprise, we need to turn a profit whenever possible."

"So?"

"So if you work for us, part of your duties will be to look for possible revenue-generating opportunities."

Shanna looked blank. "You mean—like stuff to *sell*?"

"We'll want exclusive media rights from you, for one."

"What is there to sell on Pluto?" she sputtered.

"For one thing, the experience. Everyone loves to watch other people in danger from the comfort of their living room sofa. Viktor and Julia have lived under the eye of the vidcams for twenty years. Are you willing to do that?"

"I g-guess so." A pause. "Does the camera follow them everywhere?"

"In the shared rooms, sure. In the contract. Not in their ca~~bins th~~ough."

"Still . . ." She blinked, as if she had not thought about this part. Just a kid, really . . ."It must be hell."

"It's what you want?"

The self-doubt blew away with a sigh. "Yes. Yes."

He did what had always worked at crisis points: just let

himself follow his guy instinct. Even when it was his daughter. "I'll have a contract drawn up."

Her eyes widened, and he knew suddenly that she had not really thought she would win. She rushed around the desk and hugged him, then ran out the door. "You'll never regret this! I promise," she called behind her.

Much later, as he was staring moodily out the window, he recalled one of his mother's sayings: "If you love them, let them go." *Thanks, Mom.*

The Pluto Mission Control auditorium was jammed. Newsies, bureaucrats, some lunar tourists who'd managed to get in from the big luxury hotel nearby—*Fly the Great Lunar Cavern!*—and even a scattering of scientists. All noisy, chattering. A fair fraction of the lunar population seemed to have wedged itself in. Axelrod took a deep breath and stepped out.

Applause spattered across the tiered seats as Axelrod came in from stage rear, with an apprehensive Swain a few steps to the rear. Behind them an enhanced image of Pluto as *Proserpina* had seen it from a million kilometers out filled the large screen.

Showtime! Axelrod thought. He hated these and loved them at the same time. Nobody without a streak of showmanship ever got to run a big-time business. Even in its darkest days, with an accountant type as administrator, NASA had put the best possible face on the space station debacle.

He acknowledged the applause with a short wave of the hand. The cheers were for Shanna, he knew, not for him. He stepped into the chalk-marked area staked out for the holocamera focus. Uncomfortably he became aware of the unseen eyes of Earth's billions a light-second and a half away.

"Ladies and gentlemen," he began, "we have exciting news from Pluto tonight. At 10:30 this morning, GMT— which is also our local time here at Moonbase One—we received Astronaut Shanna's latest report. Tonight she speaks to us again, and this time you are going to hear her in person. She's well over 6 billion kilometers away from us. That's 3.6 billion miles for those of you who go in for nostalgia."

This line got a ripple of light laughter in the hall, a good sign. He made himself smile. "And it won't be in supersound. But I think we all want to hear what she has to say. His eye caught the second hand of the big wall clock, closing in on a digital readout coming up on 2100, another (and expensive) concession to nostalgia. Timing his last words to end one second before the hour, he said, "All right, Shanna, come in."

The words the young astronaut had spoken from Pluto orbit hours before came booming in, overamplified, immediately covering them in a dry wash of static.

Damn solar flares, Axelrod thought, becoming once again the electronics professional. *Why'd the sun have to get so wild just now? The scientists say it's just part of the long solar cycle, but it's coming on top of all the crackle and fizz from near Pluto.* This interference was yet another sign that the bow wave of the solar system was getting pressed back, already close to Pluto's orbit. Understanding this was the second major motivation for going to Pluto. Could such distant events be significant? Or even dangerous?

As the interference continued, people stirred restlessly

in their seats. Yet the room filled with suspense, for whatever words they could get would be from farther than any human had ever spoken. A voice, if not from the infinite, at least pretty damned close. Though there had been other reports, this one came after the first surface landing.

The distortion stopped, the hiss faded. The first word from Shanna that came in loud and clear at Moonbase One and on Earth was, "Life! I'm sure of it!"

The woman's fresh, youthful voice exulted. The audience stirred. "I matched every molecular combination in the library memory against it. The Kares both checked me, but they wanted me to make the call, so here I am again, stayin' up late, swillin' coffee, on the phone, callin' home."

Axelrod smiled. The homey touch always worked, clear across the solar system.

"The *only* compound that even came close was chlorophyll *b*. So these are not only plants, they're photosynthetic ones. Back when Pluto was considered more interesting"—she didn't try to keep an edge of sarcasm out of her voice— "some hackers at JPL worked out a series of biochemical reactions that theoretically could work here. It turns out they *do*. But!—they're not powered by Pluto's distant sun. It's nine hundred times weaker than our sunlight here. There's not nearly enough energy in it."

The crowd stirred. This connected directly to the central riddle. Why was Pluto so warm, just lately? And what did this have to do with the data from the Voyager probes, which showed that the interstellar gas and plasma were intruding farther into the solar system?

Shanna talked right through the buzz. "The plants combine ammonia ice with carbon dioxide ice and get free hydrogen, carbon, and nitric acid. Presto! Then the nitric acid and the carbon recombine, releasing more free hydrogen plus CO_2 and nitrogen—and that's where the animals come in!"

Her voice lilted on "animals," and the word sent another murmur through the crowd.

"They're methanogens—eaters of methane. You have methanogenic microorganisms on Earth, kilometers down. Since the Marsmat discovery we've learned plenty about them. They branched off from our chemical forefathers about 3.5 billion years ago. Then they got pushed off to the ecological edge of things—chemical also-rans. Here they're the main show. They recombine the hydrogen and CO_2 released by the plants into free oxygen and methane. They store some of the hydrogen in their bodies, and then they can inflate themselves—hydrogen balloons! I watched two of them floating above the sea that way, apparently just passing the time of day."

Axelrod smiled. Nobody, not even that idiot press secretary, could believe Shanna was making *this* up. He had depended on the timbre of her voice. The others had ventured their explanations before the pictures came in. To prove her case, a big glossy picture of two spherical blobs came on the screen. It was at high resolution, and the two hovered over a red lapping background, half shrouded in pink mist. They bobbed and turned in vagrant winds.

The room went absolutely silent. Shanna did not.

"They also store the oxygen, near as I can tell. And they can combine it with hydrogen, like old-fashioned rocket fuel. I saw one of them escape a predator of some kind by gracefully jetting up through the air, while its exhaust froze behind it and fell into the sea."

"*Really,* now!" snorted the woman science reporter from the *New York Times.* Axelrod hoped that gibe hadn't gone out on the air to Earth. He would have shot her a frown, but he was still on-camera. Instead, smile, damn you, smile. Like it was some mild joke.

With uncanny premonition Shanna's tone turned a shade argumentative. "Yes, a predator. This is evidently a complete, balanced planetary ecology. But I don't think the one that got my first rover was just a beast. From the readings I was able to get before the rover hull dissolved, I think nitric acid ate it. Those low bushes produce nitric acid and the animals don't."

Puzzled frowns in the audience. Science reporters they might be, but high school chemistry was going a bit too deep for most.

"So the creature that ate the rover was using a plant process, see? Not necessary for its own metabolism. Using it to melt my probe, pry it apart—that's awfully close to tool-using. There's not only life on Pluto— there's *intelligent* life!"

Shanna went right on, her springy tone rolling over the shocked faces in the auditorium. "That's what we've been able to learn by remote observation. Now, obviously, we have to go down there. I'm the captain and the biologist. My job, the way I figure it. By the time you hear these words"—Shanna's voice rose in almost childlike delight—"we'll be on my way to Pluto!"

The rows of blank looks would have been funny if Axelrod hadn't felt exactly the same.

"I've discussed this with the rest of the crew. Let's say the vote was, um, divided. So as captain I took the responsibility. After all, it's my risk and my field of study.

I'm going down, with Jordin as pilot." Her voice softened. "Finally . . . good-bye, gang. And especially, good-bye to my dad. He always said nothing could really do more than slow down an Axelrod, and I'm proving him right again. Bye, Dad!"

After that, from distant Plutonian space came only a whispering hiss.

As soon as the cameras went off, Hilge growled, "You didn't give her permission to do that!"

Nobody could hear her rough whisper in the growing hubbub.

Axelrod grinned. "And I didn't say she couldn't."

5.

A DAY AT THE BEACH

THE LONG ICE RIDGE rose out of the sea like a great gray reef. Following its Earthly analogy, it teemed with life. Quilted patches of vivid blue-green and carrot orange spattered its natural pallor. Out of those patches spindly trunks stretched toward the midmorning sun. At their tips crackled bright blue St. Elmo's fire.

Violet-tinged flying wings swooped lazily in and out among them to feed. Some, already filled, alighted at the shoreline and folded themselves, waiting with their flat heads cocked at angles. The sky, even at Pluto's midmorning, remained a dark backdrop for the gauzy auroral curtains that bristled with energy. This world had grown its steadily thickening atmosphere only in the last few decades, the astronomers said. The infrared studies showed warming for maybe fifty years. Yet the gathering blanket was still not dense enough to scatter the wan sunlight, so the bowl of sky was a hard black.

Into this slow world came a high roar. Wings flapped away from the noise. A giant filled the sky.

Jordin Kare dropped the lander closer. His lean, hawklike face seemed to be all angles in the cockpit's red glow. His eyes moved restlessly over the board instruments, the view screens, the joystick he moved through minute adjustments. Shanna's legs were cramped from the small copilot chair, and she bounced with the rattling boom of atmospheric braking.

Beside her in his acceleration couch Jordin peered forward at the swiftly looming landscape. "How's that spot?" He jabbed a finger tensely at the approaching horizon.

"Near the sea? Sure. Plenty of life-forms there. Kind of like an African watering hole." Analogies were all she had to go on here, but there was a resemblance. Their recon scans had showed a ferment all along the shoreline.

Kare brought them down sure and steady above a rocky plateau, their drive running red-hot. Streamers of steam jetted down onto ice hardened like rock by the deep cold.

This was a problem nobody on the mission team, for all their contingency planning, had foreseen. Their deceleration plume was bound to incinerate many of the life-forms in this utterly cold ecosystem. Even after hours the lander might be too hot for any life to approach, not to mention scalding them when nearby ices suddenly boiled away.

Well, nothing to do about it now.

"Fifty meters and holding." Kare glanced at her. "Okay?"

"Touchdown," she said, and they thumped down onto the rock. To land on ice would have sunk them hip-deep in fluid, only to then be refrozen rigidly into place. They eagerly watched the plain. Something hurried away at the horizon, which did not look more than a kilometer away.

"Look at those lichen," she said eagerly. "In so skimpy an energy environment, how can there be so *many* of them?"

"We're going to be hot for an hour, easy," Kare said, his calm, careful gaze sweeping the view systematically. Shanna could see what he meant: the lander rested on its drive, and already, pale vapor rose from beneath, curling up past their downview cameras. The nuclear pile would cool in time, but it might sublime away ice beneath them. The engineers had thought of this, so their footpads spread broadly. Hot water could circulate through them, to prevent getting stuck in hardening ice later.

They had thought of a lot of things, but certainly not this dim, exotic landscape. The ship's computers were taking digital photographs automatically, getting a good map. "I say we take a walk."

They were live straight to Earthside, and Shanna was glad he had voiced the idea first. The mission engineers had warned them to venture onto the surface only when unavoidable. *Come this far and never feel the crunch of Pluto beneath your boots? Come, now.*

The cold here was unimaginable, hundreds of degrees below human experience. In orbit they were well insulated, but here the ice would steal heat by conduction. Their suit heaters could cope, the engineers said—the atmosphere was too thin to steal heat quickly—but only if their boots alone actually touched the frigid ground. Sophisticated insulation could only do so much.

Shanna did not like to think about this part. If it failed, her feet would freeze in her boots, then the rest of her. Even for the lander's heavily insulated shock-absorber legs, they had told her, it would be touch and go beyond a stay of a few hours. Their onboard nuclear thermal generator was already laboring hard to counter the cold she could see creeping in, from their external thermometers. Their craft already creaked and popped from thermal stresses.

Their thermal armor, from the viewpoint of the natives, must seem a bristling, untouchable furnace. Yet already, they could see things scurrying on the plain. Some seemed to be coming closer. Maybe curiosity was indeed a universal trait of living things.

Jordin pointed silently. She picked out a patch of dark blue-gray down by the shore of the methane sea. On their console she brought up the visual magnification. In detail it looked like rough beach shingle. Tidal currents during the twenty-two hours since dawn had dropped some kind of gritty detritus—not just ices, apparently—at the sea's edge. Nothing seemed to grow on the flat, and—swiveling point of view—the ridge's knife edge also seemed bare, relatively free of life.

"Maybe a walk down to the beach?" Jordin said. "Turn over a few rocks?"

"Roger." They were both tiptoeing around the coming moment. With minimal talk they got into their suits.

Skillfully, gingerly—and by prior coin flip—Shanna clumped down the ladder. She almost envied those pioneer astronauts who had first touched the ground on Luna, backed up by a constant stream of advice, or at least comment, from Houston. The Mars landing crew had taken a mutual, four-person single step. Taking a breath, she let go the ladder and thumped down on Pluto. Startlingly, sparks spat between her feet and the ground, jolting her.

"Wow! There must be a *lot* of electricity running around out here," she said, fervently thanking the designers for all that redundant insulation.

Jordin followed. She watched big blue sparks zap up from the ground to his boots. He jumped and twitched.

"Ow! That smarts," Jordin said.

Only then did she realize that she had already had her shot at historical pronouncements and had squandered it in her surprise. And her first word—*Wow*—what a profound thought, huh? she asked herself ruefully.

Jordin said solemnly, "We stand at the ramparts of the solar system."

Well, she thought, *fair enough.* He had actually remembered his prepared line. He grinned at her and shrugged as well as he could in the bulky suit. Now on to business.

Against the gray ice and rock their lander stood like an H. G. Wells Martian walking machine, splayfooted and ominous. Vapor subliming from beneath it gave a mysterious air.

"Rocks, anyone?" They began gathering some, using long tweezers. Soil samples rattled into the storage bin. She carefully inspected under the rocks, but there was no sign of small life—worm tracks, microbe stains, clues. The soil here was just regolith.

"Let's take a stroll," Jordin said.

"Hey, close-up that." She pointed out toward movement above the sea.

Some triangular shapes moved in the air, flapping. "Birds?"

She could faintly hear calls, varying up and down in pitch. Repeating the same few notes, too.

Jordin said, "Look in the water—or whatever that chemical is."

"Methane? Like molasses." Her eyes widened. On the slick, wrinkled surface, movement. Things were swimming toward them. Just nubs barely visible above the oily surface, they made steady progress toward shore. Each had a small wake behind it.

"Looks like something's up," Jordin said.

She followed and saw something odd. "Hey! What's that?"

A gray arm with a pincer at the end. Gray, lying on the sand. "Looks metallic," Jordin said.

There were bits and pieces littering the beach. "Fragments," Shanna said. "Looks like some body, torn apart."

They saw other parts along the shoreline, most no bigger than ten centimeters. "Funny," Jordin said. "Might be a machine?"

"Probably a species we haven't seen yet," Shanna said. "Gotta get a sample of that." They scooped up a few pieces, filed it away mentally under Mysteries, and walked on. When they came to a big boulder, Jordin took an experimental leap. He went over it easily, rising to twice his height.

She tried it, too. "Wheeee!" Fun. And good footage for the autocams focused on them from the lander.

As they carefully walked down toward the beach, she

tried her link to the lander's wideband receiver. Happily she found that the frequencies first logged by her lost, devoured probe were full of traffic. Confusing, though. Each of the beasts—for she was sure it was them—seemed to be broadcasting on all waves at once. Most of the signals were weak, swamped in background noise that sounded like an old AM radio picking up a nearby high-tension line. One, however, came roaring in like a pop music station. "Ouch!" She slapped on filters and then made the lander's inductance tuner scan carefully.

That pattern—yes! It had to be. Quickly she compared it with the probe log she'd brought down on her slate. These were the odd cadences and sputters of the very beast whose breakfast snack had been her first evidence of life.

"Listen to this," she said. Jordin looked startled through his faceplate.

The signal boomed louder, and she turned back the gain. She decided to try the radio direction finder. Jordin did, too, for cross-check. As they stepped apart, moving from some filmy ice onto a brooding brown rock, she felt sparks snapping at her feet. Little jolts managed to get through even the thermal vacuum-layer insulation, prickling her feet.

The vector reading, combined with Jordin's, startled her. "Why, the thing's practically on top of us!"

She eyed the landscape. If Pluto's lords of creation were all swimming in toward this island ridge for lunch, this one might get here first. *Fired up by all those vitamins from the lost probe?* she wondered.

Suddenly excited, Shanna peered out to sea—and

there it was. Only a roiling, frothing ripple, like a ship's bow wave, but arrowing for shore. And others, farther out.

Then it bucked up into view, and she saw its great, segmented tube of a body, with a sheen somewhere between mother-of-pearl and burnished brass. Why, it was *huge*. For the first time it hit her that when they all converged on this spot, it was going to be like sitting smack in a middling-size dinosaur convention.

Too late to back out now. She powered up the small lander transmitter and tuned it to the signal she was receiving from seaward.

With her equipment she could not duplicate the creature's creative chaos of wavelengths. For its personal identification sign the beast seemed to use a simple continuous pulse pattern, like Morse code. Easy enough to simulate. After a couple of dry-run hand exercises to get with the rhythm of it, Shanna sent the creature a roughly approximate duplicate of its own ID.

She had expected a callback, maybe a more complex message. The result was astonishing. Its internal rocket engine fired a bright orange plume against the sky's black. It shot straight up in the air, paused, and plunged back. Its splash sent waves rolling up the beach. The farthest tongue of fluid broke against the lander's most seaward leg. The beast thrashed toward shore, rode a wave in— and stopped. The living cylinder lay there, half in, half out, as if exhausted.

Had she terrified it? Made it panic?

Cautiously Shanna tried the signal again, thinking furiously. It *would* give you quite a turn, she realized, if you'd just gotten as far in your philosophizing as "I think, therefore I am," and then heard a thin, toneless duplicate of your own voice give back an echo.

She braced herself—and her second signal prompted a long, suspenseful silence. Then, hesitantly—shyly?—the being repeated the call after her.

Shanna let out her breath in a long, shuddering sigh.

She hadn't realized she was holding it. Then she instructed DIS, the primary computer aboard *Proserpina,* to run the one powerful program Pluto Mission Control had never expected her to have to use: the translator, Wiseguy.

She waited for the program to come up and kept her eyes on the creature. It washed gently in and out with the lapping waves but seemed to pay her no attention. Jordin was busily snapping digitals. He pointed offshore. "Looks like we put a stop to the rest of them."

Heads bobbed in the sea. Waiting? For what?

In a few moments they might have an answer to questions that had been tossed around endlessly after the Marsmat discoveries. Could all language be translated into logically rigorous sentences, relating to one another in a linear configuration, structures, a system? If so, one could easily program a computer loaded with one language to search for another language's equivalent structures. Or, as many linguists and anthropologists insisted—particularly in light of the achingly slow progress with the Marsmat—does a truly unknown language forever resist such transformations?

Shanna stood absolutely still. Those minds offshore might make something of a raised hand, a shifting foot. Not all talk was verbal.

She *felt* the strangeness. Forbidding, cold, weird chemistry. Alien tongues could be outlandish not merely in vocabulary and grammatical rules but in their semantic swamps. Mute cultural or even biological premises wove into even the simplest of sentences. Blue skies Earthside lifted the spirits; here a blue gas might be poison. What would life-forms get out of this place? Could even the most inspired programmers, just by symbol manipulation and number crunching, have cracked ancient Egyptian with no Rosetta stone?

Not moving, she sent, "Bring Wiseguy online verbal, now."

"Copy you," came word from *Proserpina*'s bridge. Ukizi, from the voice signature.

She heard a delicate pop, and there was the burr of background—Wiseguy waiting for instructions. "Hey, guy," she said.

"I am not a guy, despite your nicknaming me, but thank you," the program answered in melodious male tones.

"We're going to feed you microwave code," Jordin put in. "Make the usual assumptions, as per training protocol number three. Decode in real time."

"Now we . . . wait," Shanna said, mostly to be saying something. The chill was biting into her feet and hands, and she wanted to move, get blood circulating. "Stay still," she sent to Jordin.

"Wiseguy," Jordin said, "can you make anything of those birdcalls?"

"Melodic structures, simple," the program said.

"Thought so," Jordin said. "Maybe singing is a universal."

With the Pluto Project already far over budget, the decision to send along Wiseguy—which took many terabytes of computational space—had been hotly contested. The deciding vote was cast by an eccentric but politically astute old skeptic, who hoped to disprove the "bug-eyed monster Rosetta stone theory," should life unaccountably turn up on Pluto. Shanna had heard through the gossip tree that the geezer was gambling that his support would make ISA bring along the rest of the DIS metasoftware package. The geezer had devoted decades to it, and he passionately believed in it. This would be a field trial nobody could have foreseen.

Wiseguy had learned Japanese in five hours; Hopi in seven; what smatterings they knew of dolphin in two days. It also mastered some of the fiendishly complex, multilogic artificial grammars generated from an Earthbased mainframe.

The unexpected outcome of $6 billion and a generation of cyberfolk was simply put: a good translator had all the qualities of a true artificial intelligence. As systems got apparently smarter, the philosophers fretted over how to tell an AI from just very fast software. By now the distinction had blurred. Wiseguy *was* a guy, of sorts. It—or she, or he; nobody had known quite how to ask—had to have cultural savvy *and* blinding mathematical skills. Shanna had long since given up hope of beating Wiseguy at chess, even with one of its twin processors tied off.

"I am laboring, though I must edit and substitute," Wiseguy said.

"Okay, just hurry."

"There are six transactions capable in human languages," Wiseguy said. "To make assertions, ask questions, issue commands, wish, promise, request. Further, all can be done negatively—"

"So? Hurry!"

"If there are others that aliens use, I will not even recognize it. I suspect that is happening here. I shall place blanks where I suspect this is happening."

"Great—get on with it." She waved again, hoping to get the creature's attention. Jordin leaped high in the 0.1-g gravity and churned both arms and legs in the ten seconds it took him to fall back down. Excited, the flying wings swooped silently over them. The scene was eerie in its hush. No calls now. The auroras danced, filmy. In Shanna's feed from *Proserpina* she heard Wiseguy stumbling, muttering . . . and beginning to talk. Not in English, but in the curious pips and dots of the microwave wave trains.

She noted from the digital readout on her helmet interior display that Wiseguy had been running full bore while eavesdropping on the radio cross talk. Now it was galloping along. In contrast to the simple radio signals she had first heard, the spoken, acoustic language turned out to be far more sophisticated. Wiseguy, however, dealt not in grammars and vocabularies, but in underlying concepts. And it was *fast*.

Shanna took a step toward the swarthy cylinder that heaved and rippled. Then another. *Careful.* Ropy muscles surged in it beneath layers of crusted fat. The cluster of knobs and holes at its front moved. It lifted its "head"— the snubbed-off, blunt forward section of the tube—and a bright, fast chatter of microwaves chimed through her ears. Followed immediately by Wiseguy's whispery voice. Discourse.

The big body had small cuplike appendages. Ears? But there were smaller openings below, too, with leathery flaps that moved to track the sound of her footsteps. She guessed the cuplike ones were microwave antennas. *On a living creature*, she thought, and then put aside her sense of awe. If they were like the human-made mechanical antennas, they could both transmit and receive with them—unlike, say, eyes.

Another step. More chimes. Wiseguy kept this up at increasing speed. She was now clearly out of the loop. Data sped by in her ears, as Wiseguy had neatly inserted itself into the conversation, assuming Shanna's persona, using some electromagnetic dodge. To her ears it was just a noisy, spurting stream. The creature apparently still thought it was speaking to her; its head swiveled to follow her.

The streaming conversation verged now from locked harmonies into brooding, meandering strings of chords. Shanna had played classical guitar as a teenager, imagining herself performing before concert audiences instead of bawling into a mike and hitting two chords in a rock band. So she automatically thought in terms of the musical moves of the data flow. Major keys gave way to dusky harmonies in a minor triad. To her mind this had an effect like a cloud passing across the sun.

Wiseguy reported to her and Jordin in its whisper. It and the alien—Ark—had only briefly had to go through the "me Tarzan, you Jane" stage. For a life-form that had no clearly definable brain she could detect, the alien proved a quick study.

She got its proper name first, as distinguished from its identifying signal; *its* name, definitely, for the translator established early in the game that these organisms had no gender.

The zand, they called themselves. And this one—call it

Ark, because that was all Wiseguy could make of the noise that came before—*Ark-zand*. Maybe, Wiseguy whispered for Shanna and Jordin alone, Ark was just a "place-note" to show that this thing was the "presently here" *of* the zand. It seemed that the name was generic, for all of them.

"Like Earth tribes," Jordin said, "who name themselves the People. Individual distinctions are tacked on?—maybe when necessary or socially pleasant."

Jordin was like that—surprising erudition popping out when useful, otherwise a straight supernerd tech type. Nobody was going to find an alternative here to Earth's tiresome clash of selfish individualisms and stifling collectivisms, Shanna thought. The political theorists back home would still make much of this, though, she was sure.

Shanna took another step toward the dark beach where the creature lolled, its head following her progress. It was no-kidding *cold*, she realized. Her boots were melting the ground under her, just enough to make it squishy. And she could hear the sucking as she lifted her boot, too. So she wasn't missing these creatures' calls—they didn't use the medium.

One more step. Chimes in her ears, and Wiseguy sent them a puzzled "It seems a lot smarter than it should be."

"Look, they need to talk to each other over distance, out of sight of each other," Shanna said. "Those waxy all-one-wing birds should flock and probably need calls for mating, right? So do we." Not that she really thought that was a deep explanation.

"How do we frame an expectation about intelligence?" Jordin put in.

"Yeah, I'm reasoning from Earthly analogies," Shanna

admitted. "Birds and walruses that use microwaves—who woulda thought?"

"I see," Wiseguy said, and went back to speaking to Ark in its ringing microwave tones.

Shanna listened to the ringing interchange speed up into a blur of blips and jots. Wiseguy could run very fast, of course, but this huge tubular thing seemed able to keep up with it. Microwaves' higher frequencies had far greater carrying capacity than sound waves and this Ark seemed able to use that. Well, evolution would prefer such a fast-talk capability, she supposed—but why hadn't it on Earth? Because sound was so easy to use, evolving out of breathing. Even here—Wiseguy told her in a subchannel aside—individual notes didn't mean anything. Their sequence did, along with rhythm and intonation, just like sound speech. Nearly all human languages used either subject-object-verb order or else subject-verb-object, and the zand did, too. But to Wiseguy's confusion, they used both, apparently not caring.

Basic values became clear, in the quick scattershot conversation. Something called Rendezvous kept coming up, modified by comments about territory. Self-merge, the ultimate, freely chosen—apparently with all the zand working communally afterward to care for the young, should there luckily occur a Birthing. Respect for age, because the elders had experienced so much more. But respect tempered by skepticism, because the elders embroidered experiences when telling the young the tale of the raiders from Darkside.

"And what's Darkside?" Jordin asked. He stirred restlessly, watching the sea for signs that others might come ashore. But the big bodies bobbed in the liquid a few hundred meters away.

Wiseguy supplied a guess: "The Outer, they call it also. Perhaps meaning beyond Pluto's orbit? Far into the darkness? There are other possible interpretations I can display in order of descending probabilities—"

"That's good enough," Shanna said. "On with it."

"Hey, they're moving in," Jordin said apprehensively, mouth working.

Shanna would scarcely have noticed the splashing and grinding on the beach as other zand began to arrive—apparently for Rendezvous, and Wiseguy stressed that it deserved the capital letter—save that Ark stopped to count and greet the new arrivals. Her earlier worry about being crunched under a press of huge zand bodies faded. They were social animals, and this barren patch of rock was now Ark's turf. Arrivals lumbering up onto the dark beach kept a respectful distance, spacing themselves. Like walruses, yes.

Standing motionless for so long, Shanna felt a sharp cold ache in her lower back. The chill had crept in. She was astounded to realize that nearly four hours had passed. She made herself pace, stretch, eat and drink from suit supplies.

Jordin did the same, saying, "We're 80 percent depleted on air."

"Damn it, I don't want to quit *now*! How 'bout you get extra from the lander?"

Jordin grimaced. He didn't want to leave, either. They had all dedicated their lives to getting here, to this moment in this place. "Okay, Cap'n, sir," he said sardonically as he trudged away.

She felt a kind of silent bliss here, just watching. Life, strange and wonderful, went on all around her. Her running digital coverage would be a huge hit Earthside. Unlike Axelrod's empire, the Pluto Project gave their footage away.

As if answering a signal, the zand hunched up the slope a short way to feed on some brown lichenlike growth that sprawled across the warming stones. She stepped aside. Ark came past her, and another zand slid up alongside. It rubbed against Ark, edged away, rubbed again. A courtship preliminary? Something about their movements made Shanna venture the guess.

The zand stopped and slid flat tongues over the lichen stuff, vacuuming it up with a slurp she could hear through her suit. Tentatively the newcomer laid its body next to Ark. Shanna could hear the pace of microwave discourse Ark was broadcasting, and it took a lurch with the contact, slowing, slowing . . . Then Ark abruptly—even curtly, it seemed to Shanna—rolled away. Its signal resumed its speed.

She laughed aloud. How many people would pass up a chance at sex to get on with their language lessons? All along the shingle beach, stretching to the horizon, the zand were pairing off. Except Ark.

"Y'know, sex took a couple billion years to evolve on Earth," she said.

"Huh?" Jordin's voice sounded surprised. "Oh yeah. Here . . . well, how old is this ecology, anyway?"

"Pluto must've formed early, from condensation. This could be lots older than us."

She muted the furious bips and dots of the Wiseguy-zand conversation. Occasionally Wiseguy sent them a quick term for help— "Is this sensible?" the program asked. "Ontological?"

"Hey, is Wiseguy into philosophy already?" Jordin asked. "I dunno what that means."

"Ummm. The biology saying is *ontogeny recapitulates phylogeny*—meaning, in development of the embryo you see the past stages of the species. Once we had gills, back in our fishy days."

"Hey, pretty heady stuff," Jordin said skeptically. "So soon?"

"Well, Wiseguy did train on the SETI messages."

"Seems like it's digging at how the zand see their place in this weird world."

"Maybe canned brains are natural philosophers."

"Yeah, they don't have sex to distract 'em." They both laughed at that, releasing tension.

Here we are, Shanna thought, *the Columbuses of a new world, and we're waiting for a computer to do the introductions.*

"Y'know, I gotta move or I'm gonna freeze," she said.

Jordin grunted assent. "Feels great to move. Hey—the zand are moving inland."

"Uh-oh. Toward the lander."

Shanna walked back carefully, feeling the crunch of hard ice as she melted what would have been gases on Earth—nitrogen, carbon dioxide, oxygen itself. Low-g walking was an art. With so little weight, rocks and ices that looked rough were still slick enough to make her slip. She caught herself more than once from a full, facedown splat—but only because she had so much time to recover, in a slow fall. As the zand worked their way across the

stony field of lichen, they approached the lander. Jordin
wormed his way around them, careful not to get too close.

"Wiseguy! Interrupt." Shanna explained what she
wanted. It quickly got the idea and spoke in short bursts to
Ark—who resent a chord-rich message to the zand.

They all stopped short. "I don't want them burned on
the lander," Shanna said to Jordin, who replaced her suit
oxy bottles without a hitch.

"Burned? I don't want them eating it," Jordin said.

Then the zand began asking *her* questions, and the first
one surprised her: *Do you come from Lightgiver? As
heralds?*

In the next few minutes Shanna and Jordin realized—
all from their questions alone—that in addition to a society the zand had a rough-and-ready view of the world, an
epic oral literature (though recited in microwaves), and
something that resembled a religion. Even Wiseguy was
shaken; it paused in its replies, something she had never
heard it do before, not even in speed trials. It was learning
not just an alien language but an alien mind.

Agnostic though she was, the discovery moved her
profoundly. *Lightgiver. After all,* she thought with a rush
of compassion and nostalgia, *we started out as sunwor-
shipers, too.*

There were dark patches on the zand's upper sides, and
as the sun rose, these pulled back to reveal thick lenses.
They looked like quartz—tough crystals for a rugged
world. Their banquet of lichen done—she took a few
samples for analysis, provoking a snort from a nearby
zand—they lolled lazily in their long day. She and Jordin
walked gingerly through them, peering into the quartz
"eyes." Their retinas were a brilliant blue with red wire-

like filaments curling through and under. Convergent evolution seemed to have found yet another solution to the
eye problem.

Jordin said, "Y'know, I'll bet these guys can see the
sun the way we do."

Shanna had been snapping her own digitals. "Meaning?"

"Our eyes are tiny in comparison. We're forty times
farther away from the sun here, so these quartz eyes are
forty or so times bigger. They can resolve the point of the
sun into a disk."

"Ah. So what's our answer? Are we from Lightgiver?"

"Well . . . you're the cap'n, remember." He grinned.
"And the biologist."

She quickly said to Wiseguy, "Tell it: No. We are from
a world like this. From nearer, uh, Lightgiver."

As soon and as tactfully as possible, Shanna got the interchange turned around, so that she was again asking the
questions and the zand answering them.

Discussing the sun was useful, too. They had a calen-
dar concept of short and long warm-cold cycles that intrigued her. Obviously it corresponded with Pluto's
rotational day and centuries-long orbital "year"—an impressive feat of observation and deduction for people who
lacked a technology. Shanna soon realized, however, that
this idea was new to the zand—that, in fact, it had learned
the information that very planetary day from an untutored
genius it referred to as Old One. She pressed it further and
learned the cold arithmetic. Ark said that this very day Old
One had discoursed on such deep truths while floating
over the "amber sea."

The moment she realized those numbers' implication

for the future of Pluto, she broke off. For the first time since she had been a very small child, she blinked back tears.

Don't waste our damn time on tears, Shanna sternly told herself. *And certainly don't weep in a space suit.* But she remained silent, truly at a loss for what to say.

Do not sad, the zand sent through Wiseguy. *Lightgiver gives and Lightgiver takes; but it gives more than any; it is the Source of all life, here and in the Dark; exalt Lightgiver.*

"Incredible!" Shanna said to Jordin. "Wiseguy must be sending Ark pretty sophisticated stuff."

Jordin said, "Hard to believe Ark or Wiseguy can intuit our moods."

"And is trying to console us? Or just repeating some, well, theology."

Jordin said, "Unless Wiseguy's imposing human categories on Ark's language. Which seems likely—but how'll we know?"

Wiseguy told her that the zand did not use verb forms underlining existence itself—no words for *are, is, be*—so "sad" became a verb. She wondered what deeper philosophical chasm that linguistic detail revealed.

"Apparently," Wiseguy said, "we have settled an interesting philosophical question, one that arose with the SETI codes, before I was invented."

Startled, Shanna asked, "Which is . . . ?"

"Whether all intelligences would use intertranslatable symbol grammars."

"Uh, I see."

"The answer seems to be yes. That is why I can so readily translate the zand language."

"Um." *Lightgiver gives and Lightgiver takes.* The phrasing was startlingly familiar. The same damned, comfortless consolation she had heard preached at her grandmother's rain-swept funeral.

Remembering that moment of loss with a deep inward hurt, she forced it away. What could she say?

After an awkward silence Ark said something Wiseguy rendered as, *I need leave you for now.*

Another zand was peeling out Ark's personal identification signal, with a slight tag-end modification. Traffic between the two zand became intense. Wiseguy did its best to interpret, humming with the effort in her ears.

"Y'know, I had my doubts about using a program for first contact," she said. "But it's working."

"What choice did we have?" Jordin asked reasonably. "We can't sit down here for weeks chatting away at our low, verbal bit rate."

"Right. For one thing we'd freeze our asses off."

This all became abundantly clear for the next two hours, when Wiseguy consulted them incessantly about ambiguities, context, syntax—the gray areas where human intuition might still outclass Wiseguy's terabytes. The process was wearing, but at least she and Jordin could rove the land and get a feel for the cold twilight strangeness here.

Finally Shanna turned the translator off. First things first, and even on Pluto there was such a thing as privacy. Wiseguy had no need to hear frail humans discussing their weaknesses.

Jordin, ever the diplomat, began. "Y'know, it's been hours . . ." Even on this 0.1-g world she was getting tired. The zand lolled, Lightgiver stroking their skins—which now flushed with an induced chemical radiance, harvesting the light. She took more digitals, thinking about how to guess the reaction—

"Y'know . . ."

"Yeah, right, let's go."

Stamping their feet to help circulation, they prepped the lander for liftoff. Monotonously, as they had done Earthside a few thousand times, they went through the checklist. Tested the external cables. Rapped the valves to get them to open. Tried the mechanicals for freeze-up—and found two legs that would not retract. The joints took all of Jordin's powerful heft to unjam them.

Shanna lingered at the hatch and looked back—across the idyllic plain, the beach, the sea slick like a pink lake. *Chances are, I'll never be here again. Maybe the high point of my life . . . an incredible vista.* She hoped the heat of launching, carried through this frigid air, would add to the sun's thin rays and . . . and what? Maybe help induce a Birthing? She reminded herself that she was a biologist, here to understand, not take sides . . . *Impossible.*

Too bad she could not transmit Wagner's grand "Liebestod" to them, but even Wiseguy could only do so much. She lingered, held both by scientific curiosity and by a newfound affection. Then another miracle occurred, the way they do, matter-of-factly. Sections of carbon exoskeleton popped forth from the shiny skin of two nearby zand. Jerkily these carbon-black leaves articulated together, joined, swelled, puffed with visible effort into one great sphere.

She knew—but could not say how—the two zand were flowing together, coupling as one being. Self-merge.

Inside, checked and rechecked, they waited for the orbital resonance time with *Proserpina* to roll around. Each lay silent, immersed in thought. The lander went *ping* and *pop* with thermal stress.

Jordin punched the firing keys. The lander rose up on its roaring tail of fiery steam.

The experience had been surrealistic. Her biology training was shouting all during their time down there, *This makes no sense.* No life chemistry should work well at such low temperatures. Enzymes might, sluggishly, but no other biological machinery she knew. But the zand played on . . .

Shanna's eyes were dry now, and her next move was clear: *I've got to talk to Old One.*

6.

OLD ONE

THEY SPENT A WEEK recovering from the first landing. ISA insisted that they "restart their sleep cycle," which meant rest up. No problem; she and Jordin were exhausted.

But recovery wasn't as easy as when she'd been a teenager; they'd expended a lot of nervous energy. Still, she bounced out of the sack the first day back after six hours to find Jordin already back at work. He was fixing some gimpy gear and refitting the lander, filling supplies and kicking the tires. Engineers think of their equipment as extensions of themselves and often take care of it better than their own bodies.

They had to be debriefed. Shanna recorded a quick summary, mostly commentary on the real-time data feed they had sent. Jordin grumbled and did the same. There were the mandatory media appetites to feed, too—a contractual obligation. *Thanks, Dad.* The Consortium's race to Mars two decades back had built an enduring public for space, sold as real-time, you-are-there exploration.

As soon as possible, she got beyond *Proserpina*'s daily details and found time to think the easiest way—by pulling extra time on watch.

A darkness deeper than she had ever seen crept across Pluto. Night here, without Charon's glow, had no planets dotting the sky, only the distant sharp stars. At the terminator line shadows stretched, jagged black profiles of the ridgelines torn by pressure from the ice. The warming had somehow shoved fresh peaks into the gathering atmosphere, ragged and sharp. Since there was atmosphere far thicker and denser than anybody had expected, stars seen from the surface were not unwinking points; they flickered and glittered as on crisp nights at high altitudes on Earth. Near the magnetic poles she watched swirling blue auroral glows cloak the plains where fogs rose even at night. When *Proserpina* had first arrived, Earthside openly doubted the images they sent back. Clouds? Open bodies of liquid? Impossible . . .

Despite all their discoveries, the basic mystery had only deepened. What was delivering such heat to the icelands?

Shanna turned off the interior lights so she could see

subtle shadings in the crust. It was her nighttime watch, by preference. All the crew were asleep but for her. *Proserpina* swung serenely about the forbidding crescent of a world that made no sense. As a biologist she was adrift on seas of speculation, as vast as the pewter-gray methane lakes that winked where the sunlight struck.

The dashboard clock's blinking crimson obediently reminded her that she should have filed another report, but she had skipped it, letting Mary Kay file a nominal status check and mission parameter index. Even billions of miles away there was paperwork.

A Pluto day lasts 6.4 Earth days, so by the time *Proserpina* was fully functional, the zand were just about to wake up again. During the Pluto night *Proserpina* requested permission to drop small, rugged microwave sensors around the zand gathering areas. Earthside fretted and argued but after a mere several days, agreed.

Down they went. Most survived and began picking up zand cross talk. By eavesdropping, it did not take long to find the Old One, because it was the subject of many conversations. Old One proved to be not just old but huge— three times bigger than any zand they had seen. The Old One seemed to be a different kind of creature—though in high-resolution optical observation from *Proserpina* it did look much like the zand. Or else the zand, like some Earth species, simply kept growing all their lives, so a big zand was an ancient one.

Wiseguy was grinding at the river of zand-talk data, steadily incoming from the eavesdropping sensors. The program thought the "structure coefficients" of the microwave banter suggested a sophisticated language and extensive knowledge, both about Pluto and about their own social codes.

Very well; but why was it there? Why such intelligence in this oddly barren place?

After days of threading through the Old One's conversations they hit a startling level of complexity. Shanna had scanned through Wiseguy's interpretations, and they astounded. Here, all rolled into one, was the Aristotle, the Bacon, the Galileo, maybe even the Einstein of the zand species. Or else it was the latest in a long line of huge intellects, their knowledge handed down through many generations.

Shanna immediately requested Earthside's permission to speak directly to Old One. Again delay. Arguments. Some theorists thought that *Proserpina* had already gone too far in "interfering" with the zand. Unforgivable, one senior biologist proclaimed in a public screed. But then, they'd said the same about interactions with the Marsmat, too. Those who always advocated going slow didn't understand that people who did not live forever wanted some closure in their lifetimes. And that windows of opportunity had a way of slamming shut; ask Leif Eriksson.

After more days ISA agreed. Down went a complex microwave relay, positioned near the Old One. Jordin had labored over it, adding a small nuclear thermal generator, packing in layers to insulate the electronics against the forbidding cold. Then Wiseguy made their overtures.

The introductions and first dialogues went surprisingly well. It was almost as if the creature were expecting them. Talking to it over microwave proved dizzying. Shanna instructed Wiseguy to stop fidgeting over pronouns—which the Old One seemed to feel were irrelevant—and other such minor grammatical distinctions. She went for the big, conceptual lumps. From the speed and insight of the Old One's answers she felt the presence of a vast intellect. The zand had produced such intricate, quick thoughts! All with no written language or notational system or even a telescope, much less a computer.

Any biologist would ask the obvious: where did such intelligence come from? This skimpy environment, with few microbes and almost no fauna bigger than her thumb, seemed inadequate. At least primate intelligence had arisen in a broad, diverse biosphere . . . but maybe that wasn't necessary.

The Old One was the premier zand philosopher-scientist, and it had the advantage of time. It had lived, if Wiseguy's own beginning conversations with it were right, more than four hundred Earth years. As for how old the zand were—well, the Old One had shied away from saying. Maybe it didn't know.

Old One had blithely skipped most of the semantic and conceptual preliminaries she and Wiseguy had gone through with Ark. *These guys learn!* In fact, the native savant—its bulky, walruslike body already appearing on T-shirts Earthside—shortly had started communicating directly with the Discursive and Integrative System.

"Dis" was the Greek equivalent of Pluto, so the project's choice of acronyms was entirely appropriate. Their DIS metaprogram was a superstructure above Wiseguy, tasked with integrating results with the whole architecture of their onboard computing. Olympians, keeping their own counsel, for now.

Wiseguy had ceased including Shanna in the interchange most of the time. That would have slowed them down, and Shanna did need sleep now and then. Old One didn't seem to, so the large zand and Wiseguy exchanged sallies of semantic battle without a break. She didn't like this, but that's how advanced systems worked, a century into the computer revolution. Machines didn't bother slow-mo humans unless necessary.

And Old One, unlike some geniuses Shanna had known on Earth, had tact. When she awoke and came back into the loop, it had abruptly halted its data rate with Wiseguy. Abandoning what must have been for it a heady conversational brew, it deftly brought her up to date. As soon as she began a series of questions, it knew what she wanted to ask.

Yes, it said—her vitamin hypothesis did, after a fashion, fit the facts. The zand suffered from what amounted to nutritional deficiencies. Analogous to Earth species, they needed trace elements for full health and strength, even for survival. The remedy lay, in a sense, close at hand—and in another way frustratingly, tantalizingly far off.

That was why Old One had philosophically resigned itself to die in the next few day-cycles. It had readily volunteered this fact, as though they would understand. After all, weren't they also from Lightgiver, or at least in its neighborhood? They knew all, yes? Surely they could tell that another wave of Darksiders was coming, this time to bring a tide of death?

Lights often streaked across Pluto's somber heavens. Some of them pounded into the ice or plunged into the sea as what Old One called skystones. As soon as she heard the translated anthology word—a common translators' programming trick, nailing terms together as an approximation—Shanna knew whence they came: the cometary

Oort cloud. That great gray swarm surrounds the solar system to a depth of a third of a light-year. Inconceivably vast, its inner edge intersects the orbits of Pluto and Neptune. Pluto, nearer the cloud than Earth and shielded by less atmosphere, is far more vulnerable to hammering by meteoric debris.

But something malignant fell from the sky, too, and then roved the surface, killing zand.

Shanna's mind had skated ahead of even Wiseguy, slapping pieces of the puzzle together. The zand's life was even more precarious than she had imagined. Only by sheer cosmic accident—or as they would have said, by the mercy of Lightgiver—had a stray comet never pulverized Rendezvous. Or sent a tidal wave to roll over the zand during their breakfasting or at Birthing.

She thought about that in light of Pluto's long but odd history. Many astronomers thought it had started life as a moon of Uranus, later liberated by some impact or else by the slow tugs of gravity from some other passing body. Somehow the world had gotten free.

Maybe the origin of life here, and evolution, had started then. Maybe. Only by another accident—or miracle; give the zand their nod—had they survived the Oort cloud bombardment—

Hey—wait.

A lightning hunch, like the ones that had given Shanna a competitive edge during astronaut training, struck her, hard. *Evolve? Who said they evolved here?*

The implications of that were too much for now—she brushed them aside. But one thing she suddenly knew. The zand were metal-based life, almost like machines, but driven by a metallic chemistry. Nobody had foreseen such an exotic chemistry, blending metal's liking for oxygen—like the iron rusts of Mars—and a chilly liquid chemistry of methane. Running low-temperature metabolism demanded rare elements. Churning chemistries had to be fed.

Out there in primordial Chaos and ancient Night, in tiny but sufficient quantities, lay the heavy metals and rare earths the zand needed in their food. They harvested these, Old One said, from the skystones.

But that raised a practical problem. Most skystones fell into the large methane sea, where at sunset they irrecoverably froze. Or else the skystones plowed into the cliffs and shadowy crevasses on the nightside. Into those frigid lands the awake zand never ventured; they slept through the coming of night. But the fallen skystones then sank into the liquefying ice fields at daybreak. The methane sea came from the ices and so consumed all but a tiny fraction of the vital skystones.

She pondered this exotic biology. If a zand was lucky enough to find a skystone at dawn, before the precious stuff sank into the melt—or if it could dive into the shallows, searching for treasure on the frozen shelf . . . But the chances of that had to be so slender. *They had so little time.*

Shanna reluctantly—for such a mass of knowledge remained untapped in that mind!—bid Old One farewell, through Wiseguy. Which even seemed to sense her mood, and said, "There will be other conversations." *Hope so.*

7.

CRESCENDO

EARTHSIDE SENT THEM a blizzard of questions. Shanna tired of answering them. She had one of the crew, Chow-Lin, do a downlink transmission because he had the old NASA-style jargon down pat. Alphabet soup, with acronyms back-to-back. The message was that they had "contingency strategy worked out" to avoid "any serious danger," though they were "operating out of" their "planned parameter space." There was no "incremental creep in risk," just their "preplanned" (she always wondered what "postplanned" might be) "spectrum of exploratory responses" to a "knowledge-acquisition-driven expedition" here on the "frontier of humanity." She had always admired the way bureaucracies spontaneously produced leaden prose, blandly sliding from the mouths of people who absolutely believed everything they said.

Then they had an all-crew meeting. Around the table the rest of the crew looked grim, like a support group for hemorrhoid sufferers.

"We don't understand," Chow-Lin said. "The zand, the Darksiders—what's it mean?"

"I want to compliment you on how you handled the public angle." Shanna had taken management courses and remembered to open with a compliment, especially if one wanted to present people with plans they might very well dislike. "Quite adroit."

But Chow-Lin wasn't having any. "We don't know what's going on!"

Jordin said quietly, "Research is when you don't know what you're doing."

Mary Kay looked askance at her husband. "Or overdoing."

Shanna asked her, "You think we stayed down there too long?"

Chow-Lin said stolidly, with a heavy-lidded blink, "You were hours over nominal."

"Hey," Jordin said, "nominal is just a guess, not an order."

Chow-Lin was unmoved, lips twisted skeptically. "If you'd had a liftoff failure, there wasn't time to get you up from the surface before you froze."

"We made the discovery of the age," Jordin said, still sounding reasonable but his eyes glinting. "That tends to concentrate the mind."

Shanna recalled the old Samuel Johnson saying, something like, *Nothing so concentrates the mind like a pending execution.* She stayed silent while Jordin and Chow-Lin traded gibes, with Mary Kay slipping in worried remarks. *Overture* . . . Then even Uziki, the quiet one, chimed in. *Discord* . . . *First Theme.* Shanna recognized the tones, listening for the underlying feeling rather than surface content. They needed to get out their vexations, not about the danger of the first landing at all, but about being left out. Therapy time.

Now for *Second Theme* . . .

"Taking chances isn't the same as exploration," Chow-Lin was saying, so she countered, "What were you observing?"

Chow-Lin hesitated only a second, nodded to Uziki, who punched a command into one of the big wall display screens, which was at the moment showing surf breaking on a white beach. It flickered over to a 3-D diagram of the vicinity near Pluto, with Charon shown to the side. "We used radar backtracking of incoming masses, as discussed. There is a steady stream"—the screen showed orange dots curving in from farther out—"coming on nearly straight-falling orbits." The dots followed yellow trajectory curves, approaching Pluto and slowing.

"Not a free infall, then," Jordin said.

"No, in fact, there's considerable slowing on the approach. Then—" The dots entered the thin Plutonian atmosphere, showing flaring trails.

"Aerobraking?" Mary Kay asked doubtfully.

Chow-Lin nodded. "Yeah—artificial as hell. Somebody's dropping descent packages on the surface, and they're moving slow enough to survive the impact."

Mary Kay said, "Deliberately targeted, that's clear—this stuff isn't natural."

Shanna wondered for a moment if she had lost her capacity for surprise. *So much* . . . She thought silently for a moment as the others discussed details, and then said slowly, "All those incoming arcs—they end on the nightside."

Uziki said, "Yes, I noticed that, too. For some reason—"

Jordin said, "Even when their aerobraking trajectories wrap all the way around the planet, they end up coming down at night. Damn funny."

Shanna made her leap. "Those are the Darksiders! The

zand call them that because they land when the zand are asleep and most vulnerable."

Chow-Lin sat back, face impassive. "Ummm, an hypothesis . . ."

"It can't be an accident that the incoming prefer to land at night, when they can't even see the landing zone very well," Jordin said. "Hey, maybe that's why we found pieces of them on the beach—some of them hit too hard and break up."

"Maybe a Darkside landing is tied to the biology," Mary Kay ventured, looking at Shanna—

Who shrugged. "Could be. Night's pretty damned cold—even for Pluto. All I know from the Old One translations is that the zand are getting decimated by something called the Darksiders. If they're to be believed—and why not?—it's an ongoing genocide."

Chow-Lin frowned, fidgeting with a pen. "With the strings being pulled by—"

"Something farther out—but what?"

Uziki said to the screen, "Full outview." The screen scale expanded until Pluto was a small circle, then a dot. The infalling lines in yellow drew together, making a long, slightly curved band. The scale continued to expand but the yellow just kept going, until— "That's as far as we can track with any resolution."

"Wow," Jordin said. "They're from really far out."

"No assignable origin," Chow-Lin said crisply. "But their orbits point back to a big ice body." On-screen, a tiny dot got labeled: X. "Got it in the low infrared. It's an incredibly cold place—but warmer than anything else out here, except Pluto."

"How could anything live there?" Mary Kay asked.

"How can the zand?" Jordin countered. "No question, this is low-temperature chemistry we haven't a clue about."

"There's got to be something more." Shanna peered off into nowhere. "Pluto's is an ecology that's thin, far too sparse. No microbes in the soil—I just ran the chem check and micron-level analysis. Now, that's just plain impossible. Biology builds up from the basic building blocks. Here there are none. Just a few organisms and a spotty food supply. No pyramid of life, just a few big fauna sitting atop a set of stilts."

"So . . ." Now Mary Kay looked both skeptical and puzzled. "We're missing something."

"Or else our whole comprehension of biology is wrong. You don't build up big creatures without a huge investment in processes, chem, metabolism . . ." Shanna stopped, frustrated, but knowing what to do next.

"Let's leave it to the biologists Earthside," Mary Kay said. "We're explorers, not theory guys."

"Right, explorers." Shanna took a deep breath. "So let's explore. I say we go down there and see what the Darksiders are."

"Hey, no," Chow-Lin said automatically. "Another descent so soon? I strongly—"

"We need to get the full story here," Jordin said. "Not go running home with more questions than answers. We haven't got a clue what is driving Pluto's warm-up, and that is our mission."

This was true, but Chow-Lin's expression told them that the argument cut no ice with him. He said, "I think we've gone off the deep end here."

Mary Kay, showing some grit in her narrow-eyed expression, said, "We're at the deep end—the borderland of the solar system. It took a lot of money to put us here, and—"

"You're going to interfere in an intelligent alien society, don't you realize that?" Chow-Lin said.

"We already have," said Uziki, who usually confined herself to computers and the robots. She seldom said anything about nonengineering matters, but Shanna was glad to have her come forward. "They're part of the problem we came to solve, right? So we have to understand them."

"We can't just blunder—"

"Do I hear echoes of the Prime Directive here?" Shanna said, absolutely straight, letting the words do all the work that a sarcastic tone would have. Chow-Lin was a fan of an ancient TV show, one she had watched a few times. She knew just enough to make fun of it.

Chow-Lin said guardedly, "Well, we do have to follow some code."

"Look," Jordin said reasonably, "we don't have protocols from ISA on this. So we're free to deal with opportunities as they arise."

"You want to go down there again?" Chow-Lin countered. "It's dangerous."

"Yeah, but that's not the appeal," Jordin said, only a slight upturn at the corner of his mouth showing that this was ironic.

"We don't have permission," Chow-Lin began. "I'll enter an objection—"

"No, you won't, mister," Shanna said mildly. "That's an order."

She had carefully chosen the moment to invoke her authority. On long missions crew saw their captain sharing the scut work, doing her clothes in the washer, waking up after a bad night's sleep—and soon enough, she didn't look like a voice of authority anymore. But that didn't mean the mission could do without one. It was a matter of knowing when to remind them, a lesson learned through the decades on Mars and passed on.

Chow-Lin opened his mouth to say something, then slowly closed it. He shook his head for a moment, biting his lip, and Shanna thought she would have to deal with outright insurrection. But no; he looked down, eyes boring into the black tabletop, and said nothing.

Into the silence Jordin said casually, "Y'know, we could use a systems modification. For . . . defense."

Shanna said, "What?"

"If the Darksiders are bent on taking down the zand, maybe they'll come after us, too."

The crew rustled uneasily. Shanna hadn't thought of this possibility, and she could tell they hadn't, either. "So how do we . . . ?"

"I'll modify the chem launch sequence. Cook up a little surprise just in case."

Chow-Lin said, "That's entirely uncalled-for. Not only do we interfere with a sentient alien form, we plan an action against it!"

"Technically," Jordin said, "the Darksiders are probably the second sentient form here."

This gave Shanna an opening to help firmly defuse the confrontation. "We just don't know—and that's why we're going."

She ended the meeting, setting another for the next day.

That gave time for the rest of the crew to argue among themselves, of course. Over the next few hours she spoke privately to several of them and massaged the social angles.

The Kares, Jordin and Mary Kay, were resolutely reasonable. They took it upon themselves to make the diplomatic arguments that Shanna could not, without appearing weak. They had discovered so much already, yes. The surface was treacherous, yes. The Darkside even more so. Yes. So why go? Because it was their job, and anyway, the captain said so.

It took two days of talk and one more of fending off Earthside's alarm. But she went—with Jordin, again. Earthside wanted to use their experience.

Shanna knew very little out here, but one thing she knew for sure: the zand were worth protecting. What was that saying? *The fox knows many things, the hedgehog one big thing.* Okay, she was a hedgehog.

Darkside beckoned. She was going to become a meteor miner. *Crescendo.*

8.

DOWN IN THE DARK

ISA PLUTO DAILY SUMMARY
GMT 0940, Thursday, 12 May 2044

All hands on station:

Descent to Pluto Surface
Descent Crew: Axelrod, Kare, J.

State of Ship

- Data systems recycle and purge complete
- Thermography and ultrasound integrity check completed 0630 on lander by J. Kare; ready to deploy
- Consumables 38 percent above nominal usage rate
- Power generation rate 99.67 BOL
- Uplink rate maximum of IRSC
- Orbital parameters within profile

Five-Day Outlook Summary

Tuesday, GMT 0900: Lander profiling and resupply
Wednesday, GMT 1230: Reactor reshipping by robot teams commences—three-day lining tests and monitoring SUBT
Thursday, GMT 1030: Systems test of optical and infrared sensing
Friday, GMT 1100: Wiseguy update and Earthside UBK
Saturday, GMT 0300: Mechanicals review and monitor reboot

Crew Q&A:
Where to begin, guys?

Quote for the Day: "Details Are Our Business"

The big lander roared as it descended on its steam plume toward Pluto's nighted surface. They took it cautiously, through step-down orbits, pausing at each one to assess the surface and let the detectors have their feeding time.

Shanna watched somberly, her chair warming her against the seeping cold here in the planet's shadow. She loved the view this low, skimming. Astronomy's geometries were the essence of smooth beauties—arcs and ellipses, crescents and circles, orbs round and fat in their perpetual, serene dance. This deep range of pockmarked worlds held steep, chiseled mountains that had endured longer than whole continents on Earth. She was gaining now a sense of the deep reservoir of time sleeping out here.

But perhaps that sleep was over. The astronomers were used to seeing this deep freeze as a tabula rasa, unwritten upon since the solar system's creation, not as a dynamic realm. But now they knew otherwise.

Their nominal mission was a second sampling of the surface, this time on the nightside. Mission goal: to measure atmospheric changes as night came on, and to search for debris from the mysterious incoming orange packages—the Darksiders, presumably. Or so she had argued to ISA; but, in fact, she was seeking the meaning of this place—how it really worked. Too many things didn't add up.

"Getting something visible ahead," Jordin sent on comm.

"I see it—down below the crescent," she answered.

"Not a reflection of a star, either. Too bright."

Lights. Brimming yellow dots on the upcoming horizon. Not in the sky; on the ice. A prickly coldness ran through her. In the intense cold below they would have much less time on the surface. ISA didn't want them to do any EVA unless absolutely necessary.

Shanna wished she had questioned Old One more fully

before charging off this way. *The fox knows many things*... Could the zand tribal epic, of the great raid from Darkside in the distant past, be true?

But there couldn't, strictly speaking, be any Darksiders. All the planet was exposed to the sun in due course as it rotated. Surely "Darksiders" could come out in the zand's own territory after nightfall, right? And day-living borers and flappers and the zand could flourish on "Darkside" when it faced the sun.

Confusing. Maybe a huge mistake in Wiseguy's interpretation. She fretted. Then something like an answer came. As they drove down farther into the night, the reactor in their belly humming and thrusting, a great, sickly greenish yellow arc rose up before her, blotting out stars.

"Wow!" And just maybe she had part of her puzzle.

Ah. Charon was synchronous in its orbit—the fat gray moon hung perpetually above this area. When the twin worlds swung around into sunlight, Charon—so aptly named after the ferryman of Hades—cast a large shadow, eclipsing the tiny sun. Lightgiver would give even less warmth here than on the opposite hemisphere. This side of Pluto was forever unfavored. It would be far chillier. Even at high noon here methane snow would come drifting down. There was a Darkside, after all.

The sun was still four hundred times brighter than moonlight on Earth, she remembered from one of the briefings. Enough to read a newspaper by, but without much atmosphere, all shadows were sharp, hard.

Okay, she thought, listening to Jordin bring them down to the preselected landing zone—not far from the odd lights, she noted. *The Darksiders prefer to come in out of the night and land in the coldest portion of the planet. Now think like a biologist.*

Life filled its appropriate ecological niches, as Darwin had seen in the Galápagos long ago. One-half of Pluto was home for the zand; the other was the domain of the "Darksiders."

No, damn it! That wouldn't work. She did remember some of the astro briefings she'd had, after all. Viewed from Pluto, Charon had only started regularly eclipsing the sun within the past half century. The astro boys had nailed it finally in 2029, when both the satellite's orbit and the planet's axis had begun to drift. Big surprise. The orbital mechanics had changed.

And the waltzing worlds had swung in their crazy, new looping orbits, not giving a damn that the astronomers couldn't figure out why. By 2042, when their mission launched, Charon was eclipsing the sun regularly each Plutonian day.

Come, now! Evolution is not that swift, no way.

Unless . . .

Unless the strange orbital shift was what had brought the Darksiders out of wherever they hid—hibernated?— for most of Pluto's long orbital year.

Shanna shook her head in disbelief. Centuries ago, had Charon's orbit similarly moved to screen out the sun? *Are you getting enough oxygen?* her nagging inner voice asked. *This is strange, even for you . . .*

She brushed aside her doubts. *Follow your nose, girl. Damn the inner critics.*

Okay. Did that have anything to do with the odd—but apparently natural—radio emissions that the Space Array had discovered? The whole alarm about the big plasma storms that might be washing into the solar system, if the Voyager data were right?

Put that by for now also. Then ... And then Darkside had raided Rendezvous? Old One had said lots about that, clothed in mythic jargon even Wiseguy couldn't follow. The zand, their battle story told them, had barely survived that legendary Götterdämmerung. *Or is my liking for Wagner leading me astray here? Twilight of the gods beside a methane sea? Ooooggg ...*

And this time, Shanna suddenly realized, if the Darksiders moved to the lightside within the next few Earth hours, they would catch the greater part of the zand helpless, immobilized in the rosy afterglow of Self-merge.

Had that happened before? Probably. Something had built those epic poems Old One recited at blinding, Wiseguy-level speed. The zand feared the Darksiders for good reason. They were both predators, but somehow the Darksiders were even better at it.

Jordin was on the comm, passing numbers and "okays" back and forth with Mary Kay on *Proserpina*. When he had a free moment, she asked, "You're sure the little surprise is ready?"

He grinned. "It's too simple to go wrong. Just oxy and hydrogen feeds from our reserves. I fitted two small nozzles and tucked them into a spare cylinder I had, to make a reaction chamber. Just a li'l trick."

"Um. Li'l trick." Jordin could rig up anything on short notice, it seemed. "Hope we don't need to use it."

"Hey—look there, near our LZ." Jordin pointed. When she looked puzzled, he added, "Landing zone." And she recalled that he had started out as a Marine flyer.

"This thermal armor is pretty confining." She felt it

pinch at knees and elbows. "I know you think we need it—"

"You may be the cap'n, but I'm the safety officer." A nod of the head. "Ma'am."

Small lights moved below. Scurrying patterns. "Those look . . . alive," Shanna said.

"Maybe that's the Darksiders."

On the attack? she wondered. *Hey, don't get ahead of yourself.*

She repeated her thoughts to Jordin as they descended gingerly, pausing at each orbital level to assess the landing zone. He said, "You got this place figured out already?"

"Not really. But something tells me we don't have time to hold seminars on the local biology."

He grinned. "Not that I'd attend, y'know."

"I know."

Shanna's grandmother had dinned into her "reverence for life"—all life. Suppose the incessant motion below was a battle of some strange kind. Could she make a terrible choice, to save the zand? She gritted her teeth.

A circle of greater darkness yawned below, breaking the thinly moonlit landscape. It moved; she came fully alert. Quickly she called on *Proserpina*'s computer for data. The temperature differentials DIS could measure in the lower infrared and group into a map.

Presto! Inside a minute they had a sketch showing the walls and floor of a deep pit.

"Quite patently artificial," she said.

"Looks like it to me, and I'm just a physicist."

"I thought you were an engineer-pilot."

"Hey, physicists can do anything."

"Um. So they think. But not biology . . ." She told DIS to amp the center of the circle, use every pixel. In seconds it did. The screen before her and Jordin zoomed in.

Down at the bottom moved blocky somethings, jointed at odd angles, limbs stubby, each outlined in a blue glow. They moved, slow and deliberate.

"What's that blue from?" she asked.

"Spectral lines say—let's ee—argon."

More movement. Ghostly forms, sluggish, as though underwater. Patterns. The jerky, angular shapes were forming into neatly aligned ranks and files, like an army on parade—or a war fleet.

"Are those organisms or machines?" she asked.

"Ol' DIS can't tell us without a whole further set of assumptions, I'd say."

"I hate to go down there, not knowing."

He waved a hand at the starlit wastes below. "Out here do such distinctions even matter?"

"Good point. This pushes the boundaries." She frowned. In cold so deep as to be beyond all human reckoning, maybe there were no boundaries.

The dim forms were moving into an intricate, ordered array. "Looks like a search pattern," she said.

Jordin was busy with their hovering pattern, but in 5 percent of a g there was time to maneuver. The nuke thrummed at their backs, and its plume caught starlight in a filmy gauze. "Maybe they're getting ready for dawn," he whispered.

Too many possibilities, Shanna thought. "What *are* they?"

On an inspired hunch Jordin asked DIS to search under

"Superconductors." He added, "And match to the spectral lines below."

It took only seconds. Good ol' DIS reported. Yes—there were plenty of compounds down there rich in copper and oxygen, and alloys galore. He grinned and said, "Could be that makes them superconductors, at these temperatures."

She frowned. "So?"

"So—remember those sparks that zapped us when we were walking, last time? There's a big potential difference between the top of the atmosphere and the ground."

"Is that usual? I mean, this place is plenty odd already ..." She had never had a really intuitive feel for physics, and it was showing.

"Not so unusual. Earth's like that, too. When you're standing on the ground, there's a couple hundred volts between your feet and your head. When you walk across a carpet and touch a doorknob, you're just letting electrons from the carpet fibers make their way to the higher elevation. Zap!" He shrugged as though this was obvious.

"So knowing that, you never jump when it happens?"

To his credit he laughed. "Touché! My point here—this is a guess, okay?—is that energy is available to drive anything that can harvest the potential difference—voltage, I mean. We haven't measured it—I didn't think to—but from those sparks I'll bet it's considerable."

"But why is it here at all?"

"Umm, good point to you! Pluto turns pretty slow, and that's the ultimate source of the volts—spinning planets with magnetic fields are like generators whirring away in space. Pluto's should be weaker than Earth's ..." His voice trailed away in puzzlement.

"Somehow the whole place is getting pumped by the electrodynamic weather, you think?" she encouraged him.

He gazed at the surface, now so sharp in the stretched shadows of sunset that it looked like a drawing in black and white. "One thing the Voyagers told us was that voltages are trickling in from the Oort cloud's deep freeze somehow. Ummm . . . There's that data showing the shock wave in the solar wind. I hadn't thought that could be related."

She hadn't paid a lot of attention to the briefings and endless 3-D color visuals about the region farther out. The solar wind speed had dropped near the Voyagers, decades back, she recalled, and the physicists thought that meant Voyager was about to meet a shock wave. The multicolored graphics made it look something like the shock cone riding just in front of a supersonic airplane, causing a sonic boom. That was where the solar wind, which had thinned in its expansion all the way from the sun, finally lost out to the pressure of the plasma that hung between the stars. "That's sure a long way out," she said.

"Yeah, but that fast probe, Ulysses, found that the shock's much closer in now than when Voyager found it. They—we—call it a termination shock, and those are great at making fast particles and electric fields."

Shanna retreated to what she knew: biology. "There are eels that can store charge indefinitely, I think. Swimming batteries. They use it to discourage predators and stun fish."

He looked at her intently. "So being a battery might be a way to keep energy reserves when it's night. Then— those zand could just connect up their internal terminals and—zap!—a quick, sure source of efficient energy. I'll bet it's the same for Darksiders."

She sat upright, eyes on the main screen. "Something's flying down there."

Small wing-shaped things hovered, then lofted upward together, circling within the pit. Blue lights around the regimented ranks dimmed. "Hard to make them out," Jordin said. "But they're organizing, yeah."

"Close-up in infrared," she instructed DIS.

A dim view leaped into focus on the screen. Shanna squinted. "They're . . . pulling something apart."

Something bigger than the moving things. Jordin said, "Looks like they're slicing up a . . . zand."

Her stomach clenched, looking down at the black ice. "They attack the zand at night. The zand are bigger, but they're sleeping, I guess."

The vague forms had pulled pieces away. Quick, scurrying moves.

"Let's have a look, okay?"

Jordin nodded and started their last deceleration. Zero hour; no more time for dispassionate study and idle speculation. It felt good.

He hit the controls. The lander danced up and away, maneuvering above the center of the great pit. Their steam blurred the view.

Shanna took a deep breath. The lives below were at risk, and maybe she didn't fathom what was going on here . . . but she had to act; it was in her nature. Her pulse pounded in her ears. She had gotten here by following her instincts, the deft feel of intuition. *Even if I'll regret it the rest of my life.*

They could see better. "Yep, that's a dead zand," Jordin

said. The shapes nearby moved into a circular pattern. "They see us. Maybe hear us, too—if they have ears."

Shanna said tightly, "That li'l trick you rigged up—"

"On it," Jordin said.

"They're coming fast—"

"Man, they look—"

"Yeah, dangerous." He put his hand on a little switch on the far side of the module from her. She hadn't noticed it before, and he hadn't mentioned it, either.

So I wouldn't bump it by accident? But the call is mine . . .

More shapes swarmed in below. Jordin said very casually, "Y'know, we can't hover forever."

"Check. Okay, land in that big broad spot. Looks rocky."

"Yep, it is."

He took the lander into a bare plain, several kilometers from the Darksiders. They touched down, and the steam plume seemed to blow off the hard ice nearby without even provoking a liquid shimmer.

Jordin read off the shutdown protocol, and she echoed it. They spent several minutes checking the engine readouts, relayed the digital package up to *Proserpina*, and Jordin carefully evaluated the lander pads. "No melting under us."

"Good, let's—" Their audio rang with pops.

Jordin put their local radar on the big screen. "Yeah, I see it."

Dots were converging from all around, making local radar give off a chorus of pings.

"Let's get out of here," she said quickly.

"Done." He slapped the overrides, and the nuke flared again. A quick burst took them up a hundred meters.

"I think," Jordin said mildly, "a professional biologist would label that aggressive behavior."

"I tend to agree."

Below, gray boxes moved with startling speed. They had rushed in under the lander's plume, meeting just below. They now clustered and dispersed in quick, jerky movements.

"Ummm," Jordin said. "Walking washing machines."

"More like combinations. Legs that end in wheels. See that one? It's rolling over the flat rock, then steps over the small boulders. Ingenious."

"Wheels. Gotta be machines, not zand."

"Right. And look, they're extruding pipes out the top." She pointed where a cluster was poking narrow tubes upward. Their steam dispersed quickly, so the boxy forms seemed to ripple. More came in steadily from the sides. There were at least a hundred within view. As the newcomers arrived, they, too, started extending their tubes.

"Ummm. Don't like the look of that."

"Me, either." She felt a sudden prickle of fear.

"Like they were ganging up to . . . shoot at us."

"That switch?"

"Yeah."

"Draw them in." She thought, *Jordin and I have fashioned an instrument designed for delicate exploration of an alien world . . . into a bomb.* "Then . . . do it."

Something flickered in Jordin's face. "You—really—"

"I know, it's a big step—"

"Let's just clear out of here." His lips set firmly, resolved.

"We've got to act," she said quickly.

He looked at her. "We?"

"Okay, me. I'm captain, I'll take the responsibility."

He nodded, lips working, then nodded again. "Right. Your call." His thumb touched the jury-rigged relay. He made the lander lower a bit. Darksiders came flocking in from the sides, moving even faster. Shanna felt sudden fear. They were so fiercely agile, and in this deep cold. How could anything—

"Should drop some." Tensely Jordin counted. The minicam showed the rocks below growing larger. An instant before impact, he hit the probe's cutting torch. The oxy-hydrogen mixture exploded.

A giant yellow fist blasted out of the pit. Vapor boiled up, thick fog condensing at once into glinting crystals. Debris shot far and wide.

A shock wave slammed into the lander. The deck rocked. Something solid screeched right through from wall to wall, in and out again. Its passage rang like a giant's handclap.

Shanna was in her armor—otherwise explosive decompression would have finished her. In the air around her she saw crystals rattle down in a frigid shower. Air screamed out of the lander.

Jordin fought the lander's controls. The vehicle swayed and sank like a drunken express elevator. Deceleration jets sputtered, then coughed out. With a shriek of twisting metal the lander thumped down. *Too hard.* Three legs groaned and buckled under, canting the deck steeply.

Shanna slammed against the wall and felt blood run down one cheek. Her right shoulder hurt, sharp and biting. The silence in the shattered cabin, after so much thunder, seemed eerie. Pluto's cold gases sighed in. She saw her breath frosting over the faceplate and turned up the armor's heater. It gave a wan warm breath at her neck. She breathed in shallow gasps, and the air cut her throat. Her legs were already getting numb. *Not much more time.*

She glanced sideways, stopped. Jordin was sprawled halfway out of his couch, mouth sagging, unconscious. She shouted, but he didn't move. Dead? She couldn't tell if he was breathing.

Proserpina rasped in her ear, demanding answers.

The cold . . . A pouch near her mouth held medication designed for just such a terminal emergency. No pain, the briefers had told her; a bland taste, drowsiness, and then—nothing.

She had told them back Earthside to take it out, but after launch she found that it was still there.

No, damn it. With blunt fingers she punched in the suit command to call *Proserpina* on the hailing frequency. "We're down, hull breach, trying to—" Her throat rasped, and her voice shut down. The cold was tightening around her. Her arms and legs moved sluggishly as she got up, turned to the dead command board, then looked at the few screens still live.

Movement. A square, bulky object, outlined in cold blue light, lurched past the outside view screen.

Noise. Clanking, cutting rasps, thumping.

Sudden terror—real, little-child fright at monsters in the dark—clutched at Shanna's heart. The Darksiders were here.

The creeping, aching cold fogged her mind. Some small corner of it still knew nonetheless what it was doing. "Wiseguy! Wiseguy!"

Dazed, she got the translator up and running, a hiss in

her ears. Outside-direct interface. "Wiseguy . . . talk to them," she hoarsely whispered. "Explain . . ."

Talk to them how? Even with the simpler zand it had taken hours of eavesdropping . . .

A section of bulkhead wrenched away. Pale blue light. In through the ragged hole came a many-jointed, metallic limb ending in a . . . lobster claw. It groped along the control board.

"No—don't break anything!" she cried wildly. As if having heard, the claw stopped. Extended. It jerked forward. The arm swung, extended across the cabin, and touched her faceplate with a sharp click.

She blinked. Fast-growing frost crystals framed the claw in an ivory glow.

Tired . . . cold . . . no . . . mustn't—not yet. Poking blindly with her stiffening hands, she pawed at the claw. "Wiseguy . . . tell them . . . Warm . . ." Shanna slumped. Her icy armor stung her flesh through her padded jumpsuit.

Then she was falling through space, into an endless nighted gulf. The ultimate outrage was that a last lucid spark of awareness was able to watch it happening.

Down . . . down . . . down.

9.

REBIRTHING

LONG, SLANTING AFTERNOON RAYS stained the cliffs of Rendezvous in soft turquoise and pale gold. The thin air rang to the cracking and clanging of round, dark shells as they opened like great eggs.

Old One hovered over the placid sea just offshore, drifting lazily on the welling heat from below. It came alertly out of its meditations and deftly moved toward a stretch of barren rock shingle. There its particular young friend and mate in Self-merge drew apart like giant, slick amoebas. And there, glistening on the sand between them, feebly stirred seventeen splendid zand.

Harsh cries clashed in the cold air. Flappers, patiently poised above Rendezvous to wait for Self-merge to end, now folded themselves and arrowed downward.

With quick energy it had doubted that it still possessed, Old One flipped over. It pointed its vent apertures at the sky—and fired. The rosy flame lit its plunge. It carved the sky, swooping by the furiously flapping shapes, turning the shrill exhaust on them.

Hunger calls turned to thin screams of dying rage. Blackening flapper bodies tumbled and fell to ground. A host of small scavengers raced out to feed on the smoking remains.

Baffled, the surviving flappers circled over the beach, readying to strike again. By this time other zand came scurrying into action. They had forgone the bliss of Self-merge in order to stand guard, awaiting Birthings. A furious, snapping air battle erupted over the stony shores of Rendezvous.

The little new zand below obeyed the genetic impulse imprinted into them. Like baby turtles on tropical isles, they scrambled down the sterile stretch of beach, searching for something to give them lifegas. Not finding any, they dove with tiny splashes into the sea. There beckoned a gray scum of marine organisms. The floating mites fed on microscopic crystals of ammonia and carbon dioxide, exhaling hydrogen, the gas of life itself.

Adult zand flocked in behind the newborn and joined end-to-end in a living wall, fencing off the shallows as a swimming area for the young. One warder on the seaward side cried out as its body took the impact of a borer. Commotion, thrashing. A flapper darted in, nipped off the parasite's body behind the head, and flapped away.

"Feed the young some of this!" Old One commanded, jetting toward blue-gray scum. The zand rushed to obey, catching the wrigglers. The young ate, breathed in lifegas, squeaked. Zand warbled gratitude. With great effort the zand and their shellmates struggled up, groggy from Selfmerge, and began weakly singing the first notes of the Hymn of Birthing. All along hillsides and ice hollows of Rendezvous, other zand joined in thanks and praise to Lightgiver.

But a strange new sorrow gnawed at Old One. It joined, with the quavering of age, in the song, while inwardly it wondered—did Lightgiver truly hear? And what did the new beings mean, who brimmed with fatal heat and acted so strangely? Could they be of Lightgiver Itself?

Old One had long been certain that Lightgiver did not

move across the sky. Instead, somehow it knew that the World in its day turned toward the bright body in the sky, warmed itself, and then spun away again, in endless cycle. Putting together its own thinking with what the hot strangers had said, it now reasoned further—that in the much greater cycle from warm to cold, Lightgiver did not approach and recede from the World. Instead—the thought electrified—the World traveled in a great eccentric loop, first closer to the Source of light and life, then away.

Old One basked in thought. So far this was compatible with zand theology and perhaps even strengthened it. Lightgiver was not a wanderer across the sky but instead commanded, the unmoved center of All. The strangers had implied a stunning conclusion—that Lightgiver was, in fact, one of those strange bright points in the sky that multiplied at twilight and grew fewer, thinner at dawn.

Now, as it listened to its fellow zand sing chorus after triumphant chorus of the Hymn of Birthing, the eldest of the tribe began to understand why the strangers had been reluctant to part with this stunning information. The strong, simple faith the zand had in Lightgiver, as the knowing, caring Awakener and Nourisher of all life, had carried them since time immemorial through hunger and storms. Through the attacks of flappers and borers. Through the gathering sad and bitter disappointments of dwindling Birthings. And through much else, for cycle after hard, weary cycle.

With the new knowledge just gained of their World, they might yet prevail. But Old One decided it would not, at this critical time, share with the others a further revelation that must surely make them falter and despair. Most of the motive essence that sustained them, the strangers had hinted, did not come from Lightgiver at all.

The strangers had acted very much like followers of Lightgiver's Way. They had given, freely and without question. They had shared sadness and joy. And they had descended from the black sky, for the zand's sake. They had risked life and in their sluggish way sallied off to Darkside.

Old One did not expect the strangers to return from Darkside, of course. Much imponderable evil lurked there. Even those of Lightgiver could surely not master it.

10.

HOUSEGUEST

SHANNA WOKE.

She hadn't expected to. And none of the kinds of after-life she had ever idly visualized included lying naked in a warm nutrient bath.

She let her mind drift . . . wishing for more sleep . . . Then the green, acrid, medicinal-sharp fluid drained out beneath her. She sat up. Not a mark on her; not even, so far as she could tell by feel, a facial scratch suffered in the crash. And internally she felt fine. Ravenous but great. *Proserpina*'s life-support program was passing a test no-body on Pluto Project had ever imagined . . .

Then memory returned. Somehow Jordin had gotten

her away from the Darksiders, had kept her alive.
"Jordin!"

He came in softly, carefully. "You've had a big day."

"How long was I out?"

"I'd say 'bout seven hours. Mary Kay sedated you so
you wouldn't feel the work done on your skin." He
frowned, and his lips were set in a firm, give-nothing-
away cast she recognized. Withholding something for
later, yes.

"Freezer burn?" She tried to sit up and look but was
still groggy.

"You mean frostbite."

"That was a joke, Jordin."

He didn't smile. "We had to peel you some. Mary Kay
did it, not me."

"Ummm, yeah, privacy . . ." But her mind was racing
now. "The Darksiders?"

"They helped, kinda. I was knocked out, and they re-
sealed some of the joints."

"They *what*?"

"Some kind of vacuum welding, I guess. As soon as I
could get oriented, I lifted us off."

"You were injured!"

"Ship operations helped. Mary Kay told me how to use
the suit built-in injector, got some stimulant I can't pro-
nounce into me. Everybody helped. We had a little trouble
with the pumps. One shut down, dunno why. I'm taking it
apart now. Looks like a frozen-up valve, is all."

"But you made it! Wow!"

"Thought you'd appreciate getting back into a bath."
His askew smile was the Jordin she knew so well—never
brag, just do the job. But he was hiding something, too.

"They *repaired* things?"

"Sure looks like. Vacuum welding . . . They're smart."

"Yeah. Everybody out here seems to be."

"Uh, I've got to get back to work."

Jordin left, blushing a bit. Still with the funny set to his lips. She let herself laze about a bit, trying to read Jordin's mood, then roused herself. *Time for rebirth.* She was stiff, and her joints ached. As she stood to climb out of the tank, a triumphant wave of elation surged through her and pushed all other thoughts and pains aside. *Hooray! I'm alive!*

She set the adjoining shower cubicle for a full, vigorous needle spray and stepped inside. She took it happily, until the water recycler blinked to warn her that she was overusing. Then she let a gush of cold water pour down on her for several seconds before shutting it off. Rather than activate the air-dryer, she stepped out, tingling, and wrapped herself in a huge bath towel.

Now you should get some soup into you, her grandmother would have said now. So she did.

The chatter with crew was warming, too. She programmed the autochef for one of its most elaborate meals; the ingredients, recipe, and computer routine had been a farewell gift from France, of all places. Preparation burbled happily and she snuggled herself into a fresh coverall. Some astronauts and cosmonauts she had known, when not actually working, adjusted temperature and humidity controls and floated around in their cabins nude. Shanna, however, wore clothes every ship day for much the same reason British colonial officers in the old days, even in the steaming tropics, donned full formal dress for dinner each evening—a connection with civilization. And if crew found out she was doing nudie floats . . .

The autochef chimed; first course served. Shanna turned up the audio and put on the Brahms *German Requiem*, which, despite its sometimes lugubrious lyrics, seemed to her actually one of the most joyous, life-affirming works ever composed. Crew sat and ate and tolerated her taste, knowing she didn't want to talk. They all had unspoken protocols.

"Here on earth we have no lasting abode," she sang, thinking of the Darksiders. She had just killed a lot of them, and yet they had saved her life. And if the zand legends could be trusted, they viciously attacked the zand in the long Plutonian years. And she and Jordin had seen them with a dead zand. She was certain that only her crude bomb had stopped them from doing it again. How to judge?

Or was there something deeper happening here? She brought this up around the dinner table, all crew present except the watch officer, Uziki. Shanna was American, so she opened with that. "Would an alien outsider judge America's performance by My Lai and Wounded Knee or by Lincoln and Jefferson?"

That got them started. Mary Kay said, "Aren't we getting anthropomorphic here? What kind of consciousness—what kind of ethics—operates with a circulatory system running on liquid nitrogen?"

Chow-Lin twisted his lips skeptically. "Or did we get into something we don't have a remote chance of understanding?"

Jordin said, "We sure won't unless we try."

Shanna let the talk run. She had given the orders, and

the others weren't too happy with playing spear-carriers. Fair enough. But democracy was a luxury out here. "There wasn't time for a long discussion," she said. "Somebody had to act, if we were going to keep talking to the zand."

Mary Kay said, "Looks from the IR like the Darksiders did pull back after you lifted off. No more feelers out to encircle that zand community."

"Um." Chow-Lin looked melancholy, staring off into the distance. "Make a wasteland and call it a peace."

Shanna wanted to bark back, "Enough of this nonsense! It's done, so we live with it"—but she held her tongue.

Mary Kay said soberly, "We looked at what happened at the, uh, attack site, after you left. Toward local noon, zand came into where you blasted the Darksiders. They . . . ate the remains."

Shanna gaped, openmouthed. "They feed on . . ."

"Looks like," Mary Kay said. "Tore the body parts down, ingested them somehow."

Chow-Lin said, "Remember those parts you and Jordin saw on the beach?"

Jordin snapped his fingers. "Darksider parts!"

Shanna was awed. Here was a predator-prey relationship, of a weird kind. Maybe, maybe . . . Darksiders had the edge in the night, but zand could digest the Darksiders during the day. Overall, the Old One said, the Darksiders were winning. "Speaking as a biologist," she said, "this is making some sense . . . but . . ."

She and Jordin gazed at each other, eyes wide. "Current-driven . . ." he said.

"Biosphere," she finished.

Jordin blurted, "Enhance the chem reactions with current. Speed up all the enzymes and protein folding . . ."

"To make a chemical biosphere run as though it was a lot warmer," she finished.

Mary Kay frowned. "Why? Because whatever built the Pluto biosphere knew lots more about electricity than it did about warm chemistry?"

The whole crew stared at each other. "Sounds good," Chow-Lin said.

Shanna sat back. *Wow. Can that be it?* They needed to know more, sure, but she was captain, after all. She should let the research angle rest, get down to business, check out status reports—and then her eyes widened. "Hey, did anybody go down the checklist for the lander?"

Mary Kay said ruefully, "We were kinda in a hurry."

"Worried about us, sure," Jordin the peacemaker murmured, coming out of his distracted gaze. Something still irking him.

A suspicion clicked in Shanna's mind. She said nothing, just jumped up and was first to reach the departure bay. They searched the lander, which was going to need a lot of blowtorch-level work. The alien patch-up had been hasty but remarkably firm and tight. "This wasn't done any way I can figure," Jordin said, running a gamma-ray probe over the seam, which looked like brown, melted ice cream. "Must be low-temperature metal bonding or something."

"Spread out all over it and check every crevice," Shanna said tersely. *For what?* She had no idea.

Shanna worked methodically, letting Brahms follow her in her ear patch. Internal systems running okay. Then the external check, looking in every cranny, the underside, wiring boxes, thrusters, and—

There it was. A neat oval hole, cut all through the crumpled number four landing leg. Rimmed by an equally neat patch of a dull reddish material.

"Red?" Mary Kay said. "Never seen that on the surface."

"Only two centimeters across." Jordin took a sample. "Big enough for a clawhold. Maybe somebody hitchhiked aboard?"

They stared at each other. "So it's . . . onboard?" Shanna mentally kicked herself for not doing this right away. She had been lolling about in a goddamn medicinal bath. *Captains don't pamper themselves!*

The breach was near the lander leg's chunky top swivel joint, which was sitting a mere meter from a bulkhead that cradled *Proserpina*'s life-support tanks. (*My God, do they know our ship blueprints, too?*) Between the bulkhead and cryo tank compartment the ceramo-carbon deck was scratched and scored, as if something had dragged a heavy machine through. *Or a machine dragged itself.* A faint tang of—*ammonia? What chemistry worked in them?*—hung in the air.

"Spread out through the whole ship," she said. "We've got to find this whatever-it-is." *Darksider. Houseguest.*

They scattered. She raced hand over hand up one level, to the main ship computer console. An all-systems check gave her nothing. A light winked at her imperiously from one of the monitors. *Input for you from DIS, Shanna. Read me!* The music ended. Shanna looked at the chronometer: 1700 GMT; nearing the end of the mission's nominal day, but who was counting anymore? Two microwave schedules missed; Earthside must be frantic. She could not yet face playing back whatever worried, subtly reproachful messages they meanwhile might have sent to her.

"Mary Kay! Call Earthside, tell them what's up." Ah, the pleasures of delegating. Time to do some hard looking.

"It's in the cargo bay," Jordin said tightly over comm.

She had been fruitlessly searching for over ten minutes now and saw immediately that he had done the right thing: look where people weren't, usually. The Darksider was smart. And . . . why?

"Let's circle it," she sent to all crew, and started down to the cargo level.

It was there, all right, somehow running at a temperature it could never have evolved for. But then, machines don't evolve . . .

A boxy metal thing, with odd burned-metal spikes, like an angry kitchen appliance. It lifted a shiny, lopsided black claw toward them as they converged. Threatening? No—a scramble of microwave noise came from it, hissed into her ear processor. Talking.

DIS sent, *It says there is someone who wishes to communicate.*

"And who might that be?" she said aloud. Heads turned, eyes questioned. The whole crew was here, surrounding the thing.

If it exploded, good-bye to the expedition. She gestured for most of them to leave. The Darksider did not move when they did, but she could see glinting quartzlike sensors on each side of it.

I am unsure. It speaks very similarly to the zand. I believe they are linked in some fundamental way.

"Ummm. Even though they're blood enemies? Why's it here?"

To make us listen. To help with the . . . converse.

"With . . . ?"

Those who made this world, it says.

"And who's that?"

Something . . . big.

The feed cut out.

11.

EVIDENCE OF THINGS NOT SEEN

"THEY ARE UTTERLY STRANGE." Shanna's voice resonated in the crowded, hushed hall. Axelrod sat at a desk in a capsule above the auditorium where the gaggle of reporters sat, buzzing. He puffed on a cigar, and his very own filter system sucked in the smoke so as not to offend the entire rest of the moon. He relished the pleasure and privilege.

His daughter was sending without any visual feed. Probably because she was looking ragged, judging from the high, tight notes in her voice.

The reporters caught her anxiety as well. Their eyes narrowed.

"Even good ol' DIS is having a hard time making sense out of them, but we've figured one thing out at least. The Darksiders are not native to Pluto at all. They didn't evolve a biology that could go with this planet's chemistry. Instead, I think, they shifted Charon's orbit—in order to make Pluto's daytime under the satellite's shadow more comfortable for them."

A rustling of startled disbelief. The briefing room on the moon was overheated and bleak beneath the hard ceramic light, and the crowd of reporters and the snubbed snouts of the media feeds focused on the stage, where Axelrod stood and listened with the rest of them, his face furrowed with doubt and a skating anxiety. Shanna's tones slid through the hushed silence of the room, subdued, distant, coming from billions of kilometers into the long, far dark.

"They come from the Oort cloud. That much I'm sure of—the one onboard with us sent a strange, warped— well, I guess you'd call it a map. In three dimensions, in warped perspectives, with weird signifiers we can't figure out yet. The sun's at the far left and down, and whatever made all this happen, it's a lot farther out than Pluto."

Another rustle of disbelief. Eyes cast sideways, eyebrows raised.

She went on, not knowing how her words would be received. From her tone she obviously didn't care. "And it's clear from all the vector displays and orbits that this has been going on for a long time. It picked up when they started getting our radio signals, I guess, judging from the timeline—if we've read it right. Thing is, Pluto, for them, is a great experiment. By deliberately infusing greater energy than the planet's own low-level ecology had available, they have evolved a sentient native Plutonian life-form—the zand."

The reporters were muttering, agitated.

"Yeah, I know—evolution doesn't work that way. Well, this is *driven*. Forced change."

More murmurs and grumbles greeted this.

"What I'm saying here is that I've recognized what Pluto reminded me of. Grad school! Y'know, when you do those set-piece experiments? Testing simple biospheres-in-a-box, to see how they respond to higher salinity, or heat, or chemical drivers? *Pluto is a big lab experiment.*"

An uproar. Scientists and reporters alike jumped out of their seats and shouted. Some shook fists.

This is going to look great on vid, Axelrod thought. *Maybe we should put these press conferences only on the pay channels.*

Shanna went on, unperturbed, hours away at light speed. "You tech guys are gonna love this next part! Simple ohmic heating from currents wasn't enough. They're trying to run it all that way, the whole planet, including the borers and flappers—which I haven't even had time to study yet. So much to do!"

A famous biologist stood and started to make a speech to the audience, his face red, eyes bulging. Axelrod gathered that Shanna's views insulted not only the man's entire professional career but his culture. Luckily the audience shushed him.

"They had to apply the planet's electrodynamically derived currents directly to the 'foodrocks' the native animals consume—and their interference with Charon's orbit has messed up that process a bit. These beautiful auroras are the wastage of the experiment . . . which may well be failing."

Axelrod blinked. This was far more than he could ever

have imagined, but already his mind spun with a way to play it.

"Centuries ago the Darksiders culled the zand colony of unwanted genetic traits. The zand remember it as a battle, we figure. Remember it with terror and pride—a big event in their folklore. A cold-blooded Darwinian pruning operation, and yes—I'm having real trouble with the ethics of that. For sure. Maybe this whole damned place is a . . . well, a luxury. An experiment by beings we haven't even seen yet."

Her voice was tight, controlled . . . and Axelrod could tell she was on the ragged edge of fatigue. Not sleeping; the ship monitors said so. And from the psychers' feed line, they knew that the crew was worried about her. Sure, they said, she was abrasive and intense, and yet they tried to support her, the captain. Also their only field biologist, who was trying to put the whole jigsaw picture together. But there were limits. Her voice was thin, stretched.

Axelrod grimaced. He couldn't do a damn thing to help her. He got to his feet, steaming with energy that had no place to go.

"The Darksiders themselves—or Oort clouders, whoever *that* might be—they've . . . well, *developed* the zand. I'm unclear what's really behind this whole . . . project. Their idea seems to be to understand how life can exist on worlds. 'Warmlife,' the Darksider said—but I think it's speaking for something else. That something has tried to bridge the gap. Figuring out life on worlds. Running a big circuit, far larger than planets. Somewhere there's a voltage source, and Pluto's at the other end, the resistor. Ohm's law, big-time. Using electrically generated *chemical* energy for the ultimate purpose of exploring in-

ward. Toward the sun. Toward us. *We* are *their* frontier.
And they are ours."

This rush of information stilled the room. But only for
a moment. A storm of disbelief stirred, faces contorted.
Shouts. The noted biologist was on his feet again.

"So we can't come back. Not yet, anyhow. That big
nuke you're sending out to relieve us—we'll meet them."

"What!" Axelrod paced, hands behind back. "She can't
just—" And he knew she could.

"What happened to us on the surface was first contact,
and a very strange one. DIS got us through it. So on impulse—I admit it!—I zapped them, the Darksiders. Then
they saved my fool neck, and Jordin's, too. Figure that one
out. And now—now, as the only humans in these parts,
we're sort of elected as ambassador to Outside. Somehow
we've got to open negotiations with them. Or would you
like the next contact to take the form of a rip-roaring interplanetary war? With beings we don't know anything
about."

Axelrod blinked again. In an instant he saw destiny
wrapping itself around his daughter like a dark shroud.
"Shanna, don't take any more risks. It . . . it's not worth
it," he said softly.

Beside him Dr. Jensen spat back, "Shut up. You know
it is."

For the first time the young, confident voice wavered.
"I'm making this decision sound easy. It's not; I'm not
that heartless. It's going to be lonely out here. But my
crew agrees, and we're staying. Beyond nominal mission
duration. Beyond nominal systems lifetime even, if we
have to. There are plenty of backups onboard that big ol'

nuke you're flying out to us. Extra supplies, tech, crew. We can make it!"

Astonished silence in the room.

"And there were other things I'd hoped to do. We'll keep on making our schedules, check in regularly. Lots more to do out here!"

A long pause, then: "Good-bye, signing off for the crew of the *Proserpina*," a quickly choked-off breath, and then only the rumble of interstellar noise.

12.

A HYMN OF DAY'S DEPARTURE

COLD DIM SUNSET STAINED Rendezvous in a gray glow. A hard black sea seethed on the far horizon, awaiting the sun's banishment. Icy mountainsides lay clean-picked of any food, save for the fine dusting of brown spores that had settled when the afternoon air began to cool. Out at sea the massed zand, thousands strong, sang the long, lacy Hymn of Day's Departure. The music soared through the dimming air—a multipart canon. As each small group of zand singing its part came to the song's end, it broke away from the larger choir, its members dispersing over the lapping violet sea.

The Ark-zand swam steadily toward the setting sun. Lightgiver's rays now streamed through a gauzy veil of storm clouds, and the sea rose steaming with a rising wind. They had lingered too long, the zand feared, their chorus freighted with skittering anxiety. To be caught afloat, when the falling temperature irreversibly triggered its night-change, could well be fatal. Already, the borers had vanished into the freezing deep and the flappers were gone from the sobering sky.

And the zand had much to live for now, they knew. The young were quick, eager to learn, zestful. Nearly all of them had survived, thanks to the huge loud vessel from the sky, a miracle. It had killed many Darksiders, leaving their carcasses littering the plains. From these the zand had fed. Even Old One had shed its customary gloom and seemed determined now to live into another day, and many more.

Clouds rolled up, towering redly into the sky, obscuring Lightgiver. A freezing blast from Darkside brought the first whirling, spiky crystals of snow. Time was running out. The sea stiffened, readying to turn hard.

Lift! Lift! Together, singing, the zand decided to gamble some of their precious fuel reserves. Lifegas flared in orange plumes. They soared steeply up from the freezing ocean. Far off, looming against the oncoming storm, rose the peaks where they had spent their early morning recovery time. Arcing into deft parabolas, the zand swarm drove on hard through the fast-cooling air.

Snow came in fiercely, blowing in bitter, blinding gusts. The zand reached their steepled retreat from the long, hard night, some veering, crashing into the ramparts of a crag. Sea level dropped precipitously as the surface fluid froze, shrank in volume, and sank. The groans and shuddering spasms of the daily cycle reverberated low and strong through the sharpening air.

Late! We are late! Zand slammed into slopes, tumbled

from the gathering air, died in their dozens. But most landed and found shelter. Quickly now the surviving zand drew in masses of the new, loose snow and blew it over the foodrock that would again, as last night, serve as its cache. The foodrock brimmed with fresh energy, gathered from the crackling soil itself. Sparks still jumped when the zand tumbled rocks into place. The foodrock darkened in color beneath a blanket of freshly formed borer spores.

The Ark-zand stopped in its calls to the working ranks. Something here was different. The field of black, night-ready spores was broken down the slope by an irregularly shaped mass not made of ice.

Lightgiver be praised! The heavenly Provider from the far dark had sent the zand a skystone.

And Old One had taught it how needful the skystones were for life. A touch and they carried fresh knowledge into all who would listen. Voices from the Great Dark.

Carefully the Ark-zand moved the rough stone up to the edge of the cache and covered it with snow. In the snow blur it did not see through the blizzard's dancing curtains the small, smooth sphere which had guided that skystone down so that it would land on the world gently, without the usual ice-shattering explosion of hot vapor.

Nor did it know that the Earther it had met that day was at that moment alertly monitoring the little probe, drawing it away from Pluto's weak, icy grip.

Sighing, the Ark-zand settled into the grateful embrace of sleep. It felt a last crackling surge of energy as a current ran down from the sky and found waiting conductivity in the nearby rock. So it would be through the long night. Currents flowed, storing energy within intricate chemical balances. Though this voltage spike came from immensely far away, in thin trickles of electrons streaming across magnetic fields, to the Ark-zand it simply came from the sky in a prickly, delightful gust.

All such gifts were from Lightgiver, it thought. Or else from the Far Dark, where legend said greater entities lurked. So much to understand! The two rulers of the sky, a point of fierce light and the opposite realm of vast dark, were the twin poles of a world that did not need explanation. Creation simply . . . was.

As it ebbed into restful calm, it issued one last humble prayer of thanks. Creation simply was.

13.

POST FACTO

JORDIN GOT RIGHT TO the point. He rapped on the door of her cabin and sat in the only other chair. Crisp, efficient. His mouth not canted at that odd friendly angle anymore. Looking determined.

"Mary Kay and I have been talking."

"Yes?"

"You nearly got us both killed down there."

"You got us out, though. I'm recommending you for special recognition by—"

He shook his head, two quick jerks. "We can't be taking risks like that."

"Just being out here is risky—"

"I'm here to notify you that as per ship's regs, and contractual constraints, I'm filing a complaint with ISA." He said this in a flat monotone, memorized. He had probably written it out.

"Oh?"

Clearly he had planned to leave it at that, but he was tempted to say more, tongue darting over his lips. "The whole idea was just plain asking for trouble."

"I'm not going to debate my decisions, especially post facto."

"Earthside says you told them we crew had all agreed."

"As I recall, I said you *would* agree. When you had thought it over."

He slammed a palm on her desk. "*That's* what I mean."

"Jordin, I wasn't trained to be captain. I'm just making do."

"Not doing too well, either," he said sullenly.

"A captain isn't always right."

"And crew always has a right to their own opinions."

"True—but they don't have a right to their own facts."

"We don't think all these ideas hold up."

She shrugged—an effort, because her whole body had gone rigid. *Tired.* "Maybe they won't. That's research."

"Okay, fine, your privilege. Just thought I'd tell you. It's Earthside's matter now."

"Thanks for letting me know."

His eyes darted around the room, not looking at her, acutely uncomfortable. "You bet." Then he was gone.

She barely had time to think about that when a beep told her an incoming vid was ready, defragged. She called it up on her cabin screen, and it was from Dad. No tag title, just Axelrod the Great popping up on the screen, wearing slacks, blue shirt, auburn sweater. From the moon, in his personal study, fake digital fireplace crackling with flame in the background for the homey touch. *Personal message,* the sub tracker said.

Uh-oh . . . She paused it, got a glass of wine to brace herself, and watched.

"Hey, honey, you've got the whole world agog down here. What discoveries! As incredible as the zand vids are, the Darksiders are simply mind-blowing! Some kind of superrobots, they look like. I've—the Consortium has— gotta get some. Just think of what their tech will mean down here. Miles ahead of anything on Earth. Asteroid mining will be a cinch with those babies. *Proserpina* may be ISA, but *High Flyer* is ours, and there's plenty of room to bring back interesting cargo. I'll tell their crew to get ready."

Shanna suppressed a retort—*no sense talking back to a recorded message.*

"Sorry, got so excited about all your great work, I forgot to say how *really* worried I was about you. Don't take more chances than you have to; you're still my little girl. Pretty dangerous stuff." He paused and nervously shifted in his seat, eyebrows lifting. "And, ah, rumor is, your crew may be thinking the same."

Hmm. What does that mean? Jordin? I'm gonna be replaced? And Dad kinda agrees with him?

Even across a billion miles the rumor mill churned away—at light speed.

He rushed on. "I know, the Darksiders are alien and strange and all. But they're machines, right? Got to be some patent opportunities there. They work in cold and near vacuum. Nobody here can figure out how. Honey, you said there wouldn't be anything to sell on Pluto, except the story of going there. Not so! You just found it. Or found them—great name, too, the Darksiders. I can see a vid series, just using the title." She groaned and slapped the pause switch. *I'll watch the rest later—if my blood pressure goes down. Viktor and Julia! The First Couple of Mars! Coming in with a huge shipload of Consortium types, probably ready to strip the landscape. Gee, Dad, I can't wait.*

She was suddenly drained. She closed her eyes and drifted into a dream of electric-blue shapes with giant claws rushing toward her . . .

14.

THIS IMMENSE VOYAGE

LATER, SHANNA SIGHED and stretched in the spaceship's comfortable pilot chair. Again she was watch officer while crew slept. She liked it this way.

Earthside would come through in a few hours with their response to Jordin's filing. There would be weeks of messages slinging back and forth. Tedious, disheartening, divisive . . . she could see it coming.

Jordin might prevail. She had to admit, he had a case. She had a lot of respect for Jordin Kare. But ISA didn't like dissension, especially endangering this high-profile mission billions of kilometers away. Word would leak, and their political stock would take a dive. ISA was the role model for international cooperation; failure would echo around the globe, amped to the max.

But that was hours away, and now she had this last watch to stand by herself. Bliss. There was even coffee.

Time to take stock, girl.

The lander was a wreck, but *Proserpina*'s resources could put it back together. Weeks in the machine shop; do them all a lot of good.

Meanwhile, the sole remaining probe functioned with grace and precision. And so would she.

Proserpina—Pluto's bride—had a mother named Ceres, she recalled from the background briefings, a goddess of the growing grain; whence the word "cereal." The daughter ended up stuck in the Underworld six months out of every year, which she guessed was the way the ancients poetically figured when to get their crops in and when to plant again.

Shanna, as she indirectly helped the zand bring in their harvest, did not want to be similarly mythologized. She wouldn't communicate directly with the zand, at least not right away. They were going to have a severe enough intellectual revolution as it was, when the impact of that single meeting on the shore sank in. The price of progress is often pain. Let them thank Lightgiver, not the Earth interloper, for this gift from heaven.

Strange, wasn't it, how human and zand music, religion, and ways of caring so often paralleled each other? Or did that simply show the limitations of DIS and all semantics?

Through her gray fatigue she let her mind idle. Could she introduce into Darksider ethics the revolutionary no-tion that other sapients, even if less bright than oneself, ought to be treated not as means, but as ends? A huge leap.

The psychologists said humans learned that in childhood, only through tit-for-tat social games. Well, maybe that could work here, too—if there was time. And there wasn't a lot of time before the big nuke rocket came swarming up here, bringing more opinions . . .

Speaking of ends and means, Earth's self-appointed diplomat reflected, she had leverage; *Proserpina* had physical capabilities the Darksiders could not fathom— which she could give or withhold—

Careful there, girl.

"Sleep well," Shanna said toward the twilight view, where the zand were bedding down. Now the hard part began. Her fingers danced over the probe controls. The little globe bobbled and bowed, then shot toward the Darksiders' domain, now enjoying its pallid day.

Alone in a world of unrelentingly hostile cold and ominous dark, she was, without noticing it, supremely tired and hugely happy. That this last outpost of the sun had, however improbably, harbored life. That all the smug scientists had been wrong. That this grand mystery was just the beginning of an even deeper one.

She was a biologist, trained in the conventional litany, sure—but she knew when to abandon cherished beliefs. Some guiding hand had stitched together low-temperature chemistry and the tenuous energies of electron flow, knitting here a gossamer, lively web. Who? Why? To some godlike purpose?

Shanna mused about the lives she had blasted to oblivion, so quick in her certainty. Had those dim mechanical forms been truly alive?

Definitions, her grandmother once said, had to be like a fat man's belt—big enough to cover the subject but elastic enough to allow for change. Out here life clung to the last vestiges of possible chemistry. And she was sure, now, that evolution alone could not have forged such an intricate ecology, with so few species—not even in the 4 billion years Pluto had spun.

The topsoil samples they had brought back had yielded nothing. If Earth or even the dimmed ecology of underground Mars was any guide, life found myriad small species to kindle. Larger forms stood upon a huge, broad pyramid of microbes beneath. Bare stony soil could yield little. Yet the zand, the Darksiders—they were like cartoons of life-forms.

Woven from what?

Those things in the pit were not forged from nature's relentless mill, for *they did not know anger.*

They had not wreaked vengeance on her and Jordin when they had the chance. Instead, they had saved them both.

For a moment Shanna pictured the Darksiders at the opposite extreme, as saints, but that, she knew instinctively, was also wrong.

They were, finally, constructions. Theoretical models. More like robots than organisms, but way ahead of *Proserpina*'s 'bots. Not machines, perhaps, but something that stretched the definition of life and probably broke it.

She let her intuition rummage around a bit . . . *Yes.* The Darksiders were agents of something larger, something feeling its way, something . . . dispassionate. But what?

Pluto orbited in its elliptical sway at the very verge of that realm where chemical reactions could proceed slug-

gishly. Beyond here lay a black abyss in which the seemingly fragile bonds between molecules would not crack
before the weightless hail of sunlight. They congealed in
the unending cold.

In that dark kingdom only electricity could race and
flow, to bring motive meaning from the potentials and
gravid capacitances, hanging in the vast vacant spaces.
There, beneath distant star gleam, gossamer-thin sheets of
electrons drifted silently before the subtle tugs of induc-
tances, in vast circuits that light itself could barely span in
a full day.

She shook her head, trying to see . . .

Biologists think in terms of slow, blunt chemistry. Out
here there might be instead the rule of electrodynamics,
proceedings only a tiny fraction slower than light. Intelligence set free from molecular torpidity could dash across
immensities, unchecked by all but the gritty limits of matter's innate resistance. There the speed of light was the
natural speed of events. Of thoughts.

Something had made use of these truths, some brooding intelligence hitherto unsuspected, though the basic
laws—of thermodynamics, of electromagnetic fields—
had been known to humanity since their discovery in the
nineteenth century. Back then the laws had emerged
among people seeking to heat and light their shadowy
homes. They wanted efficiency. From such practical
measures had come fundamental truths. An old term came
to her: *electrobiology.* In the early twencen earnest physi-
cians and greedy quacks had sold appliances that meted
out small electric shocks, reputed to cure everything that
ailed the human body. It hadn't worked back then, but

something way out here was blending electrodynamics and chemistry in the hard cold of Pluto.

For some reason the forces out there had conducted an experiment on this little dab of rock and ice, blending the two sources of animation—chemistry, electricity. Frankenstein's legacy?

What's more, the experiment was still young. It looked like a work unfinished, left by giants for a better day, vast and massive but incomplete.

When would the giants return?

The sun took more than six Earth days to circle around Pluto's frozen globe, bestowing and withdrawing its heat. But something more powerful now drove this warming world. Something invisible.

What had made all this happen *now*? The prospect of Earth's incursion into this bitterly cold place?

Perhaps the entire experiment was itself a strange form of communication . . .

And the Old One . . . How had it learned so much? Superior intelligence? But what had selected for such wit and insight out here? Where was the evolutionary pressure? Or could the pressure come from some hugely larger volume?

No . . . too much. She had a gut suspicion that centuries ago, when Old One was young, something began a process of subtle tutoring. And before that, a process of deep, cerebral working among that zand's foreparents.

Otherwise how could one zand, unaided, have forged so far in explaining their bitter realm? That implied some agency had begun Old One's education long before humanity even knew the outermost planets existed.

And to what end? Shanna looked outward at the unyielding black and wondered what huge surprises waited there. And how long they would be in coming.

The new big nuke was behind them, coming up fast. If *Proserpina* burned her remaining reserves, she could forge outward into those bleak vast spaces. Keep pace with the bigger nuke approaching from below, surging up along the long sloping gravitational potential . . . out, ever outward into this space where bodies cold and mysterious circled in slow orbits, very nearly free of the distant sun's governance. And with some tricky maneuvering, *Proserpina* could find an iceball—maybe Charon—and melt some of that vast icy store for water, for their smaller nuke rocket.

They all could still be a part of this immense voyage.

She peered at the slate-dark world turning below in the vast hard cold. Thinking. *But not if I'm replaced as captain.* She sat bolt upright, fatigue swept away. *Dad! The Great A!* She flipped on the recorder and started talking.

And down among the howling winds, in the gathering gloom of methane snowdrifts now mounding about them, the zand slept on.

PART III

BEYOND PLUTO

The real voyage of discovery consists not in seeking new landscapes, but in having new eyes.

—Marcel Proust

1.

LONG WAVELENGTHS

ON THE LARGEST SCALE, Julia reflected, the solar system was a spheroid cloud of debris. She looked at the big flatscreen display of an iceteroid they were passing, gleaming dully in the dim radiance of the ever-more-distant sun.

The whole vast volume behind their ship, the *High Flyer*, was filigreed with bands and shells of flying shrapnel. Beyond Neptune, big ice fragments coasted in the Kuiper belt. At any moment a pair could smash together, or just clip each other, getting thrown into long ellipses, deep wobbly orbits. And this negligible-looking little blob of primordial gray ice and dust right here could, like the rest of the solar system's slow leftovers, now and then make a sharp hook by skimming near another piece of scrap and in a few years slam into a blundering planet. Earth's dinosaur-killer could have come from right around here.

Julia shivered, not from the cold outside. Her pod was toasty-warm, comfy. But the strangeness that lay before them was approaching, and she had no idea of even what it might be. The voyage from Mars had taken months—a miracle, at speeds made possible by their fusion drive—and there had been plenty of time to study, learn . . . and worry. *Proserpina*, the ISA expedition, was low on supplies and would have to depart soon from Pluto, under their mission plan. But *High Flyer* was bringing enough to sustain them both near Pluto for months more. *High Flyer* was to assist *Proserpina*, particularly with alien translation problems. In transit they had spent much time on the long-wave emissions from beyond Pluto. *High Flyer* would also venture out there, getting data on the bow shock. Those both at ISA and the Consortium were apprehensive about the seat-of-the-pants style of all this, but Julia and Viktor shrugged them off. They had been living that way on Mars for decades, making do. Viktor still worked on the Marsmat problem in his spare time, and when this adventure was done, they would go back to it. But now they were focused forward.

"Anything new from *Proserpina*?" Viktor hollered from the control room. He could have spoken over comm, but he just leaned back in his chair and called down the gangway. They spent enough time logged into electronics systems as it was. And a husband and wife like to keep in touch in the most basic ways, too.

"Not a peep. They're not due to report for nearly an hour."

Nervously she checked the all-sky scan, anyway. Yes—far back there, she could see through their nuclear rocket plume's virulent blue-white. Pluto glimmering, and *Proserpina*'s signifier overlaid. Two motes swimming in the black. *High Flyer* had completed its delta-V with both Pluto and Charon, looping a figure eight through, to lose velocity. They swung by and turned outward, following the streams of current that *Proserpina* had mapped. Straight out into the vast dark . . .

"Getting a lot of that odd noise again," Victor called. "Coming up in the ultralow frequencies."

"The stuff *Proserpina* picked up?"

"*Da*—stronger as we go out."

"I thought you said it was just more turbulence from way out at the bow shock."

"Earthside advises me not. Say is too low, very low frequency, for these high power levels."

"Then it goes in the mystery bin."

"I already sent to the Wiseguy compiler. Maybe someday it will tell us something, huh?" He leaned back in his flex-seat and grinned, so that she could see him down the gangway. "Before we retire, maybe even."

This was a standing joke between them. They would never retire unless the world ran out of mysteries, and out here that was quite unlikely. She grinned back. "Wrong. I have a big file processing right now. Remember, I sent your questions on? SETI Institute ran their Wiseguy, cross-compared with our data, and finally coughed up."

"I don't believe!"

"Come look." About time to peek at the processing, anyway. Her curiosity was as hungry as his.

They had reviewed Wiseguy's capabilities, read through its mediated talks with the zand, the crawlies of Pluto. A spectacular discovery, the zand, Julia had to admit. A sentient species! Even more exciting, *to talk* with them. Her and Viktor's long years of slow, difficult work on Mars had not produced anything like the same result. The Marsmat was still an enigma; many still doubted if it was self-aware.

Not that they had been just studying old data on the way out. *High Flyer* was outfitted with big phased-array antennas, to study the bow shock region. Their most intriguing work had been those electromagnetic maps Viktor had been developing.

And now he and Earthside were using Viktor's work to discern whether there were coded messages coming in from the bow shock region. Shanna's crew had picked up some hints; it was *High Flyer*'s job to sift through the sea of data, try to crack the meaning.

"Program is smart," Viktor said. "Thinks can find words, connections."

Julia blinked. She could not follow the spray of data on Viktor's working screen. But then she looked closer and thought about how they had labored over similar problems, struggling to fathom the Marsmat.

The software—Wiseguy the semi-AI, plus elaborate metalinguistic codes—had been cobbled together Earthside. It followed on detailed theories of how language builds up from basic mental architecture. For decades the linguists had used the primates as a model, but in the last few decades they had extended it to dolphins and whales.

It turned out that whale song was elaborate, beautiful—and simple. The first whale song deciphered had the structural complexity of grand opera, but the message (like most opera plots, and that was no coincidence) was, *I'm horny, I'm horny, I'm horny.* Later code work unfolded the intricate whale ways of broadcasting *I'm over this way!* and *Food here.* And, of course, *Danger!* There were other tribal messages, too, but none that could not be expressed in a sentence. Nature did not always produce sophisticated dialogue.

But why should that Earthly experience apply to the extreme low-frequency emissions from out here? The old

Voyager probes had first noted the noisy spectrum, but nobody thought it was more than plasma waves, the local weather. *Proserpina* had captured more for detailed analysis. Thousands of Earthside analysts had sweated over those, and *High Flyer*'s better data. Viktor had been handling the elaborate merging of all this, and now . . .

Now there was a new angle to the process. Viktor pointed it out, and she saw it suddenly, after minutes of scrutiny. Structure leaped out of the flow. The incoming digital streams broke into constellations that resembled words in their numerical architecture.

"And they are! So the Earthside tech types say." Julia finished her explanation to a blinking Viktor. "*Our* words. English!"

"Is impossible."

She grinned and put on her mock-gruff Russian accent. "Is not."

"Must be error."

"Unless whoever's sending this has heard us first, and they're replying."

"At ten kilohertz? No one uses frequencies that low. Waveforms are huge!"

"Oh?"

"*Da!* Even early radio, Marconi, he used only hundreds of kilohertz—pretty big waveforms already." He stopped, eyes widening with a sudden idea. "Must calculate wavelengths." He scribbled on his slate, frowned, and scratched his short, salt-and-pepper beard. "Ummmm . . . Marconi could use those frequencies because he was using really big antennas. Right."

"Right how?"

"*Da*—made of chicken wire, they were, strung between houses, like early Russian pioneers in radio—

She chuckled. "Who discovered it all first, along with the telephone and laughing gas—yeah, I've heard. Point is, my earnest darling?"

"That Marconi's antennas had to be at least a fraction of the size of the wavelengths he used. Or else they couldn't radiate very much—or receive much, either."

"That was the best he could do?"

"*Da*—and this is the best *they* can do."

"Who?" Julia was thinking about antennas, which she had worked with for decades but had taken for granted.

"The whoever that sent these signals at frequencies of ten kilohertz. Maybe they picked up our transmissions— God help us! Maybe all our radio and TV for the last century. But can't reply at those frequencies. Because, see, at normal radio wavelengths, we're talking antennas maybe a meter in size. Way too small for them. Instead, they go for ten kilohertz—because that's a wavelength they can manage."

She blinked. "Not a joke, right?"

"Nope. Divide the speed of light by the frequency to get the wavelength and therefore the antenna size. Old stereo systems had three speakers: the smallest, the tweeter, for high-pitched sounds; the big woofer was for bass notes—down to low-frequency rumbles."

Most of this was new to her, but she got the principle. "The thing that sent us these messages—the ones the Wiseguy codes are grinding away at right now—is—"

He grinned. "Really big woofer—at least thirty kilometers across. Aliens are giants."

2.

THE TOWERING ICE

SHANNA SETTLED DOWN INTO her smart couch and went through the setup protocols. Showtime!

Every time she went on watch, Shanna knew she was born to do this. From the beginning of this long mission she had found her hours on watch the most exciting she had ever known. Even after years on the mission, whose goals had veered radically as they learned more, her pulse raced when she went on duty. Being captain helped.

Telepresence duty was the absolute best. Boldly exploring, while sipping aromatic Colombian. In the 3-D environment she saw the Pluto landscape in sharp detail merely by turning her head. No sensation of movement, or of cold, but sounds came aplenty: the slow sigh of breezes, the crawler's clanking, the crunch of ice, a crisp fizz of vapor boiling off, which was a lot like bacon frying.

It had been weeks since she had actually been on the surface, and that was the crash. So this was the next best thing: phony Pluto. Digital discovery. Earthside was superworried about safety after that crash—the Chicken Little culture was quite frustrating. Politicians actually said, about every activity, even exploration, that safety was always the number one consideration.

Imagine human history if we had always felt that way, she thought. If it kept on like this at ISA, nobody on *Proserpina* might ever get to go back down to the surface.

Come billions of kilometers and stop a few hundred klicks short . . . crazy.

She peered at the landscape steadily, letting detail sharpen. Stark shadows cut across the dirty gray plain, and the sun was a glaring point. Under Charon's gloomy crescent the thin methane atmosphere scattered little light. Darkly twisted, tortured sculptures jutted from the ice sheet. The slow-motion weather here had worked on them for eons on the somber, sleeping plain. The moon loomed huge and ominous above a sharp horizon.

It held a certain austere beauty, but the mere landscape told nothing of its incredible cold. They had been drawn here by the unexplained growing warmth of this place— yet "warmth" was the wrong word. That grim, dismal view was only 120 degrees above absolute zero. Compared with Pluto's temperature measured Earthside back in the twencen, a brisk 42 absolute, this was Florida. A moment's exposure would not merely freeze her; it would snap her bones into confetti from thermal stresses.

Yet here life stirred. Incredibly. She had been down there twice, and it was still hard to believe.

Life on Pluto. Amazing enough by itself. Not just the simple legged forms that crawled and walked these bitter, barren hills—recent discoveries, thanks to telepresence, letting her drive the crawler from orbit. Or the flyers, angular or bulbous. No—there were others who descended from the sky, those from even farther out, beyond Pluto: the Darksider machines.

Nobody, not even the most extreme exobiologists, could have guessed.

Shanna resisted a morbid feeling: that the fragments of crumpled metal she and Jordin had picked up, mingled with those ice chunks, were actually scraps of ... well, flesh.

By now she knew better. Not flesh, but once living—if machines could truly live, even very smart machines like the Darksiders. But emotion yields slowly to reason; she still thought of the Darksiders as autonomous intelligences. Even after their captive onboard turned out to be a robot of sorts, able to carry out instructions well but incapable of original action.

She inched her crawler forward. Working in a comfy work pod, directing the crawler with telepresence gloves, she had to be careful not to alarm her prey. Ahead, the gunmetal-blue, oblong Darksider didn't seem to notice. Maybe it was recovering from its landing. Or playing possum.

Remember, you're the new kid out here. Maybe we don't know all that lurks in these shadows. You might look like an intriguing new kind of lunch.

She moved her hands in their command gloves and made the crawler grind forward another meter, crunching ice. Her low crawler was creeping on treads up to the Darksider at a shadowy angle. In the incredible cold here slow was always a good idea. Parts froze up without notice. Circuitry went dead, and even an emergency warm-up couldn't revive it. When the crawler stopped or pivoted, she sent a surge of electricity through it just to keep it warm. Moving here had an ominous, ponderous feel that got on her nerves.

Another sluggish move, then a wait. The Darksider didn't seem to mind.

Scavenging for Darksider remains had turned out to be easier than skystone hunting. Earthside wanted more parts, to better understand the different Darksider designs. Sky-stones, a rather poetic name for the rain of incoming mete-ors. She had come to like the whispery acoustic language of the zand, and their name fit, a combination of "zany" and "grand." They were both, speaking in long, wispy chords that skated great distances through the thin nitro-gen-methane air. Chilled words, pealing out with a rolling rhythm that reminded her of whale song. But unlike the whales, this time she caught what the zand were saying.

This was yet another wonder, but one human-made. Wiseguy had picked "skystones" as more expressive than English's "meteors." And indeed, the incoming rocks did not flare in the chilly "air" here, just slammed into the ice, carrying fresh Darksiders—from where? Their captive Darksider would not say; perhaps its narrow intelligence did not know.

"Got the target?" Jordin asked over comm.

"Dead on. Big one, looks like parabolic antennas stick-ing out of the carapace."

"Let me know, huh?" His tone was edgy. "I'm on this watch, too, y'know? It's not nice to just say nothing, leave me hanging here."

"I'll try being nicer if you'll try being smarter."

"Hey, just because I screwed up capturing that pair of Darksiders—"

"Okay, okay." She should be keeping peace, but he was sometimes irksome. And he *had* messed up the last telep-resence run. "I'm just watching it for now."

"Oh. I'll get on the spectral scan."

"Actually I thought you were napping."

In his lately familiar miffed tone he shot back, "I'm checking your every step."

"Don't need a babysitter, y'know," she said. "Catch up on your sleep."

"That an order, Captain?" Jordin said stiffly, with a subtone of derision to boot.

Yep, I'm still captain, and that's what's bugging him. "Sure. Nod off all you want. Earthside won't know."

"Might just do that."

Actually he was right. They had all been working so hard, for so long, that four days ago Earthside told her to institute mandatory days off. Nobody was going to honor that, she could tell right now. They all loved this vast, strange problem set before them. The shadowy mysteries kept them going.

Jordin signed off, though it would be just like him to keep his headphones on as he slept, just in case. She couldn't seem to strike the right notes with him these days. She knew she was getting a bit snappish, but no wonder. The approach of *High Flyer* was stirring anxieties old and new. And this long mission was rubbing personalities against each other. Plus some unusual stresses . . .

Dear old Dad had come through for her, right—but as Axelrod the Great, wielding his legendary deal-making magic. They'd had a lot of conversations the last few days—one-way at a time, of course, given the huge distances.

"I'm gonna have to burn a lot of chits to keep you as captain," Axelrod's concerned face had said. "It's going to take promises, and I'll have to make good on them. Remember what we talked about before—plenty of people want Darksider tech. They're betting it'll blow away any robots we've got here."

Meaning, of course, that the Consortium was betting.

Even though this was an ISA mission. "Well," she'd replied, "as captain I'm your best bet to get anything at all from this mission."

His answer hours later had infuriated her. "Y'know, honey, *High Flyer* can get us Darksiders, if necessary."

Lucky for tape delay; her first reaction would've been a disaster. Something on the lines of "The Mars Couple? Over the hill, Dad." Finally she'd settled for "It might be tricky for the Consortium to get around ISA's claims of first discovery. Ask your battalions of lawyers. But if I back up your claim, as the Consortium's rep on this mission all along, it'll be a lot easier. Daddy dear."

His face showed grudging admiration on the next vid. "Good point; so we have a deal. Oh, and I'm getting interest in having some small zand back here, if the exobiologists can figure out how to manage it. We want them alive, not stuffed. Possible? Nobody knows. I'll have more details later."

What a Victorian he'd have made! Zand aren't European, white, or Christian, ergo they have no rights. Without seeming to disagree, she'd sent, fingers crossed behind her back, "As they're sentient, they'll have to *agree* to go, Daddy dear." Might as well keep the edge in the dialogue.

She was still waiting for his reply.

A ping from the instrument board snapped her back to the present.

Hey, concentrate.

One more meter . . . Out of shadow now. Closer . . .

Her boards reported weak microwave emissions from the prey, but it remained stark and silent on the snow. But no, *not* a corpse, she reminded herself. The latest arrival, radar tracked from far beyond Pluto. Better to grab than pieces. Her hands moved in air like a pianist's.

Move. Close with it.

The crawler probe clanked forward and stuck out spindly grapples. Grasped. *Gotcha.*

She reeled in her catch like a fish—back to the waiting lift vehicle, in slow, deliberate moves. While the probe and its burden were still lifting off for the mother ship, *Proserpina*, the DIS computer ship-mind whirred through a preliminary analysis. Shanna watched the silvery ship rising toward them over the curve of the planet and felt sharp anticipation.

The probe made it back without incident. The crew did maintenance, getting ready to leave orbit. Shanna waited for her chance to see the new catch up close.

The new Darksider was nasty, which to a biologist meant interesting. Those fierce-looking claws—tantalum carbide, hard and tough even in supercold. The structural shell—aluminum/titanium alloy. (*Magnification, please.*) Those looked like mechanical relays of some sort, and they were made of solid mercury? Sure; at these temperatures, why not?

But what was the purpose of those patterns of rare earths? And those curves, seen in projection, looked almost like a conventionalized helix—*Oh.*

Shanna spoke into her recorder. "Hypothesis: these devices, whatever they are, contain a genetic model. Yeah! A helix, too, recalling DNA. A model of what? Of the 'ideal' zand, from a Darksider's point of view?" Her mind made a large leap. "We already know that these infalls came periodically, from dating the ones we found, centuries old.

Chow-Lin did it using isotopes, I dunno how. So—when Pluto arcs out along its steeply elliptical orbit, something hammers it with Darksiders. Been doing it for at least three planetary orbits—that's nearly a thousand years! Darksiders scan the zands. Those that don't measure up they squish."

Guided evolution? Part of the grand experiment on Pluto?

The probe clunked into its housing; she heard it ring. A conveyor rattled, taking its burden down to *Proserpina*'s low-temperature laboratory. Time to get to work.

Appropriate background? Something romantic but reflective, she decided; Schumann's *Konzerstück*.

Supported by mellow French horns, the piano chords rolled out while DIS, now in direct physical contact with the specimen, shifted into high speed. She fancied she could hear it hum.

Views of their catch filled the curved screens around her. Well, well—this beast hadn't been bent from sheet metal in a machine shop, that was sure. Coldformed, one molecular layer at a time, grown as crystals were. From the Oort clouders' massive perspective, she guessed, a delicate job of microengineering.

And the chilling thought came: from that same perspective, the injection of those "tools" into the zand culture would be no more a "raid" than the injection of antibiotics into a human bloodstream.

The thing was not dead, instruments said. Maybe shut down by itself, to save power. Or maybe orders from some mysterious Other. With care, and with the help of DIS, she could probably feed a trickle of tailored DC into its superconducting circuitry and bring it back to life. Make it *move,* clash those jagged claws, jump up and down. (*Boogie!* she almost heard Grandma say. Her father, alas, never got that loose.) Possibly attract its makers' attention that way?

If one of her own hemoglobin molecules tried to get her attention, would she notice? *That* was the relative scale between herself and the hypothetical somber dwellers in the Oort cloud, in the far dark beyond the warm worlds. Yet they had made the rickety zand biosphere, whoever or whatever they were.

They had plenty of room, too. Where the sun's gravitational grip slackened, countless icy islands swung, taking centuries to complete a single orbit around the dim home star. That archipelago stretched halfway to the next gleaming stars. As infinities went, it would do quite nicely.

They had come seeking the root of a mystery, never anticipating that the answer would be so vast and startling. At the end of the twencen, Pluto's atmosphere had seemed to start cooling off, as the planet arced outward on its slanting ellipse. Atmospheric specialists predicted it would freeze out somewhere before 2020.

Only it hadn't. Instead, even as the first probe sped outward, the thin film of chilly nitrogen and methane cloaking Pluto began to warm. Other compounds began spiking their spectral signatures up on the most sensitive Earthbound detectors: water vapor, carbon dioxide, even nitrogen wedded to oxygens.

And as the mission had prepared, a further, ominous puzzle arose: the solar system's bow shock was moving. This "pause point" is the working front where the sun's outward wind of particles meets the interstellar plasma.

This forms a surface much like the curve made by a ship powering across a lake, seen from above. Before, the nearest this bow shock had gotten to the sun was about one hundred astronomical units, a full hundred times farther than the Earth-sun distance. But now that fluttery front lay only a few AU beyond Pluto, now just a tad beyond 40 AU from the sun.

If the solar wind let that wall of molecular hydrogen behind the shock intrude into the inner solar system, Earth could be destroyed. Even approaching partway in, say into Saturn, would be very dangerous. That seemed unlikely to the specialists, but without an explanation of what was happening beyond Pluto, few found that comforting.

At first Shanna had thought the bow shock issue was pretty nebulous—after all, it was about thin gases, right?—and had to keep reminding herself of an old diagram from the early space program. It showed the solar system plowing through the interstellar spaces, pushing gas and plasma before it like a snowplow. If a voyage from the sun to the nearest star were like a marathon, in reaching Pluto the runner would have gone only fifteen feet. Both Voyagers and Pioneer had passed into the outer realm, genuine interstellar space. But if the solar snowplow weakened—or the pressure of the interstellar gas increased—the boundary would intrude farther in, brushing the planets. One swipe with molecular hydrogen and Earth's oxygen would combine, making water and a lot of energy. The biosphere would get hot and breathless within days. Even little trickles of hydrogen could hurt a lot.

She often gazed at the old NASA sketch—from back before it joined ISA—of the region they were now ex-

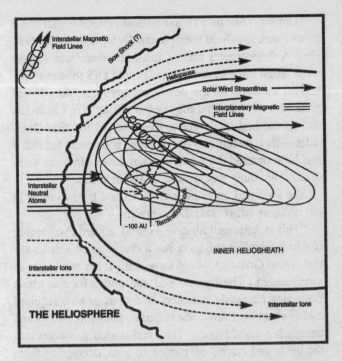

ploring. All very clean and scientific. No mention of lethal weather.

And now Pluto held life. Not just chilly slime molds and small crawly creatures, but a few species in all, crowned by the self-aware zand. And her bet was that these in turn were being altered by the skystones that fed them . . . and the Darksiders that bled them.

Earthside scientists now bet that Pluto was driven by energies somehow imported from where the bow shock roiled and frothed in plasma arcs bigger than planets.

DIS said, "Transmission due."

"Ummm." She owed it to Earthside, after the grief she'd given them, to at least keep punctually to their radio schedules. A fundamental rule of missions: there was always *some* damn thing interrupting. She told DIS to start trying revival methods on the newly captured machine. It had gone silent shortly after they began talking to it. Chow-Lin and Jordin had spent weeks trying to get the first Darksider—their hitchhiker—to respond, and concluded that it had been ordered (by what?) to shut down. Now she wondered if anything would work on the new one.

She switched on audio and visual and tried to relax in her obliging smart chair. Deep breath—

"This is Astronaut Shanna Axelrod, aboard *Proserpina*, in Pluto orbit." It still gave her a charge to be able to say that. (And Grandma would have warned her not to get so swellheaded.) They would edit and polish for the whole brimming Earthside audience, of course, as now required by full-disclosure laws. She hoped no laser-link pirates had caught her latest reports. They had started to swoop into the beam and carried off choice nuggets, decrypting them and bootlegging them in time to compete with the cleaned version. Embarrassments galore, unless she kept close to the vest. But who could, all the time?

In the background Schumann sang, and DIS clucked and ruminated, while she talked. Arpeggios rose from sonorous lower octaves. The longer this mission went on, the more she needed music's sense of human connection, of grand prospects. For that, the romantics were better than even Bach, for her.

"Not much progress on the Darksiders. The ones in the cold lab talk for a bit, then shut down. DIS is working on it, but my guess is they're unable to run very long without instructions—from where, though?"

She felt a fluttery twinge of unease. Minimal speculation, ISA had ordered. Earthside thought she was moving too fast. She wanted to *know*—and it was *their* lives on the line out here, right? *Easy, now—keep your tones proper and level.* Or should she record these little reports and have DIS take out the stress-diagnostic frequencies? Yep, she should consider that. Tomorrow.

"So, zilch. The local Pluto life-forms, the zand especially, I'd love to take the time to study them. But they're maybe a sideshow, Jordin and I—and the rest of the crew—think. You're just going to have to rely on our judgment."

She took a deep breath. Even after years of talking into silence, knowing that her message would take hours to get to its listeners made her uneasy. Humans need conversation, not oration.

Then there was the psychers' explanation. Reminding her of how far away they were from help? With one exception, yes.

"And, speaking of the zand, I've had some second thoughts on what to do about their situation. They're on the wrong end of a predator-prey dynamic. We can help them, sure, though that goes way beyond our mission profile. And we're using the Darksider-type strategy! Hiding from sight and occasionally sneaking a meteorite in amongst them might be as bad for them as to have Lady Bountiful descend from the clouds in full view. It could make them completely passive."

Amateur psychoanalysis, sure, but it made sense even

for aliens. Skystones will fall when needed, right? Light-giver will provide; *they* need do nothing.

"There's quite enough external control over their fate as it is, with even their genes—if I can use that word impre-cisely—messed with by outsiders. I'd like to see the zand stand up on their own feet, even though feet are something they haven't got."

Hopeless anthropomorphism: she could all but hear Dr. Jensen snap out the words. *Hey, it's a metaphor, guys.*

Avoid argument, Shanna told herself; *you're really in charge out here, calling all the shots. Captain! But get some advice first.*

"So"—pause for the beat—"I'm having DIS plot us a new course, toward *High Flyer.* I want to link up with them. I know, I know—*Proserpina* wasn't made to go out into the comet-rich inner disk. But we've picked up a lot of easy water here, heating the ice. We had the lander haul some up on the return from recon descents, using our 'bots to do the grunt work. We're fully fueled. The mysteries of Pluto can't be solved on the planet alone, and we'll make a powerful team out there, with *High Flyer.*"

There, it's said. Not crazy, no. Hell, Earthside sends a totally new kind of ship out to explore further and wants us to meekly head on home? As the original mission plan called for?

The rest of her crew agreed, of course, but not strongly, and *it was my decision, damn it! Mine alone. Captain.*

Proserpina's pokey fission nuke drive could only make it far enough to nip at the fusion-burn heels of *High Flyer.* She made herself take a long breath. *We can stay in the game.* "I want you to consider this as an add-on to our mis-sion. Also backup for *High Flyer.* We—"

Clanging. Loud, rasping alarms.

Shanna leaped from the immersion pod, heading for the pilot's chair. "All hands up!" she sent on comm. A whole row of instrument lights winked red. The hull was overheating.

But how? Panic flailed her. Heating from atmospheric friction? Maybe—were they falling out of orbit into atmosphere?

But, no—the holoscreen image of the planet and its satellite showed *Proserpina* precisely on its looping curve, where it should be. What could be heating the hull and blasting salvos of static into her music deck? Reflexively she shut it off.

Radio and microwave readouts jumped to the top of their scales. The external cams flared with light. Sheets of rippling electricity, swathing *Proserpina*'s hull and rebroadcasting like crazy. "What!"

Could any get in here? Flashes of light current? And how much microwave dosage was she getting?

Best get into her insul-suit—and fast. "Crew! Go to insul-suits." She shucked her coverall and squirmed into antiradiation garb that looked like a silvery wetsuit. It clung coldly to her bare skin. Jordin came through a hatch, doing the same.

Banging. Thumps. Screeching metal on metal.

From inside.

"Oh damn! The Darksiders—" Shanna raced hand over hand, down a tube, around a corner. She could hear crew footsteps thumping in the corridors above. She slipped, hit the wall, rebounded from a bulkhead, swiveled—and stopped before the view port for the cold lab. Cracks snaked across the frosty circle.

The alien body inside had revived. Its tin-gray parts moved with jerky purpose. It jumped and jittered. A claw swung at the view port again and stopped. Shanna flinched away.

It—or the intelligence controlling it—must have realized what would happen if it broke out. Emerging into ship temperature, the rules of superconduction would be suspended. Ordinary electrical resistance would prevail. Heat would build up as its currents suddenly met resistance. *Zap.* Death by Ohm's law.

She watched the thing jitter around uncertainly. The Darksider body must have reacted reflexively to the input surge DIS had tried. It came to life and automatically fought to escape. And then thought better of it . . . Now it stood motionless on the cold lab's examination table amid the restraining straps' tangled ruin. Shanna fancied that it glared.

"What's up, DIS?" she asked.

"I am trying to integrate its behavior patterns with input." The voice was coded to be male and warm, tailored to her tastes, but it still managed to come over as canned.

"Any ideas?" Jordin asked.

"It has some limited autonomy. I gather from inductively reading its inner currents that it is caught in a behavioral dead end."

"Something like a logical loop?"

"Perhaps."

Without being asked to, DIS had switched from lab analysis to dealing with the immediate emergency. *Good ol' DIS.* The heating of the hull, its sensor monitors informed Shanna, affected the surface skin only. Those secondary, lightning-bright lower-frequency discharges were annoying—obviously she wasn't going to finish her message to Earthside just yet—but nothing more than that.

"Jordin, keep an eye on it," Shanna said. "I'll brief the crew and check the hull."

She relied on her training, got that done, then got herself calmed down. Getting her immediate adrenaline-pumping alarm to fade, her racing heart and gulping breath settled back to normal—with meditation skills, that took two minutes. Then came a wave of fierce joy.

She couldn't reach out to the presumptive aloof denizens of the Oort cloud. But quite evidently something had come exploring on its own and touched them instead. Rippling currents along their hull, prodding its emissary Darksider 'bot.

What could do that? Time to gather the crew and do some brainstorming. The burden of being captain was the detail, but the reward was seeing the problems, having first crack at them. Maybe have a little party afterward to celebrate leaving Pluto orbit. They were all getting irritable, even the once amiable Jordin. So she gave herself one more minute and listened to good ol' bombastic Wagner.

3.

INSTIGATOR

THOUGH THE GALAXY APPEARS to be a swirling pinwheel of light, most of it is nothing. Emptiness. Utter black oblivion.

Or so it seems to small mortal eyes. Yet huge resources abound in the dark. Entities move there, unseen. They witness the ebb and sway of worlds from far beyond. Their perspective is larger, longer. This is how they see the inner, warmer realm:

The forms of life that arise on planets, encased in flesh or carapace, in fur or fin, see the universe through a narrow slit of the spectrum, light's brimming wealth.

Evolution prunes and whittles its subjects so they take advantage of the greatest flux their parent stars can offer. Seldom does planetary life evolve to sample the lazy, meter-long wavelengths of the radio or the pungent snap of X-rays.

So they do not witness the chaotic tumble of great plasma clouds between the stars. They see nothing hanging between the hard points of incandescent light, and so they falsely assume that what they call space is just that.

Yet stars, those brimming balls of radiance, continually spew forth matter which fills the void. The starwind streams out, expelled by snarling magnetic storms.

A human hand dipped into this gale from a spacecraft would snatch up only a few tens of molecules. By the time the thinning gale reaches the rim of the solar system, the density drops to a thousandth of that handful. Then this billowing wraith wind thins further—and meets the colder, denser fog that hangs between the stars.

There, between sun space and interstellar space, the comets coast, waiting for a chance collision to begin their weary inward journeys. Something happens in that realm that is no mere meaningless dance of matter and energy. Though invisible to human eyes, the banks of clotted plasma moving there are complex and forbidding. And alive.

Seen in an immense radio lens, the vast reaches would seem to have knots and puckerings, swirls and crevasses. Here the particles thicken, there they disperse into gossamer nothingness. And moving amid this shifting structure are thicker clots still. Some huge eye, sensing radio waves a kilometer long, would see them as incandescently rich. Their skins would shine where magnetic constrictions pinch and comb their intricate internal streamings. Filaments like glistening hair would wave and shimmer in the slow sway of ancient, energetic ions.

An even larger "eye" could hear the booming calls and muted, tinkling cadences of their conversations. Their talk began before the birth of the arrogant star nearby, now blaring away its substance in winds and magnetic whorls.

These Beings are unseeable by anything that evolved on simple, raw planets. They live through the adroit weaving of electrical currents. They feed on the electric potentials that trickle through the comet clouds. Their interiors are highly ionized plasmas, filigrees of ions and electrons in their eternal deft dance, long strands smoldering and hissing with soft energies. Moving at tens of kilometers per second, these inner cores sweep up magnetic fields and harness the induced electrical fields.

Even the best astronomy of small, planet-bound, chemically driven intelligences could only glimpse the momentary flaring of these plasma veins. The larger arteries and organs of the Beings would be beyond all but truly immense radio eyes—certainly far larger than anything contemplated by humans, even after the rocket-powered breakout into their own solar system. Each of the Beings stretches across a light-day of thick plasma and molecules.

If the entire solar system, including dim Pluto, were reduced to the size of a human fingertip, the bulk of the Oort cloud of iceballs would lie ten yards away from that finger. Yet these spaces could still encompass only a few hundred of the Beings, and have for billions of years.

Bodies so vast must run by delegation. A pulsing stomach busy digesting induced currents cannot know immediately that a distant molecular arm hungers for this spark of life. The intelligences that evolved to govern this huge bulk then resemble parliaments rather than dictatorships.

Yet even assemblies have names. And must at times speak with one voice.

The habit of these particular Beings had long been to assign names by the principal traits each displayed—age-old but not immutable. Still, to other intelligences these traits themselves were mysterious, fundamentally unfathomable. To represent them by the signs and conventions of mortal discourse is to falsify.

Further, over the yawning eons, Beings formed linked pairs, an electromagnetic yin and yang. This proved to have greater stability, since countercurrents repulsed, keeping nearby Beings from merging destructively. Most moved and grazed on upwelling fresh fields, in company with a Being of opposite polarity. Assigning the linkmates gender, as she or he, is a human convention only.

Outlining the unknown begins with a gesture toward the known. To convey even a sliver of the flavor, though, demands simplification. One must remember that the gift and curse of language is to render complexity into clarity, through a simplicity that must lose much. This can make profundity appear commonplace. Yet it must be.

What follows should best be understood as singing.

<Let us end this pernicious search *now*,> Forceful broke a long, tense silence.

<Absolutely,> Serene echoed. This was no surprise. She had opposed the Inbound investigation from the start.

From Ring, Forceful's grim linkmate, came ringing agreement. A quick chorus of assent forked forth from Mirk and Chill, their social offspring, now grown beyond the early stage of Protos. Beings shaped natural, recently born Protos into members of their community.

The young ones liked the far, cold reaches of the Vastness beyond all stars; it kept them agreeably out of reach. Soon, despite the time delay that waves took to span these reaches, came assents from them and their linkmates, Sunless and Dusk. These were echoing calls, hollow-sounding and rich in bass ion harmonics.

<Someone is trying to force a cusp point, a crisis—and before we can recover from the bad news,> Recorder mused.

They formed a block of six: Forceful and Ring, their Protos Mirk and Chill, and their Protos' linkmates Dusk and Sunless. Thus far they had been able to outweigh with firm argument the others, the Eight, who still wanted to press on. That faction desired to plunge in past the outermost planet's eccentric orbit and into the hot lower depths.

Only once before had any Being ventured into those treacherous regions. The ancient, woeful tale of Incursor had taught the Beings not to venture inward.

That Incursor had been brave was never doubted. In the

Beings' early era, when they first evolved to consciousness in the bow shock, much had been ventured. Incursor's aim had been to fathom fully their own origins. He had voyaged inward, in an expedition assisted by many Beings, a faction known still as the Inbounds. Incursor discovered much, but in studying an inner world he became lost. Legends spoke of occasional bursts of Incursor's unique voice, but the messages were tangled in the starwind and never lasted long. Sobered by this, the Beings took as an article of faith the Outbound view—that exploration of the stars was their destiny.

But the Inbounds never quite gave up. Instigator had slowly marshaled her strength. For long eras she had worked to understand how life of any kind could arise inward, and her experiments were renowned. Instigator's findings were already revered by Beings around distant stars.

And now the balance had been thrown even further the way of the Inbound Eight, by disaster.

Rumors had whispered in from distant Beings—remote even by their own vast standards for measuring space—who fed near the older stars. Strange tales indeed. Stories of the surfaces of many little rocky worlds tucked in close to stars, which had lately been rotting into life. Here *"lately"* meant on the proper scale of high intelligences—the time needed by a star to trace out its orbit around the center of the galaxy itself. A respectable time.

The words from the stars spoke of a low, obscene, hot life. *Solids.* Not powered by the clean transformations of electromotive force, but by the clumsy building up and tearing down of molecules.

These rot-born beasts were *swamps.* They seethed with

the messy contaminants that made up the cometary ice-balls. Their spectral signals the Beings had deduced from their explorations of the icy motes that would, on occasion, loop in and out of planetary systems, swinging into lethal zones where heat clawed at them.

<They are cropping up everywhere in the galaxy,> Instigator had told her fellow workers. That was some time before, when she had first reported on the genetic experiment she had started on this local system's outermost world, nearly a galactic cycle ago. <They are quick! And quite successful! They spread.>

Forceful shot back, <You are making copies of this lore, are you not?>

Instigator sent fluttering coils of turbulence at this insult. <I use the ample data that flowed down in the star-messages.>

<Mere imitation,> Forceful dismissed.

<None of us has ever before made a solid being!> Instigator shouted.

<None ever wanted to,> Sunless and Dusk sent in their gibing, hollow tones.

Even in this argument they and Mirk and Chill followed the ancient convention, that subordinate generations spoke as one. If they disagreed among themselves, they remained silent—which was often a blessing, their elders strongly believed.

<This achievement, though only partial, is like that of older Beings, such as Incursor. He ventured inward, sent back knowledge, then was lost,> Instigator sent. <Like Incursor, I am doing this for us all.>

Forceful rejected this in plumes of incandescent effrontery. <You are doing it from vain pride.>

Ominously Instigator coiled portions of herself into dark striations. <I do not tolerate insults well, as many here know.>

<You have had quite a bit of practice at that,> Recorder noted. <I feel some of us have been intolerant of . . . eccentricity.> The pause before the last symbol-term was significant, placing Recorder midway between the factions.

<I have had quite a bit of provocation!> Instigator shot back.

<You arc over to a conclusion-state without just cause,> Forceful said.

<I got the basic plans and methods from a long starmessage—the pealing chorus that sings to us from the distant plane of the galaxy. Profound truths! They are of the very greatest wavelengths and require much study to comprehend.> Instigator purled off portions of herself to show disarming openness. <The passages were laden with import and a call to alertness.>

Forceful sent coils of skepticism. <Not all such messages live up to their grandiose billing.>

<But they can,> Recorder observed. <In this case— but mind, with no promise of future agreement—I side with Instigator. We must prepare prudently.>

<How?> A chorus of Ring, Forceful, Mirk and Chill, Sunless and Dusk—all sent the same doubtful interrogation.

Recorder showed startled puzzlement. <By allowing Instigator to act according to her character. We must all go to the Cascade soon, to feed. Let us do so in a proper spirit. We must allow some freedom to each other.>

<You are being too soft!> Forceful sent with quick,

angry striations. <Your hunger for the Cascade speeds you to hasty decision.>

Recorder sent rumbling bass notes of discordance. <Careful what you say. I, the local eldest, feel that we can afford to continue experimenting with the solid mechanisms.>

<It is full of risk!> Forceful countered. <We could be vulnerable to disorders we do not know. Even the starmessages you cite say this!>

Recorder sent firmly, <The risks of contact with such unbearable, beyond-all-reckoning *cold* are incalculable. Our bodies would condense out upon solids—that is why even you, Instigator, do not directly touch worlds. We deal in electrical energies and dance with magnetics. Such dangers of contact—actually touching solids!—are in the end attractive only to the rash, the occasionally foolish— that is, to Instigator and its many parts. Let Instigator digest the risks, I say.>

<As I do,> Instigator sent.

<We need Crafter!> Dusk sent. <One who knows how to work with tiny things.>

<I speak with Crafter often,> Instigator said. <We collaborate on these problems. He will want to be part of the contact.>

<Crafter should speak to us,>Ring said with an indignant aura. <Directly.>

<Crafter likes solitude,> Instigator sent mildly. <To craft.>

<Very well.> Recorder paused to let their momentary angers dissipate along the intricate magnetic field lines. <Let us go to the Cascade in a goodly spirit.>

Derisive laughter came, but in such long wavelengths

that the Being—or Beings—who sent it could not be resolved, even using the antennas of the largest of them, Recorder. Vexing, but Recorder had suffered such insouciance before.

<Come,> Recorder said. <I am hungry.>

4.

THE SOLAR RAMPARTS

SHANNA GAZED at the pale crescent of Pluto falling behind. Its moon, Charon, looked outsize, fat. It was, at about half Pluto's diameter. Thirty years ago, the astronomers said, it was just an iceball. Now it brimmed with a filigree of warming nitrogen and water, as Pluto did. Pale gas rimmed both crescents.

The source of the energy that drove this lay farther out from Pluto. And Uziki, the shy physics type, had found out how. After Ferrari's death, the remaining five had reshuffled duties to cover the tasks. Her original crew position was in engineering and computers, but she had a Ph.D. in plasmas. She had found that the energy came in subtly, as electrical currents in a thin plasma column, pointing straight in toward the sun.

The nuclear drive rumbled hard at her back, rattling the decks. *Proserpina* was now riding along that column's outer sheath. The plasma physicists Earthside thought they could learn a lot about how the whole mechanism worked by looking at the conditions at its boundaries, for some reason.

Not her field of expertise, but it made sense—something was confining the current flow, shaping it neatly toward Pluto. What lay at the other end of this mechanism nobody had even guessed, so far. Something big and strange, for sure.

"Picking up a lot of turbulence," Jordin said from the side couch.

"Plasma waves?"

"Yeah, a lot like the stuff coming from the bow shock zone up ahead, I'd say."

"Low frequency? Like *Voyager* picked up?" About plasma physics she knew at least enough to ask questions, but not much more.

"Sure is. Pressure waves, running down this sheath, keeping the currents nicely aligned."

"A kind of . . . plasma pipe?"

"Yep. Energy flow pipe, with Pluto-Charon at the far end of the circuit." Jordin was intrigued, fingers working in his command gloves. He waved in the space before him, and pretty colored displays outlined the flow patterns. Currents arcing in, nose-diving, finally captured by the crusts of the two worlds. The heating effect flared visibly as a dull orange glow in the icy crusts. Filigrees ran under the blue ice sheets, melting the thinnest layers into gossamer vapors. Clouds fumed into the gathering atmospheres.

"Damned odd," was all Shanna could think to say.

"Not an accident, no way," Jordin whispered, eyes intent on the constant play of pattern.

"What kind of thing can set up magnetic pipes bigger than planets?"

Jordin shrugged. "I dunno. Earthside is still talking about all this as a whole new kind of biosphere, driven from outside by currents—"

"I'll say!"

"—but natural. The astrophysicists are playing games with the bow shock region, tying its moving into all this commotion on Pluto."

She snorted. "That just moves the problem back a step. What made the bow shock boundary move in from 100 AU?"

"You don't get the game." Jordin grinned. "Moving the cause into their ballpark means they get to make the pitches. Get the hurry-up funding. Make headlines."

"So young and already so cynical."

"You expect scientists to be loftily above it all?"

She nodded grudgingly. "Okay, now you're starting to sound reasonable. Time to up my medication."

It took six days for *Proserpina* to overtake *High Flyer*. Its exhaust burned diamond-hard against the black. Escape velocity from Pluto was 1.1 km/sec, only a tenth of what it took to escape Earth's grasp. Orbital speeds were low out here, too. Pluto moved at a paltry 500 m/sec, not a whole lot faster than a jet plane. Out there in the Oort cloud, speeds got even slower. Shanna had a momentary comic picture of herself running to catch up with a planet . . .

And there it was, a bright dot rushing into the far dark.

High Flyer was a huge thing, like a skyscraper with a big bright rocket flare stuck on one end. Most of it was gray bottles of water blocking the hind drive from the living quarters.

In space geometry is the only guide to size, and even

geometry needs a measuring stick. Here the only guide to her eyes was the air lock, the bulky structure a mere small cap near the top third of the craft.

This was a *big* nuke. And the first fusion rocket of major scale, built for both speed and distance. No mere pod sitting atop a big fuel tank, which in turn fed into the reactor. Of course, the parts had to line up that way, no matter how ornate the subsections got, because the water in the tank shielded the crew up front from the reactor and the plasma plume in the magnetic nozzle.

To even see the plume, *High Flyer* had a rearview mirror hung amidship, out ten meters to the side. The whole stack was in zero g, except the top thick disk, which the crew seldom left. Forty meters in diameter, looking like a dirty angel food cake, it spun lazily around to provide a full Earth g at the outside. There the walls were meter-thick and filled with water for radiation shielding. So were the bow walls, shaped into a Chinese hat with forward viewing sensors. From inside, nobody could eyeball the outside except through electronic feeds.

The whole ship was well over a hundred meters long. Built like a barrel, it rode a blue-white flare that stretched back ten kilometers before fraying into steamy streamers. Plasma fumed and blared along the exhaust length, ions and electrons finding each other at last and reuniting into atoms, spitting out the actinic glare. The blue pencil pointed dead astern, so that at the right angle the whole scene was an exclamation point, with the sun as the dot. *Proserpina* hauled up within a kilometer, and the two ships fretted over the details of making the transfer.

In the end Shanna won out. *Proserpina* was cramped and showing wear; and she wanted to see inside the bigger ship. She, Jordin, and two other crew would come across in the shuttle. Part of her wanted to play status games and make them come to her, but her own curiosity won out. She wanted to see what this monster of a ship looked like, and it would indeed be good to get out of the house for a while.

Not that she looked forward to a tech-talk fest. Whenever ship crews got together, there was a lot of talking shop, but out here she could use some simple human contact. Being captain always kept you at a distance from your crew. And the hyperlink to Earth was no substitute for real talk, either. Last week she got a memo that said, "Cascade this to your people and see what the push-back is." It put her off reading her e-mail for days.

They wedded to the air lock gingerly. The lock was big and bulky, like everything here, with fancy safety bells and whistles. *Mass to spare*, she thought sourly.

They cycled through, in formation. For Earthside audiences *High Flyer* was recording every greeting, handshake, joke, and guffaw. They got through it, agreed to turn the cameras off, and Shanna had a moment to assess this Julia Barth, senior woman among astronauts, legendary for a crusty exterior that concealed a sharp intelligence. She stood straight, shoulders back, smaller than Shanna had expected; the great should be larger, to match the reputation. Julia was compact as all astronauts were, maybe a tad stringy. Her face was lined, mouth cocked at an assessing angle, eyes quick. Suntanned, too, from working in the Martian domes. Already, Shanna was sizing her up.

Her husband, Viktor, was quiet and gruff, big and muscular among the slim astronauts, eyes flicking from one face to another as the conversation moved. Equally famous, just as at ease. They both seemed energetic but calm. Maybe the Mars Effect was real. Shanna wondered how they were in bed together . . .

Everybody knew each other's profile, had read their books (some ghost-authored, some even eloquent), and they passed through the usual compliments. Shanna knew she would take an industrial-strength makeover to be presentable, but the *High Flyer* men all told her how great she looked. One, Hiroshi Okada, had gleaming eyes and a mirthful grin. She liked him at once, and not just because his compliments didn't seem forced.

In cultural profile *High Flyer*'s crew was like hers. By no accident, most spacers were from North America or Asia. Those were the cultures, mid-twenty-first century, where young people still asked, *When can I do X?* The Europeans usually said, with dread, *How do we stop people from doing X?* And *X* could be just about anything technological. Genetically modified food, screening for future disease risk, opening up the asteroids for mining of scarce metals, living longer through genetic tailoring, beaming microwave power from space, living half-time in virtual villages, sending a beacon signal to the stars.

ISA was mostly backed by Asians and Americans. Euros didn't go into space—You could die! It would cost a lot!—and were busy shoring up their aging societies with plentiful taxes and fearful politics, eyeing the ever-growing population of Muslims in their midst . . . Shanna was quite glad to be out here, away from the swamp of Earthside.

They sat around the ship's pedestal mess table, a polycarbon white circle. An awkward moment. Everybody beamed, glad to see fresh faces, but nobody spoke. *An epic moment far from Earth. All sorts of firsts here. How to start?* Then Viktor produced, improbably, two bottles of champagne to mark the moment. That loosened everybody even before lips touched liquid.

Sure enough, the first socializing was about the latest Earthside news, most of it just the usual wrangling and angling that passed for politics. That done, like dogs sniffing noses, they relaxed.

Shanna let the chatter run for about half an hour. They all had the zand interpretations, the spotty information on the Pluto biosphere. So they concentrated on reviewing the data, dancing around hypotheses. Viktor reported on his idea that the wavelengths received from farther out meant that the radiators were tens of meters in size, at least. Maybe that's just their antenna size, Chow-Lin said. Franklin agreed. After all, our antennas are pretty big, too.

But, Viktor countered, the signals are from places where there are no worlds at all. Certainly nothing remotely as large as Pluto. They got into a technical discussion, and momentum flagged. Tit for tat, counters, hedges. Shanna let it run as long as she could bear before saying, abruptly, "What do you make of our . . . hosts?"

Viktor's face was veiled as he said, "You think big things make the small Pluto things?"

Wow, he knows how to cut to the chase. "Somebody did," Shanna said. "We're not looking at natural evolution here, for sure."

"Julia thinks so, too," said Viktor. "She is pretty good biologist. Has intuition."

Shanna felt a stab of jealousy. *Damn, she's good. How did she come up with it so fast?*

Jordin sent her a look she could not decipher. "We haven't actually discussed all this yet."

Good old Jordin, undercutting my claim to first discovery, Shanna fumed.

"The antenna-size argument," Chow-Lin pointed out, "just sets a lower bound. The creatures could be far larger. We're lots bigger than our eyes."

Viktor said, "All assuming that the antennas *are* eyes— I mean, not a technology. Because we see no technology out there, just empty space."

Julia's mouth tilted skeptically. "I rather think these zand of yours are not naturally evolved, but how can something bigger than a mountain—maybe the size of continents—make them?"

"Not a clue," Shanna said. "But they didn't evolve on Pluto. That's not a biosphere back there, not a truly integrated system. It's a base camp, getting by on energy rations."

"And run by electrical power that comes from way beyond," Jordin added.

Julia's wary gaze did not alter. "No chance Pluto's been running that way for a long time?"

Jordin shook his head. "It looks . . . well, recent, contrived. The whole planet's got a narrow pyramid of life, few microbes, just a handful of amino acids—the minimum to make it work."

"Built by something *really* strange," Shanna said.

Viktor said, "So we invoke that rule, the knife something—"

"Ockham's razor," Shanna said. She had been reading plenty of philosophy of science; it seemed a good investment, out here amid the truly weird. Plus science fiction, of course—lots of Arthur C. Clarke. "We've got two strange things, so maybe one causes the other."

"*Three* strange things," Julia said matter-of-factly. "You got the transmission Earthside sent forty-two hours ago? They've decoded that low-frequency stuff that keeps washing over us."

Shanna raised eyebrows and nodded reluctantly. "I can't follow it all, but . . . okay, one more mystery."

"Getting to be lot of mystery out here," Viktor observed.

Hiroshi nodded. "I've been running codes, along with the Earthside spectral analysis. They're—the big things— sending stuff in English, that's certain."

This was new. There followed an extended discussion of how to decode. Mary Kay said, "That's my area. Transcendental Grammar, the Earthside cryptanalysts call it."

Shanna said, "Isn't that secondary, compared with the basic biology?"

"Not at all, Captain." Mary Kay's tone was just civil. *How come?* Shanna thought. *Long-mission syndrome, as Jensen called it? Or do they all just dislike me?*

Mary Kay went on in a stiff, I-am-being-professional manner, "Whoever is sending, they don't use punctuation the same way we do. Commas, periods, semicolons, dashes—they all help organize the relationships between parts of the sentence, yes?" She smiled brightly, as though this was obvious, though Shanna had never thought of it that way before. "Semantic amplifiers, they are, adding precision and complexity to meaning."

Jordin nodded, backing up his wife. "Increases the information potential of strings of words."

"The trick," Shanna said, hiding exasperation, "is to figure out what they are, not just how they talk."

"Not talk," Viktor said. "More like writing, by the time we—DIS and its handyman, Wiseguy—get done."

Shanna said, "Because we can't hear it?"

"Writing is a million times weaker than speech," Mary Kay said incisively. "No inflection, tone, smiles, winks, raised eyebrows, hand moves. Got to allow for that."

Chow-Lin said, "Sort of like a hieroglyph competing with a symphony?"

Mary Kay nodded, and Viktor said skeptically, "You think they have such things?"

Chow-Lin shrugged, an example of what he meant. "There's plenty in the wave spectrum we can't decode. Look, I'm kinda reaching here."

"And I'm getting lost," Shanna said. "I'm a biologist, not an information theorist. I think in terms of species, biospheres. I want to get down to what kind of creatures these things *are*."

Julia said, "Our Wiseguy has been working on their low-frequency transmissions. We can eavesdrop. They call themselves the Beings."

"Also the Diaphanous," Hiroshi added precisely.

Shanna narrowed her eyes. "You should have sent this information over."

Julia smiled. "We wanted to explain in person."

Shanna said, "Diaphanous? Imagine—what a vocabulary."

"I had to look it up," Viktor admitted. "And I'm human. Wiseguy said was good synonym for a whole constellation of meanings."

Julia smiled at him. "Most of the time."

"They must've been listening to us—to all Earthside—

a long time," Hiroshi said carefully. "It is the only way to explain how it can—"

"How they can," Jordin interjected.

"Right." Hiroshi nodded vigorously. "How they can know so much of our language. English, anyway, though there were pieces in German—*Ich muss diese Frage verstehen,* as I remember. 'I must understand this question.' "

"Hey, join the club," Chow-Lin said, which got a laugh all around.

"Maybe they have only one language." Shanna laughed, too, but made herself stay on the problem. Even though it was risky for a captain to think out loud. *But here I'm just one of two.* "So they eavesdrop on some Earthside broadcasts and include it all, thinking German is just some English they don't understand?"

"Um." Hiroshi thought. "German's close enough to English, one of the two roots of it. Maybe they can see that. Incorporate the German?"

Viktor blinked. "What a mind."

"Minds," Jordin corrected him. "Earthside has gotten clear conversations in every batch. Interplay. Cross talk. We're overhearing them."

"But they're sending to us directly in English, too." Viktor frowned.

"Earthside has cracked their language," Jordin said. "Throw a few thousand crypters at it, you get results. We can eavesdrop on them now."

"I am still amazed that anyone could figure out what so strange a thing was saying," Viktor said disarmingly. He gazed at Jordin and Mary Kay. "Can explain?"

This brought them a beaming smile. Shanna knew well by now that Jordin was a frustrated professor and would no doubt be a real one someday. For now he was stuck being a mere astronaut. "The key is the chromatic scale. You know, the way notes are arranged on the piano. Our Western *do-re-mi* is a subset of that. Turns out, people worldwide put *extra emphasis* on tones that correspond to the notes of the scale. We like doing it. You record people talking, they put more energy into those special notes."

Julia said, "Really? I never noticed."

"Nobody does. We think it's natural. And it *is*! That's the breakthrough. Once we found this out, half a century or so ago, everybody thought it was a biological thing. Maybe we as primates heard bird song, invented some crude music, and after that learned to talk. Kept the same scale-note structure, see?"

Shanna had heard all this before, but it was fun to see the others react. Sure, they'd gotten squirts from Earthside about all this, but who had time—or more important, given how badly written most of it was, who had interest—to make their way through it? The *High Flyer* crew was enthralled, champagne forgotten, except for Viktor, who sipped automatically. *Maybe likes the alcohol a little too much?* She would have to remember that. Maybe he was the weak link in *High Flyer*.

"But for a long time," Jordin went on earnestly, "the math folks thought the scale itself came from harmonics, the ratio of numbers, all that Pythagorean stuff. Ancient history! Only it turns out to be right. See, the scale gives us pleasant harmony in music. That's why the twelve-tone garbage back in the twencen was the end of classical music."

Blank looks all around.

He hurried on. "They forgot the scale! We're conditioned by evolution to like the harmonics, the basics of music. So do dolphins, whales, birds! All of us."

Viktor scowled owlishly. "Am losing you."

"Oh. Sorry. A liking for harmony is apparently a universal—that's what I deduce from all these waves we've been getting. Whatever's sending them, they're singing!"

"Can see data?" Viktor looked unconvinced.

They spent half an hour looking at spectra on screens, Jordin and Mary Kay doing most of the talking. Jordin said, "Those intermediate-frequency plasma waves we detected coming out? Turns out there were plenty more picked up on the Deep Space Network—Goldstone and all those others, Parkes in Australia, you know—at least the higher-frequency modes, the upper hybrid ones, the descending helicons that go"—he whistled—"and they *all fit*. Lotsa data there. Plenty of cross-correlations. One big conclusion. In these 'Beings' speech—both the stuff they send us in English and the substuff, the cross talk they're having with each other—in that speech there is the same spectrum of harmonic emphasis."

Viktor took another sip of champagne. Nobody said anything. Viktor's eyes squinted as though he were looking upwind into a gale. "Is meaning?"

Jordin did not take this clue. "That the Beings communicate by a coding system that is like ours."

In Viktor the light dawned. "So . . . on that your crew— no, Earthside—can hear their talk? And Wiseguy deciphers?"

"Yes," Mary Kay said. "Soon we'll be able to talk back—through Wiseguy."

Innocently Viktor said, "Can hear their inner thoughts?"

Jordin blinked. "Those may be the plasma waves we're getting. Can't understand them, though."

Julia said, "Thought isn't like singing, I suppose?"

Jordin spread his hands. "Guess not—our thoughts aren't, right? Not mine, anyway." This got a laugh. He went on, "Maybe the stuff we don't understand is leakage. From whoever is sending the talk. I dunno." Vigorous head shake.

"Amazing," Julia said. "We'll have to integrate our data with yours, through Wiseguy."

Shanna let out her breath. It was going to be hard to break in on all this, but she had to get some things straight. "Say, let's take a break, gang. How about a tour of your ship?"

This was fun, especially watching the 'bots working near the drive systems. Robotics plus nukes were the future.

Cameras tracked the impromptu tour everywhere; the Consortium would wring every dime out of the footage. After an hour of this, when she and Julia were out of view, Shanna said, "You and I have some stuff to discuss. Don't want to bore everybody. Can we take it into another cabin?"

"We call them rooms," Julia said slowly. "Seems better, more homey. Uh, of course, let's."

They slipped away with a nod to Viktor, who was leading the tour, holding forth as host. Julia led the way through a circular hatch rimmed by pale emerald emergency phosphors.

Shanna followed briskly. They came into a compact compartment she assumed was Julia's office, though no adornment of the inward-sloping faux-mahogany walls testified to this. There were contour chairs made of something pale effervescent blue and so thin that when she lifted it the 0.38 g field to face Julia, Shanna flung it toward the ceiling—and, startled, let the revolving chair spin with classical slowness into the corner. "Uhhhhh—oops." She retrieved the chair with one quick swoop of her left arm, flicked on the magnetic anchors, sat—

And wondered how to start. She had fretted for weeks about this moment, but now, actually in Julia's presence, she marveled. The years had lined that face, but it was still the one Shanna had on her dorm room wall in college. This woman had changed space travel, revolutionized biological studies. Julia didn't just take part in the first manned mission past the moon but stayed there and made a home, back when astronauts were still hopping up and down from space like it was hot water they couldn't stand to stay in. Shanna swallowed, and set aside her hero-worship attitude toward Julia. *Face it—you want to be like her, the benchmark of greatness. Which means you have to keep hold of your results out here, not let the media feature the Mars Couple every other minute . . .*

The absurd chair gymnastics seemed to break the ice between them. Unplanned, but who knew what the unconscious could do? Shanna had learned to go with the flow of events and surf on it when she could. It was the only wisdom she could pretend to herself that she had actually discovered, instead of just reading about, but maybe it was enough. Anyway—"Let's talk as captains, eh?"

"I'm actually not captain," Julia said.

"What? Earthside—"

"I'm in charge of scientific matters. Viktor's Captain, but he and I are married, so we have split the duties. That's our style."

"That's completely contrary to—"

"Chain of command, I know. We cut a deal with Earthside. Whatever they want to call it, fine."

Shanna kept her face as impassive as a firm wall against getting irked and losing it. "Because you're famous, you think you can abuse—"

"Use, not abuse." Julia leaned on the slim black poly table between them. "Having the Axelrod name must've been useful in keeping your captaincy, eh?"

"That was a little matter—"

"Look, we're 6 billion klicks from Earthside regulations—"

"And you and Viktor," Shanna spat back, "the oldest crew in the astronaut corps, you're going to be in charge?"

"Not at all," Julia said mildly. "Experience does count, seniority might matter—but we have two ships, so we have two captains. As we're all on the same scientific expedition, we have to agree on methods, results, risks. Viktor and I have more experience than you—"

"On Mars, which is an oven compared with Pluto. Why, we've had telepresence crawlers freeze right into the regolith, first day out! Took steam piped from the ship to get it free. I've had a lot more experience—"

"Than we have at superlow temperatures, yes." Julia's eyes narrowed, her mouth twisted wryly. "But the biggest problem out here, the reason for the gigabucks spent to put us here at top speed, is the bow shock."

"*If* it's a threat." Shanna's words rapped out. "Earthside weather hasn't shown any changes—except for the global warming, of course—even though the shock wall has gone from 100 AU to 42 AU in thirty-some years."

"I know the data, for goodness' sake! But a hell of a lot

of numerical simulations show big effects in the offing. The molecular hydrogen that's leaking into the inner solar system, it'll build up and start reacting with the free oxygen in our upper atmosphere."

"And make water, big deal. Nobody knows—"

"Plenty of energy yield there, that's the point. Heat up the upper mesosphere, and that drives big changes below. Screws up the stratosphere temperature profile, and pretty quick that heat moves down toward the business end, where *our* weather gets made."

Shanna sniffed, nose turned up. "I see where you're going with this. We should be looking mostly at the shock edge, find out what's driving it. But Pluto is *key* here. That's what my, our discoveries show. Something's running all this, and it isn't stupid."

"Nobody said the problem wasn't interconnected."

"This isn't about dumb weather!" Shanna tossed her head back, her hair cascading slowly in the low gravity.

"Okay, smart weather, then. Point is, the zand are pretty interesting. You were lucky to have stumbled into first contact with a self-aware species."

Shanna felt her defensive walls come up. "Not stumbled—more like ferreted out," she shot back. "Some people thought I was just imagining the whole thing, that I was faking the data, even."

"To be sure. The early criticism was unwarranted, but that's often what you'll get from Earthside. A lot of second-guessing and tall-poppy cutting."

"Huh? I don't get it." Shanna looked perplexed.

"Aussie slang. Grow into a tall poppy, people slice you off, whittle you down to size. Put another way, the Greeks felt their gods punished excessive hubris. It's the same thing."

"Oh, I see. Hm. Never thought of it that way."

"It helps not to take the automatic criticism personally. Save that for the important objections. The trick is to tell them apart."

Shanna felt some of her anger ebbing away. In her defense against coming across as a hero-worshiper she'd forgotten that Julia had endured decades of scrutiny and bad-mouthing. Julia pressed on. "But we're moving beyond the zand, now, to contact with the movers and shakers out here—that's the main event. And if I may offer a bit of advice on the zand, you have to get over pretty fast your claim of exclusivity. You don't own the zand just because you discovered them. Hundreds of scientists Earthside are now reworking their research agendas to focus on the ecology of Pluto. No, make that thousands. Not to mention all the ink that will be wasted by the 'What does it all mean?' crowd."

"You want to have a crack at them?" Shanna resented the rebuke.

"Look." Julia sat back, shaking her head. "We can't start out like this, with a fight. We cooperate out here or we die."

Shanna nodded, thinking furiously for a way around this woman, to hold her own. *Go crying to Earthside? Not again. Try to marginalize her in future? Hard to do, on another ship. Okay, put that aside for now, but keep looking for an advantage.* "Okay."

"I know Axel—sorry, your father—spoke with you about our taking some Darksiders back with us."

"Hey, 'Axelrod' is fine. I didn't see him much as a

child." She made a wry face. "Yeah, I know he wants them. I even agreed to deliver some, if we can." She felt suddenly drained. *Time to end this conversation.*

Julia sat, unmoving. Shanna made herself smile slightly. *Bad beginning. She looks tired. My turn to try to lighten this up.* "Hey, my father thinks we're both bad girls."

Julia made a small, thin smile. "We are, no doubt. Maybe we're both a bit, how to say, heavy-handed? One thing you learn as captain is that there are very few problems that can't be helped by orders ending with 'or die.'"

Shanna sighed. "I discovered that myself. My crew is irritated with me."

Julia studied her. "You've been on duty too long. You're worn down."

Shanna's eyes flashed. "Uh-uh. I and my crew are as fit for service as anybody."

"I'm sure," Julia said stiffly, getting up. "Look, you and I haven't exactly hit it off—"

"I'll say!"

"—but let's keep it to ourselves."

"Right. Professional." She cocked a wry smile. "I guess this day was a total waste of makeup."

This made Julia smile faintly, grudgingly. "It wasn't wasted on my crew, believe me. The guys have had only two women to look at for a year, me and Veronique."

"Same on *Proserpina*, me and Mary Kay, only it's been years."

"Not easy, working in tight quarters. The hormones get going."

"Sure do, and not just among the men."

"Ha!—I'll say. Luckily I have Viktor."

"Yes, a husband. I neglected that point before shipping out."

Julia smiled without mirth. "You may not know this ancient history, but our being married was a, shall we say, 'condition of employment.' Marry or be replaced."

"Huh? That's Victorian."

"They felt that an unmarried woman couldn't go into space for years with three men."

"Who? The Consortium?"

"No, Axelrod—your father."

Shanna opened her mouth, closed it. The silence stretched. Julia said softly, "Luckily it's worked out terrifically. We made it alone on Mars for two years without killing each other."

Shanna just stared.

Julia looked tentative, half turned, then looked back. "A piece of advice . . ."

"In dealing with the men?"

"Yes, and not just for the men." A thin smile. "Always keep your words soft and sweet, just in case you have to eat them."

5.

STRANGE SYMPHONY

JULIA WAS GLAD to see them go.

She had thought that she would be very glad to see fresh faces, but they wore out their welcome in a day.

Maybe she was getting too old for this spacer stuff. Or maybe her diplomatic skills were wearing thin. Had that been behind the trouble with Praknor? Anyway, the Shanna woman was abrasive, self-obsessed, smug—and those were her good points. Julia suspected that in a pinch the woman might also be careless, the one sin reality never forgave.

The first hour had told the tale. Of course, they had more techy discussions, crews getting to know each other, all aware of the collaboration to come. But the edgy distance between herself and Shanna had been an undercurrent beneath every moment. Everybody felt it, but thank God, didn't talk about it. Until they were gone.

"You need rest," Viktor said flatly when the lock clanged down.

"Yes, sir, Cap'n, sir."

"Really."

"Point taken. That Shanna really wore me out. The way she tosses her hair back, showing off—*arrggh!* That's always irked me. Worse than dealing with that Praknor—hey, think it's a generational thing?"

"Hope not. Am not ready to be 'old fuddy-duddy generation.' "

She looked at Viktor appraisingly. "I'd choose your old fuddy-duddy over any young guy."

"According to Praknor, many women Earthside agree with you."

"Ah, the sperm king!" She laughed and collapsed into a lounger. The logistics and tech issues had dominated everything, as one would expect of astronauts. But somehow all the time she was seeing their ship anew, through the others' eyes. They thought it wonderful, ornate, opulent compared with their fission-driven craft. Fat cats of *High Flyer*. Well, fair enough—fusion had come available at just the right time to make *High Flyer* a whole step up, and it showed. A great way to sail into the abyss, indeed.

High Flyer's designers hadn't much consulted any of the future crew about interior design—it had all been done on the hustle—so it reflected Earthside's latest notions. Appliances and even furniture looked as though they had grown there—ductile, rounded, even drippy as if recently melted. The style was called blobjects, and this look made them seem organic, natural.

But, in fact, they were the opposite, stuffed with smart chips that processed data without letup. If a crew member was carrying a virus—no medcheck caught all of them— *High Flyer* wanted to know it. If you had fallen asleep in the common room and were about to miss your watch, the room noticed and *High Flyer* beeped you awake. Even in the stringy little microgravity "beds" at the axis for low-grav sleep, they could mommy you to death, if you let them.

Like many of Earthside's cities, the "smart ship" embraced its inhabitants, keeping tabs and worrying over health, safety, supply and demand of air, moisture, heat, power, the works. She had found it weirdly claustrophobic at first and for weeks did not sleep well, feeling that some *thing* was watching. Then as they flew at great speed into cold, dark spaces with no humanizing glimmer of promising light, *High Flyer* seemed to become warm, comforting, restful. Home. Which was the idea of her designers all along.

"The Vid Kids hauled off their stuff," Veronique reported briskly. She was trim but managed to have an Earth

Mother persona, a real trick in the astronaut corps. She was the crew comic, too, hearty when all the rest were withdrawn. Valuable beyond measure, on a long mission.

Viktor nodded. They had labeled the *Proserpina* crew with that name because they had anxiously asked for the latest vids the *High Flyer* might have brought—indeed, it was a big part of the "mail" they'd asked for from Earthside.

"Maybe they don't like their own company too much by now," Viktor said with a wry eyebrow lifted.

"How long have they been gone?" Veronique asked.

"Two years, five months," Julia supplied. "Time wears out the best of friends. Be grateful we're riding a fusion torch, not a fission one."

"They also tried out the smart-ship functions," Veronique said, stabbing at the air irritably. "One of them I found ordering a martini from ship's stores!"

"I know, I came in after you stormed out," Julia said wanly. "And ship was delivering, too. I never thought to ask before."

Veronique said sharply, "You should've protested! Hospitality is one thing, but—"

"Yes, is waste of ship time and resources," Viktor said mildly. "But is diplomacy here, too."

Veronique wasn't buying this, Julia could tell. She was a brilliant all-round type, good at six different skill sets, but a bit wearing when she got on a cause. Viktor started speaking in his mild, calming manner, and she left that job to the resident expert. Julia needed to get away from them all. *Far away.*

Decades of Mars duty had taught her to create her own privacy. Nothing like cramped quarters to concentrate the mind! She had learned to disappear within herself, walling out sounds and smells and vibrations, to create a still, silent space where she could live, rest, think. In the continual noise of the hab she had learned to hear well, diagnosing the ship's vibrations. But just as well, she knew how to listen carefully, or to deliberately not hear. An essential skill, taking years of daily practice to master.

Living in space created rituals and customs, even taboos, to keep buffers between people. This extended even to language, allowing her to politely avoid any question she didn't want to answer.

So she had insisted on this cabin artfully crafted of paper walls and tatami mats and small, delicate decorations. Simplicity made it easy to stay within her mass limit. And illusion helped. If it was high-resolution enough, even knowing that a view was phony did not rob it of its effect.

She sat cross-legged.

Watching a sunset on a personal wall screen was perfect for this. Listening to the interior rain—the fall of vapor sheets on each wall, images playing on their thin surfaces—brought delicate splashes into her concentration . . . and the present vanished.

The simple thatched hut sat on thick hardwood pylons above a sweep of immaculate white sand. Maples surrounded it, and she approached it on stepping-stones so perfectly set in the moss that they seemed to have grown there. On the veranda were sitting cushions, for seldom would anyone want to sit inside, in the single room of hewn beams and rustic screens. This ceremonial teahouse was for tea and thought alone.

All hers for now. She shared it only with Hiroshi Okada, and he was on 'bot duty. Crew needed their retreats, and Julia had in the long decades on Mars come to understand well the Japanese cultural way of dealing with an ever-pressing crowd you had to get along with. Getting away was the only strategy. She and Hiroshi had pooled their allotted ship space in this way.

She rose and entered the massless retreat she had fashioned herself—the essentials of a classic garden: stone, water, bridge, pavilion. They all hung in the spaces of her own private place. Only visual, but still telling, restful.

It was a cylindrical volume of falling mists, each a thin translucent sheet that descended in the light air as holographic projections played on its surface. A few feet away the pleasant moisture tingled in the nose, and the images framed the room into the Harmonies Garden of Wu Xi, a classic spiritual retreat. Cinnamon camphor trees perfumed the air. A tinkling waterfall splashed on worn stones. She sat in lotus position on a tatami mat and watched the cascading stream leap over convoluted limestone. The walls had curious cylindrical holes that had been worked by flows millions of years ago.

Stone.

Water.

Bridge.

Pavilion.

Until her next watch.

*   *   *

Three days later, the bare nugget sun now lost in the glare of their blaring fusion torch, she sat with Viktor and Veronique and tried to make sense of their new discoveries.

Veronique played them the complex waveforms, souped up from their original very low, infrasound frequencies around ten kilohertz, into the audible. It was the strangest symphony anyone had ever heard.

At times the haunting low notes were like the beating of a giant heart, or of great booming waves crashing with aching slowness upon a crystal beach, playing the ceramic sand like a resonating instrument. Julia felt the notes with her whole body, recalling a time when she had stood in a French cathedral and heard Bach played on the massive pipe organ that sent resounding through the holy stone box wavelengths longer than the human body, so the ear could not pick them up at all, but her entire body vibrated in sympathy. It was a feeling like being shaken by something invisible. It conveyed grandeur in a way beyond words.

And now the thing that made this strange symphony was tolling like an immense bell that itself enclosed an entire cathedral, and used it for the slow, swinging clapper.

Into her mind came the memory of a whale she had sighted offshore Sydney, breaching fully into the summer air. The long shape had burst nearly free of the sea, flukes turning lazily in the sharp sunlight. She had bought many recordings of their songs. Even if they had simple messages, she found them haunting.

Sitting back, she tried to envision what would radiate waves tens of kilometers long. To such creatures, humans might be as inconsequential as the lice that pestered the skin of a blue whale. The longest wavelengths *High Flyer* had detected (barely) were truly gigantic, up to a million times longer than those that ushered in classical radio astronomy. A century ago the center of the galaxy was detected by an amateur astronomer, Grote Reber, using a backyard dish strung from ordinary household wires on a wooden frame. He used wavelengths as big as a human. What could humans glimpse in wavelengths a million times larger?

Julia reminded herself that it was only because they were out here, beyond the dense plasmas blown out by the effervescent sun, that they could detect anything at all in this region of the electromagnetic spectrum. By accident *High Flyer* had strung its antenna elements along its great length, so they were seeing with an "eye" effectively hundreds of meters long. Yet even such an aperture could sense wavelengths of many kilometers only dimly. But they had detected those waves, and that had changed everything.

The great virtue of discovery, she mused, is that it raises more wondrous questions than it answers. She had a quick image of humanity's perceptual universe, expanding outward in a sphere from the sun. To be sure, they came to understand what lay in that increasing sphere's volume, in time. But the price—or reward—was that the surface of that sphere, the edge of the unknown, also increased. There was more known, but always more to be known.

Yes, she thought, *and the unknown can masquerade as the unknowable.*

She thought of the actual sphere of the solar wind and wondered if the sun at its center kept these huge beings at bay. Not so long ago, humans kept wolves prowling at the rim of their campfires—but not venturing farther in—out of fear. Did something like that keep these huge beasts from plunging into the realm of the planets?

And if so, should a mere ship venture into that dim twilight beyond the fiery campfire, where truly gigantic wolves might lurk?

6.

TINY THINGS

<THEY ARE COMING,> Serene sent from afar. She was cautious and wanted no part of any strange tiny things that intruded.

<This is your work!> Forceful said to Instigator.

<I did not bring this forth,> Instigator said, her intonation deflecting criticism. <And we did all approve my studies and experiments on the small world, to learn more of the ways of small life.>

<I sense danger here.> Mirk's signal worked with worried low notes.

<All due to you Inbounds,> Sunless said.

<This is yet another risk!> Ring charged. <Recall Incursor's fate!>

Instigator said sharply, <We do not know what befell Incursor.>

Mirk sent, <He was among the inner hot worlds. Perhaps he touched one, condensed, knew a True Death.>

<If anything happens, it is your fault, Instigator,> Chill said sternly.

<Isn't making things happen what we wish?> Instigator sent. <We seldom enjoy such opportunities to sample anything from the Hot.>

<We want discovery without danger!> Chill said.

A chorus of voices agreed. Subharmonics made a droning chorus of dread.

Recorder said slowly, as bespoke its age, <The two seldom go together.>

7.

SPIDER NET

VIKTOR WAS IRKED.

"Damn! We're flying straight, straight as arrow—and they're not."

Julia sat down in the parallel acceleration couch and for some reason, staring at the sprawled array of data and indicators and views fore and aft, remembered when she had been a teenager and had lived in a comfortably neat world, had believed utterly in the civilizing power of fresh lipstick and combed hair and not talking out of turn. Things had changed.

"Not being proper and orderly?" she asked him lightly.

"Making this plasma wire trick hard to work."

"They're not holding to course?"

"Getting buffeted, they say. Lighter ship, could be so."

"Display the net?" Julia asked Veronique. She did.

Proserpina was jiggling slightly, yes. The ships were thousands of kilometers apart, two piercing flames in the obsidian void. *Proserpina*'s fission glow was muted, its plasma not long lived. *High Flyer*'s flared brilliant blue-white behind them, fusion plasma alive with a vibrant in-candescence formerly seen only in the hidden hearts of suns.

Except—at higher resolution the image picked out ten-drils of snaky blue, each a thread connecting the ships. A spider net of plasma strands, the only way to listen to the deeps beyond. A grid for receiving waves of a scale no one had ever contemplated until now.

Their plan had been worked out by myriad plasma physicists sweating over test chambers and calculating pads, back Earthside. The first idea had been to eject a wire with tiny rockets at both ends. Fired off, they would uncoil the wire from a central processor and power supply, all left in *High Flyer*'s wake.

When the rockets played out, they would detach, leav-ing a wire a thousand kilometers long. This would unfurl the largest simple dipole antenna humanity had ever made. In the 1890s Marconi had made simple antennas like this, though those were about the size of himself—and he had changed the world. This time, a mere 150 years later, they might use such an antenna to discover beings beyond the imagination of anyone in the nineteenth century—except, that is, H. G. Wells.

It had been a pleasant image when Julia first heard of it. Stringing wire, like the radio pioneers. But too awkward, the engineers decided; too . . . well, massive. Even hair-thin wires thousands of klicks long add up.

So their ships carried plasma guns, not wires. The guns were marvels of artifice, able to emit steady streams of bar-ium ions and their court jesters, the electrons. These beams ran from *High Flyer* to *Proserpina*, slender and elegant.

Their own electrical currents provided the magnetic

fields that confined them to threads a bare centimeter wide. Unlike bulky wires, which can stretch quite little, twist only a bit, and often break, these plasma beams inherited the infinite flexibility of magnetic fields. These wrapped themselves around the currents that passed between ships. The bands of invisible magnetic loops could flex and swerve and contort to accommodate the varying distances between the huge spaceships. They kept contact going.

But they were also simply current carriers, like wires, only far more insubstantial and vulnerable. They worked as the effective wires of an antenna, stretched between the speeding ships at velocities of tens of kilometers per second.

These plasma pinches could pick up the waves incoming from the outer reaches, just as ordinary wires could. Processors aboard both ships then deciphered the oscillations in current and voltage as signals. H. G. Wells had never thought of this, much less Marconi.

"But what could make *Proserpina* jounce around?" Julia asked. "This is empty vacuum, after all."

"Not quite," Veronique said. "We're getting close to the bow shock. Ah yes—there, that ruby glow ahead." Diffuse radiance filled half the sky.

"But that's just where the plasmas meet. Thin stuff."

"Put it into a resonant wave, just about the size of your ship, and the effect piles up," Veronique said. "Like wind forcing oscillations in a bridge. Acting all along the side of *Proserpina*, it can hit that resonance. Or maybe just as bad, it's like a steady wind on a car. The faster we go, the bigger the effect."

"Ummm." Julia frowned, alarmed. *A threat in empty*

space? "Should we dive straight into the nose of the bow shock?"

"*Da.* Is closest part, the nose," Viktor said. "Like the prow of a ship, bow shock spreads out from it. We want to know what's up, best place to go."

Julia reminded herself that Viktor was captain, even if she was sleeping with him. She would keep her worries to herself for now. "If it can shove *Proserpina* around that way . . ."

"We are much bigger, heavier." Viktor grinned wickedly. "So is *Proserpina*. May lose the antenna, yes, but need the shock data. And will be fun. First persons to cross into interstellar space!"

Julia laughed. "Once a pilot, always one," she whispered to Veronique, not so soft he wouldn't hear.

"Not just for thrill," Viktor said soberly.

"You haven't forgotten that we're down to 28 percent on water?" Veronique said timidly.

Viktor glowered. "Of course not. We can run another month on that."

Veronique said evenly, "We're not supposed to run less than 20 percent."

"We'll find iceteroid, no problem," Viktor said decisively.

"I thought they were supposed to be pretty far apart out here," Julia put in. "We passed one a couple weeks back, though."

Viktor said bearishly, "We do not turn back."

"I didn't mean we should," Veronique said. "Just—"

"After we blow the nose"—Julia grinned at him as she said it—"we'll look for some ice to melt down."

With a curt nod Viktor said gruffly, "What I had in mind."

Julia could see that even after more than a year of crewing with them, Veronique was still working out how to deal with a married couple who could read each other's every unspoken cue.

"Check spectrum locus, eh?" Viktor said, pretty obviously trying to change the subject.

Veronique called up the mapping their plasma-net antenna was making. Spotty, but the conclusion was clear: "Most of the really long wavelength stuff is coming from around the nose," Veronique said.

"It's not just noise?" Julia asked.

In answer Veronique flipped on the audio. Long, humming chords. Thin leitmotifs atop that, skittering down the scale. A spray of sharp notes like harsh shouts in a distant fog.

"Working on the decoding?" Viktor asked, eyes never leaving the displays.

"You bet," Veronique said crisply. "I think I can break it into words soon."

"Words already? You're using just the SETI codes?" Julia asked wonderingly.

"Well, with a bit of spin of my own." Veronique grinned. "I think the other side is making it easy for us."

"The . . . source?"

"Sources. Near as I can tell, there are plenty of them."

Julia blinked. "You can tell them apart?"

"Except the rude ones. They talk over the others."

Viktor nodded. "Too many of us like that."

Julia was amazed. Decoding the low-frequency, long-wavelength signals had been a feat of intellectual daring.

After all, what could humans share with them? If the things that made the signals were large, in the depths of space beyond stars, maybe they were not even used to stable structures. She sat back and mused.

One could think of them as being like jelly creatures maybe, awash in a dark environment. They might not think mainly in terms of numbers, but of geometry. Their mathematics would be mostly topology, reflecting their concern with overall sensed structure rather than counting or size. They would lack combustion and crystallography but would begin their science on a firm foundation of fluid mechanics, of flows and qualitative senses.

But others Earthside argued that no matter what the environment, creatures that made it in a harsh place would evolve basic ideas like objects, causes, and goals. Still . . . what objects were hundreds of kilometers in size? Iceballs, all right, but creatures? And what about causes? Even in quantum mechanics the idea wasn't crystal clear.

Still, every environment had limits. Scarcity would bite, forcing the idea of realizable goals. Hardship would reward those who caused goals to come to pass, acting on whatever objects the vast creatures could see.

So maybe there were universals among intelligences, even if a bit abstract. The critical point had come with the realization that the harmonic structure of sound had a numerical key, that the notes of the scale were the ratios of whole numbers. This unlocked the code. *Do-re-mi,* a child's rhyme, had turned out to be fundamental.

A noted twencen physicist, Richard Feynman, once said, to the horror of some philosophers, that "the glory of mathematics is that we do not have to say what we are talking about." So sense could fly on the wings of mathematics, of encoding, without having to point to common, shared objects—chairs, sunsets, bodies—to make a sentence that made sense.

Beyond that, the argument descended into ornate relays of mathematics. Or maybe it ascended; anyway, Julia could not navigate the logic.

"What are they saying?" she asked.

"Sounds like . . ." Veronique paused. "Maybe warnings. Maybe threats."

Viktor grimaced. "Hard to know which I would prefer."

"Wiseguy is having problems. Context related. But it can translate to know they're talking—singing—about danger."

Julia had a momentary vision—an intuition, but from where?—of a spongy, swarming thing like a cloud. Yet also a thing of currents and whirling motion, a thinking tornado. And a thin extruded tendril of it—hesitant, flexing, touching, feeling . . . inward. A giant's rub.

8.

CASCADE

THE ETERNAL COOL GALE came howling in from Upstream. To meet it, a constant roar of the starwind came soaring out from the eternal, prickly Hot.

Sheets of heavy spray slashed at the Beings as they came to feed. Hot plasma streamers curled and smashed howling against their outer wings. The curling waves were steep and breaking into coils. Some of these gnawing whorls were large enough to engulf an entire Being, and when one did, it carried the hapless, rubbery shape of intense magnetic order down a slope of ravening turbulence, to dash it into rivulets that scoured its hide.

Then the Being would be buried gloriously in the food it sought—gorged on it, lacerated by the very energies it needed to live. This paradox dwelled at the center of their art and philosophy, the contradiction between feeding and being ravaged.

At the worst, not merely to be flayed by the frying of dying magnetic fields but to be cut, seared, feathered, and frayed. Diminished.

Most Beings knew how to skirt the worst of it, skating the edge while absorbing magnetic whorls and digesting them into stronger fields within themselves. They valued the helicity above all, the twisted fields that carried the tight strands like rubber bands, that enabled a Being to confine itself. Sinew gave strength.

Yet the awesome power of the Cascade never deterred, for this was the peak joy for them all. They rolled and basked and breached in the slide of the interstellar plasma, a torrent eternally incoming, smashing against the resolute wind from the distant Hot.

Together as always, Mirk and Sunless were hogging over the crests of blithe helicity, sliding down their slick slopes. Their very perimeters sagged and staggered under the chop, absorbing energies and being seared by them, a thousand eating tongues forking into their magnetic skin.

Joy came sliding in with the spitting fear, always. Some Beings dreaded the necessity of the Cascade. Others longed for the shaking, slamming, pitching verve of it.

Chill and Dusk broke with glee through mountainous crests, skating on the seethe. Battered, they lunged into the roar of magnetic storms and spitting ions, rolled and swamped by them, besting them with cries of triumph. Hissing fires lit in their bufferskins.

Swimming, they sang.

<Ah, the young,> Recorder said, feeding sedately on minor vortices.

<They are older than some stars,> Ring chimed.

<Tell me again whose Protos they are,> Forceful said.

<Some of ours, once. We helped in their upbringing, as I recall,> Ring sent in diplomatic calming notes. <Time erodes such specificities.>

<Merriment has its place, and this is it,> Instigator sent, lolling from one great churning crest of magnetic twist to the next. <Ah!>

Instigator adroitly sucked in the morsels of delicious helicity, absorbing their angular momentum. Pleasure suffused its body, a shape sleek and slim and the size of planets. It loved basking in the surges of energy as some of its unwanted hair-fine fields—ugly, with frayed ends, unsightly tangles, and nets—dissolved in heat and plasma jets. Knots that Instigator could never unwind it let meet other such repulsive, contorted messes fresh in from interstellar space.

Fizz! Hideous, snarling wrath dissolved into balmy energy. Whenever fields of opposite direction were shoved together, the opposites canceled. Their energies flared beautifully along Instigator's lean flanks, lighting up its best features. It thought its elegantly tapered in-mouth was the best, a purse like no other among the Beings. And its marvelous antennas: streams of elegantly confined plasma, arcing to and fro as tasteful advertisement. Through these it knew the Whole, and what other agency of itself should be as beautiful?

Part of the refinement of this harvest was in just *this* state, Instigator thought. Bliss, while tumbling mouthlong into the abyss. The Cascade.

For they were shooting down the coiling rapids. At their backs pressed the Upstream, heavy and eternal, cool and certain. Here came the interstellar plasma and gas, the charged and uncharged wedded by their long association, all coasting along at their minor velocities between the stars. Until the Hot came plowing along its great path, the arc that would take it all the way around the Hub in due time, circling the entire galaxy. In the frame of the Beings, carried along by the Hot's slow sway, the Upstream was the eternal storm that fed them. Manna.

All along the parabola of the Hot's province, vast turbulence negotiated the collision of Hot and Stream. Squalls larger than worlds perpetually broke there, in energies comparable to the pale Hotlight that shed upon this.

<Something coming!> Mirk called.

<From the curl!> Chill supplied.

Curling out of the churn, they all caught the low-frequency wave front.

<Hotcloud!> Sunless shouted. These came seldom and could be rich.

<I sense it is fruitful,> Recorder said slowly. <Thick, fresh—not collisioned, dulled, and slumbering.>

Hotclouds were the occasional nuggets that came forth when the Hot raged. Furious and doomed, Hotclouds came from storms that burst into froth. As they rose, they ebbed, died. The Hotclouds' bounty was gained at the expense of a framework that might have made a Being. But it would be a rebuke not to feast upon the vagrant energies remaining in the Hotcloud, after all. The cloud was thick plasma, cooling and clasping its fields poorly. It was child's play— and if a child were nearby, it would be encouraged to be the first—to rip this poor bag and eat its momentary wealth.

Ring began, <We may have children nearby, Protos.>

<The nearest is hundreds of Beings away,> Recorder said. This was the old way of measuring distance, though Beings varied greatly in size according to age and whether they had ever been Diminished. <And this coming thing is not good food.>

It smelled wrong, scorched and bristling. Too . . . alive. Hotclouds had settled into decay and were easily torn. This torch cut upward through the waves, not minding the curl of them, boring, cutting outward.

<So tiny but so angry,> Ring observed warily.

<We should back away!> Chill said, the nearest to it. Chill flexed away from the speeding bite.

Forceful spoke for the first time. <All avoid it. Now!>

Too late. The Hotpoint punched through the strong field blanket Chill had raised to protect itself. Fields flared and died as the onrushing lance of plasma punched through Chill. Long, agonizing peals came from Chill. Shells of opposite currents peeled away. Dusk, Chill's linkmate, fell away in a panic. The very tones of Chill's outcry shifted as layers swamped and filled with virulent plasma, stifling chords.

<It is too quick!> Recorder sent.

<Catch the plasma shells as they uncoil!> Dusk called, struggling toward Chill's raked image. <Chill's mental architectures will die quickly if we cannot—>

A sudden searing wail froze them. Chill was being stripped by the warm, fast electrons. Flowing faster than field knots could impede them, they made new conducting paths within the vast body. Charges long held apart suddenly united. Frenzy. Memories and structural parts of Chill popped and moaned in pitiful low tones . . . and fell silent.

<Pull away!> called Mirk from afar, but it was far too late.

Chill splintered now. They all rushed to capture parts of Chill as he shredded. Shards of plasma caught in magnetic traps fumed free, lost. Colossal flares burst along the body as fields, newly connected by the ravening plasma, canceled each other out. This liberated raw energy blew apart more parts of the rupturing body.

<I can see the center of it,> Instigator said. <I matched speed with it—so fast!—and above the center all is dark.>

<An object!> someone called.

<Your damnable small cold things!> Sunless shouted.

<It is tiny,> Instigator went on carefully. <Not anything I—we—have made, I assure you. It is one of the small hot solids from the inner worlds. I did not think it was dangerous.>

<Do not mind what it is, kill it!> Forceful sent in shrill tones.

Instigator said, <I think the hot plasma spews from the cold ship.>

<Impossible!> Sunless sent. <Hotter makes hot, not colder.>

<Not now.> Instigator's words carried menace. <I will try to stuff the plasma hotness into the tiny cold creature. See what it can withstand.>

Mirk sent mournfully, <Parts of Chill! I am finding shards . . .>

<I compacted myself.> Instigator was grim. <I clasp the Hotpoint plasma—now.>

Mirk sent, <. . . that is all there is now.>

<I have it! I choke it!> Instigator cried in triumph.

9.

RAM PRESSURE

"DRIVE FAIL!" VIKTOR SHOUTED. "Right in middle."

"Burn failing in the core?" Veronique asked. "I'll—"

"No—getting back pressure." Viktor's hands flew in the command gloves, but the complex, luminous display hanging before him did not change. "Plasma coming back into the magnetic nozzle. Damn!"

"How can it?" Veronique called Hiroshi for backup while the picture before them both worsened. The plume they saw from two aft cameras was bunching up, as if rippling around some unseen obstacle. The logjam thickened as they watched. Vibrations came through the deck, all the way from hundreds of meters down the long stack.

"Getting a lot of jitter," Veronique reported. "Building up."

"Ram pressure is inverting profile," Viktor said crisply. "Never happens, this. Not even in simulations."

"I can *feel* it," Veronique said. "This much vibration, this far away, the whole config must be—"

"Too much plasma jamming back into the throat." Viktor gestured to where the side profile of the engine showed the blue magnetic hourglass-shaped throat. No matter could survive the fused plasma that flowed along that pinch-and-release flaring geometry. Made of fields, it could adjust at the speed of light to changes in the furious ions that rushed down it, fresh from their fusion burn. But it could only take so much variation before snarling, choking—and blowing a hole.

"I must shut down," Viktor said with icy calm.

"But we'll—"

"Go to reserve power."

"That won't last long," Veronique said as she did it.

Hiroshi worked sending data, his voice grim. "*Proserpina*'s behind us; seems okay, though. We're getting lots of plasma pressure. Must be the bow shock."

Julia burst in, face flushed. The sphere of electrosensors registered her presence and decided to ignore her. Viktor's hands moved in the air, capturing and changing ship controls. "What's—," she began, and seeing Viktor's face, stopped in midsentence.

A long, low note rang through the ship. No one had heard that sound since training. The drive had not been off since then. Muted, yes—as they maneuvered near Pluto—but never gutted and silent.

Over audio came a buzzing. "What's that?" Julia asked.

"Not from the engine," Veronique said, "that's for sure."

"Can you localize?" Viktor asked, eyes not moving from the control space before him.

"Yeah, it's—hell, all around us." Veronique looked puzzled. "Low-frequency stuff."

"Listen," Julia said softly, "it's almost like a song."

10.

SORE DIMINISHED

<You killed it!> Ring cried with glee.

Dusk echoed all their joy. <Crack the cold tiny thing!>

<I cannot,> Instigator sent. <I have no way to hold it. It has done something, turned inward. The fields at its hot end, they withdrew, sucked back into the cold body.>

<Afraid!> Forceful celebrated. <The tiny thing is quite properly afraid.> Others joined in its joy.

<How is Chill?> all wanted to know. Even distant Beings, just hearing on the fast frequencies of the attack, chimed in, much delayed.

<Fragments. Sore . . . Diminished.> Dusk was dazed, slow.

<It will repair,> Ring said. <I will give of my parts to rebuild.>

<Thanks to all,> Mirk broadcast as others poured in with promises of help. Already, streamers of augmented field nuggets began to arrive near the Chill spaces. Gingerly parts of the great body began the slow labor of remaking their inventories, pressures, currents, and knots. What memory remained within Chill itself would, of course, be honored in the reconstruction and spliced in seamlessly. But some was lost forever. To be so rudely, abruptly Diminished was the worst of fates. It meant strands of selfhood cut, continuity amputated. Among all Beings near and far, a loss.

<I am alongside the fragments, wrapping around.> In-

stigator sounded firm and sure, but with an undertone of apprehension it could not disguise.

<Very good,> Forceful said. <I am coming to help.>

<It is a small cold shard now, slippery in my grip.>

<I will coil in from your topmouth, to help,> Forceful said.

<I feel the pressures again,> Instigator said. <It feels like—>

In defense Instigator had made a hollow column of itself. Actinic violence flared there. Instigator screamed. A white-hot lance gouged in its bowels. The cutting sword shot out of the cold thing, roaring in mad rage. Instigator unwrapped, coiling away from the flaring plume. She tried to veer away from exploding radiance but left shreds of herself behind.

Panic. A chorus of screams pealed into the distance as Beings sensed the eruption.

<I am burned,> Instigator sent. <But safe.>

<I am alongside!> Forceful called. <Hurry, it is going fast away.>

<Clear away from its path!> Ring ordered all those younger, who were many. They scattered, sending pips and yelps.

Recorder sent, <It is so small, on the end of this lance. Can we use that?>

Forceful said angrily, <We can knock the cold vessel off the hot jet! Make it turn.>

<If all together—yes, come!> Instigator was almost joyful. <If we all together—>

In a rush, pressures gathered from all those Beings within range. Magnetic fields can thicken and flex as quickly as light, bringing vector forces to bear.

<All on one side!> Forceful sang, in its element.

They heaved and worked, all Beings nearby sliding sections of themselves together into a thin disk. This sliced against the tubular throat at the base of the small cold thing. The arc shuddered and fought along its length as the throat that formed it worked feverishly to adjust to sudden sideways thrusts. The system could not cope with the canny way the magnetic disk cut, moved and tilted, cut again.

<It is toppling!> Forceful sent in triumph.

11.

DRAGONS IN THE NIGHT

"DAMN! HAVE TO SHUT DOWN again," Viktor said grimly.

They were all rotating slowly, hanging sideways in their couches. The entire ship moved as it had never been meant to. Creaks and groans ran along it, big booms and warning clangs echoing down the softly lit passageways.

"The throat's going?" Julia asked.

"Malfing." Viktor spoke clearly through clenched teeth. "Big error signals. Does not explain itself."

"Yeah, systems analysis says it doesn't know why," Veronique added. "No simulation—"

"Shutting down now," Viktor said. The rumbling aft faded. Eerie popping noises came through the support beams around their cabin. Creakings. A sour stench of something scorched. The display space before Viktor and Veronique seemed calm.

"That buzzing again," Julia said.

"I got better directionals this time," Veronique said firmly. "I rotated some aft antennas, the sideband controllers, too."

"Where's it from?" Viktor asked. "Around us, yes?"

Veronique frowned. "Intensity plot—well, look at this. Max on the sides. I thought it'd be in the rear someplace. Something to do with the nozzle shutdown."

Julia watched the shape form up, a filmy blue image on the screen before them all. "Damn," she said. "A wedge of magnetic fields and plasma. It's running alongside us. Keeping up. Even though we're tumbling."

"The emission region, look. Big, yes—we have found the source of the low waves," Viktor said. "Nasty, too, they are. Trying to kill us."

"What'll we do?" Julia asked. *We went looking for dragons, and now we found them.* "We can't tumble like this forever. The plasma antenna grid—it's out of commission, like this."

"These things won't go away, I bet," Veronique said. "What *are* they?"

"Dragons," Julia said. "Dragons in the night."

Viktor grimaced. "So we punch back. I'll fire a small side jet, rotate on the other axis, take our aft around on them."

Julia saw what he meant as his hands traced a command system into being in the space before him. A faint rumbling began. The ship began to slide sideways, or that's how it felt to her. Multiple-axis accelerations had never been her strong point in training, and that had been decades ago.

Her head spun, her stomach lurched. Yet she felt awe at the presence of these immense . . . things.

Viktor glanced at her, frowned in concern. "Is okay?"

Julia said softly, "I'm glad somebody knows what to do."

"I try, is all." He winked.

The sliding feeling got worse, and something strummed deeply, amid more popping noises.

"Ready power up?" Viktor called to Veronique. "We be fast now."

"Roger."

The surge made Julia's gorge rise. Whirling, wrenching—she held on.

"*High Flyer*, coming in on port approach," came Shanna's clear voice. "We're out at 1,237 klicks, closing slow. Gather you have trouble."

"Something we can't see with eyes, yes," Viktor called back. "But on-screen . . ."

"Dragons," Julia said. "Stay well clear of the plasma emission zone, Shanna."

Viktor brought up a picture with *Proserpina*'s bright flare at its center. Wisps of ivory luminescence crawled across the image, blurred as if out of focus. "To port. Acquiring your close-upped image. Your burn looks stable."

"Right, but between us there're some vague shapes," Shanna said. "Like worms, coiling around each other."

"Plasma discharges, I'll bet," Veronique said. "I saw some, back in the days when I did lab work at Caltech. They're diffuse, like a neon light, but they're long threads. Means there must be pretty powerful magnetic fields around them."

"Ummmm," Viktor murmured, staring at the traceries

that moved like kelp in the slow wash of tides. "Magnetic pressure we can counter with plasma pressure, right?"

"Good idea," Shanna said sharply. "Bringing our tail around."

"*Da.*"

Proserpina's image began rotating. The bright flare of its drive glared as it came around to point in their direction. Julia could see filigrees of exhaust licking out across the great distance, moving at tens of kilometers per second, to judge by the scale. Where the wash of it struck, the threads of ivory plasma shredded, blown apart. Their soft glow dissolved.

"Got them!" Shanna called.

"Copy that. Pour it on," Viktor called happily. "I'm bringing ours around, too."

More lurching. A nasty rumble in the deck. Julia hung on.

12.

HARD PLASMA

<IT CUTS!> MIRK CRIED. <Sharp!>

<The other hotshot has turned!> Dusk called. <It expands now—so fast.>

Mirk called, <We are caught between them.>

<Back away, all!> Recorder sent at high amplitude.

<I am wounded,> Forceful reported calmly.

<I, too,> Dusk admitted, her tone laced with skittering pain.

They were all withdrawing, trailing some fields they would lose in their haste. The example of Chill had brought caution to them all.

<It burns as bright as ever,> Instigator said ruefully. <We did not hurt it, only interrupt.>

<Let us keep pace, however,> Recorder said. <We are not so hurt as to let this affront pass.>

<No, no, no,> all chorused—all but Chill, who was silent and would probably be so for some time. With Diminishment came not only damage but loss of status. <Do not let them escape.>

<To where?> Recorder said. <Both came from the Hot but show no signs of wishing to return.>

Mirk sent, <See—they turn, as if to run alongside the Cascade.>

Their pursuit had carried them safely upstream of the roaring Cascade, but they still felt vibrations and shocks from it reverberate through their bodies.

A long silence hung between them. Each mended its skin and currents, rebuilding where hard plasma had torn raw gouts in filmy magnetic structures. In the quiet, upstream from the thunder and boom of the Cascade, a faint whispering came to them. Jittery spikes came from the two tiny cold things.

<Hear that?> Sunless and Dusk sent together.

<It is not froth from the Cascade?> Ring asked. <So busy!>

Sunless sent a slick burst of layered nuances, piling language into stacks. <See? This is how they arrange their speech.>

<You think it is speech?> Dusk asked. <So noisy!>

<We can decode it, I think, in time,> Sunless answered. <See you, it is not too greatly different from the orderings we receive in the startalk frequencies. There is a mathematical ordering here. If we can find its cues . . .>

<Do this work, yes, Sunless,> Forceful said. <There must be sense to all of this.>

Recorder sent a long, thoughtful roll of waves, whose import was, <Do we think—is it possible?—this an intermediary from Incursor?>

Mirth greeted this. <Impossible!> Forceful said.

Dusk dismissed the idea. <Such as we surely cannot grow from tiny cold kernels.>

<We came of grander stuff,> Ring added. <And not cold! Not solid!>

Recorder recoiled a bit from the chorus of derision. <But these come from inward, and so may know how Incursor fares—if he lives, still.>

<Such motes?> Forceful said. <What could they know?>

Dusk added, <No true intelligence can reside in chilly specks!>

Someone farther out sent, without an identity signature, <The Laws of Beings do not permit it. Obviously.>

Recorder said patiently, <We should always ask ourselves how to use any new thing, to gain access to the Well.>

Forceful sent striations red with disagreement. <We are living in a fortunate time. The Cascade presses in toward the Hot, as it has not done for a long era. Let us take advantage of this moment! Use it to destroy the tiny life on

the inner worlds. Stop them from coming out here, or else we shall share Chill's fate.>

Recorder's aura became uneasy. <I remind us all that the last time the Upstream delivered such high flows, forcing the Cascade inward, we made no progress in learning of that fearsome region. We surely do not want to venture so far in that we would meet Incursor's fate.>

Forceful bristled, shimmering its outline. <Past failure is not an argument.>

<We have experienced many of these inward incursions of the Cascade.> Recorder sent them all a picture of past ages. Images laced among them all—of eras when, under the Upstream's rising pressure, the Cascade had pressed in upon the orbits of the giant worlds. <Each time, we venture a bit inward but fail to learn much that is useful.>

<Remember those who became trapped inward,> Dusk added, <and are lost to us.>

<We have not forgotten,> Ring sent mournfully, tinged with a sad aura.

They all knew that Ring was the closest relation to Incursor, lost long ago to inward, near the Hot—a tragic, historical agony.

<Do not forget our successes,> Instigator insisted. <Remember how we pushed some of the little iceballs inward, carefully targeting them to strike the inner worlds. That was a triumph!>

<So from the flares of the iceballs' impact, we learned some of this 'chemistry' you love so much,> Ring said adamantly. <I am not impressed with knowing such dirty facts.>

<All learning can be useful,> Instigator said firmly. <Will be useful, in time.>

Dusk sent, <Far better to learn at a distance, never venturing Inbound. Instigator learned much of chemistry that way. Incursor sent us the molecules that can copy themselves, recall. *That* was a triumph! For which it paid dearly.>

Instigator said, <Without those I could not have assembled and tuned my experiment on the small, near world. Even with them I had to resort to electroshaping them. Then I was forced—with noble Chill and sly Crafter—to devise the Darksiders, all to prune and tune my little coldworld experiment. Troubles, yes—but knowledge demands this.>

Into the middle of this came a long, pleading note. <I petition to address you all.> It was Chill.

Forceful sent, as custom required, <Approach and speak.>

<I apologize for my failure in our engagement with the small, cold, solid thing. I am humiliated by my wounds and ask to be Diminished.>

A rustle of concern washed among the Beings, who had drawn nearer.

Forceful said, <We need your abilities, not merely your presence. Diminished, you would be of less use to us at this pressing time.>

Chill replied with a clear shame aura. <I have begun to compose my poem-song, that by custom I should create.>

Consternation swept through the Beings. This was a major step, one that left no doubt about Chill's resolve.

<Oh no, please do not!> Dusk sent.

<I must.>

Beings could fray, dissipate, then recompose. Feeding lustily in the Cascade ran the risk of such erosions. This was where the more primordial of Beings had learned the arts of suffering loss and then rebuilding themselves. By oozing soft currents, carefully using the eternal laws of induction and conduction, those early, rather dim intelligences had with agonizing slowness mastered Resurrection over Diminishment. The galaxy had spun in its eternal gyre fully fifteen times before the Beings had fathomed how to become immortal.

But only if they wished. Resurrection soon—on a time scale whose long unit was that gyre—became of far greater significance. The Resurrection skills allowed Beings to manifest in fresh form. To choose Diminishment—not merely to *suffer* it from the outrageous surges of the Cascade or the magnetic insults of a passing molecular cloud—was an act of nobility and honor. It could lead to the highest status among all Beings, near and far.

One's fate in life, all Beings held, was set by deeds performed in past Manifestations. Previous wise acts yielded, in time, superior magnetic shapes in this present life. Bad or stupid acts gave the reverse—poor character, low status, even ruin.

Since the Origin, Beings had passed through many Manifestations. Some traces of these past lives and deeds still lingered in core memory. Those feather-light remembrances were the breath of eternity, the high wisdom of previous selves.

How beautiful life therefore was, and how sad. How fleeting, suspended in a limitless *now* that embodied all that had come before, but was still now, the only time one could change. Eternity stretched away in both time directions, while a Being was pinned to the moment. Such was the state of Being.

<I forbid it!> Forceful sent.

Chill insisted. <I ask permission to subtract by humble self-reconnection.>

<We need you now,> Dusk said anxiously.

<I could use a time, going into the great void before Remanifestation.>

Recorder said, <Permission refused.>

<Might you approve later?> Chill asked plaintively. <I beg again to end myself.>

Recorder said, <You are needed.>

<Then I apologize. Allow me to do something of hazard, that I may redeem myself.>

Instigator fizzed with excitement. <I do have an idea, one you could aid in. Chill, you are a smaller Being— deft, agile. If Crafter's arts can be brought to bear, you might be able to insert yourself into these tiny solid bodies. Thinly. It would be dangerous. But we need now to make direct contact, to test if intelligence lurks in such microscopic scales.>

The other Beings sent cries and shimmering auras of alarm. Some fizzed with anger at the very idea.

But Chill answered, <Show me how.>

13.

BURNT-YELLOW FINGERS

IN THE AFTERMATH OF the assault, Julia retreated into her meditations. After time in the sliding vapor world of her Japanese garden she knew what to do next.

Years before, while adapting to Mars, she had discovered by Web browsing the melancholic poetry of A. E. Housman, an English poet dead now well over a century. A particular piece of that man's wisdom she and Viktor had applied:

> Ah, spring was sent for lass and lad,
> 'Tis now the blood runs gold,
> And man and maid had best be glad
> Before the world is old.

Sex, after all, was the flip side of death.

So she and Victor had a ritual. They answered every brush with danger—and there were many, particularly in the years they held on together at Gusev—by making love, laughing, shouting out their joy in the moment, thumbing their noses at gloomy ol' fate. *Ah!—yes.*

Afterward they talked. The crew could keep track of the electromagnetic blizzard their plasma net was delivering. *Proserpina* was flying in clean formation now, so they could use all their gossamer plasma-web ability. Earthside was gobbling up the broadband data feed, analyzing, theorizing, decoding the long strings of mystery.

They talked about mysteries, too. The discovery of life on Mars had ignited an ongoing debate Earthside, of course. The prevailing view now emerging was not that of the chattering classes of the long-dead twencen. Back then, all the smart folk thought that the universe was a pointless cosmic joke, on us.

Now the Martian experience—delving into whether weird, world-spanning, and ornate molds were sentient— had opened the plausible case that the universe was a meaningful entity. Increasingly it seemed to be made down at the lawmaker's level to generate life and then minds. Brute forces seemed bound, inevitably to yield forth systems that evolution drove to construct models of the external world. Inevitably those models worked better if they had a model of . . . well, models. Themselves. A sense of self.

So if even archaebacteria could evolve in Martian caverns into thinking beings, then a whole landscape of mind opened. Admittedly the Marsmat had rather inscrutable traits. Still, the tantalizing suggestion had emerged, from all their fieldwork. Could evolution yield up, along strange paths, beings who could discern truth, apprehend beauty? Maybe even yearn for goodness and define evil, experience mystery, and feel love? Even allowing for the human habit of projecting their minds' traits onto other species, that was a compelling possibility, to just about everybody. Yet Julia had to remind herself that yearning was not proof.

Viktor was, of course, ever the skeptic. "What of these things that try to disable my ship?"

Julia grinned, suitably relaxed. "We're on their turf. Remember, when Leif Eriksson landed in the New World, the first thing to meet him was a flight of arrows."

Viktor scowled. "These things, big as buildings—already I see on Net that ignorant people Earthside think these are gods or something!"

Julia poked him and wrestled around among the bedding until she was sitting on top of him. "So what if they do?"

Viktor snorted. "Is childish. People want gods who pay attention to them, is all."

She held his wrists down and demanded, "You mean, can humans claim any spiritual special status? Compared with what?"

He gave her a broad, silent smile that said he could easily tumble her off but wouldn't. She persisted, "Look, we both came out of a Christian background."

"Not me! Was brought up to be proper atheist."

"Yes, another gift of the Soviets." She remembered the church her family had attended, pillars and vaulting white as plaster, like a cast around the broken bone of faith. Still . . . "Christianity has the most to lose from intelligent aliens, right? Jesus was *our* savior. Dolphins and gorillas and supersmart aliens—he didn't die for them."

"Um." Viktor sighed, resigned to a discussion. "Jesus was God's only son, yes?"

"The Bible says so."

"So unless God has the same son go around to every planet . . ."

"Or wherever these things we've found live—"

"Dying at every one of them? I am no expert, but— seems cruel."

"Worse, it means part of God has to go around dying all the time."

"Am glad I'm not a theologian."

"Me, too. I looked up this stuff, and there's even a quotation about Christianity and extraterrestrials from Thomas Paine, the American revolutionary—over two centuries old! He said"—she glanced at her notepad, on their side table—"Let's see, *He who thinks he believes in both has thought but little of either.* Ouch!"

"I wonder if is right way to think of intelligence, anyway. These big creatures—have consciousness maybe, but how about ethics? Sin?"

"I'm pretty sure they'll fear death. Sin? Hell, I don't believe in that! And ethics—well, sure, in the sense of social rules."

"Social rule is like take off hat when enter room. Ethics, you need philosophy."

"Okay, any social being will need some philosophy. But—"

"I am social, do not need philosophy."

She grinned. "You only think you don't. We don't know how to think about ETs, that's for sure. Can one become a Muslim? A Jew?"

Viktor gave her a soulful look, big brown eyes liquid in the hard incandescent light. "Your meditation, the Japanese thing—it's about this?"

She sat back uncomfortably. "I suppose. The Buddhists and Hindus seem the least threatened by advanced aliens—they took the Marsmat in stride, remember?"

"Does idea of alien Jew make sense?"

"To who? Maybe not to us. But they do have a big, open idea of God."

Viktor frowned and grunted skeptically. "Those Baptist and evangelical guys who attacked the Marsmat finding . . ."

"Right, they're the opposite. But they've been losing out lately, Earthside."

"So now we have a big God, coming out of cosmic evolution, give us the biological universe? Better than the supernatural one of the ancient Near East, sure."

"I'll buy that."

"Only, makes me wonder. These things we find—are they extraterrestrials?"

She paused. "Oh, I see—do they have a planet?"

"Maybe they live on iceballs, maybe not. Hard to see how they get so big, on small worlds."

She frowned. "But they must've."

"Or are they maybe this big God you talk about?"

"Oh, come on."

"This God might show up in person—wrong word, but you know what I mean—sometime."

"Now? Here?" She chuckled uneasily.

"God needs only be better than we are. Not perfect."

"I see . . . Never mind who made the whole universe, maybe there are bigger minds than ours already in it?" She laughed, head tilted back. "So until the Creator shows up, we can get by worshiping something that's better than us?"

"We are at edge of solar system. Maybe once we get out of our cage, we get a prize."

"Hmmm . . . And you said you didn't deal in theology."

An alarm clanged. Their comm beeped. Hiroshi said, "We're getting a lot of high voltages in the plasma net. Big signals."

"How's drive?" Viktor demanded.

"Running hot and smooth," Veronique said.

"Coming!" Viktor called.

They hustled into clothes and got up to the bridge double time. The audio piping in a spectral summary of the electromagnetics was blaring through the spaces where the entire crew was on duty. Julia said, "Turn it down," and from the lower frequencies came again the strange symphony she had heard, haunting in its sense of meanings layered in harmonics.

"Big voltages in the whole antenna system," Veronique said tersely.

"Damn!" Hiroshi waved his hands in the active control space, trying to keep ahead of the surges. Viktor barked orders to them and the other crew, all in their work pods. A sour smell of tension crept into Julia's nostrils, and the scent was not all her own.

"We're getting feed-through," Veronique called. "Something's putting big inductive voltages in the whole damn plasma array."

Viktor blinked. "How far away is *Proserpina*?"

Veronique rapped out, "One thousand seventy-three klicks."

"What can put voltages all along a plasma conductor *that* long?" Veronique asked.

Nobody answered. The visible control display surged with red readings. "We're getting in deep here," Julia said softly.

Veronique cried, "Systems crash!"

Hiroshi leaped up. "I can't shut down the antenna systems at all. It's feeding *back* into us—"

A yellow arc cut through the space before them. They all bailed out of their couches and lay flat on the deck as the snapping, curling discharge twisted in the air above. Viktor called, "Stay down! It's some high-voltage phenom—"

The crackling thing snarled around itself. Sparks hissed into the air. Coils flexed, spitting hard orange light. When a coil approached the metal walls, it veered back, snaking into the open space. A smell like burned carbon filled the air. The foot of it flared into blue-white, keeping contact with the wall terminals where the antenna systems all fed. Julia watched it, keeping flat on her back.

Viktor said, "To break down air, the voltage is—"

"Megavolts," Veronique snapped. "Stay flat. Stick your head up, it'll draw current, fry you."

"They—it—is trying to kill us," Hiroshi said through clenched teeth.

The audio raged. Sparks snapped. Nobody moved. Then the discharge arched and twisted and abruptly split. Yellow-green strands shaped into . . .

"Human shape!" Viktor said. "Making . . . like us."

The shape was like a bad cartoon, never holding true for long. Elongated legs, wobbly head, arms that flailed about in crimson disorder, hands jutting out, flailing, and then collapsing into sizzle and flicker.

Julia felt her heart thump. "They can see us! So they're sending us an echo, an image to—make some kind of . . . communication?"

The figure wriggled and sputtered. Julia raised her right hand slightly into the singed air. A long moment. Then slowly, agonizingly, the figure moved, too. It raised its left hand, mirror image. Wavered. The hand flexed, and with a feeling of visible effort, shaped itself carefully into . . . fingers. Thumb. The skin of it was yellow-bright, surging like the surface of the sun in hot brilliance. Meanwhile, the body faded into a pale ivory discharge, an electrical fog flickering on and off as if barely able to sustain the sizzling voltage.

The Marsmat did something like this. Somehow they know we are visual animals. Maybe this is a universal way to make contact. Get into the other's frame of perception . . .

Julia slowly flexed her fingers. The echoing fingers moved, too, suffused in a waxy, saffron-mellow glow. It hovered in the air unsteadily, holding pattern, all energies focused on the shimmering, burnt-yellow hand.

"Let's try—," Viktor began.

The arc snapped off. There was nothing in the air but a harsh, nose-stinging stench.

Veronique was sobbing softly. Hiroshi jumped up and turned in all directions but could see nothing to do. Somehow there was in the space an aching sense of vacancy.

Viktor patted Veronique on the shoulder, her mouth open and working but unable to say anything.

Hiroshi said, "They . . . want to talk?"

"Talk?" Julia recalled what Viktor had said: *This God might show up in person sometime.* She laughed with a high, nervous edge.

14.

STICK-OUTS

<THEY ARE TRULY TINY!> Chill cried, awed.

<Who?> Crafter's tones were, as always, somber and

of exceptionally long wavelength. The other Beings had to strain to hear them.

Chill's voice wavered up the narrow spectrum. Long tones came from the blanket Chill had formed around the solid, moving ships. It kept a gingerly distance from the spewing plasma plumes. <The motes. I slipped in—such small spaces!—and framed my eyes into receiving antennas. I saw them! Shaped so odd. Not like a classical figure at all. Not elegant, like us. Is there such a thing as a chemical shape, Instigator?>

<I have no idea,> Instigator sent, deeply confused. Chemistry was the province of itself and of Crafter, because they were the only ones who cared for such ugly, liquid matters. But a chemical *shape*? What would masses driven by such blundering energies make themselves into? It strained the imagination. <Send describing images.>

<Five stick-outs from a rectangle—I can say picture no better. I saw four of these shapes.>

A chorus of disgust, wonder, alarm. <How did they change?> Ring asked.

Chill's aurora surged with excited puzzlement. <That is the oddity. They kept shape! Instead, one of them moved one of its stick-outs.>

Instigator was beginning to doubt all this. Chill might be merely having delusions, brought on by the extremity of what it had attempted. Even with Crafter's help the task was probably impossible, after all. <How?>

<They hold to shape,> Chill answered. They could all see that he had unwrapped from the speeding mote, careful not to diffuse into the plume of hard plasma that bloomed behind it. <Sticks-outs upon stick-outs—very strange. Then it moved. I moved to echo. It did, too!>

<Chemical intelligence?> Forceful fumed redly. <Nonsense.>

<Not!> Mirk shot back. <Chill has redeemed itself supremely. Has discovered more than even Instigator.>

Forceful said, <I will go into the thing. I do not like these motes. Crafter! Come—help me.>

Crafter was silent.

Chill sent, alarmed, <Do not!>

Ring screamed, <I can't go with you.> She fearfully unlinked from Forceful.

<Must.> Forceful made its way toward the flaring, killing plume. <Must.>

15.

THE VIOLENCE OF THE AMPERES

THEY WERE STANDING AROUND, babbling in the way people have when tension is suddenly released, an aroma rising from them, all nervous and quick-eyed and chattering. Primate patterns.

Then the alarm clanged again. Hair stood on end.

Julia dove for the floor. Veronique did, too, but she was the last to do so, and she paid for it.

The burnt-yellow discharge surged from the antenna board, snarling. The air bristled. A tendril shot forth and caught Veronique as she fell. She crackled with the violence of the amperes that surged through her. Julia watched as Veronique's mouth opened, a shrill shriek escaped—

and then the mouth locked open, frozen. Smoke fumed from her hair.

Veronique jerked, screamed. Her blue coverall sparked at the belt. She struck the deck, tiny fires arcing from her fingers. Her hair burned away in a flash. She shuddered, twitched—was still.

A vagrant spark struck Hiroshi. He jerked, screamed. His jaw slammed shut, opened, yawned, slammed down again. *"Ahhh—!"*

Again the electrical energy vanished.

Seared silence. The acrid air stung their nostrils.

Viktor said bitterly, "They want to talk, do they?"

Hiroshi's breath whistled between broken teeth.

Julia sobbed beside Veronique's singed body.

16.

TUBE WORM

SHANNA FLINCHED. THE VIDEO feed was all too clear.

"The damned thing's invisible!" Jordin said. "I can pick it up on all the low-frequency bands, sure. But it's not even plasma."

On-screen, Shanna gazed at the charred lips of Veronique's corpse as the *High Flyer* crew lifted it, carried it away. The whole face was swollen, bruised, already darkening. The fingers were blackened by the discharge. Only a few days before, she had seen that mouth lifting in a smile, laughing, sipping expensive champagne that fusion power had hauled 100 million miles.

"It's whatever holds plasma," Shanna said. "See? Those strands, they're confined by magnetic fields. Just like our plasma receiver net. Currents lock in the ions and electrons."

Jordin nodded. "A magnetic intelligence?"

"Thousands of kilometers long," Shanna said. "And we thought the zand was a strange form of life!"

"It was—is. But this . . ." Jordin stared at the video feed, then looked over at the multiple screens that showed the sources of the low-frequency waves they were receiving. "I've got that new software running, pulling these weak cyclotron harmonics out of the noise. Look—"

Shanna had trouble focusing on what he was saying. But indeed, there were images, flickering at the very edge of detectability, on the whole-space screens.

Jordin's hands swept the air, sharpening the images. "There's a *shape* that's making those waves. Wrapped around *High Flyer*. Look—"

Once he pointed it out, Shanna could see the filmy, foggy form. A long tube with many small openings, like puckers or pores. And a big tubular opening—a mouth?— at the head of it. Head? Yes, it moved forward, and the front weaved as if it was scanning its surroundings. A huge magnetic tube worm.

"So that's what they look like," Jordin said wonderingly. "But look beyond—in the higher cyclotron harmonics."

Shanna felt a visceral nausea. "Disgusting."

He upped the register and drew out of the background

more faint traceries. "Those are much farther away. My God, they must be *huge*."

"This one's closer, smaller." Shanna's mouth narrowed, lips pressed pale.

"Yeah, it's wrapped around in a closed shape."

"Let's give it some of what it gave us," Shanna said bitterly. She had met Veronique when *High Flyer* arrived and liked her immediately. Hiroshi, too. His front teeth were shattered, only stubs left. The medical team was patching him up.

She grabbed the controls. "Where is that bastard?"

17.

SUDDEN PRIDE

THE DARTING FIRE CAUGHT FORCEFUL. Burning hard plasma blew away its outer layers in a single gout of raging fire. He veered to avoid, but the flame followed.

<Come, help!> Forceful called.

<We come!> Crafter's low drone was welcome, but it came from far away.

<The two motes are turning. Both!> Ring was alarmed. <They concentrate the plasma on you.>

<I flee!> Forceful turned and wriggled away. Its magnetic columns flexed into quick, darting parts. It could dissolve into smaller, coherent structures and run faster, it knew, but the price would be a long, agonizing reassembly.

And some humiliation, too. Sudden pride filled its strands. It bellowed, <To flee before the enemy! No!>

Resolute, it turned. <I flee no more.>

The hard plasma came into it, and the searing pain was suddenly everything.

18.

THE EATERS OF GODS

JULIA FELT WAN, PALE, SAD. Her breath came slowly, as if dredged up from far below.

They were drifting now on minimal thrust. It seemed plausible that the magnetic creatures were drawn to the plasma of their fusion drive, for some reason. So this coasting was an experiment. The Beings seemed to have withdrawn. Viktor had ordered double watches, looking in all directions and in every wave band they had. The ship rang with tension. They all needed time to recoup. Veronique's death had shattered their peace of mind. They all knew it was dangerous out here, but *this* . . .

And what of those creatures? Downloading Jordin's improvements on the signal/noise software that Earthside had sent to upgrade Wiseguy helped. The *High Flyer* crew numbly looked at the images traced out by the weak cyclotron emission.

The wormlike thing that had electrocuted Veronique was moving away, shredded and pocked. Beyond it, the entire sky seemed filled with dim images of many more.

The scale of them, implied by the intensity and apparent size . . . Her mind boggled.

So huge, they were like gods. Or were they worse? Could they be the eaters of all the gods that humanity had ever imagined? Brrrr . . .

Only hours after Veronique's death, when they had to get back to work—a spacecraft under boost needs tending—did Hiroshi discover that their antennas were dead. External cameras showed that they were fused. The intensity of the current-voltage surges had simply melted their fragile wire webs. So they had to fix those, and right away. If their attackers returned, *High Flyer* needed to know about it. Hiroshi was aft, getting the robots set up.

Viktor worked beside her as she stared mutely at the images. Ever the practical one, he was assembling radar images of their vicinity. "This one looks good," he said.

"Oh?" She came out of her daze. A pale greenish blotch swelled in one of the side screens. "An iceteroid?"

"We better try to refuel. That last time, I burned up a lot of water."

In the end all long-distance rockets are steam rockets. Whether liquid hydrogen married to liquid oxygen, or water passing by slabs of hot plutonium, or through a fusion-burning core, they all flashed into plumes of steam.

Real space commerce demanded high energy efficiency. Realization of this returned to NASA in 2005, with the hesitant first steps of Project Prometheus (every bureaucracy loves resplendent names). The first rush of Mars exploration had proved the essential principle: refuel at the destination. Don't haul reaction mass with you. Nuclear rockets are far easier to refuel because they only need water—easy to pump, and easy to find, if you pick the right destination. Nearly all the inner solar system is dry as a bone. If ordinary sidewalk concrete were on the moon, it would be mined for its water, because everything around it would be far drier.

Mars is another story. It bore out the general rule that the lighter elements had been blown outward by the radiation pressure of the early, hot sun, soon after its birth. This dried the worlds forming nearby and wetted those farther out—principally the gas giants, whose thick atmospheres churn with ices and gases. Mars proved to be wetter overall than Earth, though without much atmosphere. Not massive enough to hold on to its atmosphere for long, its crust had been sucked dry by the near vacuum. But beneath the crust are thick slabs of ice, and at the poles lie snow and even glaciers. So explorers there can readily refuel by melting the buried ice and pumping it into their tanks.

In time the moons of Jupiter and the other gas giants would become similar gas stations, though they orbit far down into the gravitational well of those massive worlds, demanding a lot of delta-V, tens of kilometers a second, just to get to them. This makes Pluto a surprisingly easy mission destination. Small, deeply cold, with a large ice moon like a younger twin, it takes only a km/sec delta-V to land upon.

Of course, the ice was rock-hard, taking a lot of therms to melt. But the nuke had therms to spare. And beyond it, now, the refueling targets were even easier.

"What's its size?" she asked.

"Looks to be two three seven klicks diameter," Viktor read off the flickering scale. "Surface grav, maybe a hundredth of a g."

Easy to approach and hang alongside. Hard labor, lugging the hoses around, melting that incredibly tough, deep-frozen ice. But it would be R&R, too. As her mother used to say, *Your mind working too much? Use your hands instead.*

"How far?"

Viktor beamed. "Two days flight, with some time for delta-V. I was worried maybe we not find much ice near this bow shock."

"Enough time to fix the antennas?" Julia asked.

"Some, anyway." Viktor grimaced. "We'll have to run the all-'bot teams. And get them ready to operate on this iceteroid, too."

Julia finally managed to rouse herself from her lethargic depression. She had lost team members in the long decades on Mars, starting in the first expedition, with the two who had ventured into Vent A on their own. But never quite so brutally. And never to an enemy other than carelessness and bad luck. "I'll go help."

Veronique had been principally in charge of the robots. Her loss meant they would all have to pitch in. Hiroshi volunteered right away. Julia found in the first hour that she was rusty. She had telepresence skills learned in the generations of workbots sent to Mars, but these were the very latest designs and built for different tasks. In the flight outward Veronique had done too much of the work and tutored too little. But then, they had all been infernally busy. A new ship is a fresh menu of troubles.

On *High Flyer* robots did maintenance and repairs outside and in the fusion region. If they got hot near the reactor, they then cooled off in a shielded vault, nestled beside the huge water cylinders, until ready to use again. They never entered the living quarters. If they themselves needed repair, the work was done by other semiautonomous robots, operating under smart telepresence.

"How're they looking?" she asked Hiroshi in the mid-pod, between life systems and the water columns.

"Cranky." He looked distracted, punching in commands to a big, cylindrical stack of multipurpose armatures. The many arms made it look like a very dangerous Swiss Army knife with jets attached.

"Lemme see." She started on prep.

None of the ship's robots looked remotely human. A two-armed, two-legged 'bot would be maladapted here. Spindly ones operated in the zero-g sections near the axis, and on the hull when they were not boosting. Other bulky ones had multisocketed arms, so they could lurch from socket-hold to tie line in the rugged radiation environments of the drive. Slender, snaky forms labored to check and patch the vast water cells that had to be kept from freezing. Water circulated by sluggish pipes to the warming zone of the reactor, but the joints had a tendency to pop.

They were smart 'bots, of course, because they had bodies. This elementary point had eluded the twencen AI savants: intelligence builds up from sensory-motor experience, not from logical rules. Start with a body and build a mind.

So the rise of the robots, starting in the early twenty-first century, meant that form of AI came into its own. No more software and wiring diagrams; bring on the neural plasticity and learned patterning. A working robot was not a set of abstract reasoning software walking around in a metal skirt. It was instead a mind brought up on a diet of inertia, friction, torque, and balance. All along through the 2020s and 2030s, machines learned from animals, not from logicians. In space they crawled and slithered and even flew—all using methods mimicked from worms and rattlers and octopi.

She told the hull 'bots to check for flaws and damage, delegating a special, spindly team with big hands to install faraday shields around the microwave antennas, once another team had replaced them. These were just wire cages, with grid spacing greater than the emitted micro-wavelengths. Since the big power they were getting came in far longer wavelengths, this should protect their comm gear against overload and blowout.

Robots grew up in a techno-universe that was getting embedded, smaller, sneakier, and everywhere. *High Flyer* was not made on the mode of the stalwart *Titanic*, splendid gray iron in hull and hammering engines. It was instead a moving bulk ruled by a nervous system of chips and 'bots—buggier, not just bigger.

"Hey, Viktor, we need zero g now," she was finally able to send on comm. "Gotta get these 'bots out."

"Was quick," he said approvingly, and the rumble of the drive cut off. Julia clung to a beam, and the 'bots went into their automatic, gyro-stabilized positions, ready to work. She wished Hiroshi were there to help, but he was sedated.

Out the 'bot hatch they went—a long tube leading to an automatic air lock. They popped into space, got oriented, and started. Julia watched and corrected.

She could feel the whole system at work, in the working immersion pod. Tuning into the embedded, fixed sensors, she picked up the whole-body feel of the Swiss Army cylinder balanced intricately on a gas jet. It was remarkably like sensing the entire *High Flyer*, because the perception space was the same. When Viktor let her immerse in *High Flyer*, she could *feel* how its fusion flame adjusted its flight, sense the throb as pumps moved its arterial water and air through capillaries. She saw the framed scenes as artificial eyes peered into circuit tangles and even the fusion hellhole.

She would never forget the first time she saw their drive, from the inside. She had never paid much attention to fusion, believing—as the skeptics had said for half a century—that controlled fusion power plants lay twenty years ahead, and always would.

But the sudden advent of a high-quality fusion rocket made her hit the books—or rather, the Net—and fathom the magnetic doughnut that held the ions of boron and hydrogen. The ions snaked around the geometry and then slammed into each other, giving forth brimming radiation, spitting hot alpha particles out. Then the doughnut collapsed. Ions let fly. The rocket engine was this flickering, come-and-go doughnut, holding the plasma, then letting it fly as the doughnut died.

This called up the memory of scuba diving in Hawaii, on the north coast of Oahu, offshore Turtle Bay. The wonder of it had charmed her. Hanging upside down above a coral reef, she had learned to blow bubbles that, rising, formed into rings. They were magically exact, thinning into hoops a hand wide but of thickness less than a little finger.

Toroids, she remembered from high school geometry. A fat one was like a doughnut. She floated thirty feet down, utterly relaxed, and watched the floppy bubbles shape themselves into beautiful rings, order emerging from chaos, another of nature's miracles.

Like now: another doughnut of fierce fires, dying. The

ions escaped down a magnetic gullet that became a throat, shaping the plasma into a ferocious fire that jetted out the back. The doughnut died, crumpled magnetic field lines sagging. *Another torus*, she remembered from Hawaii, seeing them shape magically into toroids, into rings. Nature found so many uses for the same geometries.

Tending the 'bots was not so romantic. When she switched the immersion pod to the 'bot world, she sensed the moving, momentary minds of the working 'bots. Those methodical programs puzzled over their driver problems, moving flanges and lifting hatches and turning tools—all to do the myriad minor jobs a giant needed. But a proper ship 'bot worked as a simple AI, all done below consciousness, please—like digestion and excretion, not suitable subjects for meaningful discourse.

They spent days on the litany of the big, complex ship—maintenance, maintenance, maintenance—before attempting any new mission. Days later, when Julia got back to their quarters, frazzed out, there was a vid tagged *Personal* from Axelrod.

She watched it with Viktor. Axelrod came on splendidly dressed, probably after some big corporate to-do. His suit was artfully formfitting, concealing the bulges that lower lunar gravity seemed to ordain, especially around the middle. But his smile was sunny, and she knew the look from experience. Self-satisfaction beamed forth, confidence radiating, and as he spoke, his voice fairly bubbled with gurgly chuckles. His teeth were perfect, and his smile broadened even further at the end of sentences, stretching as if the smile were shooting its cuffs.

"I think it's just great that you're following your nose

out there," he said grandly. "Find out how those Darksiders get made! We can use every scrap of detail. Take samples! Hell, take Darksiders! I told Shanna you'd be there to take them in charge."

"What?" Julia shot back to the screen. "We haven't even seen the damn things yet!"

"Maybe take whole iceteroid," Viktor said sardonically.

"I've just been at a meeting of our backers, and they're 100 percent behind you. Take every precaution, of course"—he beamed—"but take every opportunity, too!"

"Does really think we need pep talk?"

Julia nodded. "It's all he can do. For executives you can't just do nothing but wait. Not allowed."

Viktor curled his lips in a knot and turned off the vid. "For this I, too, can wait. Until we are done."

19.

ICETEROID

THEIR NOZZLES BURNING SOFT and pale at low drive levels, the two long cylinders swooped down toward the pale gray iceteroid.

The astro folks Earthside said there were over forty thousand iceteroids like this out in the dark, at least. Pluto wasn't really a planet, they said, just the biggest of these "cometoids" that others wanted to call Plutinos—so maybe it wasn't surprising that there was one fairly near the nose of the bow shock. Still, it was suspicious, because the blocky body *looked* odd. They expected the usual dirty-gray ice, but it was a dull green.

"Lots of current in the plasma around us, too," Jordin reported.

"Reminds me of Pluto," Shanna said, frowning. "Warmer than it should be—look, there's a funny brownish haze around the thing. An atmosphere!"

"Now, that's plain impossible," Jordin said. "A chunk of ice can't hold on to a gas at all."

But it was there, all right. "Methane, the spectrum says," Jordin admitted.

"One other thing . . ."

"What? It's pretty thin stuff, not much of an atmosphere—"

"No, the spin." Shanna pointed. "It isn't."

The chunky, potato-shaped mass held steady on the screen. Jordin said, "Ummm . . . maybe it's really slow."

"No, been tracking it for hours. Zero spin. Never saw a natural object that didn't have some."

They came gliding in carefully, *High Flyer* on the other side, to provide maximum coverage of this miniworld, which they had decided to call Iceball.

Shanna sent one of her bulky 'bots shuttling over to gingerly touch down. *Proserpina* had no need of water—they had refueled on Pluto's glimmering ice fields—but Shanna wanted to see if further clues to the zand could be here. The incoming Darksider machines that dropped on Pluto had to come from somewhere, and Iceball was upstream of the currents from the bow shock. Somehow, all this diffuse energy had to fit together.

High Flyer was deploying 'bot crews on the other side. Their teams set to, hauling out pipelines to melt ice and suck up water. *Proserpina* would have first crack at the science, then. Their spidery, many-armed 'bots hit gingerly in the microgravity, sinking anchor lines through the odd green-brown splashes that covered about half the ground. They had all crew available running 'bots, the comm air alive with fretful cross talk. Jordin ran the chemical analyzer 'bots, Shanna the patrol 'bots. Her point-of-view choice was a 'bot that didn't anchor, jetting instead over the visibly curved, bumpy surface. *Bird 'bot*, she thought.

"Y'know, this is damned strange," Jordin said on comm from his control pod.

"Tell me about it." Shanna's 'bot had arced over a brown crest. Beyond stood a complex construction, house-sized and spiky with contorted flanges, tubes, valves, chutes, and prongs like a big arc-welder rig. "Got an artifact here."

"A Darksider?"

"Maybe the factory that made them."

"A working factory?"

"I can see parts moving. Some dust in a column, spinning around. Purple sparks, too, jumping around inside the column. There are pipes, transparent pipes. With fluids pumping through them—liquids I can see shining by their own light."

Jordin said, "Wow. Me, I'm getting boring readings on methane and ammonia and—wait, looks like maybe complex organics in the stew here, too."

"Y'know what I think? This is somebody's workshop."

"Like Pluto, you mean. Yeah. Sure ain't natural."

"Hey, the fluids are awfully bright. I wonder if they're—well, metals? In some kind of plasma discharge, not solid—but metals, yes."

Jordin's doubtful tone was clear even over the raspy comm. "You got spectra?"

"Here." She shot the data over and was gratified when, in less than a minute, he replied, "Yep, there's iron and nickel and copper. Uranium, too."

"So it's—what, a plasma foundry?"

"Yeah. Here, where ambient's, lemme see—wow!—46 Kelvin!"

"And we thought *we* were engineers."

Shanna watched as a scoop slowly descended from the porcupine-like structure. With a huge claw it scooped up material from a tray and deposited the man-sized pile in a hopper. Something sucked the material into a cylinder, and some actinic flashes came from the studded walls of it. Then the tray began moving away on invisible jets, lifting and sailing over the horizon.

Shanna made her 'bot lift some dirty ice a meter and let go. The ice took an eerie minute to fall, straight down. "Y'know, the zero spin makes sense. Moving something takes nearly nothing, and it's easy to get it to drop where you want, when there's no rotation to mess you up."

"Easy if you're a machine calibrated that low, yeah," Jordin said. "Not easy for our 1-g reflexes."

"This"—in an instant she was sure of it—"this must be where the Darksiders get made."

"Yeah?" Disbelief colored Jordin's voice. He sent his 'bot scooting after the loaded tray. Spindly and light and as big as it was, it still moved well. "Let's see."

From the 'bot point of view the gray ice shot by below. Small gas bursts altered its straight-line path to curve around the close horizon. Jordin was hard put to keep the tray-flyer in view. The ice here was crusty, spattered with brown. Then something new bulked up, large, a tangled structure rising over the horizon's icy rim. Columns of moving, electric-blue dust whirled in the vacuum, somehow confined. They passed through the dark struts and corridors of the—*Well*, Shanna thought, *might as well call it a factory; it sure looks like one*—and electric-green arcs flashed every few seconds, sending weird shadows stretching across the plain and up through the twisted towers above.

"Look there," Jordin said.

The flying tray had disappeared somewhere into the labyrinth. On the dirty ground at the factory's edge stood half a dozen constructions, in various stages of assembly. Small machines worked over them. "I'll bet when they're finished, they'll be Darksiders."

"No bet—good call." They watched silently as myriad small machines prowled the strange, shadowy structure.

One passed nearby, and Jordin did a quick spectral scan. "I wondered how they handled seeing. Those big eyes are calcium carbonate."

Julia came in, voice faint. "Can't be. That's the stuff of the white cliffs of Dover. Biological."

Shanna made a superior smirk. "Plenty of nonbio chemical ways to make it, though. Trilobite eyes were made of it, 400 million years ago. There's a transparent, crystalline form, and the trilobites used that—a unique invention, never duplicated later. So somebody designed these to use calcite crystals. Maybe they work better at really low temperatures."

Julia's voice was etched in doubt. "Oh? Never heard that."

Jordin seemed to sense the edgy tension rising, and said

quickly, "So trilobites and these things could both give you a stony stare, huh?"

The women laughed, maybe a little too much.

They got to work, taking pictures and working their way through the complex. Shanna liked immersing herself in the shadowy lanes and weird worked architectures, losing herself to the strangeness of it. Ice crunching, the 'bot's clanking. An hour went by without her noticing it, in part because their link to Julia dropped out and she could work without always thinking about the other woman. But then—

"Hey down there!" It was Julia on comm. "We're in good range again."

"Can't talk much," Shanna said. "We're watching the natives." She sent a cam-view attachment on a sideband and was gratified to hear Julia's gasp.

"What are they?" Julia whispered.

"Minions," Jordin whispered back. "I always wanted to use that word, and these sure seem to fit."

"Minions of what?"

"The magnetic beasts, I'll bet," Shanna said. "Certainly not the other way around. Ever since I saw my first zand, I was sure it couldn't be natural. I mean, couldn't have arisen and evolved on Pluto."

Jordin made his 'bot extend a tool, effectively pointing to a team of three small devices that skimmed out from the edifice, over the ice, and then swarmed around a partially finished Darksider. "Right, no way. There's not the complexity of a natural biosphere. No pyramid of life, nothing. Just raw materials and . . . machines."

"Ummm," Julia said. "Like a biosphere designed by something that didn't know the steps?"

"Or wanted to cut to the chase," Shanna said.

"Something in a hurry," Jordin said. His breath came fast over the comm, but his voice was calm.

"Now the diplomacy begins," Shanna said. "We're on the ground, might as well introduce ourselves."

"Think they'll notice?" Jordin asked quietly. "They've sure ignored us so far."

"Look," Julia said, "ants crawling across your desk don't know they're interrupting a superior being reading e-mail. They don't notice you at all."

Shanna nodded. "So we use something they will notice."

Julia asked, "What? We don't—"

"We hauled it all the way from Pluto, and it's been itching to get out. Let's deploy that Darksider I caught."

20.

TOROIDS

FORCEFUL HURT. <I should be grateful . . .> He paused to summon energies. <. . . that I did not suffer more . . . Diminishment.>

<You were brave,> Ring sent. <Gallant!>

<I was damaged,> Forceful sent sourly. <And they both got away.>

<Not far,> Sunless said. <They are within the outer skirts of my own body now.>

<They are at the Orb?> Instigator asked with alarm.

<Very near, yes,> Sunless said. <I did not think that significant, compared with Forceful's losses.>

<Never mind Diminishment, even if suffered from such motes as these,> Instigator said. <Quick, what are they doing?>

<Nothing,> Sunless said. <Drifting. Their fires burned low and now are out. They hang like the dead beside the Orb.>

<They are attacking my experiments!> Instigator sent.

<We must converge,> Recorder sent to all. <This series of incidents strongly suggests that we are suffering an incursion from life-forms who wish us no good.>

<But the two fire-breathers together! How—> Sunless cried.

<We will surround them.> Forceful sent weakly but with a calm ruthlessness. <With our fields concentrated—intermingled—we may be able to apply enough pressure to gutter them out.>

<You wish revenge,> Chill said carefully.

<Who would not?> Forceful's voice was fading.

<Very well,> Recorder said, signaling an end to discussion. <Together, now—>

21.

WANJINA

JULIA TOOK A LONG break from the 'bot-controlling job and walked to her private preserve. The water collection went on, most of the crew running the 'bots . . . and she needed to think. There was something brewing here, events moving too fast, and she needed to be centered to fathom it. She shut out her ship's eternal hum and concentrated.

The sliding sheets of water again caught the projected scenes she had not seen in person now for decades. One of the obliging, scanty comforts of Mars had been its sometimes eerie similarity to the great red interior of Australia, where she grew up.

So she called up in the walls around her the abrupt scarps of sandstone in Australia, the lashing rains pouring over them, and shortly after, the scorching summer turning the rock to furnace heat. Yet the grand rocks looked redder after the rare rains, standing out in sunsets against lush grasses as wide swags of pearly cloud hung over the floodplain. In the northwest she had once seen wall paintings of spiritual beings, *Wanjina,* with huge eyes and no mouths—beings who saw all but judged nothing.

The memory came to her abruptly. The human legends of higher creatures *who saw all but judged nothing*—yes. The pressing human need, embodied in legends of goblins and angels and golems and trolls and faeries and so many—the need to find another voice in this indifferent universe.

Was it so demented? Pathetic?

And now here was the possibility.

But how to talk?

She remembered a classic story from Kyoto lore.

Two men were watching a beautiful pool and the koi fish that swam just below its calm, clear surface.

"The fish are happy," said one man.
The other asked, "How can you possibly know?"
"How can you know if I know?"
"How can you know I cannot?"
"That is not the point," the fish said.

So how to think about this?

Expect the unexpected.

Sighing, she left the security of her personal space and trudged out into the command deck. Viktor was there, dealing with details as their complex sensorium sampled and delved and fidgeted with the immense landscape presented by the panoply of sensors *High Flyer* carried. The new software gave them a holistic view of things never glimpsed by the human eye: magnetic fields, plasma fluxes, the slow clash of pressures and shock waves at the boundary of Things Solar and Things Stellar. Humans had evolved in the flat dry plains of Africa, and their sensory inputs (to use a computer freak's terms) were of a blithe Euclidian geometry in obliging finite spaces, flat planes, and simple forms. Human eyes were not made for the surge and suck of such three-dimensional turbulence. But they tried.

Instead of talking, that blunt medium, she simply embraced him.

Took him to bed. Made love and made it matter.

There is always something ultimately fatal about sex. How did that poem go . . . ?

> *What use to rise and rise?*
> *Rise a man a thousand mornings*
> *Yet down at last he lies,*
> *And then the man is wise.*

But it doesn't have to be so, she realized.

Something clicked.

"I've got it!" she said.

"I thought you just had," Viktor said, lounging, grinning.

"No, not that—I mean I understand."

He snorted. "Having done experiment, we now get theory?"

"No, the magnetic things, creatures, whatever. They can reconnect their field lines, the way the Earth's magnetic fields do after they've been battered by a solar windstorm. They can rebuild! So they don't have to die."

"Everything dies. Is evolution."

"Not evolution out here! They don't *have* to die. Imagine a creature that from the very beginning, however they first were born, had the ability to tailor its cells, its basic units."

He blinked. "Animals do not know they will die—is almost definition of animal, right?"

"Animals, yes. And maybe that's the big difference between us and these things. We fought them off. But to them this may have just been a maneuver, a temporary loss—nothing really important."

"I thought the scans showed that we wasted the magnetic bastards."

"No, just that some of their field structures—those arcades and archipelagoes, remember?—they glowed and seethed and then—*zap!*—they were gone."

"We maybe killed them—it—whatever. *Da.*"

"No, we didn't. Damaged but not dead."

"So this stuff I see on all the screens, closing in on us—it's the same things? The Beings?"

"Creatures, yes. And they know what happened, they were there. We can negotiate with them."

"They seem not interested in negotiation."

"That first appearance in the ship, it seemed to want to connect with us. It mirrored my movements."

"Second time, though—"

"Maybe that was a mistake, a miscalculation. How could they understand what is dangerous to us and what isn't? They don't even have solid bodies! Electrical discharges sustain life to them."

"We can kill them with plasma? Disrupt their electromagnetic fields maybe."

"But they won't be dead! So to them all life is a negotiation, 'cause they never die."

"All measures are temporary?" He wrinkled his forehead.

"In a way we can't ever know, yeah. Everything's temporary. Like the weather. The only thing that ever lasts is *them*."

Viktor arched his heavy black eyebrows, bemused. "Interesting theory, m'dear. Makes our job out here maybe easier, though."

His words jerked her out of her gauzy speculations. "What?"

"Bow shock coming closer and closer, and these things may be the cause. And we cannot hope to kill them."

She nodded. "But they have killed one of us."

"We have a job to do, and if we keep letting them damage us . . ."

Julia sighed. "We have to let them know that we mean business? I had hoped we could learn . . ."

"In way, makes communication job easier. We can damage them but not kill. So they learn."

"Learn to . . . fear us?"

"Maybe best to think of them as animals—who don't know about death, either. But they can learn to respect."

She eyed him. The analogy to animals had a point. "Veronique . . ."

Viktor frowned. "*Da.* We are small, they large. They may respect us if we can hurt them."

22.

FREE RADICALS

"I'VE GOT IT FIGURED," Jordin called joyously. "I know what makes those lichen possible."

Shanna was carefully maneuvering the captured Darksider toward the factory complex, using slight shoves across the soft starlit plain. But she, too, had wondered at the puzzle of how anything managed to live on a dab of ice under lower illumination than a flashlight. "Oh? Fill me in."

"My chem-sampler 'bot—it's fished up a whole soup of stuff, yeah—but the telltale is, this iceball is *rich.*"

"Um." The Darksider was twitching, but her 'bot had it in three claws and wasn't letting go. Whatever had made Darksiders, it had little appreciation for gravity. Her 'bot, on the other hand, could maneuver in a full Earth g if it had to. It was maybe a hundred times stronger than the

Darksider, and she had to be careful not to cave in the Darksider carapace with too swift a movement. The two machines scooted slowly toward the spindly dark factory. "Uh, yeah?"

"It's richer than Earthside ocean water. See, thing is, this iceball has been here in the dark many billions of years, doing nothing but sopping up cosmic rays. Free energy. The high-energy cosmic rays barrel into it and create ionized atoms. On Earth it's warm enough that they find each other right away and recombine. Not here. The radicals stay frozen, ready for the lichen stuff to eat."

"Yummy." She brought the 'bot over the horizon, made it survey for suspicious movement, then went ahead. None of the Darksiders parked in front of the factory showed any reaction.

Like most tech guys, Jordin took any vague murmur as encouragement. "So the simple molecules can sometimes find others, build up more complex stuff—just like in our ocean, only at 50 degrees Kelvin. Amazing!"

She slowed and lowered the 'bot. A long moment of sliding silence, only her own breath rasping in her ears. No reaction from the lined-up Darksiders. So she let hers go. The captured 'bot settled to the surface, taking a full minute during which Shanna concentrated for any sign of reaction among the others. Jordin was talking organic chemistry, carbon and its many friends, her least favorite subject in university, and it went right by her.

"Not only that, the ice has plenty of uranium 235 in it. Another energy stock. That's what this fungus stuff we see is doing—burrowing through the ice, collecting the U-235. Uses it for warmth, eats the organic compounds left by the cosmic rays—it's a whole ecology. Ice worms crawl around and gobble up the fungus."

"I don't see any gobbling going on," Shanna said warily. Her Darksider was shuffling forward toward its kin. "Things're pretty slow out here."

"Well, sure," Jordin said with undiminished enthusiasm. "Low temperatures—but lots of time, maybe since the galaxy formed 10 billion years ago. The turtle beats the hare—it's wonderful."

"Hey, they haven't beaten *us* yet."

The Darksider convention was in slow motion. Hers lifted one of its odd, X-shaped grapplers and touched one of the others. A pale yellow spark arced. Nobody moved. Then another spark, but this time from the other Darksider to hers. "And they look like they're communicating with jolts of electricity."

This interested Jordin enough that he tapped into her 'bot sensorium. "Ummm, makes sense, kinda. So damn cold here you have to give somebody a smack just to get their attention."

Shanna blinked. The Darksiders suddenly moved, forming a circle. They projected arrays of wires above their "heads"—knobby tool assemblies, really—and a sudden crackling came into her ears. "They're sending something in microwaves," she said. "A . . . buzzing."

"Sure," Jordin said happily. "They're talking to their gods."

"What?" She got the sudden impression that her Darksider had sent a status report, and now all of them were . . . praying? "No, maybe just reporting in."

23.

PLASMA DRAGONS

FORCEFUL SAID FIRMLY, <We must attack. These cold, solid things will cause us much damage if they suddenly flare to life, spewing plasma.>

Mirk added, <When we are bunched together so, yes. We have not met this way in how long? My memory of such an event is in long-duration storage, and slow to revive.>

<Too long, by my measure,> Recorder said. <But I know—nearly one galactic rotation.>

<So long!> Ring responded quickly, since it was so nearby. <I can feel the strums of us all, our digestive juices flowing, our dim internal murmurs.>

<But wait!> Instigator called. <I have touched my experiment. It calls to me. One of my emissaries to the Large Cold Place has returned—brought by those solids!>

<Impossible!> Ring derided.

Instigator sent reassurance underlain with perplexity. <Not. I can sense them grouped. The emissary I sent to adjust the life-forms there. To subtract what was not according to plan.>

Ring shot back, <But your theory of life in the Hotsphere is that it has no plan.>

Instigator sent subtonics of admission-with-riposte: <I have altered the life-forms a bit.>

<To achieve quick results?> Mirk sent insinuatingly.

<The Hotsphere began to bear simple life not long after

our origin—or have you forgotten the last few findings sent by Incursor? He had begun his own experiments with those forms. A great long age ago! I did not wish to take such a long time to gain some understanding.>

Recorder said formally, <We can review your work later. Now we meet a true antagonist—one you gave us no warning of.>

Instigator retorted, <Who could imagine that cold solids could spew out hot stuff-of-life?>

Recorder spiked back, <You. You were supposed to discover the potentials of solid life.>

They awaited a reply, but Instigator paused, puzzlement creeping into its emission. <The mechinicals I formed, developed—they signal me. To report strange things. There is one of the several-spoked things near them.>

Dusk ventured, <They are . . . studying us?>

<Through Instigator's inventions,> Sunless said. <How symmetric.>

<How so?> Recorder asked.

<We were persuaded long ago to let Instigator proceed to study the Hot by making actual solid manifestations. Tools. Now they study us through our own tools. The several-spoked things—do they look like our tools?>

Instigator answered, <No, not at all.>

<Then the several-spoked are tools, too, I would wager.> Sunless bore down upon the point. <Symmetric.>

<Then the large solids that burned poor Chill and Forceful?> Recorder pressed. <What are they?>

<They must be the true intelligences. They are plasma dragons!>

A tremor swept through them all, detected as fast ripples in the basic background magnetic field. The spatter of this fizzy noise sobered them.

<That is an old, discredited legend,> Recorder said primly.

<These are real!> Forceful insisted. <They spit plasma of a hardness and sting we have not known.>

<That does not mean they are the ancient dragons. I firmly believe the conventional wisdom of the far voices. Dragons were descended from a mongrel form of sun, slight and bristly and always angry at the other suns because of their far greater size. Those explode in wrath, leaving only the dragons. Then the dragons spit and fume and damage such as us—who never did anything to a star, and surely are the very children of the suns.>

Instigator said mildly, hoping to calm them all, <The plasma dragons these might be, but they are small. We can overwhelm them.>

<Yes!> Forceful seized upon the moment. <Let us!>

24.

CREATURES AS GAUZY AS LACE

"THEY'RE COMING!" JORDIN CALLED. "The big guys for sure. Lots of strong magnetic waves on the ship antennas."

Shanna was watching the 'bots maneuver on dirty ice. "Damn! I want to see what they do next."

"Look, the Beings made those."

"Sure, but we can *see* the Darksiders."

"Darksiders've called down their makers, I'll bet." Jordin was agitated. He pulled out of his sensorium hood and said directly to her, a meter away, "We'd better tuck in, and pronto."

"Okay." Shanna jerked her head out of the confines of the sensorium hood and looked around. In the mild, air-conditioned deck nothing seemed awry. Yet she knew huge things were coming, creatures as gauzy as lace but as deadly as a viper. "What'll we—"

The deck shook. Circuits in the wall fizzed with over-load currents.

"Julia!" she called. "What're you—"

"It's slamming us around. Hard." Julia's voice over comm had lost her usual calm, Great Lady of Space tone. That alone shook Shanna. "We've got to damage these damned things!"

"Damage?" Shanna felt a quick burst of irritation. She had felt that way, sure, but—"They're trying to communicate! I think they're monitoring this Darksider, learning from it. Even Veronique's death, that might have been—"

"You don't know any of this."

"I . . . call it intuition."

Julia's tone was cool. "I felt the same way as you, but we must remember. They've done us damage, invaded a ship. They're quite probably behind the bow shock that's moving in. Viktor has convinced me that we have to put our mission first."

You never know what goes on inside a marriage . . . "We don't know that they're behind the bow shock phenomenon." Shanna struggled to keep this civil.

"We can't kill them, I think. They've killed one of us. We have to make a show of force."

"I don't agree."

"We're under orders from Earthside to stop the bow shock from moving farther in, if I—we—possibly can."

"Thanks for adding the 'we,' Cap'n."

"What's that mean?"

"Sarcasm is just one more service we offer out here—to newcomers."

Julia's voice was suddenly tight, controlled. "Captain, you *will* assist us. *High Flyer* has overall command of this expedition."

"Don't remind me."

"And Viktor agrees with me."

"I'm so surprised."

Julia ignored this gibe. "I want us to coordinate our thrust vectors. To bring our exhaust plumes to bear on the same volume of space. That should maximize—"

"We've got to *talk* to them. I damn well didn't spend a year on Pluto to see you just come in and—"

"You *will* comply, Captain. Switch on your full screens—I noticed from your internals that you've been too busy arguing with me to tend to business—and run the new software we got from Earthside. The signal-to-noise enhancer. So you can envision the magnetic structures."

"We've got it up, sure." Shanna frowned. "Why, what's—"

"So we'll know where we're shooting."

Shanna sucked in a dry breath, made herself breathe out—*calm, calm*—and nodded to the rest of the crew. Their eyes were white.

Jordin muttered under his breath and sprang to the central position on the bridge. They both strapped in as other crew dashed to their stations. Shanna watched the screens anxiously as the ship rattled and creaked with stresses.

Jordin and Mary Kay got the full software running, calibrated. Shanna studied the images. Was Julia right? She sensed the hand of Viktor in this shift.

On the screens the fluxes whirled and merged, mere digital analogs of a reality no human eye could grasp—beings bigger than continents, sweeping in on them like furious tornadoes with a grudge. Or were they? She felt them all swept forward, emissaries in a collision of beings that neither side could have foreseen. *And I thought the zand were exotic!*

Pluto had been a lot easier.

25.

SMOKE RINGS

JULIA FELT HER SHIP shudder. Considering its immense length and mass, this spoke powerfully of the net pressure even a filmy, lacelike filigree of magnetic field could exert.

"Let's go!" she ordered Viktor. "Give them some prop wash."

High Flyer surged onward, a relentless kick in the pants, accelerating on jetting coils of fresh, snarling plasma. The mottled iceball fell away. Far off, *Proserpina,* too, flared and followed. Between them snaked forth bright electron beams, marked by their gauzy radiance where they excited the clotted hydrogen that backed up from the raging bow shock. Starlight sprinkled the ship as auroral fires danced along its flanks. Energies born of magnetic fields pressed at them.

"I'm getting a lot of that same low-frequency hash," Viktor said.

"The high-power stuff that started all this?"

"*Da,* is same." He looked significantly at her. "Your creatures."

"Hey, they're not *mine.*" Though she had to admit to herself that she didn't want to kill them. Still—"They're drawing in close?"

"I'm not getting a good image." Viktor thumbed over to the *Proserpina* link. "Send latest, eh, Jordin?"

Their screens brimmed with twisting shapes—slow, smooth. Julia had learned to make out structures in the shifting magnetic topo maps, like looking down on hills that kept moving around, growing taller or shorter, restless blobs. "Bunching up at our tail, looks like," Julia said.

"Time to spring trap?"

Julia wondered. Poking them with the fusion drive's lance might just get more of her crew killed. She doubted that anything could dismember such moving mountain-sized things for long. She called out, "Shanna! Come alongside us—we'll have to use both torches."

"Mine's a lot less cutting than yours," Shanna sent back. They were both gunning it and weaving together in programmed dodges, to throw off their pursuers. But flies can't dodge trucks, as many windshields have proved.

Julia could see big bunched masses of high magnetic fields converging on both ships.

"Let's get close together, then turn our thrust at the maximum field points," Julia said.

The idea of dueling with such beasties was laughable, and both their ships were like lumbering tank ships. But Viktor sent *High Flyer* into a long curve toward *Proserpina*.

"Punch that way!" Shanna called. "DIS—navigation override: DEC 48, RA 23."

They seared the sky together.

Fuming, the magnetic whorls backed away. But the ships could perform this gravity-free gavotte only so long—then their plumes drove them apart. Long minutes ticked by as both crews watched their screens. Nobody moved, not even to get coffee. The magnetic stresses crept back in. Feelers filled the spaces.

"Damn!" Viktor said.

"We can't do this forever," Julia said.

"They'll figure out a new trick," Shanna said. "This is their turf."

Julia took a long breath of the ship's dry air, smelling the sweaty fear around her. Nobody spoke.

She had to get them out of this trap, this endless cycle of violence and terror. *"That is not the point,"* the fish said.

"Yes, but how to break the . . ." She pursed her lips. *Some problems just curve back in upon themselves, and that is the only solution.*

Was that it? *The figure that curves upon itself.*

She said to Viktor, "The fusion equilibrium, it's a torus, right?"

He was busy, and his fingers danced in useless, fretful patterns. "Is working fine, don't worry."

"Can you clean the system now?" she pressed him.

"What?" he sputtered. "We do that only to go to shut-down."

"I know. You pulse the top magnetic fields, force the toroid down through the magnetic nozzle."

"But only to finish the burn!"

"Do it."

"What?" Disbelief.

"Now."

He peered at her for a long moment. "It is our defense, the exhaust—"

"They gave us a humanlike figure. We could show them something like themselves. It's all we've got."

"But the danger! Will take time to reconfigure the drive, stabilize—"

"Now. Please."

It took more long minutes, but he did it. The great circulating doughnut shape squeezed downward, heating further as it compressed through the knothole of the curved magnetic nozzle, and popped free.

It was hotter than the ordinary exhaust and brimmed with fresh virulence, burning saturation holes in their aft view screens. The doughnut expanded, cooled, and traceries worked along its slick surface. All this they witnessed on the same grid display that showed the magnetic structures. The toroid was small, tiny compared with the Beings. But it grew. Dimmed, cooled, but swelled as its magnetic field lines tried to straighten out. The plasma inside cooled, recombined, gave off a flash of blue light.

Shanna called, "What the hell is this?"

"Calculated risk." Julia said it forcefully, but she was suddenly full of doubts. She had acted on impulse, on a hunch. She had done that on Mars before, and it had worked. But here . . .

She whispered, "Viktor, better start building a fresh toroid."

"I will have to reset the induction coils, prime the Marshall guns—"

"Please, yes. In case we have to . . . well, run for it."

Shanna said, "You sure flip-flop. I thought you were the one who wanted to zap them."

"I, we, do—but something I remember . . ."

Then the screens brimmed again with furious activity. In the whorls of magnetic turbulence she saw again a spinning, spitting torus—the shape she remembered from Hawaii, when she had blown bubbles and seen them shape magically into airy toroids; in the core of her own fusion rocket, the magnetic torus that kindled ions—a geometry so sought by nature that it appeared in vastly different places. Now it condensed into an immense, wobbly doughnut shape. Both ships speared through the hole of it.

"Like a noose that can choke us," Viktor said sourly. He turned back to work on rebooting their fusion core.

"Or . . ." Julia let the word hang in the tense air.

"The toroid," Shanna said. "They're making themselves, all of them, into one huge—"

"They're echoing us," Jordin whispered.

Julia watched the giant structure form, a curve thousands of kilometers long. Capable of pressing against their ships, yes. Or doing another job?

"They echoed our human shapes."

"And killed Veronique." Shanna's lips pressed so thin they turned white.

"Yes . . . still . . ." Julia was guessing, but it felt right, and she had learned to shoot such rapids with no qualm. "Now they're echoing our fusion doughnut. But it's *their* shape as well this time. So they know there is some sort of basic kinship between us. A love of geometry—particularly of geometry that works."

Viktor laughed dryly. "Euclid would be pleased. His language!"

A call from Mary Kay interrupted. "We've gotten low-frequency communication from somebody. Big wave train. DIS put Wiseguy to work on it." She paused. "*High Flyer*, are you getting it, too?"

"Yeah, big amplitude."

Long, coasting minutes . . . Mary Kay said, "They say they'll withdraw a bit. Want to speak among themselves."

Julia shrugged. "I wonder if we can eavesdrop?" Viktor nodded.

Mary Kay said, "They've put up some sort of . . . well, screen. A blob of plasma, wrapped around us. Both ships."

Shanna sent, "We're seeing that, too. Wow, it's building in density."

Jordin came on. "Maybe that's to give them some privacy. If they talk to each other in low frequencies, it won't come through that blob because the plasma frequency is higher. Just like Earth's ionosphere—we can't receive low-frequency stuff through that, either."

Viktor said, "How long they want talk?"

Mary Kay said, "There's a phrase here, Wiseguy just delivered. 'Half period of small world.' What's that?"

Viktor said, "Hope is not orbital period—that's centuries. Must mean rotation—few days."

"Well, at least it buys us time." Julia shrugged. "Let Earthside worry for a while."

At dinner they slurped up the meaty stew ravenously and crawled into bed. Julia was exhausted. More like completely drained. Looking at Viktor, she could tell that he was, too.

"I wonder if the Beings sleep?" she asked, yawning.

"No reason. No day or night out here. So they talk for next few days. About us."

"Thing is," she said, "I can still do a hard day, maybe two in a row, but then I've got to recoup."

Viktor grunted assent. "Not youngsters anymore, the two of us. Wish for more of Mars Effect. But remember motto: age and cunning can defeat youth and strength anytime."

She drained the last of her hot cocoa and snuggled down into the covers. "Unfortunately we're on the same side as the youth and strength brigade. We're supposed to cooperate with them."

Viktor was looking blearily at a laptop screen. "Speaking of which, we got urgent message from Praknor. Too busy earlier to look at it."

The last thing Julia heard before slipping into blackness was Viktor's quizzical tone. "Big things happening on Mars, same time as here."

PART IV

COSMIC UNREST

It appears that the radical element responsible for the continuing thread of cosmic unrest is the magnetic field. What, then, is a magnetic field . . . that, like a biological form, is able to reproduce itself and carry on an active life in the general outflow of starlight, and from there alter the behaviour of stars and galaxies?

—Eugene Parker,
Cosmical Magnetic Fields

1.

UNIVERSALS

BOTH SHIPS HAD TO wait weeks, through long and sometimes tedious translations, to discover the truth—or at least a version of it.

Astronauts are obviously not ambassadors, nor are they experts in linguistics. But they made do.

Slowly the complexity of Being society emerged—often through misunderstandings. Wiseguy groused—unusually vexed, but then, it was a truly advanced self-learning program—that matters were made more difficult by the Beings' habit of using no particular word order in clauses that made up conditional statements. Everything seemed to depend on everything else, so a sentence could mix up word order, and yet to the Beings it meant the same thing.

Perhaps this came from their having no sharp boundaries, so flow and flux were the basics of life, not barriers. Some human senses are like this: we feel that metals are cool even if they're as warm as the room, because we sense the rate of heat loss, not the temperature itself. Yet the Beings could count. They knew basic arithmetic and were whizzes with an intuitive feel for calculus, particularly integrals. For gigayears they had been integrating fluxes that nourished them.

Only a minority of them were interested in the Hotness,

which seemed to mean the realm of planets and sun. Most were engaged in conversations or works that even the Beings could ill describe. Wiseguy finally gave up trying to translate into human terms, though the closest approximation seemed to be "the Long Dance."

So with plenty of Earthside computational help, they let Wiseguy assume a role in the dialogue, one that Dr. Jensen christened "Gofer to the Beings"—with only slight irony. Wiseguy's orders were to focus on the bow shock problem.

"Got a call in from Shanna," Julia heard in her headphones, from the watch officer, Doug Killings. "Forwarding."

Julia sighed. She was trying to keep their ships working together well, but Shanna wasn't making it easy. When Shanna came on, she started right in: "I'm picking up a lot of movement from some of those Beings, the ones who pulled farther out."

"So?" Julia was trying to thread her way through a lot of Wiseguy results and did not like her concentration broken.

"Ukizi broke the Dopplers down. There's some spikes, looks like small, fast things."

"Um. So?"

"Well, anything new makes me recall what happened before. Veronique."

Julia said stiffly, "She was in my crew. I'll take responsibility."

"Not what I meant. Be warned, is all."

"Roger. Out." The old pilot-spacer jargon worked well if you wanted to be abrupt.

Julia sighed with relief. Back to Wiseguy. Wow, was

this dense stuff. The program's most probable interpretation was that the Beings were not instigators of the bow shock intrusion—even though one of them went by that name and seemed to have earned it. Instigator had started the whole agenda of duplicating "hot" life on Pluto.

Earthside had a consensus theory for the Beings, garnered both from Being talk and from their movements. Whole teams had followed the gusher of data the two ships had sent back, and applied vast computer resources. From that trove they had tracked the Beings' movements using the *High Flyer* and *Proserpina* radars. With more intricate work Earthside had outlined them and picked up features of their geometry, all seen by their plasma wave emissions. These last sounded in audio like fizzing howls played against a basso background.

Legions of "experts" (whatever that meant) had profiled from this lode. The Beings, they thought, were opportunists. Every now and then, the Beings said, clots and clouds drifting in the realm between the stars would wander into the path of the Hotness, which apparently meant the sun. Those big clouds had increased density and mass and smacked into the prow of the solar system. For a "short while"—which seemed to mean centuries—the interstellar wilderness where the Beings thrived would press inward. Most Beings avoided that turbulent zone. But this local group relished the chance to feast on an enhanced Cascade—their harvesting of incoming energy.

So they ventured inward. And fed. And instigated.

It was not clear why. Certainly the turbulent zone where the solar wind met the interstellar plasma was ripe with energy. And as that boundary, the "heliopause," bulged in, forced by the increased interstellar pressure, the Beings moved with it.

Perfectly natural, *follow the food*. But why the Pluto experiment? Julia felt that they were just born curious. Maybe that was a universal, too, among intelligent creatures. Perhaps curiosity was how they got smart.

Shanna, in her role of discoverer of Plutonian life, thought there was some ancient driver. She asked Wiseguy to scan carefully the Beings' word choices, for terms like "ancient," "epoch," "age span," "eon." "I think they want to find out where they came from," she had said. "Which seems to be 'the Fount,' whatever that is."

"Somewhere in the solar system?" Viktor had scowled doubtfully at Shanna's screen image.

"That's what they say—I think. These codes in Wiseguy aren't perfect."

"Unlike her," Viktor said out of range of the microphones.

The codes were fast but blunt, yes, but in time they served. One thing was clear: the Beings seemed troubled. Some of their party had departed in a rage. These Earthside had identified by their "color"—low-frequency emissions, apparently leakage from their interior thoughts. The Beings left behind kept up a running debate—on which *High Flyer* and *Proserpina* eavesdropped, with Earthside's legions kibitzing—about what to do. Some felt they should break off contact because it was dangerous, new, frightening. New opinions came in daily, from Beings so distant that the light travel time was just getting to them.

This was another clue that the Beings had an ornately complex society, which one might well expect, given that their apparent age was 3 or 4 billion years. This Wiseguy eavesdropped from conversations; their time scale used as a unit circuits of the sun around the galaxy, which is about 250 million years. Not much younger than the sun itself. And at least one, called Recorder, said it had been around back then.

This conclusion had taken a while to check and even longer to get used to. They had invited Shanna and some of her crew for a discussion of it.

"Cannot be creatures who live forever," Viktor maintained.

Shanna and Julia agreed, which surprised them both— brows furrowed, eyes carefully not looking at each other—even though they were both biologists. "Evolution always trades off long-term traits against short-term advantage," Shanna had said, her tone implying that she had not expected this from Viktor. "That's why we age."

Viktor had shaken his head. "We wear out, is all." He had sprained his foot the day before doing some repair work and illustrated his thesis by limping across the dayroom deck.

Julia said helpfully, "Look at our hearts. They work fine for a while, when we're mating and bringing up children, but then they get clogged and fail."

Viktor grinned. "I know theory. But these Beings, they say they do not reproduce."

Both the women biologists blinked at this. How a Being could arise without natural selection through reproduction was a mystery. Even beyond carbon-based molecules, the principles were supposed to be universal. "This feels pretty damned anti-Darwinian," Shanna called it, shaking her head.

"But they are here." Viktor grinned again.

"Must be they started off growing from some kernel," Julia ventured. "Their *growth* was selected for."

"Um." Viktor was not convinced; his mouth twisted at both sides, in opposite directions. "So they get smarter when get bigger? Or started smart?"

"Traits evolve," Shanna said, "they don't just pop out full-blown. Each step has to give the organism some incremental advantage."

"Oh?" Viktor shrugged. "Maybe Darwin not so universal."

The biologists agreed to leave the theory for later. Viktor judged this to be a victory, though it was unclear for whom, and brought out some champagne he had hidden deep in the bowels of *High Flyer*. "Hard times lately," he observed. The sound of popping corks pleased everyone.

2.

MASS IS BRUTE

FORCEFUL COILED ITSELF about a metallic slab of matter—gingerly, gingerly. The mass tumbled in blackness, glinting with ice. Yet the Beings could sense its hardness, its slow-yielding mass.

Sunless sent, <I wonder if this act is a goodness.>

<Do not question now! We left because we are at the

critical cusp time. Someone must act! Now *help* me.> Angrily Forceful intensified its magnetic fluxes near the tumbling mote. Arcs of spitting ions sprayed the lump.

To Sunless this place was already uncomfortably warm. They had abandoned the others, then followed an arc around, to harvest energies near the Cascade. Then they converged, conversing softly, planning, gathering their strengths. Plasma gnawed at their boundaries, irksome and itching. The Six spiraled near each other restlessly, some light-minutes away from the solid ships. Sunless and Forceful had broken off from the Eight as soon as the solids sent a confirming signal, the small shape of a toroid—the basic form of Being life.

Now there would follow some tedious and disagreeable exchange of signals—*talk, talk, talk,* endlessly. The Eight would debate the meaning of such motes knowing the toroid, and whether this in some elemental way meant that motes could attain the status of Beings. Such ideas were too much for the Six. They seethed with impatience.

Forceful had gone to the rest of the Six and made his case. If their goal of Outbounding was ever to come to pass, they would need the Eight. But Instigator had captured the attention of the Eight with its dangerous experiments on the cold world. Now the vermin from the Hotness threatened them all. The case was clear: <We must find a way to destroy these tiny things and the machines they fly,> Forceful finished.

Dusk, now Forceful's new pair-partner, had necessarily gone along, but remained quiet. Ring and Serene were distant, pondering matters. Mirk, now paired with Sunless, was similarly reluctant. Out of politeness Forceful dragged along the forlorn, shrunken Chill. Though Forceful had mentored Chill, Forceful bristled with spires of pinched, angry energy as it towed the pale and withered, Diminished Chill. None could bear to see the ragged shreds of murmuring plasma that festered from Chill's boundaries, pathetic and diseased.

Forceful asked them all with due formality and quite politely: would they join in another attack?

No. Somehow the novelty of the moment had shattered the Six.

But not Sunless and Forceful. Each seethed with rage, sending snarled traceries down their field lines.

Forceful spat as he worked. <I have paid strict attention to that strange voice, the one that says it speaks for the cold ones, the Chemicals.> Forceful had shaped itself, cupping its speech to broadcast outward. Those Beings farther out would hear his fury song. Perhaps they could be allies in future. <It seeks to blunt the Cascade! Asks the help of Beings to push the Cascade outward. Arrogance! From tiny things.>

From the outer reaches came a calming song. <Do the Chemicals not realize that even they were governed by the spirit, too? That we must live in balance with the natural spring? That the Cascade is the source of us, unquestionable? Surely even the slow, sloppy surges of their bodies also somehow capture some whisper of this wisdom.>

Forceful fumed and did not deign to answer. It radiated a fury pure and righteous.

Sunless replied in a voice studied and calm. <They come to injure us. It seems their way. Alien beyond knowing.>

Forceful continued to work but let no sign of this mix with its radiations. His tone was lofty, in case the Eight heard. <When I asked that voice of the tiny machines—so loud it is, but with no Being body attached—to give its legends, it answered. Such fantasies! The drooling fears of the young, before they discern the scheme of life.>

This provoked relieved mirth from the Six. Forceful always knew how to shift discussions in its favor, winning with charm. He fumed, ripe with thoughts now, burning his stored reserves in his fury. <There were slight signs that they did fathom bits of higher truths. They had a legend about a Chemical pinned to a piece of dead matter and allowed to die that way—Diminished to extinction! Apparently a commonplace among Chemicals. Yet after this fearsome loss, the identity emerged from its full subtraction—to claim life again. Such a desperate story! Elementary knowledge tells us that such things do not happen, of course. But the existence of such an ancient story suggests how much they yearned to not be governed by their own blunt, chemical ways.>

Sunless knew to let Forceful talk. Now she slid in with, <Understandably. Extinction! Total subtraction! Why do they persist in remaining Chemical at all?>

<They could bring doom to us,> Forceful said. <They can cut us and yet do not possess wisdom. Even their legends are primitive.>

<These tiny things—why, then, do you play with them?> Sunless said.

<We must! I have a grip on it.> Forceful was not skilled at tiny operations, having long ago left that to the likes of Crafter. <Get another such. They have mass but no other useful property.>

The two Beings were in essence flexing fields. Only in long-term memory did they have need for a realm, tucked in deep inside themselves, for permanent fields that could hold memory for the ages. There, static arrays held fixed their core personalities, built up over billions of years. External forces could destroy these. Indeed, a Being named Thoughtful, legendary in wisdom, had been rendered stupid by a passing shard of cold matter that sliced through its central web of magnetically hoarded memory. Such a mass as the one Forceful now grasped, tugging it and slinging it about, uncertain but angry.

<I can barely hold it,> Forceful said. <Matter struggles against—help me!>

Sunless had gone looking for another such metallic, conducting fragment. They were uncommon, but over her vast expanse she grasped several. She suspected that Forceful had been holding this one nearby somehow, ready to use. Now was the time. Sunless gripped the shard with her own magnetic fields, though it was slippery.

Stalks of current mingled between the two Beings. Fine sprays of atoms, dancing forever in buoyant fields, clashed with electrons to make a pinch. Together they snaked the fragment around in a circle, calling to each other to achieve balance and heft. A luminescence sprang between them where energies surged.

<We must make it gain velocity,> Forceful said.

<It is so small—>

<These solid ships are hollow, and so they are soft. At high speeds this dense solid will pierce their hollow packages.>

<I do not understand this physics, but if you so say . . .>

<I will deal with the mechanics.>

<Yes, yes, but the others will be angry if—>

<Let them be.> Forceful swung the shard around roughly in his fields, using to the full cold matter's natural rejection of their fields. <This must be what it is like to have solid touch.>

<Are you sure you understand these solid mechanics. I am afraid—>

<Do not fear! The solid creatures are weak. And small!>

Mass is brute. It required powerful surges of currents, yet a delicate sense of timing.

With Sunless to help he whipped the conducting rock around in a last surge, then loosed it—collapsing his fields at one side, letting the mass escape. Toward the ships. Fast.

<Let the tiny things deal with this!> Forceful sent with joy.

3.

INCOMING

CHOW-LIN SAW IT FIRST. "Incoming, small object, seven klicks a second."

Shanna's head jerked up from the mid-deck worktable, where she was having coffee with Julia and other crew. "How big?"

"Maybe . . . um, size of a house. Twenty meters across." He summoned a pixilated radar image on the big screen. A rough, tumbling rock.

Julia was acutely conscious of being a guest, not in control, and this froze her for a moment. A day had passed in conversation with the Beings, and Julia felt that she needed to confer with *Proserpina*'s crew, and especially Shanna. They had been holding fixed relative ship positions. Shanna had invited some of the *High Flyer* crew to come across, mostly to bring *Proserpina* new supplies. They had barely begun.

"Damn!" Jordin sprang to the control board.

"It's dead straight targeted on us, too," Chow-Lin said. "Accurate. Matched velocities. A couple hundred klicks out and due here inside a couple minutes."

Julia called to Wiseguy, "Get onto them! Those Beings! Ask what this is."

DIS answered in a resonant baritone. "I am mandated to respond to crew and Captain's orders, not to visiting guests."

Julia sputtered. Shanna shot back, "Belay that, Wiseguy—ask them. Now!"

A long pause while Wiseguy worked and they all conferred. Then: "They believe this act comes from a . . . faction. It is not condoned by the majority."

"Fine," Shanna said swiftly, "but what can they *do*?"

Silence. Wiseguy was talking, all right, but the immensity of these Beings now struck home. The light travel time to them—and through them—was minutes or more. Transmission time delay could be fatal now.

Jordin said, "I doubt we can move these ships fast enough to dodge."

Julia called Viktor, and he agreed. "Dodge is impossible—too much inertia, loaded with water in tanks. But . . . let me think."

"We've got less than two minutes to impact," Chow-Lin said, deliberately calm.

"Can we use the exhaust against it?" Shanna said.

"Worked on the Beings, but not on this," Viktor answered on comm. "It's got a lot of mass."

"Who's it going to hit?" Julia demanded.

Franklin said, "*High Flyer*. Seventy-eight seconds."

Julia froze. "Victor!" she cried. She was not looking at the radar images Chow-Lin had called up on the big screen. She stared into empty space. "Can you use the drive against them?"

"Not much time," he said. "Drive cannot stop big solid thing."

"Then—"

"Joke—when is weapon not a weapon?"

Julia cried, "What are you—"

"When is a space drive." Viktor's voice came absolutely flat and calm. "Am rotating."

"What?" Julia asked.

"Best to turn about axis." Viktor's voice was still controlled. "Cannot singe, cannot dodge, can do the—is French?—pirouette."

The radar image showed the long mass of *High Flyer* turning about its center, side jets flaring white-bright and hard. Chow-Lin sharpened resolution, and it was huge, jagged.

The rock came by in an eyeblink. Just a few meters to the side of *High Flyer*.

They applauded and cheered. Viktor's calm, steady tone said, "Comes another."

Julia's heart leaped. The radar showed a half dozen more, all homing in on *High Flyer*, all as big as houses—

enough to stave in the big nuke and blow it into history. She watched the now spinning cylinder of *High Flyer* torque and swerve, pulsing its aft nuke jet, spinning, a grand waltz set to the tune of circumstance—and it worked. Nuggets of primordial metal and rock arced past and never struck, spinning by in curves but never hitting solid. One of them sheared off an aft antenna, but there were backups. Plenty.

Wiseguy said calmly, "I find urgent traffic at high frequencies. The focus is one called Forceful, the source of these . . . pellets, as they call them."

Shanna said, "They're as big as continents, so why not? Flicking goddamn spitballs at us."

"And here's ours," Chow-Lin said tersely.

Tumbling rocks, three of them. Fast spectroscopy showed them to be mostly iron.

"Good conductors," Jordin said. "Easier for a magnetic slingshot to get a grip on."

Proserpina was smaller and so easier to turn. Since the incoming bullets were from a single source, they could make one rotation, to align the ship's cylinder with the rocks. Then they used attitude jets—magnetic nozzles affixed to the larger exhaust nozzle—to push the ship sideways.

It was touch and go. The burst of rocks came speeding in over a twenty-minute interval, tense seconds ticking by as *Proserpina* surged and rumbled. Viktor had shown them how. He sent hoarse, quick suggestions. Every hand fell to, doing calculations, checking on firing sequences. They barely had time to suit up for possible decompression.

"Not that it'll make much difference," Shanna said. "If something that big hits us, it'll take out entire decks."

Here was where Shanna's insistence on maintenance paid off. *High Flyer* came under attack again. Both ships were alive with cross talk.

Then it was over. No more salvos against either ship. They stood tensely and listened for radar pings. Nothing.

Wiseguy said in the silence, "The Beings send signals of concern."

It was not funny, but they all laughed.

Even in a crisis there is maintenance. Julia found doing routine jobs calming, and in the hours after their game of Dodgeball With Beings, she needed that. One of Julia's tasks was regulating waste disposal. She had actually volunteered for it, recalling the first Mars expedition.

By the time they had reached Mars encounter, they had over a ton of "human waste," which meant mostly dung. Rather than use up fuel landing it, Viktor wanted to dump it.

The engineer, Raoul, had to do an EVA, anyway, to check out externals. First they had to blow the bolts to free the centrifugal-gravity cable. Away flew the snaky line and the empty upper stage they had used for the counterweight. They had watched the cylinder dwindle as the habitat abruptly went into zero gravity. The crescent of Mars hung in the distance, its bright pink hues a welcome touch of color after six months in the dead black of space.

Raoul went out with Viktor, carrying a hundred kilos of trash they could leave to interplanetary orbit for a few millennia. Julia and Marc, their geologist, trained the two external cameras on them. An estimated 100 million others were watching in real time from Earthside.

Raoul's news from the Habitat Landing Module's outside was good. No discernible damage to their exterior, and the water patch they'd had to make looked as though it was holding well. Raoul put another fresh layer on, hoping that would get them through the violence of aerobraking without another leak. Even if it didn't, fresh water was waiting at the landing site, manufactured by the Gusev chem plant.

But before the adventure could start, they had to dump the dung—a ton of it. Julia had pulsed the line pressure in the waste system, pushing the solids farther into their plastic lining. Raoul and Viktor had to pull it out, helping the pressure at the other end. She recalled easing up the pressure, nice and smooth . . .

And it had stuck. Julia was doubly glad that Axelrod had vetoed live interior coverage of this part. The external cameras would give their audience a striking view, and who wanted to see crew just staring at dials? So had gone the argument.

So the subscribers did not get to watch Julia break out in a sweat. Viktor's swearing did not help the basic indignity of the moment, either, so the Consortium monitors just edited it out. Which meant that Viktor said very little through the whole high drama.

They got it free after an hour of aggravating labor. Raoul had tied it off with a huge twist-it. Grunting, the two shoved it overboard. They pulled the gray plug straight out of the cylindrical waste tube, an unpleasant analogy.

When Viktor did their burn to enter the upper atmosphere, the ton of dung had continued on into interplanetary space.

Ah, nostalgia. Now Julia simply popped the valve on their disposal system, which blew it directly out into space. Nothing jammed, because they had plenty of overpressure. Modern conveniences! She could scarcely believe how far deep-space engineering had come. In two decades she had moved from a Porta Potti tugboat to a nuclear fusion *Queen Mary*.

A day after the bombardment Julia and Viktor opened the vid from Praknor. The woman was terse, but something in her eyes betrayed confusion.

"We're getting all sorts of activity in four vents, especially Vent R. I've pulled teams out, for safety. We're monitoring with cameras and instruments alone."

Pictures of vapor layered in the air near the Marsmat. Currents ran in the walls, measured by meters. "Spectrum analysis of the currents shows complex patterns, but we can't seem to make sense of them. There are even a few of these—"

An image taken at night at the Vent R opening. High up, the stars were sharp, but vapor poured from the broad vent mouth and blurred those on the horizon. A pale shaft of light played up through the mist, a cone opening to the sky. It pulsed in a long, slow rhythm.

"Several vents do this now, about once a week. I read your early reports about one beam of light from Vent A, but not seen again. This seems to be a repeat of that, but now far more often, and from other sites. Clearly we are witnessing some new manifestations. Perhaps attempts to directly communicate with us? Or with other mat sites around the planet? Judging from the increased electrical current levels, there may be a general rise in mat response." Praknor paused, looking at the camera with concern. "The geologists have found that those currents are driven by piezoelectric effects—that is, by rock layers responding to pressure. How this ties to the Marsmat is far from obvious. What makes the pressure? I am sending by tightbeam several papers written about this and submitted to Earthside journals, principally to *Nature*, perhaps for a special issue."

Praknor's hesitant manner cut off, and she concluded, lips a thin pale line, "Any comments on this work would be sincerely appreciated by us all."

Viktor turned it off and sat staring at the screen. "Wish I was there."

Julia said softly, "Me, too."

They were kept busy monitoring Wiseguy's talk with the Beings, trying to penetrate the aliens' snarled syntax and layered meanings. "Like Mandarin Chinese," Viktor said, then admitted that he had only heard it was a mannered, opaque tongue.

In came another vid from Axelrod. "More Mandarin corporate-speak," Julia muttered, but took a break and watched the vid. A mistake. Within minutes after Axelrod's greetings and cheerleading she was fuming.

"Hey," Axelrod said, "I had this crazy idea. Sure we want Darksiders, the tech that makes them, the works. Plenty market there in space fabrication. But . . . what if we could bring some zand—small ones, of course—back to the moon for, uh, study?"

"Study?" she yelled at the screen. "You want a god-damn zoo for the tourists! But they're sentient!"

"—can cool it down for them, like those penguin exhibits at zoos Earthside, then maybe pump up the atmosphere so they could fly around. Pluto on the moon! I've tried this on the ISA people and they're okay with it, but Shanna, well, she's kinda emotional lately. Anyway, you should think about it. You gotta do some more work on what they eat so we know what to feed—"

She hit the pause switch, blood boiling. *Good old Axelrod! He'd have made a fine Victorian explorer, stuffing natives into cages!*

And Shanna had reacted just as she did, probably. Julia blinked. Maybe they were more alike than she had thought.

4.

DYNAMICS

FORCEFUL WAS ADAMANT. <We should not be surprised that we failed. The point is not to give up.>

Chill said wanly, <We are not powerful enough. And Recorder has threatened us all with involuntary induced subtraction. Further Diminishment!>

Sunless said, <Only if we return to within their reach.>

Chill sent fretful undertones. <Surely we will not . . . flee?>

Forceful rebuked the shrunken Being with, <The weak should be silent.>

Sunless said, <We try to move brute matter, as we have seldom done before. Only Instigator has studied those arts. She knows dynamics and can work on tiny scales—>

<You propose asking Instigator?> Mirk asked in derision. <She would rebuke—>

<No, I say we should not try to apply forces to small things at all. Not when the true enemy is larger.> To underline the implication, Sunless let its notes trail into the background noise of distant conversations.

Forceful said, <Yes—we can exert pressures over a larger area. Very good!>

Mirk paused, silky striations running through it, then got the idea. <Their carrying machine.>

5.

ZEUS

JULIA PUT EARTHSIDE, ISA, and the Consortium out of her mind—they were sending indigestible messages that would have taken all her time just to read—and fretted. While Jordin and Shanna worked with Wiseguy, they put the whole rest of the crew to work methodically checking all the ship's systems. If another attack came, they had to be ready for new methods. *Prepare for the unexpected . . .*

But what? Zeus hurling lightning bolts? No, that they'd already done, killing Veronique. Shotgun blasts of rocks, wide enough so they couldn't dodge? She didn't like to think of that, because there seemed no defense. She talked to Viktor, and he suggested that if the faction now called the Outbounds wanted to, they could push against the ship itself.

"Tumble us, maybe even break us in half." He blinked owlishly.

"You really think so?"

"They use magnetic pressure, and we're a big cylinder of metal." He shrugged and raised his eyebrows, a picture of Slavic fatalism.

"Gee, you're a real morale booster."

"You asked. We are mice among elephants."

"And just hope they don't learn to dance?"

"Is dangerous out here."

"Looks like time to bring in the diplomats."

"And we have none. Shanna, she is no diplomat."

Julia grinned. "No kidding. We're still barely getting along. Yet we're supposed to deal with invisible aliens the size of the Earth."

"Back on Mars we had mat that may be one connected organism. So was big, and we didn't understand." He spread his hands. "This is similar, yes?"

"Ummm. Maybe . . . It's still alien communication. And with Wiseguy it's plenty easier than the decades we spent trying to sense what the Marsmat was about."

"Is true. Maybe time to become better friends with Wiseguy. Not that it seems very wise, no."

So Julia and Viktor met in the dayroom with *High Flyer* and *Proserpina* Wiseguys linked and in attendance—which meant they had a lot of Wiseguy's running time allotted to them—and worked through the fat file of Being signals. Jordin and Mary Kay attended over comm link. Most they could throw away as just plain too hard to understand. Let the next generation of data hounds mine it for their theses. In a sly gesture of revenge Julia sent the entire file Earthside, just to let them know what it was like to get buried under digital files.

The latest attack had been reviewed by the Beings. A faction they called the Outbounds—Forceful and Sunless, plus others—had thrown the rocks at them. Something called Recorder solemnly intoned that the offending Beings had been penalized by "involuntary induced subtraction."

"Ummm," Julia said. "Off with their heads?"

Jordin said carefully, "I think it's more like a little finger."

"For trying to kill us?" Viktor demanded.

"Even a little finger hurts," Jordin said reasonably.

Julia and Mary Kay had been trawling semi-independently through the massive intercept files. They had Wiseguy group and sort the identity tags, based on time and position of their transmissions. *Even Zeus lived in a society* . . . Julia laid them out on-screen.

(Chill, Dusk) (Mirk, Sunless) (Ring, Forceful)

"Maybe that's the Six the later messages refer to," Mary Kay said.

Julia pursed her lips, pointing at correlation functions displayed in three dimensions. These showed where in the sky paired signals came from, and when. "But look. Later there are paired signals, linking two others."

(Dusk, Forceful)

Viktor leaned over her shoulder. "Look at earlier source-points. We killed Chill, I bet."

"Not killed," Mary Kay said. "Maybe wounded. See these later signals with its identity tags? Weak, but there."

Viktor studied the three-dimensional functions. "But not paired with the Forceful tag. So they . . . broke up?"

Julia had put more pairs on the screen. "Maybe these are the Eight?"

(Instigator, Bright) (Recorder, Quiet) (Joy, Solemn) (Vain, Eater)

"Why paired?" Viktor asked. "Have two sexes?"

"Hard to imagine how electromagnetic creatures could," Mary Kay said.

Viktor grinned. "Lack of imagination is not an argument. Especially lately."

Julia said, "In our biology, having two sexes lets us blend traits in each generation, always shuffling the cards to get another hand. Maybe they're making use of that."

Viktor shrugged skeptically. "Don't need to make new ones, if they live forever. Not that I think they do. Got to be accidents, bad luck—the only universal maybe."

Julia nodded sourly. "We haven't a clue how life works out here."

They all looked at each other and nodded. More and more it seemed that nothing from traditional Darwinian theory applied to these huge beasts. Viktor argued that the Beings' habitat was unlimited. They could fill the regions between the stars. So the lessons learned from Earth's bounded biosphere might not apply at all.

Wiseguy had picked up discussions among the Beings about something called Distants, who were apparently behind the low-level signals that came rolling in from all directions. These murmurings were so far impossible to decipher and might be in another language entirely than that used by the Beings they knew. These were continuous across the sky, unlike those of the Eight and Six, whose long, curling songs came from local patches in the sky.

"The Distants apparently lie beyond what the Beings term 'the desert between the suns'—or so I infer, in preliminary fashion," Wiseguy said. Julia wondered if it had deliberately obsequious subprogramming.

"Interstellar?" Mary Kay blinked. "Beings around other stars?"

Viktor shrugged. "No reason our star should be special. Is Copernican principle."

Wiseguy had no opinion. Apparently this level of inference was beyond its capacity. However, Wiseguy did feel that the opposite faction, the Inbounds, wanted to "deal."

"Um. Means . . . ?" Viktor asked.

Wiseguy said formally, "They say 'to help them get to Hotness and understand it,' approximately."

"Um. Means . . . ?" Viktor asked.

Wiseguy processed silently, then: "The inner region— planets. And something called the Fount."

Julia said, "How? To help them get beyond just developing the zand?"

"Apparently." Wiseguy had programs that made it seem to be carrying on a conversation, though "apparently" signaled a certain level of probability they could look up on a scale.

"You asked them the big question about the bow shock moving?"

"Of course, madam. They say there is a diffuse molecular cloud pressing against the solar wind. It is half a light-year thick, along the axis of the sun's velocity. The Beings have known it was coming, at an angle across the sun's orbit around the galactic center, for quite some time. Apparently."

Julia sighed. Measuring the physical problem was one of their major mission goals, and this sounded like very bad news. "And this pressure—once the molecular cloud fully arrives, how far in will the bow shock go?"

Wiseguy said blandly—and Julia thought, *Of course, it has nothing at stake!*—"They say, inward of 'the circled one,' which seems to mean Saturn."

"When?" Viktor asked.

"In about a century. It is like the weather, local conditions not well predicted, but the climate overall—"

Viktor said crisply to Julia, "Let us get word to Earthside about this—quick."

Part of Julia wanted to say, *Yes, we only have a century to go,* but she resisted.

"I have," Wiseguy said, to their surprise, "as part of my retrieval architecture. This sharpens the data. Using the information from the Beings, we received a projection done by the U.S. National Science Foundation Heliopause Working Group. It says that incursion of the hydrogen wall to within the Saturn orbit would introduce molecular hydrogen into the Earth's atmosphere, by diffusion, to an unacceptable level."

Julia was impressed with Wiseguy's abilities. Then she realized that it was undoubtedly using all Earthside computational reserves, allowing for the time delay and working well ahead of the mere humans. Linked with those resources, even with an hours-long hindrance, it had vast abilities. Plus the time to be submissive . . . Earthside had "adjusted" the *Proserpina* Wiseguy that had been snippy to her.

"And all this is already heating up all the Earthside media, right?"

"Yes. Such implications are impossible to suppress in—"

"I know, I know." Never mind that the bow shock was a gossamer brush of a delicate veil, compared with the brute momentum of planets. Panic would spread, anyway, in the hothouse media. But sullen mass and inertia were not the full story, because a steady rain of molecular hydrogen, drifting down into Earth's air, would combine with the free oxygen to make steam. That would heat the atmosphere's outer layers, sopping up oxygen, adding to the warming already stirring the air, worsening the clashes of climate.

"That analysis, it's certain?"

"To six sigmas of reliability, I believe." Wiseguy always used statistical measures. "The molecular hydrogen will combine with oxygen, generating a flooding rainfall and reduced breathable oxygen. I have the chemical rate equations available—"

"No need," Julia said. "It sounds bad enough."

"They speak of an earlier Being called Incursor. It went into the Hotness, they say, and never returned."

"What was it after?" Viktor asked.

"Knowledge. It wanted to understand the Fount—though what that is seems unclear, except that it is in the Hotness."

"Fount? A planet?" Viktor asked.

"They do not seem to know. Or else it is a . . . excuse the use of a human term here . . . metaphor."

"Look, cultural exchange time is over," Viktor said adamantly. "To business, yes? Earthside wants to know how we can stop bow shock from moving in. Can these Beings do anything about it?"

Wiseguy's voice was still flat, unemotional. "I do not know. They do not seem to have tried before. To them it is now a boon."

Mary Kay asked, "Why?"

"The bow shock moves in, toward Pluto, where one called Instigator has been for a long time conducting its 'experiments' in 'warmlife,' which I suppose means the zands. And maybe us."

"Pluto's sure not very warm," Julia said.

"It was the best they could do . . ." Wiseguy's words were coming slower now, as the discussion taxed its inferential processors. This was the boundary where an artificial intelligence was strained to its limits. ". . . to understand how life could arise in such . . . for them . . . bizarre places. Planets."

Julia snapped her fingers. "To make Pluto work, they needed energy."

"They have not mentioned this," Wiseguy said circumspectly.

Viktor beamed, slapped Julia on the shoulder. "That is it, *yes*. The bow shock moves in, there is plenty electrodynamic energy. Close to Pluto, easy to use. So they make the currents run into the planet, instead of around the bow. Feeds warmth—and electrical sparks—to the planet."

Wiseguy had nothing to say beyond "I must consider . . ." Slowness signaled its limitations. It began reviewing its interpretations of the slabs of Being cross talk, and Viktor told it to process on its own.

Julia nodded. "They need the bow shock energy to run Pluto. So they won't want that to change."

Viktor nodded ruefully. "They have no reason to help us."

Mary Kay said, "We can talk to them, ask for help." Fine crackles of static blurred her words.

Viktor's eyebrows arched. "They might not bite. What if they decide their research is more important than our lives? What will we do then?"

Julia said, "The Eight seemed sympathetic when the Six attacked us."

Viktor said, "But the Eight run the Pluto experiment."

Nobody had anything to say to that.

When Julia ended the session with Wiseguy and *Proserpina*, she returned to their quarters. On the wall screen prompt was a new message from Axelrod. She sighed and punched it in. But after the first few seconds of identification data there was only hash. She called the bridge.

"Yes, sir, Cap'n," Killings said, brow lined with worry. "Your message got cut off. We lost transmission with Earthside eighteen minutes ago."

"Why?"

"There's a big solar storm brewing. It's swept past Earth already and is blocking our lower-frequency links. You want I should send Earthside a prompt, saying we want that last vid on higher frequencies? They're pretty crowded with system telemetry, but I could get some room at 7.8 gigs, if you say, Cap'n."

Julia was tired of endless data. "No, I don't really want to see it. When—"

Viktor said, "So . . . we are on our own."

His slow, studied words gave her pause. "How soon will the storm be over?"

"It's a big one—unusual, too—so nobody knows." Killings was apologetic, one corner of his mouth fretting.

"Not your fault, y'know. Come this far," she said, "you'd think we wouldn't be worrying about Earthside's weather."

6.

TIP

THE TORRENT OF SOLAR wind drew their attention, mostly because it did the same to the Beings. Of the Six they had heard nothing but murky signals, probably (the Eight said) deliberately muffled and shielded. The Eight were like distracted dinner partners, digging into the main entrée and neglecting conversation. For the first time in a while the crews of both ships had time to stop and think. Julia, though, spent her time looking at the display screens. There, with *High Flyer*'s antennas turned back toward the inner solar system, she could see the show.

To live on Earth or even Mars was to give the sun a bit too much importance. Here it was just the brightest of the stars, not a disk. And now, Julia mused, they knew that electricity, not sunlight, fed the distant glow of Pluto. Solids were deeply cold out here, but the filmy plasmas worked with raging energies. Their equivalent temperatures were measured in the thousands of degrees, and there lay the necessity for life to harvest this bounty.

She close-upped the sun and saw there the shadowy speckles that had cast out such a withering gale. These were the ruins of solar coronal arches, dark only by contrast with the brilliance around them, but still hotter than any furnace. Yet these were the remnants of a fury that had peaked months before. The gout of plasma it exploded into space had been traveling nearly a year. From there the snarling knots came climbing up the gravity gradient of the star, through the orbits of the planets, onward without losing a fraction of their power.

Only when it intersected the tightbeams between *High Flyer* and Earth did they know of its arrival. On it came, a roiling smear now detectable only in the radio, yet glowing with the power of a billion hydrogen bombs. She could see from the Doppler readings that its speed was now several hundred kilometers per second, and so it had been plowing outward for months, undiminished and evolving. It was an oval blob, fraying at the edges but radiating halos of plasma fizz. She could see it by its own emissions.

As it approached, finer structure appeared in the shorter wavelengths. Intricate coils bigger than worlds, shattering

explosions—all testified to the recombining energy of the
fields. The plasma inside it was the junior partner now to
the festering field energies. Their radars were hopeless,
compared with the bright fountains coming off the blob. It
spun, trailing ragged arms bigger than planets. Julia
thought for a moment that it looked like a troubled hurri-
cane seen from orbit. The next moment it was more like a
spiral nebula shining forth, twisting and changing before
her eyes, as if she were suspended in time like a god of
eternity.

She wondered if this mass could do damage to *High
Flyer*. The ship was drifting under no thrust, its squat living cylinder rotating to provide onboard centrifugal gravity, and was running its reactor only for power. Working
with Jordin and Viktor from the emission signatures, she
was able to estimate the density. She gave a dry chuckle.
Though it blared with furious energies in the high microwave frequencies, it was less massive than the gauzy
glows inside neon lights. Its voyage out through the planets had thinned its anger. If it had struck a slab of Earth's
air, the collision would have crushed it.

The stormy blob was nearly to Pluto, and she thought
she could see the onrushing apparition swell as it spun.
Storms fought across it, but the structure held. By sliding up in frequency she could cut in through the spiraling
arms and see more fine detail toward its core. These frequency bands showed rivers of flame tracing out their
paths, wriggling and flaring in gleaming drops bigger than
Pluto. Shorter wavelengths brought knotty images,
gnarled in tight echoes of the overall structure. Small spi-
rals were spinning off a furious, dense core. It was as if the

overall structure was making tiny, incandescent eddies that in their turn evolved into coherent knots.

"Viktor," she called. "Look at the ninety-gigahertz image when you have a chance."

He was watch officer and had scheduled a detailed interrogation of the ship's systems, conducted using telepresence from the bridge. So it was several moments before his voice said in her headphones, "Same shape. Been visible for minutes. Implies—what?—some nodules hold together, if they have it?"

"You'd think the little ones would get sheared into pieces," Julia said. "Look at all the turbulence around them."

"Look small, but are size of Africa."

"What's with the Beings? This might be trouble for them. They apparently live off the turbulence of the shock, but this is a *big* storm. Huge energies."

"The Eight. Seem okay. Wiseguy reported they are feasting on the bow shock."

"What about the Six?"

"They seem to be quiet."

Julia asked, "Lying doggo, you think?"

"Means?"

She smiled, pleased that after all these years he didn't know every corner of her mind. "Aussie slang, or maybe old Brit. 'Playing possum,' I think the Americans say."

"Yep, that's right." Jordin's voice came on intership comm. "I'm looking at *High Flyer* from the side and wonder if you've picked up the magnetic configuration behind you."

"Behind is where?" Viktor asked. Julia could see antennas rotate at Viktor's command on her screen display.

"Outward from you, toward the bow shock."

"Um, yes. Cyclotron emissions, pretty low frequencies . . . but rising."

Jordin said, "Yep, checks with my spectrum. Lots of spikes in the hundred-megahertz bands."

"Odd, magnetic fields building . . ." Julia turned her head and saw Viktor punching in commands, studying screens.

"Hey, stay focused." She had lost a few of the lower-frequency antennas, and her view of the storm approaching was degraded in resolution. "Jordin! What's with the Eight out at the bow shock?"

"Big banquet. Not answering questions."

Viktor chimed in, "I can see on some of mine. Seems they are maybe singing, too. Very pretty. Here, I send—"

The long, low notes came to them on magnetic waves. They resounded with deep harmonics with high, tinkling overnotes. She remembered listening to the beautiful, long whale songs and wondered what the Beings would think of those. She should ask Earthside for some.

"What is?" Viktor asked.

She had no answer. Sunward, the storm was rising.

As the huge ball of fields and plasma approached, it seemed to be bristling. Tiny, lacy patterns grew. They connected and spread from each new node, and Julia had the sensation of watching something not just swelling but growing. Intricate structures solidified, working into greater webs. Each moment brought it thousands of kilometers nearer.

"I'm getting high fields nearby," Viktor said.

"Must be this storm," Jordin sent.

"No, is from behind us," Viktor said. "Is definitely not inward."

It struck Pluto, and the planet left a blank hole in the oncoming magnetic filigree. In seconds fiery fibers were creeping into the long, conical gap, illuminating it. A whole world had made only a momentary obstacle to the structure rushing out at them. The traceries laced together, and soon no trace of the dark spot remained.

On it came. The distances that had taken them weeks to cross took the spinning slug of plasma only moments. "Here comes," Viktor said, and he could not disguise the tight high notes of tension in it.

Nothing. Not the slightest rattle or surge followed the impact. Viktor had swiveled some of their microwave antennas forward, so they saw on-screen the true size of the bright fibers. One sinewy fiber passed between them and *Proserpina*, emitting a darting hiss in the low radio channels. The next nearest was hundreds of kilometers away. Julia had seen thousands of them linking and weaving in the last hour, and only now felt in her bones the size of the plasma island that was passing by. A vast continent, gliding in the night.

This close, they could see the intricate magnetic fibers that coiled and flexed as the structure fled onward and outward, into the far dark where it would dwell.

"Is just the front," Viktor said. "This magnetic architecture is deep and is passing by us. So fast! Quicker than anything else in nature, this."

Streamers of magnetic fluff shot past on their screens. Outside, in the narrow band available to the human eye, there was only the solemn black. To the vast interplay of plasma and fields their vision was blind.

Julia felt a lurch. "What's that?"

Viktor said nothing as his fingers flew over the control board. Julia felt a strumming vibration through the deck. "We're tilting," Viktor said. "Something maybe hit us."

But the pressure seals were fine, and there had been no audible impact. Vibrations in the deck got deep, strong. "What could have happened?" Killings sent on comm.

"We're getting a shove from side," Viktor said on general comm. He threw a starfield up on the main screen, the view from the forward 'scope. Slowly the center mark crept toward the right. "Is tipping us."

The deck began shuddering. A low note sounded. *High Flyer*'s nose was turning faster now, and the starfield slid visibly to the right. But the short, rotating drum of the living quarters fought the change. It was like holding a turning bicycle wheel by its axis and then trying to tilt it, Julia thought. Angular momentum didn't want to change. At the axis the coupling collar was protesting. Bearings ground against a fluid universal joint and shed vibrations into the whole ship.

"Not built to take this quick tipping," Viktor muttered as he worked at the board.

Killings said from the status board, "Mechanical linkage is getting stressed. We're going out of performance range."

"Whatever's tipping us, it's steady." Viktor's voice had gotten tight, not a good sign. "Not impact, no. Something else."

Jordin's voice came in, flat and calming. "I can see you tumbling. There's a lot of magnetic field built up on your port side. All that, acting like a pressure on the ship's metal."

"So Beings are tipping us over." Viktor now spoke in his calm, deliberate voice. "Mystery solved. But what to do?"

Killings said, "Step on the gas."

Nobody said anything. Killings went on, "We fire up the reactor, pulse-start it, get up to high specific impulse. We'll follow a spiral path, getting larger as we accelerate. A moving target. That'll make it hard to push against us."

Elegant. Viktor muttered thanks and got to work. Julia felt the rumble of fluids moving from their aft water tanks. The water was a good, thick absorber, blocking any reactor radiation. It captured the vagrant neutrons that spilled out as the reactor shot up in temperature, ready within less than a minute for fuel. The thumping pumps fed the hot chambers streams of water, and she visualized the gushers bursting into superheated steam, a hundred meters behind them. A pleasantly reassuring push eased her down into her acceleration couch. "Here we go," Viktor said, running the reactor temperature to a high spike.

They gained velocity slowly at first. The magnetic side pressure kept pace, still rotating their nose to the right, but within minutes this began to work in their favor.

"Y'see," Killings said eagerly, "the faster we spin, the more our exhaust turns against the pressure that's pushing us to rotate."

"Beings behind this, now they get burned," Viktor said gleefully. He notched up the reactor, and the ship rumbled around them. To Julia it felt like the stirrings of a great beast, roused from slumber.

She felt tremors run through the ship. They were rotating more now, and she felt the local gravity shift. She closed her eyes, but that just made her feel dizzy. She glanced around and saw that others were holding on to their couch arms and gritting teeth. If this kept on, they would soon not even be able to walk.

Abruptly she recalled the harrowing moments—decades ago, but leaping fresh to mind—during the aerobraking of the first Mars expedition. Just like then, her mind stopped thinking about ideas and spoke in declaratives. *That noise! That shaking! I'm going to die!*

She clenched her teeth and forced that away. Focused—

Jordin sent, "Seeing some movement in the magnetic pressure zone. Kinda cloudy . . ."

On-screen he sent a mixed image, ordinary optical plus a radio topo map. The ship was tumbling visibly now, its bright yellow-green plume forking around behind it. Turbulent horsetails of it sliced through the magnetic cloud topo lines. The natural resultant of the force vectors made *High Flyer* into a pinwheel, spinning in ever-larger arcs as it spat hard, hot plasma.

"Getting a big increase of cyclotron emission," Jordin sent.

Julia could see it in the all-channel summary. Spikes, quick high flurries, broadband rumbles. Silently, in bands no human ear could sense, a great howl arose from the densely packed Six.

7.

PROTO

FORCEFUL CRIED OUT in pain. <The plasma is hard, sharp, too quick!>

A searing, cutting edge swept through them. The Six were entwined, to exert the maximum leverage on the tiny traveling machine. It had been exciting at first, to work together—a closer merge than any had ever attempted— and then to start the object tumbling, end over end, as Mirk had foreseen it would.

Now the tiny machine spat back. Because the Six were so immersed in each other, they could not quickly flee. Mirk took the first cut, as ions fried down his field lines. The particles soon found his tucked-in recesses, where electrical potentials held lodes of knowledge and skill. These shorted out in ruby, snapping bursts. Mirk felt a sheet of pain shoot through his side, and heard the cries as small parts of himself seared away.

<Unbind!> Ring cried. <The hot arc—>

Ring screamed as currents stung it. Sunless and Dusk jerked away from Ring, knowing they were next. The searing sliced into them as they struggled to free their entwined lines of force.

Cries, angry and fearful, shot through them all. At close range their emissions directly pressed against the bodies of each other, fevering the vacuum with calls.

There came a larger, booming tone, the Summed Voice

of the Eight. <This plasma is spewing everywhere. It must be contained!>

<Contain it yourself!> Forceful countered, scrambling away from the agony that clawed at it.

<We are far away. You Six caused this, so you must obey the governing imperative. Have you forgotten that the Proto is near you?>

A silence. In fact, the Six had thought the Proto, a New One, would be far enough away from the struggle. But now that the machine was slinging plasma at high speed in all directions, nothing was safe.

<Alarm!> The call went up from each. All thought of tumbling the machine now fled from them.

Forceful yanked free. Now it could expand its view beyond the constricted focus necessary to press against the tiny machine. All around, for several light-seconds, the sky worked with the snaking strands of the Proto. On its long birthing flight up from the Fount, through the hazards of the planets and the vagaries of the storm, this Proto had left behind the shattered, dying shards of many thousands.

Selection had pruned away all but the robust. First came the simple forms, fields twined together and barely capable of self-organization. During their growth—as the great storms drove them outward, away from the strong trapping fields of the planets, and at last free of the roving turbulences of the Hotness—they competed with each other. Fields curled and died, plasmas fizzed and fought. Most structures died. The better were able to digest the energies and field strengths of the lesser. But as the survivor Protos approached the Cascade, they dimly became aware of its threat. The churning vortices there could break a

Proto and splatter it into rivulets. Some slowed, avoiding the whipping violence ahead.

Forceful vaguely recalled doing that, so long ago. Few Protos who shot through the Cascade lived.

And this one now—it brimmed with bristly intelligence, knowing itself for the first time. It reached out with tendrils of coiling flux, felt and heard . . . and braked. It slowed, gaining the time to assemble itself all the better.

To one side it sensed the brute energies of young plasma. It had not dealt with these virulent eating swarms since its first moments. Then, an enormous solar arch had ripped open at its top and spilled out whorls and cusps of magnetic field. Most of these died within seconds, eaten through by blind gouts of plasma. Many of the young knots screamed in waves of magnetic flux . . . and fell silent forever.

This Proto remembered that. It began to move sluggishly away from the pinwheel gusher of voracious plasma. But slowly, as it was tired from the long voyage.

<Screen the Proto!> Mirk called, though still racked with fevered pains.

But the Six were gnarled and fevered, frayed and damaged. They oozed sluggishly away from the searing torch that played among them. Panicked, they babbled and fled.

All but Chill. Diminished, feeble, it was now a thin disk of spinning fields and chilly plasma. It skated upon the virulent energies now all around it, catching waves and stealing a morsel of momentum where it could. The Six had not brought it to bear upon turning the tiny machine; Chill was far too weak to matter.

It hung spinning in the sky where the plasma arc cut. Slowly it dragged itself up the field lines, trying to maintain its own coherence. Memories flitted through it, dim shadows of a past it could barely recall. Yet it knew the struggle around it mattered, and above all the Proto must survive.

Here came the arc, on another revolution. Again the plume bit and seared away part of Mirk. Again the plasma jutted out toward the Proto beyond—and Chill thrust itself forward. In its webbed lattices valences shorted out. Potentials burned and died.

The snakes of exhaust plasma sparked and ate and in turn died.

Chill had time for one last signal, a simple waveform of ripples that ran out along the stretched field lines of its outer carapace.

I go to the True End. Make my death worthy . . .

In moments Chill lost structure, decaying by fitful inductance. Fragments spun away. Loops of coherent fields drifted into the tides of flux.

The Proto moved away now, seeking distance from the deadly pinwheel. It sensed its new world dimly, but enough to know danger and pain.

The pressure of Chill's destruction flung out shards of memory. Kernels of skills arced away, driven by the energies of dying. Some small, faster motes of this wreckage caught up to the Proto. Knots of magnetic structure sped by, some snagging in the Proto's diffuse fields, buzzing like flies caught in a web. The Proto reached out with burgeoning strength and spooled them in. Here were age-old recollections, shards of times long past.

The Proto tucked these within it, for study and use. It was willing to learn from anything it encountered. It did not know the concept of genetics, but it would, in time.

8.

TORQUES

"THEY'RE GONE," KILLINGS SAID. "No emissions from nearby."

They all groaned, rose, stretched. It had been four tense hours. Slowly they had reversed the tumbling rotation and reduced the torque on their living cylinder. Through all this they all kept watch at their stations, remembering that the attack had come out of nowhere. The coffee machine had emptied long ago.

Days before, Viktor had remarked in passing on the basic physics the Six had used. But it was difficult to see how they could have prepared. They were all exhausted and glad to be alive.

Julia took a break and spent half a day by herself. The sliding sheets of water in her meditation room were perfect for her mood. Mars had been a quiet place, so now the ship's unending background noise had to be shut out. In her quiet room the embedded electronics threw a calming white-noise blanket. These days Earthside's pressing populations walled themselves off behind thickening barricades of earplugs, triple-glazed windows, and sound-canceling electronics. She wondered uneasily if this meant she was becoming more akin to Earthside urban dwellers, whose lives got more deadened, like permanent cotton in the ears.

After some simple rest time, and before her watch came up, she made herself go through the big list of in-

coming vids. Those from Axelrod were diplomatic but
kept returning to his idea of bringing back both zand and
Darksiders. "Fah!" she said, shutting it off.

The next, from Praknor, was even less promising. More
data and description of the Marsmat phenomenon. Somehow she was not in a mood to get back to the subject that
had obsessed her for decades. Something tugged at her attention, a vague, ghostly shadow of an idea. She felt the
gnawing suspicion that ultimate reality lay elsewhere,
glimpsed out of the corner of her eye, sensed just beyond
the glow cast by the mind's conscious campfire, heard in
the slow movement of a Mozart quartet . . .

She prowled through the sliding sheets of data and
graphs and listened to the water sheets falling in the distance, and then there came . . . a moment.

Hours later Julia said, "Wiseguy, we're all here, connected. Ready."

Julia kept her voice steady, though she could *feel*
Shanna's heavy presence even over the comm link. Was it
her imagination, or, in the seemingly endless cross talk as
Julia tried to get across her revelation, did Shanna try to
import some of Julia's ideas into her own "biospherics
model" for Pluto? (Leave it to Shanna to use whatever
was the current Earthside jargon.). From the edge in
Shanna's voice, that woman was kicking herself for not
making the connections Julia had just explained to them
all.

But how could she have? Shanna hadn't spent decades
slogging away at the Marsmat problem.

"Bring on the Beings, then," Killings said enthusiastically.

"I am staging through the introductory greetings," Wiseguy said in its usual warm, male, though somehow flat tone. "They still must have explained that your individual names do not bespeak qualities."

Viktor said, "You said this before. So how do you do it?"

The short pause was unusual for Wiseguy. "I . . . assign qualities to you."

"Oh?" Jordin said dryly. "What's mine?"

"Jordin Kare is Steadfast."

"Um," Jordin said, "gotta agree with that."

Then all the rest of the crew wanted to know theirs. Julia was Introspective, Viktor was Victory, and so on. Julia wondered how the intricately linked software had decided on their qualities. Voice tones? Diction? For that matter, how did people do it with each other?

This took moments, provoking both laughter and dismay. Julia marveled at how Wiseguy, a self-learning system, had gained personality as they interacted with it. Maybe this was a lesson in itself, she mused. The Beings were magnetic structures that embodied—somehow—information, memory, architectures of personality. With names! They self-organized and adapted and learned, and very little of it seemed to be described well by the Darwinian mechanisms she had learned. The rising, self-making storm they had witnessed, borne out by the sun, had made her rethink her whole conception of life. And then, to think anew about the decades on Mars.

Julie said, "I want to talk to Instigator first."

"Done," Wiseguy said quickly, as if the artificial intelligence was glad to get beyond the names.

"Instigator, we want you and the Eight to know that we have found Incursor."

9.

A PATH INTO THE HOTNESS

FORCEFUL SAID NO. The actual message rendered literally used both hierarchies and webbed cross-correlations, and so had to be squashed to resemble a human sentence:

{[leaving] | [unbreakable]
[scorn] | [pity]
[[binary rebuke]] ~ [negation]}

Instigator replied, <There is no need for you and Dusk to depart. There is a great Inbound cause now! We must go to Incursor.>

<Impossible,> Forceful said. <The tiny things say they have found him, trapped in the crust of the fourth world out from the Fount.>

<At least we know where he is—and that he is *alive*,> Joy and Solemn sent together, to stress their point. <After such long ages!>

<We have no means *whatever* to free Incursor from such a humiliating snare,> Forceful shot back.

Bright insisted, <The tiny ones say they will help.>

Forceful sent a seethe of amused contempt. <They are

nothing compared with the scale of Incursor, by their own testimony. How could they help any of us?>

<How could they bring any of us to the True Death?> Quiet sighed, nearly inaudible.

Recorder observed, <This is what makes Inbounding such a valiant quest.>

Sunless said, <Inbounding is just seeking Diminishment.>

Recorder's helicity-mate, Quiet, sent, <We seek a path into the Hotness. There we can learn.>

Forceful began, <We are only a few of the Outbounds. We will join other Beings—yes, perhaps smaller than us and of less consequence—who are of like mind. We shall traverse the desert between the suns! We fear no obstacle—>

<Not at all,> Dusk sent. <I do not depart.>

Forceful seldom paused when interrupted, but this time: <What?>

<We have a Proto. I would rather cast my lot with it.>

Forceful asked, <Why? With such prospects before us—>

<To bring this Proto into full Being. To . . . Perhaps to replace Chill.>

Forceful let two full transit-times between the Beings pass, making a long silence. <We are Outbounds. We cannot carry Protos on such a vast odyssey.>

<This Proto I propose we call Chill.> Dusk's tone carried a hard edge no Being had heard from her before. These events had changed Dusk, and they no longer knew her.

Forceful sent fretted wave packets, no discernible content beyond a foul mood.

Recorder slowly murmured, <The Proto has pealed forth elementary waveforms. Yet . . . they do resemble the signatures of Chill.>

<We have not met this vexing quandary since the Long Times,> Vain sent—a Being who seldom spoke, like Quiet. But when it did, the Eight listened. Vain was paired in helicity with Eater—who was feasting on the fringes of whorls now stripping off the edges of the fresh solar storm—and so all understood that this was some form of consensual voice for the both of them. <Chill is *gone*!>

And so Vain sent them again to consider the deepest dilemmas that confronted Beings. Of course, they did not fear Death—an idea almost wholly theoretical—precisely because it was very rare.

Instead, they had all through their long lives suffered the Diminishment, losing whorls and thus fractions of memory and self. Such was life. To trim intelligently was ideal; to do it brutally was subtraction. But neither of these was the theoretical absolute . . . was Death. That province no one knew—by definition of Being.

And yet to this end Chill had now delivered himself.

The Beings found Chill's motivations mysterious. Perhaps some state of depression had forced him to Die? Some considered him deranged. Others felt that choosing Death meant, obviously, that some higher state was thus made available. Creation simply would not permit intelligences to *stop*. Perhaps, these said, the whispers heard from the Distants were, in fact, from those now living on another plane.

This was one of the primary reasons cited by the Outbounds for their agenda—particularly by Forceful, who now sent, <We may well find Chill ourselves, in some other state—across the desert.>

This reply sent rippling, complex waveforms among the Eight and the Six alike (though the Six were Five, with Chill gone). Their vexed talk pivoted around a paradox at the core of their existence. The bow shock turbulence could shear off parts of Beings, here in the most lively zone, the Cascade. But it also energized fresh whorls—giving food plus building materials. Beings could tease these into self-sustained magnetic cells, to stock more memory, more "body," more skills. The ultimate source of the shock wall was the sun's momentum as it orbited the mass of the inner galaxy. So the Beings owed both their origin and their growth to the remorseless momentum of that sole scintillating dot, the Fount, brimming with promise.

<So we leave!>

The Six, now the Four—(Mirk, Sunless) (Ring, Forceful)—set off to swim through the desert between suns. The voyage would be long, and quite probably they would not survive. The wastes before them held shadowy presences, legendary pitfalls, and the unending terror of the shadowy unknown. All this they knew.

Their seething plasma wakes throbbed as they steadily stroked outward. They chose, of course, to move laterally, crosswise to the unending torrent from upstream, where the interstellar gas and plasma came brawling in from the stars. Never swim against the current. They all knew that the distances were immense, the spans of time daunting even for the Beings. But the Eight sensed something fundamental, as did those lesser (and far more numerous) Beings who hung back from the Cascade. From them rose a long, rolling chorus in farewell salute. They all knew that after an age-old debate the issue was settled. Most would stay, but the Outbounds had the courage to go.

Though perhaps its end would never be known to the Eight, an epoch voyage had begun.

10.

THE SUNBORN MAGNETICS

JULIA SAT AND WATCHED as the spectral monitors—set in the microwave and radio ranges, to pick up the avalanche of talk from the Beings—sprayed their arrays onto screens. The solar storm had passed, carrying the Proto into the outer reaches. There it might survive, grow, self-organize in the filmy reaches far beyond the raw rub of matter. The society of Beings would tend to it. After all, the Sunborn were their future.

So much. She sighed, suddenly tired. "I hope this convinces them," she said wanly.

Viktor patted her hand, concerned. His forehead wrinkled, and his eyelids fluttered, holding back emotion before the rest of the crew. "You sent the entire lot of data we got from the Marsmat, so is all you can do. Was brilliant, when you saw that the waveforms in the Marsmat correlated with the Beings' language. And that this Incursor, lost in the inner planets, was trapped. So might still be there. Have a signature, anchored in the crust of Mars. Electromagnetic waves, they do not lie."

The rest of the watch crew—those not doing maintenance, anyway—nodded silently. They were waiting, too.
For her to explain the Leap.

That a Being, sunk into the crust of Mars somehow,
billions of years ago, would find a link to the emergent
biological forms there. That somehow—what labyrinths
remained to explore in this!—the Being had learned to
squeeze rock with its magnetic fields. It used that ability
to provoke other currents in the crust. That the electric
potentials it produced would resonate with the microbial
mats covering the early, warm and wet period of Mars.
That a symbiosis would arise. That a collaboration—a
dance?—would come from such strange musics. So
much . . . all in one leap. The unconscious, doing all the
heavy lifting . . .

Killings asked quietly, earnestly, "How'd you know
that the low-frequency emissions from Mars—stuff
you've been seeing for decades—was related? I mean, assuming it is."

Julia threw her head back—not tossing her hair, no;
she hated that—and thought. How *had* she seen it? Not a
clue . . . Okay— "Not a clue. It just came to me."

Viktor slapped her knee. "My girl! 'Just came to me.'
Means she looks at everything, lets it cook—presto!"

She beamed. "Uh, right." Nobody knew where ideas
came from, so what was the difference? Certainly
Wiseguy's spectral breakdowns had been crucial. She had
stared at them for hours. Days later, for a break, she had
looked at the regression analysis data Praknor had sent
along, mostly for Viktor. It was a compilation of years of
the magnetic "noise" in the southern Martian hemisphere.
Then she had slept, woken up, did routine work . . . and it

came together. The hard work was always done by the unconscious, while you're doing something else.

And here they all were, waiting for the Beings to respond. She said, "Let's do a systems check and inventory while we wait."

It helped keep her mind off matters. An hour passed, and it was as she had feared: they had expended more water these last weeks than planned. *Going for broke.* The spiraling-out maneuver to stop their tumbling had cost a good deal.

They all groaned at the news. "Need to melt more ice if we are to keep going," Viktor said.

Killings made a face. "Working the 'bots on that ultracold ice is a bitch. It'll take weeks—we lost two 'bots last time, the heavy-duty drilling ones that're hard to fix."

"Can cannibalize for parts," Viktor said. "But right— is pain in posterior."

"Unless . . ." Killings was shy about making suggestions, but this time his eyes were resolute. "Unless we cut the mission short. We can do a big burn out here, drop fast into the inner solar system."

They all looked at each other, eyes wary. A pregnant silence . . .

And Wiseguy said, "The Eight say that they recognize the Mars signals. It is their Incursor."

They cheered. "And it asks for help freeing itself. There is a long story about its expedition into the Hotness and how it tried to inspect signs of life on the fourth planet."

"On surface?" Viktor shook his head. "Is none."

"There was once," Killings said, nodding toward Julia. "You found those fossil plants, right?"

Julia said, "They were from around 4 billion years ago."

"So this Incursor has been caught in the Mars crust for that long?" Viktor blinked. "Then it had a hand—okay, is way wrong image, has no hands—in evolution of Mars-mat?"

Julia whispered, "So the sentience of the mat is not just a result of simple evolution. It's a . . . collaboration. Between these things and simple microbes."

"Operates through the piezoelectric, I bet," Viktor said. "That's what nearly fried me, back in Vent R. Squeeze rock—which can do if you are made of magnetic fields, and strong ones—and that drives current."

Julia smiled. "So when you nearly got electrocuted, it was Incursor answering."

"Um," Killings said. "Bone-crushing handshake."

Wiseguy said, "The Eight now refer to their kind as the Sunborn Magnetics."

"That's a synonym for Beings?" Viktor asked.

"Apparently," Wiseguy said. "And they have a proposition. They want you to help them reach Incursor."

Viktor frowned. "They are big, strong. Can't they just go to Mars?"

Wiseguy answered, after a pause that probably meant it was going back to the Beings for confirmation, "It is too dangerous for them. The solar wind streaming out carries magnetic turbulence—'vortex pain,' as I translate it—that tears these Beings to shreds."

"How did this Incursor get so far in?" Viktor persisted.

"They say it used a 'buffer' of plasma, forced ahead of it. The plasma came from a huge comet that Incursor evaporated, to provide a shield for it."

"And it still got caught? So others, they are afraid. Humph." Viktor gave them all a canny look. "We told them about bow shock, okay. We want it not coming into solar system. They might bargain for that?"

"So I gather," Wiseguy said. "Though the Beings have an ornate system of ideas about deals. They do exchange plasma or information or skills—apparently their major commodities, though something called helicity is bigger than all those."

"I looked into that," Killings said. "It prob'ly means giving a twist to a magnetic field. Helicity helps make a snaky tube, which can better confine plasma. There's plenty helicity in our own li'l ol' fusion reactor, sitting a hundred meters away."

"Indeed." From its tone Julia wondered if Wiseguy was enough of a persona to get irked when interrupted. "Customarily, when exchange occurs, they also shear off fragments of their own minds, duplicate these, and embed them in each other."

Julia was startled. "So each becomes slightly like the other?"

"Apparently." Wiseguy paused. "It seems more like a moral act than a commercial one."

"So . . ." Viktor stared off into space, thinking. "We get inner solar system protected *if* we can get them to Incursor. Then what do they do?"

"I do not know. Perhaps free it? Wait—" Wiseguy again asked the Beings, and Julia thought how odd were these simple conversations.

Even a Being the size of the Earth could think across its entire body at the same speed that synapses convey blips of thought across the human brain. Far larger Beings thought more slowly. One the size of the distance of the Earth from the sun, an astronomical unit, could trickle a thought across itself in under ten minutes. Since Beings of such a scale seldom confronted problems that demanded instant attention, this had not been a problem in their evolution. Until now.

"They will be content to visit Incursor. Saving it comes later." Wiseguy itself seemed awed by the scale of this idea. "They speak now of time scales greater than millennia, just to think over the matter."

Viktor asked, "And if we don't—can't!—help them get to Mars, then what?"

"Then they will not move the bow shock." Wiseguy spoke as though this were perfectly reasonable, a disagreement between gentlemen. "The shock wall is now close enough to Pluto to drive the electrical ecology there. To move it back will kill the life-forms there, the zand."

"Okay," Julia said. "So it can keep the shock there, save the zand. But no farther. Deal?"

Wiseguy took a long time to speak with the Beings. They all watched the microwave and radio spectral screens anxiously. These spiked and roiled—plainly much was being said. Julia felt intensely how thin and fragile a tendril they were here, poked far out into the deep darkness, dwelling in a place evolution had never designed them for at all. And yet this realm was connected to Mars in a way they would never have guessed, if they had not come here. All human history had been that way. Of the three types of chimpanzee, the first two—ordinary chimp and bonobo—never left Africa. But the humans came from those who did, always pressing against the far horizon.

Climb to a distant peak and look back and see the landscape anew.

Then Wiseguy said, "Deal."

11.

THE DEEP

SHANNA LOOKED ACROSS THE table at Julia and thought, *The deal with utter aliens was easier to strike than this one will be. We humans know too much about each other. Chimp rivalries. Julia has made yet another goddamn discovery, and now she'll lord it over me . . . forever.*

Viktor was working in the main cabin, and Shanna had asked for this little side cabin for just the two of them. For weeks the crews of both ships had been tiptoeing around the clash between the two women, but now Julia had asked Shanna to come over for a "powwow"—with no further explanation.

Shanna sipped her tea and watched Julia line up her pen and notebook in just the right, rigid order and say, "We've got to act together on this."

"Seems to me you've been acting all on your own just fine," Shanna shot back. "Making big discoveries. Co-opting Wiseguy's running time—nice work-around with Earthside on that, by the way, so I didn't hear a word until I get orders to let *High Flyer* have 'as much time as it takes'—without saying what 'it' was."

She stopped; her words had come out in a torrent.

Julia nodded. Silence. Then: "I admit, I had advantages. But you, after all, are the daughter of Axelrod the Great."

"I did take advantage of that out here," Shanna said sternly, "but only to hold my rank of captain."

"I know. But now maybe you should use it."

"Why?" Shanna looked guardedly at the calm woman across the narrow gray table and wondered if Julia could be trusted. She would give this a few minutes, tops.

"Because neither ship can stay much longer. Your mission is already nominally over turnaround time. ISA will start barking, if they haven't already. And we've expended more water than we thought we'd need, so we're right at full 'on-site duration,' as they say in ISA-speak."

Shanna said, "I think we can stick it out a bit longer. Cut rations—"

"Can, maybe. Should, no. There's too much at stake."

Shanna looked at the wall screen behind Julia and thought. It showed one optical 'scope's view of Pluto hanging in darkness, its crescent fevered with an air now coppery with snaking light. Once, in what now seemed to be the far past, she had puzzled from orbit over such filigrees. Now she knew that the Being called Instigator was at work, driving huge planetary currents to unimaginable ends.

"I want to stay here, study the zand," she said. "You're a biologist, you—"

"You can't sustain yourselves without supplies."

"You transferred quite a few. We can hold here another half year—"

"And then go home. But at greater risk."

"You're starting to sound like Dad."

Julia bridled at this, her lips twisting. "Just the opposite, in the long run. I've dealt with him as much as you have, and almost as long."

"He sees the zand as *zoo exhibits*." She did not try to keep the scorn from her voice.

"True—but we can use that."

"What?"

"Look." Julia spread her hands. "Face it, the zand are something biologists never met before: an artificial species."

Reluctantly Shanna admitted, "Yes . . . but . . ."

"We have to study the zand and the Beings *together*—because that's the fundamental system."

"So?" Shanna had come prepared for a fight, but this was a seminar.

"So we work toward a permanent station here. With you as head."

The idea dazzled, but she narrowed her eyes suspiciously. "Why are you being this way?"

To her credit Julia looked genuinely puzzled. Good acting, or had Shanna misunderstood the Queen of Mars? "I'm trying to heal a breach," Julia said. "I propose that we agree to dislike and disagree with each other. Fair enough. But we have to know that we must work together against a common enemy."

"What? The Beings?"

"No, Earth."

Shanna tossed her hair in frustration and caught the look in Julia's eyes. "What is it?"

Stiffly: "I have always disliked women throwing their long hair about like that."

Shanna's eyes widened. "That's . . . so . . ."

"Stupid, yes, I quite agree. Left over from school days in Adelaide, alas. But my hair won't work well at length, so I suppose it has become an automatic reaction."

"Based on . . . envy," Shanna said in disbelief.

"I suppose."

"All this time I envied you, Queen of Mars and all."

"Queen?" Julia laughed, not merrily. "Why not prisoner? I can't go back home to Earth ever again."

"Well, could've fooled me. That first meeting of ours—"

"Yes, awful. Dreadful cockup."

"Cock what?"

"Aussie slang." She grinned. "Nothing to do with cocks. Look—" Julia sat forward across the table, hands clasped. "Whatever we think of each other, we must be allies. A few dozen of us out here, ten billion back there—"

"Lousy odds."

"—but we have the biggest discovery in history. Axelrod wants Darksiders, thinking his Consortium buddies can lift a lot of technology tricks from them."

"Yeah, just like for the zand, a 'profit center' to—"

"So let's give them to him."

"Huh?" Shanna sat back, shocked.

"These aren't species out here, they're products."

Shanna flared, eyes widening. "They're living beings, intelligent."

"But it's a manufactured intelligence, installed in them."

"So we meekly hand them over?"

"We bargain, using them," Julia said. "For a permanent

station here, working on the zand and Darksiders and the Beings who're behind it all. We knit together those with the Marsmat."

"Unified biology, of some sort."

"There's truly no term for this yet, is there?"

Shanna ticked off items on her right hand. "I've been thinking. The evolution of the Beings is actually pretty Darwinian. There's plenty of variation, right? You think they're emitted as those Protos, some sort of self-organized embryo structures from the sun. Then there is immense selection pressure on them as they move out through the solar system. Maybe you really have the analog of sexual reproduction in the way the pairs of opposite-helicity Beings mentor the young Protos. Providing some plasma and information from both partners to the youngster, right? Pretty damn close to recombination of genetic information from the parents in a fertilized egg."

Julia nodded. "Could be. But then there's the big question: why are they smart at all?"

Shanna said, "Maybe humans did it with never-ending selection pressure through warfare versus cooperation."

Julia laughed. "Just like us two, eh? We evolved ourselves in a kind of social one-upping, predator-prey relationship?"

"Which fits with how you and I got along so well? Right? Our ancestors switched back and forth in the roles of predator and prey constantly, as new aggressive technologies developed. So I get your drift. Did the Beings likewise go through warfare, territory protection, weaponry?"

Julia blinked. "Why else would they need such high intelligence? Unless there really are dragons out here . . ."

Shanna said in a spooky voice, "Good ol' H. G. Wells. 'Intellects vast and cool and unsympathetic.' Brrrr!"

Julia smiled. "It's good to think outside the box, but we have to have a negotiating position with Earthside, y'-know."

Shanna thought, then said, "Okay—for starters, I won't take zand unless we can figure out how to protect them in low-temperature environments."

Julia nodded. "Goes without saying."

"And that means we have to look at a lot of problems. One, where is the nervous system in a zand?"

Julia topped this with, "Two, how is genomic information stored and translated into effector action in a zand? Is it done with low-temperature analogs of DNA and proteins?"

Shanna shot back, "Three, what do zand use for muscle, bone, and blood? How does temperature affect that?"

Julia spread her hands. "I say we just ask them. They—or the Beings who made them—must know."

"And we must have their consent."

"I imagine they would, once the Beings let their feelings known."

"Just as for the Darksiders, it all comes back to the Beings, doesn't it?"

Julia shrugged. "They run the outer solar system. Apparently always have. But you've hit the nub of it—how do we get them to cooperate?"

"Do what they want and take a Being to Mars? Impossible. Hell, they're bigger than gods!—but afraid of what to us is just about empty space, close in to the sun. Go figure."

Julia chuckled. "I wish I could. Unless we can give

them a visit with Incursor, they will have little motivation to stop the bow shock from pushing in, near Earth. Instigator will probably be happy to get more energy from the bow shock boundary as it moves in. All the better to power its experiments—the zand and all that skimpy biological substructure—on Pluto."

Shanna sighed, sitting back and looking beyond Julia again, at the wall screen. It had cycled to a view straight out, at the stars themselves. It combined spectra in the microwaves, infrared, optical, even mild X-rays. A madhouse collage, until you got used to it. Each band had sprinklings of color-coded information, lacy strands against a pervading black. She now thought of that blackness as the Deep.

Living with it had made her see its beauty—stark, subtle, and old beyond measure. A flickering cold glow of plasma discharges. The diamond glitter of distant starlight on time-stained ices; a thin fog breath of supercooled helium, whirling in intricate, coded motion: these were the wonders of the Deep, as she now knew them.

Shanna sighed, then smiled. "There have got to be a thousand doctoral theses in understanding that—what did you call it?—skimpy biological substructure. Ha! So true! Instigator just kludged together bits of essentials, rudimentary chem, plus mechanics. Run it all with electrical currents—hey, that's what makes the Beings tick over, too—and let 'er rip. What an experiment! A whole world to tinker with! And all to understand how the inner planets might work."

"What was its point?" Julia shook her head. "Alien goals . . ."

"To figure out what might be on Mars?"

"Um. We can't suppose that beings with lifetimes in the billion-year range could even be bothered with the mayfly issues of humans. They think *long*—and probably knew that Incursor got hung up there, sunk into the crust, way back when Mars was young. Still . . ."

"What?"

"I wonder if they picked up radio and TV from Earth."

"Ummm. Could be. So we—more than a century ago—started all this?"

Julia shrugged. "Why haven't they said so, then?"

"Hey, they're aliens. Maybe they've been working on Pluto since the Roman Empire. Or far longer. Some things we may never figure out."

Julia sat back and stretched. "I learned that lesson, in a different way, on Mars."

Shanna reached across the table. "Look—let's bury the hatchets, okay? I envied you, right. But now I'm over it."

"Done." They shook hands.

The two women gazed at each other, smiling, each liking the idea of not saying anything. The moment stretched, then eased away. Shanna stood. "Y'know, we were doing pretty well there . . . until I realized that we don't have what it takes to make this deal go."

"True." Julia, too, stood. "I'm just happy we aren't fighting anymore."

"Me, too. If only we had some idea of what to tell the Beings—"

A knock on the door. Viktor edged it open. "Have had crazy idea."

12.

THE TINY ONES

<After all,> Recorder said, <the tiny ones have some intelligence. They can help us.>

<I assume you mean for my grand prospect,> Instigator sent.

<Your experiments? To create more of the chemical life on cold orbs? Farther in?> Mirk asked.

<No, no,> Instigator insisted. <To find our origins. They, the tiny ones, they can lead us inward. Assuming they do not die. They seem to be extremely mortal.>

Recorder was skeptical. <Find our origins? Discover what makes the Protos? This is more ambitious than I can fathom. How?>

Instigator admitted, <I do not know . . . yet.>

Recorder said, <Historically some think that the central Hotness, circling the Fount, is their origin.>

Joy countered, <Impossible! One cannot make Life from cold, hard non-Life. That is surely a paradox.>

<I disagree. Fundamental logics show—>

<That would explain why it refuses to speak with us,> Solemn interrupted his inner ruminations to inject, tones rolling out. <The Fount is a higher entity, as are the others we dimly sense so far away. Only Founts can make Protos. They deliver it to Beings, who form and shape Protos. This is the basis of Life. Perhaps in some way Founts make the tiny life we have encountered. That was Instigator's purpose, recall: to discover how planets can make

anything at all. And she did achieve some insights. Her constructions are toys, granted. But they are a beginning toward understanding the forms that now fly out to us in the ships that can kill. Astonishing that the greatest of sins is open to such small intelligences! All this may be a way for the Founts to manifest themselves. The tiny ones call the Fount a sun, and they come from near it. This is all we can know, and perhaps it is all that is worth knowing. Certainly Founts are above us Beings and do not deign to speak to such as we. And thus the stars are gods.>

A gliding silence, then: <I disagree,> Recorder said. <But if Instigator can find a way to go Inbound, to see—>

<That is *far* too dangerous,> Joy said.

<Of course,> Instigator sent with skating glee. <That is the fun of it!>

13.

EIGHT-FOLD HELIX

A MIND ONCE STRETCHED by a new idea never goes back to its same size. So Julia thought as *High Flyer* departed, rich again with water chiseled from the iceteroids. *Proserpina* had left days before, following a long arc sunward that *High Flyer* would follow, at first, providing backup in case anything went wrong in the first stages of their joint deceleration.

To descend into the inner solar system requires gaining tens of kilometers per second of orbital speed. To acquire this, a ship fires its thrust against its present orbit and falls. From this plunge gravity gives it fresh speed, enough for a new orbit, closer to the sun. To lose and gain in this gravitational gavotte is the stuff of orbital mechanics, well understood by Newton himself. But making it happen moment by moment is both craft and art, especially while using a new class of interplanetary ship.

High Flyer ran in hot mode. Passing through the throat, exposed to ceramic plates packed with uranium, its water burst into steam. In the last, longest section the plates were closer together, neutrons flew between them in torrents, and in striking the molecules of live steam blew them into plasma—ions and electrons, then shaped by magnetic fields into a blaring torch. The plume burst out behind *High Flyer* in a gauzy rosette.

Once free of orbit, the ship plunged down the gravitational gradient. Its nose pointed at the stars, and soon its speed was enough to billow the cloud behind it, forcing it out into a wide, scalding plane.

For weeks *High Flyer* fell, led downward by its own furious exhaust. To the human eye the ship's long steel cylinder rode a hard, hot line of light that fanned out into a wide, fading skirt. But the plasma had spread so far its ions and electrons could not find each other again, and so remained lively, clinging to magnetic fields and spreading farther into a broad front—forcing its way into the inner solar system. A shield.

No human eye could see the long, tapered shape that followed behind *High Flyer*. Instigator had curled herself into her smallest possible tight helix, wrapping and rewrapping back upon herself. By now she knew that the tiny ones carried their self-information in a double helix form, and for this unprecedented task Instigator had shaped herself into an eightfold helix—slender, supple, feeding off whorls in *High Flyer*'s backwash.

Behind that vast plasma screen she was safe from the licking flares that boiled up in the solar wind. She sent signals back to the others of the Eight, full of both complaint and triumph.

Instigator sent, <I now admit that part of my quest was always to seek not just Incursor but Venturer as well.>

Recorder replied, <Venturer was your helicity-mate, so long ago? I can scarcely recall.>

<Venturer became lost to whorls. I miss his voice. Yet sometimes I think I hear him on the solar wind.>

<How could that be?> Joy asked.

Eater took moments from its own pursuits to propose, <If Venturer survived, there might be a place of refuge for us elsewhere, and inward.>

<In the Fount?> Joy, despite its ages-old name, was derisive.

<Protos come from there,> Recorder said.

<They are raw materials, no more.>

Instigator received the fruits of their work as well. Linked, the Seven could hear the faint waves that seemed to come from all around them. <I have found some hints, in the whispers we receive from the Distants,> Recorder said. <Beings such as us may thrive there, and if I am right, their messages may speak of other warmlife as well.>

They all knew by now that all warmlife was mortal, compared with the immense duration of structures and geometries Beings knew. So for those tiny ones, meaning loomed large. To go gallantly into that final night—that was the deep, uniting urge of warmlife forms. To make their short spans matter.

And so perhaps their duty to each other, to other warmlife, however odd or repellent, was to make the random universe have meaning, even for the momentary, passing minds clustering near the sheltering suns.

There was more work for the Beings as well.

A great Toroid of Beings was condensing, drawing strength to itself by hoarding magnetic fields. It tightened slowly into a knot, a tight gathering of fields that bunched against the inner rim of the bow shock.

Slowly, carefully, the Beings *shoved*. To ordinary eyes it was a battle between invisible forces. Their collective ram pressure agonizingly pushed against the bow shock. It would take years to slow the inward brute pressure. Decades more to begin to nudge it back outward. It would be an epochal struggle, for the pressure of the incoming rogue molecular cloud was vast and abiding.

It would be the work of . . . well, epochs, age spans, eons. It was a debt to be paid.

The Beings understood that this was needed. For now. For the tiny lifetimes of the chemical motes.

Julia said to Viktor, "We've got to finish that transmission to Praknor."

He wrinkled his nose. "Must?"

"Must."

"Is biology. Politics. You do."

So she set up the recorder and piped in the latest data and gave the opening speech. She seemed to have spent most of her life now talking to the snouts of cameras, imagining her audience, trying to keep it perky and interesting and always wondering if it worked. She hoped Praknor would have the sense to edit before retransmitting to Earth.

"We're coming back—you heard. Not going to be all fair dinkum with you, I'm sure, but it's got to be." Might as well be direct. "We're guiding in, like a tugboat into a harbor, a *Queen Mary* of a Being, bigger than Mars itself. We hope it will help us talk to the true animating intelligence behind the Marsmat."

Cut, pause. This was going to be tricky. Best to face it directly.

"The discovery of the Being called Incursor on Mars is going to be a tremendous shock to the entire community of Marsmat researchers, of course. Imagine spending twenty years studying something only to find that it is only a puppet for some other life-form. Gad! Lewis Carroll posed the problem a long time ago, in a poem titled 'The Hunting of the Snark.' What if the Snark turns out to be a Boojum instead?"

Praknor, loyal Consortium factotum that she was, would give this to Earthside for broadcast as an "intimate chat" with the Queen of Mars. Better be a bit more diplomatic. Translation: cover your scientific ass. Oh well, can always edit . . .

"Just occurred to me—how will the *Marsmat@Home* people react? Here they've been dutifully letting their online computers be used to compute the cross-correlations and filter functions of the ever-growing Marsmat data. Now we find that the Marsmat has been linked to a magnetic intelligence. We haven't been studying a microbial system alone. I can hear it now—'All that science, wrong, wasted!' Only it's not."

She shrugged. "Y'see, that's how science works. You make a model, you test it, then something flies in from offside—sorry, soccer jargon—and you think again. I remember all the worry about what we biologists call quorum sensing. That occurs when bacteria kick out light signals, or chemical signals, to 'know' each other. See if they are many or just a few. We spent *years* fretting if the Marsmat's big pulses of light were quorum sensing."

She stopped, took a drink. Where was this going? Well, she didn't know. But that was the joy of it, right? Step forward, part the veil.

"None of the above. That's often the right answer, and bugger the exams. We were wrong for decades about the Marsmat. Wrong! It's something we hadn't thought of. The glows and displays come from a magnetic-microbial collaboration way beyond our experience on Earth. And until a short while ago, no one would have recognized the Beings as life-forms *at all.*"

How to say this? "We make our theories, but they are bounded by—surprise!—ourselves. Natural selection turns out to work without molecules or direct reproduction—no sex, either!—or maybe even death. Darwin had only one case to study—Earth—and he sure came up with a big idea. But maybe collaboration is not just the Holy Rule for the Marsmat. Maybe it's a bigger idea."

She cut the feed and took a swig from her orange juice. Viktor was hunched over, running some more regression analysis data on his wall screen, so she tiptoed over to the refrig and slipped out the vodka and added some to her healthful juice. *About time. This is work, thinking aloud . . .*

"A Being came to a Mars that was warm and wet,

maybe 3 billion years ago. It got caught. Went native. Helped the microbials to grow up. Meanwhile, Mars and Earth were in a mutual slugfest, throwing meteorites back and forth, carrying cells and microbe passengers, screwing with each other, fertilizing each other."

She took a taste of the enhanced orange juice and thought, *Okay, Viktor, all this sex talk, I've got a li'l plan for something to do later.*

"So we're all a collaboration. Between things that would look like neon lights the size of the solar system, if our eyes could see them at all, and the stuff that grows between your toes, and us—the primate princesses."

She wondered how she had come this far, from far Adelaide. The whole universe seemed *connected.*

"Think of all the new research this opens up. Biology is never going to look the same."

The great magnetic envelope flexed like a great, coiled snake.

Instigator hugged the plasma shield provided by the braking fusion rocket. The plasma winds from the Fount howled at her edges, stripping away minor fringes of herself.

Joy! I am descending into the Hotness. A noble quest. What might this grand expedition bring?

As *High Flyer* crossed the orbit of the Ringed World, Instigator sent to her brethren, <This is where legend holds that Incursor began to suffer. Slicing winds afflicted him. Yet I am moving inward at last—snug and fed, behind a mere machine.>

Aboard that machine, Julia took time to be alone.

She flicked on a wall screen. Far inward, Shanna's ship flared bright yellow in the pervading dark. They had zand aboard, and Shanna was happily working to keep their habitat cold. Liquid helium pumps, a chemical wonderland of interlacing systems—they were busy, and happy, and, in Wiseguy-moderated conversations, learning. Grist for those thousand doctoral dissertations.

She had a sudden warm feeling for Shanna. How strange, but it felt . . . right. She indulged unashamedly in a bit of pop psychology. Some of their problems might have been personal, not spawned by who controlled the mission. After all, Shanna was the right age for the daughter she had never had; she, Julia, the mother Shanna had never known. No wonder they had fought, at first. She hoped their new, supportive relationship would be more enduring.

Proserpina would reach the Earth-moon system about the time *High Flyer* made it to Mars, decelerating all the way. What happened to Instigator then, how to keep it safe near Mars, how to free Incursor—all problems for tomorrow. Whole corps of scientists Earthside were worrying through those riddles. They would think of something; of that, she was sure.

And she and Viktor would be back on Mars. Armed with new knowledge, ready to make more descents. She wondered what it would be like next time going down into Vent R.

Julia sat cross-legged and let her mind fly free.

She thought about what her own science might be like, after it had digested the lessons she had barely glimpsed out here. That task would occupy centuries. Mars Effect or no, she would not live to see the flowering of full understanding.

The evolutionary routes are many, she knew, wending through the howling wilderness of the maladaptive, on to their severely narrowed destinations. Biology abounded with convergent examples, destinations arrived at along very different paths. Fruiting bodies of slime molds and myxobacteria alike evolved multicelled advances. Warm-bloodedness came forth several times, as did live birth and even penile tumescence. The eyes did indeed have it—as seen in the camera-like eyes of vertebrates and octopi, and the similar tiny perceptors of worms and jellyfish. Nature invented over and over again the mechanisms used by diverse organisms to hear, smell, echolocate, sense the prickle of electric and magnetic fields.

So for her it was not a huge leap to see the Beings and the Marsmat as parallel ways of first acquiring complex information and then sharpening the means to handle it better.

Since the Marsmat, biologists had suspected that waiting in the wings of the theater of consciousness there were other minds stirring, poised on the threshold of articulation. But they had never guessed that long before rude hominids sharpened flints, minds of utterly different strategies had met and merged beneath the drying plains of Mars.

Now a possibility brimmed ahead. The last smart species had learned to voyage between worlds and so had brought the three together. Was some joining of them possible? Evolution was ingenious.

Until now scientists felt a tension between a cosmic loneliness and a suspicion that there might be other minds, yes—but that they were unfathomably distant in a huge, echoing conceptual space. No more. Now the links were known, close by.

Julia sighed and tried to imagine where it might all lead.

Perhaps the Beings were members of the only truly galaxy-spanning culture. Outcroppings of organic life might be rare, while plasma was common—spewed out by stars, drifting in the black. Could this be why radio SETI had found so little? The Wiseguy program had arisen in response to the few weak signals, yes—maybe there were few organics to send.

Since the Proto had risen toward her, and it had dawned upon her what it was, she had been forced—yet again!—to rethink. About how life could evolve without the style of binary reproduction Earth's life used.

And since then, another idea beckoned.

The Proto had been blown out in an immense solar storm, from the brute eruption of a magnetic arch. If nascent plasma beings are growing in the sun—at far higher plasma densities and different magnetic fields—could they not evolve there? Could a natural cooperation arise between the Beings of the Deep and solar plasma life? Or could there come some inconceivable conflict?

Plenty to think about here—of that, she was sure.

There was more to come. There always would be.

Afterword

Perhaps it's time for an old-fashioned voyage of interplanetary discovery. *The Martian Race* was that, updated a bit, and this novel is a sequel to it. Some have felt that our backyard solar system is just too plain dull for much exciting fiction. I disagree.

In writing this novel I took the frame of outer solar system ideas from an earlier novella, *Iceborn*, coauthored with Paul Carter in the 1980s. Paul had written a novelette about exploring Pluto and came to me for advice on how to expand it; we ended up collaborating. (Indeed, the critic and novelist Brian Stableford pointed out to me that I may have collaborated on novels with more writers than anyone else, surely an odd distinction. Writing is a bit lonely, and my experience in science has accustomed me to working and writing papers with others. Perhaps science fiction inherits from science the propensity to merge talents and viewpoints; certainly there is little collaboration in mainstream fiction, which may be the poorer for it.) Paul also helped with ideas and prose, and created the Old One and other characters in this novel. I owe him a great debt.

In merging the outer solar system with the inner, I am following recent research. We now believe that our solar system formed in an active, violent region of the galaxy. Nearby giant stars hammered with intense ultraviolet light the accretion disk, from which planets formed. Supernovas sprayed the early planets and iceteroids with radioactive nuclei. The outer solar system was not just leftovers, failed worlds. Instead, it played a role in bombarding the early Earth with comets, and the young sun blew out colossal bursts of high-energy winds. The implications of this are just beginning to get worked out for astrobiology and other fields.

So I thought it would be enjoyable to make a true imaginative leap, conjuring up life far beyond the chemical avenues we know. I've left out some fairly arcane thinking along these lines, distilled from my own field of plasma physics—this is a novel, after all, not a doctoral thesis. But there are good physical reasons to imagine that molecules and dilute solutions are not the whole story of life in our universe.

There are many scientific sources for this novel's background. Especially I want to thank Ken McNamara for the figure from his *Stromatolites*. The major inspiration for the first part of this novel was visiting the striking stromatolites of Shark Bay, Australia, in 2004.

For background on Gusev Crater on Mars, thanks to Nathalie Cabrol and Edmond Grin. Their early help convinced me that Gusev Crater was a likely landing site, so I chose it for *The Martian Race*. So convincing were they that they won the competition for landing sites, and the Spirit lander has had phenomenal success in Gusev since December 2003. Calculations about walking on Mars are from Adam Hawkey's paper on human locomotion on Mars in *Journal of the British Interplanetary Society* 57, pages 262–71, 2004. Joe Miller of USC provided scientific ideas about Martian life, with cogent criticisms of the biology and plot as well. Mark O. Martin of USC gave background on microbial biology. The "cartoon" of solar wind flow around Mars is from a paper in *Geophysical Research Letters* 29, 37, 2002.

While much of the biosphere of Pluto is my own invention, the ideas about chemistry at very low temperatures flow from the late Robert Forward's groundbreaking essay, "Alien Abodes Between Neptune and the Stars."

I must thank those who gave great help in reading and criticizing the several drafts. Jaime Levine gave me the longest letter I have ever gotten about the manuscript, and even outlined the book. Sheila Finch provided telling insights into language and translation; her Lingster stories have many ingenious ideas about alien linguistics. Elisabeth Malartre found my many Homeric nods, as we politely term them. She was the unacknowledged coauthor of *The Martian Race* and took time to contribute strongly to plotting this sequel.

Is more to come? Another novel beckons, about the two decades between this and *The Martian Race*. Not right away, but we'll see.

September 2004

ABOUT THE AUTHOR

Gregory Benford is a professor of physics at the University of California, Irvine; a Woodrow Wilson Fellow; and the recipient of the Lord Prize for contributions to science. One of the most honored authors in the history of science fiction, Benford wrote *The Martian Race*, the Galactic Center series, and the classic *Timescape*. He has won two Nebula Awards, the John W. Campbell Award, the British SF Award, and the United Nations Medal for Literature.